Off the Ice

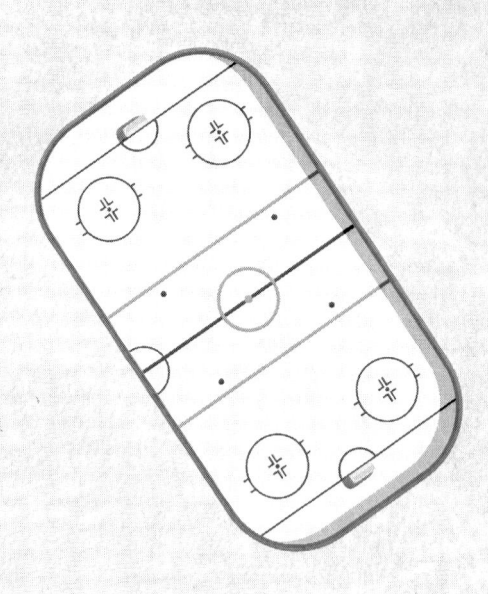

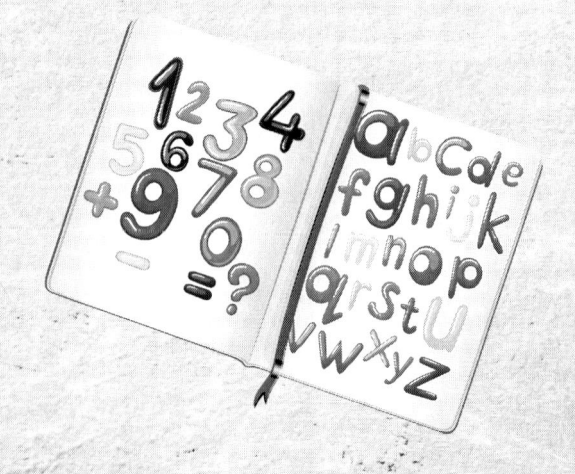

CASSIE

Off the Ice

EMMA O'DEA

Off the Ice

Copyright © 2025 by Emma O'Dea

All rights reserved. No part of this publication may be reproduced, stored in a retrieval system, or transmitted in any form or by any means, electronic, mechanical, photocopying, recording, or otherwise, without the prior written permission of the author, except in the case of brief quotations embodied in critical reviews and certain other noncommercial uses permitted by copyright law.

This is a work of fiction. Names, characters, places, and incidents are either the product of the author's imagination or are used fictitiously. Any resemblance to actual persons, living or dead, events, or locales is entirely coincidental.

Cover design by Megan Jayne Designs
Interior design by Alt 19 Creative

She said I think I'll go to Boston.
AUGUSTANA

CHAPTER ONE

Cassie

For some, the idea of being covered in the bodily fluids of another person might be repulsive. Me, however? I've come to accept it as my fate in life. Tears, drool, snot—oh God, the never-ending snot. I've been covered in it all and then some. It's not pleasant, but it's life. At least, it's my life.

"No, thank you, Adrian," I said tersely, frowning down at the five-year-old whose mouth was firmly attached to my wrist. "Teeth are *not* for biting people."

The boy blinked up at me with wide brown eyes before unclenching his jaw, allowing me to pull myself free from the death trap that was his teeth.

"It's like your parents are razoring your teeth each night," I muttered, rubbing the red spot on my arm where his mouth had just been. "No kindergartner should have baby teeth that sharp."

"Ms. Cassie," Lilian wailed in the background, "She won't share!"

Still gripping my sore arm, I turned to look at the curly-haired girl who stared up at me with expectant eyes and a pouty lip, waiting for me to solve her conflict.

"What happened, Lil?" I asked, bending down to her level.

"She-she-she," the girl stammered, her little mind whirling as she tried to get her words out. "She has the doll I wanted, and I used my words like you said, but she still won't give it!"

"Well," I said, kneeling before her, "were you holding it first, and she took it from you?"

"No, but I wanted it. And I used my words like you said. I said, 'I'm using this,' like you said."

"Right, but Lil, that only works if someone takes something you're already using. You can't use it to take something from someone else." I smiled at her encouragingly, trying to explain delicately.

"But I want it," she repeated, increasingly frustrated.

"It's hard to wait our turn." I nodded softly. "But maybe while we wait, we can play with the horse you like—"

Taylor Swift's melodic vocals erupted from the cell phone in my pocket that, apparently, I'd forgotten to silence. I pulled it out, ready to reject the call, when I saw my boyfriend's name flashing on the screen.

I answered the call, tucking the phone between my shoulder and ear to keep my hands free as I reached for Lilian's other toy.

"Dave?" I asked, answering only because he knew better than to call me when I was at work. "Is everything okay?"

"I don't *want* the horse!" Lilian cried as I held the offensive object in question in front of her.

At the sight of her tears, I dropped the horse, scrambling to find something else that might distract her while I figured out why Dave was calling me.

"Jesus, it's loud in there," came Dave's answering reply.

"That's kindergarten for you." I laughed. "What's up? Is something wrong?"

He was silent on the other end, causing my heart to plummet into my stomach.

"Dave?" I asked again, my voice a bit desperate. "What's wrong? Is everything okay?"

"Not really, no," he replied cautiously. "We need to talk."

"Oh my God, is it my mom?" I blanched, the mayhem of the classroom fading into background noise.

My eyes darted around the room until I found my coworker casually scrolling on her phone in one of the tiny chairs beside a girl coloring.

"Julie," I called across the room, "can you take over here?"

She looked up slowly as if she'd forgotten she was in a classroom. With a barely perceptible eye roll, she put her phone in her pocket and came over to where I was standing, giving me a chance to dart into the hallway, mumbling a "thanks" to her as I left.

"No," Dave said. "It's not your mom. It's—"

"Oh, thank God." I heaved a sigh of relief, feeling like I could finally breathe again. "Well, honey, I love you, but I've got to get back to—"

"I think we need to break up."

And just like that, the air was gone again.

"W-what?" My lip actually trembled. "What do you mean? I-but we- but... what?"

"I'm sorry," he said awkwardly, "but I just really think that it's for the best."

"For the best?" I repeated numbly. "What's for the best?"

"For us to, you know… break up," he explained as if I were an idiot for not picking up on it.

And you know, maybe I was. Maybe I was the biggest, most naïve idiot in the world because I thought, after six years of being with someone, there would be no possible way they'd spring a breakup on me out of nowhere over a phone call.

"Why are you doing this *now*?"

"I've just been thinking lately. All my friends are single, and they've been giving me a lot of shit for being tied down for so long," he trailed off. "You know, we started dating so young. I never really got to experience what else is out there. And you didn't either, right? That's what I mean when I say I think it's for the best. For both of us."

"But we can talk about this," I pleaded, desperate for something to fix the agony that was tearing through my chest. "We can try—"

"No, Cassie," he interrupted. "I've thought about this a lot, and I'm not going to change my mind. I hope you can understand."

I nodded, but of course, he couldn't see that. Just like he couldn't see the way the tears rolled down my cheeks or the way my fists clenched by my sides until the nails dug into my palms hard enough to leave a mark, all because of his words.

"Okay," I said, my voice barely a whisper. "Well, um. Thank you for all that. And, um, good luck out there, I guess?" I laughed sardonically, not sure how to conclude a conversation I never imagined having.

"Cassie—" he said, but I ended the call and then promptly turned my phone off, wanting to be unreachable for the rest of the day.

I closed my eyes, wiping the tears on my sweater before heading back into the battlefield that was my classroom.

In the corner, Julie was scrolling on her phone again while Lilian still sobbed, clutching the sought-after doll she had wanted just moments prior.

"Lil, what's wrong?" I went over, grateful to have someone else's crisis to worry about for the moment, no matter how insignificant it seemed to me. "It looks like Kenzie gave you a turn with the doll?"

I looked to where the little girl was playing joyfully with the stallion toy that Lilian had not so delicately rejected.

"Yes." She wailed miserably.

"What's wrong then?"

"I want to play with the horse." She threw herself into my arms, sobbing.

But what were a few more tears on my already sadness-soaked sweater?

CHAPTER TWO

Liam

I wouldn't call myself an asshole just because I like things a certain way, enjoy my privacy, and would rather drop dead than engage with some meaningless interviewer who wants to ask about my favorite color, what makes me cry, and—most importantly—what I look for in a woman.

The tabloids, though? They have no issue using that particular label generously whenever my name shows up in some vapid article. Which, unfortunately, is often. Apparently, girls love assholes because—as my teammates so lovingly showed me—I was ranked the number one most, uh, *fuckable* NHL player across the board.

It was humiliating—and honestly a little dehumanizing. But according to everyone around me, it's the life I signed up for. As if playing the game I've loved since I was a kid entitles the world to treat me like some kind of public trophy.

"Look, another one." Brody, our goalie, dangled a magazine in front of my face. It had my face blown up and edited to an almost unrecognizable level.

I groaned, skimming the article, spotting a few rumors, one or two facts, and then a handful of blatant lies before I turned my attention back to the photoshopped picture.

"Why the fuck did they give me *rosy* cheeks?" I scowled, crumpling the magazine and tossing it across the room. "It's just a bunch of bullshit, anyway. I didn't talk to any reporters."

"*You* didn't." He shrugged. "Doesn't mean someone else didn't."

"Yeah, well, this shit is getting old," I muttered, running a hand through my sweat-drenched hair. "You'd think they'd find something better to write about by now."

"But what could be *better* than the star player of the Harbor Wolves, Dreamy Mr. Liam Brynn himself?" Brody snickered, moving around the locker room with ease.

"You would think that the number of times they refer to me as an *asshole* would knock me down a few spots on their—what the fuck do they call it—their sexy scale?" I said, unlacing my skates.

"Nah, man," Brody responded, shrugging off his jersey. "Girls love that stuff. The bigger the dickhead, the better."

I snorted. "And you know this how?"

"Because I have sisters," he rolled his eyes in explanation. "Trust me, years of tears, tantrums, and drama-filled stories have taught me a *lot* about how the other side lives and operates."

"Right," I said, nodding along sarcastically.

"Trust me, if I had even fifteen percent of the whole dismissive, asshole vibe you've got going on, I'd have a line of puck bunnies out the door just like you. It's the whole unattainable thing. Drives them crazy."

"Unattainable?" I raised an eyebrow.

"My sister Tara explained it to me. Girls go for the guys who are hard to get. It's like—well, I guess it's like winning the Stanley Cup after a season that started off really shitty for us, right? It seems so out of reach, so totally unattainable at that point—so we work our asses off to get there, and once we do, it's all the more satisfying than if the whole thing had just been easy. You follow?"

It made sense, all right. He'd just put into words exactly what pissed me off so much about the whole thing. I was a *person,* for fucks sake—not some prize to be won. That's why I hadn't bothered with dating since I'd gotten into the NHL. It wasn't worth it. I didn't have the patience to deal with the endless stream of people who thought I existed solely for public consumption.

But right as I was about to unleash years' worth of media hatred on one of my best friends, someone equally important to me walked into the room.

"What the hell are you doing here?" I asked, watching as Maggie strode into the locker room as if she owned the place.

"Hello to you, too." She frowned, settling a hand on her hip.

A heavy clunk sounded in the background, and I turned to see Brody reaching for the gear he'd fumbled all over the ground. My sister raised her brows at him before turning her attention back to me.

"I'm here to see you," she said, batting her eyes in a way that was Maggie-code for *I need something.*

"I'm exhausted, Mags," I said, standing to head to my locker.

Like a shadow, she followed me. "Too exhausted for *me?* Your sweet, baby sister who loves you so much?"

"Yes," I said, shoveling stuff into my bag. "Since apparently whatever this is warranted an in-person visit, I can confidently say I am too exhausted to deal with it right now."

"Lose the attitude, Liam," Maggie said, hand shooting out to smack the side of my head. "You're no fun to be around anymore."

Brody coughed in the background, a failed attempt to cover the laugh that had me glaring in his direction.

Between the media, the pressure of the game, and the incessant needs of everyone who wanted something from me, how the hell was I supposed to be fun to be around?

I exhaled a sigh, shutting the locker door harder than necessary. "What is it, Mags? Do you need money?"

"Okay, jackass," Maggie said. "Never mind. You've clearly lost all sight of how to be a semi-decent guy. Go about your day." She scowled and turned to leave.

"Wait," I called after her, blowing out a breath. "Mags. Stop. I'm sorry."

She turned, raising a skeptical brow. "Are you?"

"Yes," I said, meaning it. She didn't deserve to be talked to like that just because I had a crap day. "What can I do for you?"

"Well," Maggie started with a nervous smile, "you know my friend Cassie?"

"No?"

"Yes, you do. Remember? You always say her boyfriend sounds like a tool?"

"Oh, *her?*" I asked. "The girl whose boyfriend left her at the concert, and she had to Uber back from, like, four hours away?"

I knew who Maggie was talking about, all right. I'd never met the girl, but my sister had told me stories. Mostly ones revolving around the recurring theme of the boyfriend being an asshole.

I'd always been slightly amused and halfway convinced Maggie was exaggerating, if not flat-out, making the stories up. Because really, who could be *that* big of a dick? I always asked why the girl didn't just get rid of the guy, but Maggie would shrug and just say her friend couldn't see it.

"Yes, exactly." Maggie nodded. "And you were right. The guy is a major tool. So, I'm sure it won't surprise you to hear that he dumped her over the phone while she was at work. Oh, and then texted suggesting she find somewhere else to stay."

"Oh, that blows."

Brody winced in the background, apparently eavesdropping on our conversation.

"Right?" She nodded along with him, clearly pleased by the solidarity.

"Like I said." Brody looked at me smugly. "Girls love dickheads."

"What?" Maggie's face contorted in confusion.

"Nothing," he said, face flaming. "Forget I said anything."

"Mags, are you seriously telling me you came all the way to the rink just to tell me a story about your friend's shitty boyfriend?" I cut into their conversation, trying to figure out the point of this surprise visit.

"Ex-boyfriend." She frowned. "Weren't you listening?"

"Yes, but I don't understand what the point is?"

"Well, you just have so much space in your condo…" Her voice trailed off. "A whole spare room and everything."

Realization washed over me. "What the fuck, Mags? No."

Her face fell, "Don't say that, Liam. She really needs some help."

"Well, I'm sure she can go literally anywhere else in the world for help. Doesn't she have family?"

"Not really," Maggie said. "I mean, she has her mom, but it's not really an option to stay with her."

"A hotel, then!"

"Liam! Not everyone is as rich as you. Do you have any idea how expensive it would be to stay long-term in a hotel?"

"Do *you* have any idea how annoying it would be to have some random girl *living in my house* long term?" I enunciate each word to try and get the point across. "Besides, she'd probably spend her time prying around, trying to find some secret of mine to sell to the media."

"She's not like that!" Maggie scoffed, insulted on behalf of her friend. "She doesn't even know who you are. She's not into sports, like at all."

I grunted.

"Really! I've invited her to come to your games with me loads of times, but she's never wanted to."

"Still, she doesn't have to be a hockey fan to know she could make good money by running to the press with news about an NHL player."

"Are you serious, Liam? Don't you trust me at all?" She looked wounded.

"I trust you," I confirmed, "but not some random girl I've never met. I mean, come on, Mags. This is a lot to ask."

"I know it is, Liam." She sighed. "But it's not for long. One month. Two tops. She just needs a little time to find her footing. Just a bit of breathing room. I'm sure you, of all people, can understand that."

I inhaled, taking her words into consideration. "And what about you? Why isn't she staying at your place?"

"Because Mom's already staying with me, remember?" She referenced a detail I apparently was supposed to have known. "And there's barely space for the two of us, never mind adding Cassie to the mix."

Maggie's apartment was outrageously small. I had to give her that.

"Unless you'd rather have Cassie move in with me and Mom stay with you," she suggested with a pointed look.

"No thanks." I visibly shuddered.

Our mom was… fine, as far as they go. Overbearing but kind. Not to mention the way she got way too involved in my personal life whenever the smallest window of opportunity opened for her.

Besides, there was something extremely unappealing about being a twenty-six-year-old man who had his mother living with him. Even if it was just for a few months.

"I'll pass on that. Why can't you just stay with me and let Cassie crash at your place?"

Maggie let out the most dramatic huff before exclaiming, "She's heartbroken! I'm not going to make Cassie stay with our mom while she's trying to get over a breakup."

"So, you'd rather have her be heartbroken at *my* house?"

"You'll give her plenty of space. And you're, like, never there. It would help her out a ton. It's not just the breakup. She has a lot going on, and trying to immediately find a place to live would be too much right now."

"Mags." I groaned. "I really don't want to do this."

My place was the only privacy I ever got. It was my safe harbor. The only place I knew I wasn't being watched, commented on, or criticized. Having some random girl there would take all that away.

"Please, Liam." Her green eyes widened in a silent plea. "It's really important. And I swear to you, it's not for long."

I thought about it, considering every aspect. Truth was, I'd been a shitty brother to Maggie for the last few years. And for some reason, she still cared about me, which said a lot about the type of person she was. If there was one small thing I could do for her, maybe it would show her that the old me was still in there somewhere. The brother who had always been there for her, who was able to pick up the pieces of whatever mess she'd found herself in. The brother she had before the NHL and the media, and the fans drained the life out of his soul.

"Fine," I said shortly, causing an ungodly-sized grin to take residence on the lower half of Maggie's face. "But here are the conditions. She starts looking for a place *immediately*."

"Of course." Maggie bobbed her head in agreement.

"I mean it. I don't want her to think she can sit back and take her time looking for her dream home or whatever. She needs to get on top of it because I *am* going to be enforcing that one-month rule."

"One month. Great. Two tops."

"*One* month, Maggie. I mean it."

"Fine, whatever." She waved my concerns away. "I'll help her look myself. But I'm sure that'll give us plenty of time to find her somewhere safe and cheap to live."

"And you better give her the rundown. I like my space. I like my privacy. Absolutely no pictures in the house. No telling people my address. Really, I'd like to keep my interactions with her to a bare minimum."

Maggie rolled her eyes dramatically. "Yeah, yeah, yeah. You know, I really think you actually might get along with her. You know, if you take your head out of your ass, that is."

I put Maggie in a light chokehold, rubbing the top of her head the way I had when I was just a regular big brother who liked to torment his little sister for the fun of it.

"Okay, okay." She laughed, wriggling in my grasp. "Get off of me, you meathead."

I let her go, feeling the foreign sensation of a smile on my face. God, it'd been so long since I'd done something as simple as laugh.

"Really, Liam," Maggie said, fixing me with a sincere look as she leaned on her tiptoes to kiss my cheek, scraggly and rough from a few days of not shaving. "Thank you so much. I knew I could count on my big brother."

"Yeah, yeah." I shrugged off the thanks. "Just give me a heads up of when she's planning on coming."

"Oh, yeah." Maggie bit her lip guiltily. "About that… she might already be there."

"Jesus, Maggie!" I swore under my breath.

"Sorry!" She held her hands up in surrender. "I just knew you'd say yes, and she really didn't have anywhere to go tonight, so I sort of let her in?"

"You're really something, you know that?" I said through gritted teeth.

"Love you." She grinned. "Be nice to Cassie, okay? Don't go around muttering your insensitive comments around her, alright?"

"I won't be muttering *any* comments around her. Remember? You said she'd give me space."

"Right, she will. And I'm sure she'll be sound asleep by the time you get home. Don't worry about anything."

Before I could say another word of protest, my sister fluttered out the door and left me with her latest mess on my hands. And this was one that wouldn't be as easy to clean up as credit card debt or a flat tire.

I let out an exhale containing more than just the stress of the day.

Just when I thought my bad mood couldn't possibly get worse, Brody's voice interjected the whirlwind of negativity brewing inside my head.

"You never told me you had a hot sister."

CHAPTER THREE

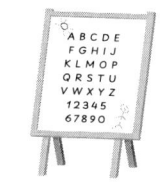

Cassie

You think you know someone after four years. Like, for example, the girl you consider to be the closest friend you made in college.

Sure, we'd chatted about our hopes, goals, and dreams. But somehow, in all that time, she'd never mentioned that not only was her older brother super rich but apparently in desperate need of a roommate.

Thank God, because if it weren't for him, I probably would've spent the night sleeping in my car outside of the elementary school.

Staying with my mom wasn't an option, and after my big splurge of, um, paying rent that month, my checking account disagreed with the idea of spending the night in a hotel.

I'd called Maggie earlier in the day, not so much looking for a solution as for the emotional support that came with ranting to your best friend. I should've known she would try to solve the trainwreck that was my life. But her suggestion of rooming with her brother caught me wildly off guard, even coming from her.

"Your brother?" I had asked skeptically.

She'd mentioned him plenty of times, of course. Vague references to their childhood and a few more recent stories, but nothing super concrete. I knew they'd been close when they were younger, but there was a lot of pain when she mentioned their relationship now. I guess they had sort of grown apart over the years.

Besides that, I knew next to nothing about the man other than the fact that he liked hockey or something and apparently needed a roommate.

Though, now that I was here, I was quickly realizing there was absolutely no way that I could afford to live here. Even for the month or two that it would take me to find somewhere more my paygrade.

Not that I would want to stay longer. It was beautiful, sure, but something about the excessive spaciousness freaked me out. I wasn't trying to be picky, but would it kill a guy to buy a cozy throw? Light a candle? Put up some art?

The whole place felt like a stainless steel, dark mahogany cave—nice, objectively, but completely devoid of warmth, fun, or personality.

Unless that personality was hockey, which apparently Maggie had drastically underplayed. The guy didn't just *like* hockey. He was obsessed. Harbor Wolves merchandise hung all around the apartment, proudly displaying the blue and gray colors of our local NHL team. While I was pretty indifferent to sports, I wasn't oblivious to the fact that as far as hockey teams went, they were a pretty damn good one.

My mom and dad had both loved sports, but I guess the gene didn't get passed down to me. I would watch with them when I was younger, in some desperate attempt to try to be included in their world, but it didn't matter anymore. Dad was dead, and Mom was… well, I shook the thought of her out of my head. It was too much to think about the breakup, the living situation change, *and* her all at once.

One thing at a time. I reminded myself, taking a steadying breath.

I couldn't bear to go back to the apartment for my stuff, so all I had were the clothes I'd worn to work, the big bag that I lugged back and forth between home and school every day, and my newly broken heart.

Maggie had brought me here and listened to me cry for a bit before looking at the clock in bewilderment and running out as fast as she could with some half-hearted excuse that she was late to get somewhere.

I thought it was odd before realizing that maybe even she couldn't handle all the messes I had going on in my life. I needed to learn to just keep it to myself.

Not knowing which room was mine since all the doors were shut and not wanting to snoop in her brother's space when he wasn't there, I settled down on the couch and waited. I felt more awkward than I'd ever felt in my life, but if the guy was so desperate for a roommate that he had begged Maggie to find someone for him without even meeting them himself, then I figured I didn't have anything to worry about. Besides, it was only a short-term rental anyway.

Across from the couch, a flat-screen hung on a brick-paneled wall, flanked by tall, arched windows spilling moonlight across the room. It was late, and my body was heavy with exhaustion, but my mind wouldn't stop spinning.

So, I sat there.

I thought about turning the television on, just for some noise to drown out my thoughts, but it didn't feel like my place to do so. I wanted to find the bathroom, but I had no idea which door it was. I considered grabbing a snack, but rummaging through someone else's fridge felt weird.

More than anything, I just wanted to go home. Back to the comfort of my routines. My space. My boyfriend.

Not whatever unfamiliar hellscape I'd landed in.

Suddenly, the idea that Dave had made some terrible mistake entered my head. I was sure that if only I went home and talked to him, we could figure it all out together. It didn't have to be this way. We didn't have to lose the last six years of our lives over what was surely just some silly quarter-life crisis.

I jumped to my feet, deciding that I needed to go home. What was I doing here? In some random man's apartment? It was insane. The only reason I had agreed to it was the expected lapse of judgment that comes when your world shatters. But now that I realized it didn't *have* to shatter, I had newfound inspiration. Everything was going to be okay!

Racing to the front door, my bag on my arm, I had energy buzzing through me and a smile on my face as I manifested the reunion Dave and I were going to have in a few short moments. My hand reached to pull open the door, eagerly forming a script in my head of what I could say, when it hit me.

Literally.

"Ouch!" I groaned, rubbing my now red forehead from the door that was now partially open.

I jumped back from the impact, revealing the towering form of a man who looked equally surprised and irritated with a hint of loathing all in one go.

It was impressive, honestly, the way he could mesh so many emotions together into one scowl and furrowed glance. And if his intention was to intimidate me into submission, he fully succeeded.

I backed up, clearing the way for him to enter the apartment. I had no idea if it was even Liam, but the way the man was glowering at me gave me the impression it was better not to ask any questions.

"Um, hi." I raised a hand awkwardly in a wave, feeling idiotic as soon as I made the gesture.

He dropped his duffel bag, flicking a switch beside the door, which illuminated the place in warm light, showing his displeasure all the more clearly. That, and his massive frame. I searched his face for any similarities to link him to Maggie but found only vague references to my friend in him.

He had tousled waves of dark brown hair, where hers was pin-straight and black. Where she was slender, he was broad and solidly built. His nose might have resembled hers slightly, long and narrow—but his eyes were what sold me. The same exact shade of sea glass green that I'd always fawned over in Maggie, framed by thick dark lashes that looked too good to be true. It really wasn't fair that some people were gifted with traits that you would think only an artist could come up with. He and Maggie were those people, I guessed.

"I'm Cassie," I said, now more confident that this was, in fact, Liam Brynn I was dealing with.

He looked me up and down in a way that made me feel like he was holding up a magnifying glass to me. I crossed my arms over my chest, shifting from foot to foot, waiting for his final assessment.

He frowned, and I held my breath in anticipation of his words. Usually, meeting strangers didn't phase me, but I'd never seen someone as intimidating as the man standing before me. It felt uncomfortable to be in his line of vision, the sole focus of his scowl.

"Do you make a habit out of sitting in the dark?" he asked in a tone I couldn't quite detect. "Or, in this case, sitting two inches in front of the door?"

"Um, no." I let out an awkward laugh. "Not really. I just, I didn't know where the light switch was and—"

"Why are you covered in paint?" His dark eyebrows arched as he looked down at my rainbow-splattered jeans.

"Oh, we were finger painting at work today," I explained. "And usually I change after work, but you know, I didn't have any clothes on me. And I couldn't exactly go home to get any because- well, I'm sure you heard that part, but—"

"Finger painting at work?" He looked at me incredulously.

"I work in an elementary school." I laughed at his confused expression. "You know, with kindergartners. That's why a lot of the paint is in the shape of a handprint. They can be sort of grabby with adults. You know, they haven't learned about boundaries and personal space and all that yet."

He looked at the two inches between us with a pointed look, apparently trying to inform me that my boundaries were hazy as well. I took an immediate two steps back, giving him room to enter deeper into his apartment.

"Thank you for letting me stay, by the way. It really means a lot. It was a really generous offer, but—" I rambled, ready to tell him about the mix-up and how I'd actually be headed home after all, leaving this night of awkward encounters decidedly behind me.

"I didn't," he said, in a tone as cold as the stainless steel of the fridge he was currently scrounging through.

"I-uh," I began, watching him take out a carton of eggs, butter, and spinach. "Sorry, what?"

"I didn't 'let' you. I didn't offer it. I had nothing to do with this." He spoke volumes with those sea-glass eyes of his.

"Oh," I started, trying to make sense of his words as he turned his back to me and began prepping his 10 p.m. breakfast meal. "Right, like not me specifically. I know we haven't met or anything, so of course you didn't let *me* stay. But when Maggie said you were desperate for a roommate—"

"Maggie said *what*?" His reaction was immediate, his reflexes even faster as he spun to face me.

"I mean, she didn't make you sound desperate!" I held my hands up quickly, not wanting to offend him. "I just mean, she told me how long you've been looking for one and that I would do as good as anyone else,"

"Maggie told you that I was *desperate* for a roommate?"

The intensity in his eyes was extra unsettling when accompanied by the knife he held in his hand. Of course, logic would lead me to believe that he was going to use it to dice the tomato in front of him, but frankly, I didn't know him well enough to be a hundred percent sure.

I swallowed, my cheeks flaming furiously. The downfall of my pale complexion was that it showed *everything*. Fear, anger, embarrassment. My face might as well be a display screen showing the world the inner workings of my mind.

"I mean, yeah?" I shrugged. "She told me you had this big apartment and all this empty space and that you'd been wanting a roommate to feel less lonely... so, here I am." I made a hand motion as if to say, "Ta-da."

Liam threw his head back and laughed out loud, and I giggled along with him because I didn't really know what else to do. When he finally caught his breath, I realized Liam found this situation about as funny as I did, which was to say, not at all.

"Let me make this very clear. I'm not lonely. I have never wanted a roommate. And the only reason I agreed to this is because I've been a bit of an ass to my sister lately, and she begged me to let you crash here *short term*."

My heart dropped, plummeting into the deepest parts of my stomach. I was humiliated. Not only because he didn't want me here and the way he put it so bluntly, but because it exacerbated a feeling that had already been gnawing inside of me all day long: that no one really did.

He didn't want me, my boyfriend didn't want me. My mom was too wrapped up in her own issues to really pay me any mind. It was all too much. I hated myself for being so fragile and weak. How come some girls could rock the whole independent, I-don't-need-anyone thing, but I found myself constantly craving love from all the people who wouldn't give it?

My ego had been bruised more than enough for one day, so I went to work attempting to repair it on my own.

"Oh, okay." I painted the fakest of smiles and hoped he couldn't see my lip tremble. "No biggie. It's just a misunderstanding. I get it. And, lucky for us, it turns out I actually *don't* need a place to stay after all. So, thank you for, you know, letting me stay here, against your wishes and all that," I trailed off, not entirely sure how to thank someone for something they hadn't actually offered. "But I'll be heading out now."

With my thumb pointed toward the door, I took off, scurrying away like a mouse being chased off by a fox.

I'd nearly reached the door when his sigh thundered through the kitchen.

"And where will you go?"

"Well." I turned, smiling brightly at him because the last thing I needed was fake pity from a guy who clearly couldn't care less. "I actually was going to go home and make up with my boyfriend. I think it was all just some silly mistake. Nothing we can't work through."

I hope.

Liam replied with an answering snort. "Isn't this the guy who called you at work and broke up with you over the phone?"

"Yes," I said, hating him for shattering my pride all over again. "But—"

"And how long have you been dating?"

"Six years." I crossed my arms defensively, narrowing my eyes at him while waiting for him to get to the point.

"And not only did he not think you worthy enough of an in-person conversation, but he also told *you* to find somewhere else to live without even discussing it?"

My cheeks were on fire, but this time not only from shame but also fury. How dare this guy rub my breakup in my face when he didn't even know the full situation?

"Well, I'm glad that you and Maggie are so close that she thought to share every humiliating detail, but you don't know the full situation."

"Oh?" he said in a way that invited more details.

"He's been under a lot of stress, trying to figure things out with life, and work has been hard for him lately, and—" I rambled, listing off the reasons I'd spent the night convincing myself of.

"Fuck that," he cut me off, fixing me with a glowering stare.

"Excuse me?"

"You don't treat your partner of six years like that. Hell, you don't even treat a stranger like that."

I stared at him, mouth agape at the harshness of his words. "Look, I don't know what type of relationships you've had, but things aren't always black and white. Sometimes people make mistakes, or they get scared—"

"No," he interrupted, his tone icy and absolute. "People don't 'make mistakes' like that when they care about someone. That's just an excuse. He was looking for a way out, and he found one. Don't kid yourself into thinking otherwise."

I flinched, his words stinging worse than I could've expected. Tears welled up, forcing me to blink them away quickly before I could give the guy any more ammunition to use against me. He might have been right, but hearing it out loud, from a stranger no less, made me feel exposed, like he'd just peeled back a layer of my skin and took joy in poking right at the rawness underneath.

"You don't understand."

"No, I think I do. I think you're upset that you wasted your time on a guy who you let walk all over you for years. I think you're trying to justify it in your mind that if you get back together now, all those years won't have been for nothing. But I also know that if you go back to him and somehow forgive him for everything he's done, you're going to have a miserable life until you end up middle-aged, divorced, and in the same spot you're in now."

At that, the floodgates burst open. Tears spilled dramatically in a way I hadn't let them in years. At least not when anyone was around. They streamed down my face in ugly, wet blobs until I felt my cheeks soaked with my own misery.

Liam froze, wearing an expression of shock and horror that might've been humorous on a man his size if I had been calm enough to appreciate it.

"Shit," he muttered, staring at me in bewilderment, like I was a bomb he couldn't figure out how to dismantle. "Stop crying. Please. I didn't mean to make you cry. Damn it."

Turning off the stove burner, he came around the kitchen island so he could stand in front of me and give his orders up close.

"Stop," he blurted out. "Don't cry. Maggie's going to kill me."

His eyes darted around frantically, maybe looking for a tissue to give me, maybe looking for an escape. Who knew?

Finding a hint of amusement in his franticness, I used the sleeve of my sweater to wipe away the tears and snot that had taken residence on my face before staring up at him.

"Crying girls are your undoing, huh?" I said through red-rimmed eyes.

"Look," he breathed out, running a hand through his dark hair. "I'm sorry, okay? I didn't mean to be so harsh. I just don't think it'll do you any good to go back there," he explained, seemingly genuine. "I know guys like that. They're not worth it."

A small, hiccupping laugh escaped me, the absurdity of the situation cutting through my sadness for a brief moment. He was this towering, brooding guy who could probably intimidate an entire army, and here he was, practically flinching at the sight of my tears. It was almost sweet in a weird, messed-up way.

"Well, I hope you're happy," I said, rubbing my nose on the back of my sleeve, "because I definitely can't face Dave now. Meaning, I might need to crash here after all."

"It's fine," he said, and this time, there was considerably less aggression in his voice, making me think he really meant it.

"But only for tonight. I promise. Tomorrow, I'll be out of your hair. You won't ever have to see me again. In fact, I'll be gone before you wake up."

"Cassie," he said, startling me with the use of my name. "Really, it's fine. I'm sorry I was a jerk. We can stick to the original deal, and you can have a few weeks to figure out a plan."

"Yeah, right." I snorted out a laugh. "After that welcome parade you greeted me with?"

He winced.

"I'm kidding. I get it. You're a guy who likes privacy. That's totally fair." I personally couldn't relate, considering I was the type of person who hated space so much that I would obliterate the solar system if given the chance, but hey, to each their own. "So, I'll take you up on the offer, if you're actually making it this time, to stay for a few nights, and in the meantime, I'll be working on living plans. Pronto."

"I am. Offering, I mean," he said, looking relieved.

"Well, thank you," I said, giving him a small smile. "I really don't have anywhere else to go. Obviously, this isn't super ideal for me either."

"We'll make it work." He shrugged. "It's not forever."

"Right, exactly." I nodded, appreciating his sense of perspective.

It would've been terribly uncomfortable for him to view me as an intruder for the entirety of my stay here.

"You can stay in the guest room upstairs to the left. It should be all made up and everything."

A big grin settled on my face as I looked up at him, biting back a laugh.

"What?" he asked.

"Now, why would a guy who likes his privacy so much need a guest room?" I smirked at him.

"It came with the place." He shook his head, but he wore an answering smirk of his own. "And Maggie decorated it herself, so hopefully, it's girly enough for you."

"And what makes you think I like things to be girly?"

He looked at me up and down, probably noticing my bright pink sweater, flower-embroidered jeans, and floral print sneakers. "Just a hunch."

He was right, but I wasn't going to admit it. But I didn't have to because my stomach erupted in a growl that was loud enough to shake the house.

"Are you hungry?" he asked a bit stiffly, as if taking other people's needs into consideration wasn't something he was used to.

"Uh, a little." I downplayed my starvation, "But I'll live. I'll just go to sleep and grab something at the coffee shop in the morning."

"Sit, I'll give you some eggs," he said, maneuvering back around the counter.

"Oh, it's okay. Those are for you—"

"Cassie, relax. Just… eat, okay?" he said, spooning some food onto a plate before pushing it across the counter toward me.

"Well, thank you," I said gratefully.

"You don't have to thank me for basic decency." He frowned, making his own plate before sitting down across from me. "Where's your stuff, anyway?"

"Oh," I said between bites of food. "I was too embarrassed to go home and see Dave, so I just didn't?" I shrugged in explanation.

He shook his head. "So you don't have anything to sleep in?"

"I have the clothes I'm wearing," I said because I didn't want him to think I was going to sleep naked beneath his sheets or anything creepy like that.

He stood up from his spot, making his way across the room to one of the many closed doors. I wondered if that was his departure for the night. He didn't exactly seem the type to wish me 'goodnight' or anything like that, but I figured he'd at least give some type of conclusion to the conversation.

I'd finished my plate of food, washed it in the sink, and put it on the drying rack, but then I heard footsteps.

I turned to see Liam holding a pair of gray sweatpants and a blue long-sleeved t-shirt. When he extended them out in my direction, I realized they were for me.

"Oh, you didn't have to—"

"Take the clothes, Cassie. You're not going to be comfortable sleeping in jeans."

I blushed, hating that I had to take even more from this man after he already told me he didn't want me there in the first place. I hated being a burden, and I hated more that I had to accept it.

"Thank you," I said, my hand touching his as I took the clothes from him.

I snatched it away quickly, not wanting to upset the guy who clearly had a lot of issues with personal space.

He nodded, moving back to the counter to eat. I held the shirt out in front of me, looking at how its size would swallow me up. The growling logo of the Harbor Wolves Hockey Team was staring up at me from the shirt.

"You're a big hockey fan, huh?"

His eyebrows furrowed impossibly. "What?"

"It's not a bad thing!" I quickly amended. "I was just noticing how you have tons of sports stuff in here. I take it you're a big Harbor Wolves fan?"

He blinked incomprehensibly.

"I get it. It's cool that there's a big team so close to us. If I were into sports, I'd probably support my local team too."

"Uh." He scratched his head as if not knowing what to make of me. "Yeah. I guess you could say I'm pretty into hockey."

"Nice, well, maybe some time you can explain the rules to me or something. It seems pretty intense, as far as sports go. Definitely the most violent, it seems. I mean, what's up with these guys ramming each other against the glass? I know they have gear and everything, but they have actual *blades* on their feet." I shuddered, thinking about all the potential injuries. "Not to mention how bad it hurts when you fall against the ice. I haven't skated in a while, but a few falls on my butt, and I'm bruised for a week after."

"Well, typically," he said, the faintest hint of a smile playing at his lips, "professional hockey players don't fall."

"Right, of course not," I agreed, reminding myself that I probably shouldn't criticize any of the things he liked after he finally offered to let me stay. "So, anyway, goodnight, Liam. Thanks again."

"Goodnight, Cassie," he said, his eyes unreadable.

Before I could say anything else to humiliate myself, I scurried up the stairs and into the guest room, the weight of the day seeping into my bones.

I flipped on the light, and relief washed over me at the sight of the bed—large, inviting, and practically calling my name. The room was simply decorated, free of anything too personal, but somehow, it suited me more than the rest of the apartment's sleek, neutral aesthetic. It felt calmer here.

There was a bathroom, a closet far bigger than any 'guest' would ever need, and miraculously, even a desk that looked just right for writing lesson plans after a long day of teaching.

No. I corrected automatically. *I wasn't going to be here that long.*

Sighing, I shimmied out of my clothes and into the ones Liam had given me, sinking into the cozy warmth of fleece pants that I needed to roll three times at the waist and a sweatshirt that threatened to swallow me whole. I wasn't a short girl, but Liam was huge, and his clothes reflected that very clearly.

I climbed into the bed, thinking I must be mentally deranged to be as comfortable as I was in a place where I knew I wasn't entirely welcome. But even though he didn't want me here, he at least wasn't kicking me out, which was more than I could say for Dave.

Still, finding somewhere else to stay was definitely the number one priority. Liam might've claimed he was fine with me staying for a few days, but I couldn't bear the hit it would take to my ego to be living somewhere I wasn't wanted. Especially not after everything that happened today.

Tonight, I had no choice, so there really was no harm in enjoying a peaceful night of sleep, but tomorrow? That's when I would start work to get my life back on track.

CHAPTER FOUR

Liam

The verdict was in, and despite years of telling myself otherwise, it had become overwhelmingly true last night. I really was an asshole.

I'm sure she'll be sound asleep, Maggie had assured me.

She sure as hell wasn't. But it would've made my life a hell of a lot easier if she had been. I could've come home, gone to bed, and found some way to gently send her packing the next morning before this whole situation spiraled into what it had, keeping my privacy intact and her self-esteem a little less shattered.

Driving home from the arena, dread had settled like a rock in my stomach at the idea of finding some random girl in my space. I realized how completely absurd the whole arrangement was. There were plenty of ways to make up for my shortcomings to Maggie that didn't involve playing host to a stranger. The whole ride, I'd rehearsed exactly what I'd say to let her down gently—that I was sorry, but my life was too busy, my space too sacred. She'd just have to figure something else out. I was sure she'd understand.

But then, I saw her.

I opened the door, and there she was. Whatever carefully crafted speech I'd put together vanished the moment she looked at me. Instead of handling it like a civilized adult, I acted like the exact kind of asshole everyone always claimed I was.

I was an ass. I'd been ticked off that Maggie had spewed a bunch of lies, wrapping Cassie and me both in a situation bound for disaster. And more than that, I was frustrated that I needed to be the one to clear it up.

Then, like a switch had been flicked, all that anger inside me evaporated the second her face fell. I watched the change in real-time—confusion giving way to realization and, finally, that unmistakable flicker of hurt settling across her features.

God, she looked like I sucker-punched her. I felt it like a blow to my stomach. I mean, her lip fucking trembled. It was too much to bear. But even after that, she didn't tell me off for being a dick. No, she forced herself to smile at me, continuing the conversation as if I hadn't just made the worst day of her life a hundred times harder.

And then, when she said she was actually going back to that asshole ex to try and work things out, that's when I really lost it.

For years, I'd heard Maggie's stories about this guy who took the 'shitty boyfriend' archetype to a whole new league, and now that I had to stare at the face of the girl who was on the receiving end of that, I couldn't handle it.

It only took two minutes with her to realize that she didn't deserve to be treated like that. The thought of her going back to someone like that, trying to repair things just because she was scared of the unknown, was infuriating. She deserved better. Anyone would.

And that's exactly what I tried to tell her. Except thanks to whatever screwed up, miswired part of my brain that's responsible for thought-to-speech processing, whatever came out sure as hell didn't get that point across.

No, it just made her cry. *I* made her cry. I'd been looking at her since I got home, thinking, *what type of asshole can make a girl like this feel so shitty?* And then I proceeded to do exactly that.

I'd tried to make reparations, telling her that it was fine for her to stay while she looked for somewhere else because, as much as I valued my privacy and space, the idea of her going back to that guy just didn't sit right with me.

She probably would've gotten back together with him, and I would've been responsible, and Maggie would spend the rest of her life continuing to tell me stories about Cassie's shitty relationship. And now that I'd put a face to the name, there was no way I could live with that guilt on my conscience.

So, there she was, now sleeping soundly in the room above me, and I felt a little bit of the tension I always carried ease up.

At least I could do this one good thing, to make someone else's life a little easier. It didn't matter that my space would be taken up for a little bit. I could handle it.

I stayed in the kitchen late, listening to her pad around, the presence of someone else in the apartment feeling strangely foreign. I'd guarded my privacy so fiercely for years that I guess I'd forgotten what it was like to have someone around.

And really, it wasn't the worst thing in the world to give her a few weeks to find somewhere else.

But for just a few weeks, I was sticking to that. Because no matter how endearing she was with those big blue eyes, I couldn't afford to let a stranger disrupt the life I'd worked so hard to keep in order.

And something told me her presence would be no small thing.

CHAPTER FIVE

Cassie

I'd like to think of myself as a hopeless romantic—the kind who dreams of someone catching one glimpse of me, falling head over heels, and vowing to spend forever by my side.

Which, in retrospect, might explain why everyone who knows me always strongly advised against one-night stands. Apparently, they didn't always come with that happily-ever-after guarantee I'd been chasing.

That was why, when I found myself trying to sneak out of a man's apartment for the first time in my life, it came as no surprise that I was awful at it.

But, considering our less-than-stellar first meeting last night, I figured it would be for the best for Liam to see as little of me as possible.

Hence, the sneaking out before the sun had even risen, as if I were some sorority girl trying to make it back to her dorm. It wasn't exactly the walk of shame you heard about in movies, but after the way I blubbered in front of a total stranger, there was definitely a heavy amount of mortification involved.

I'd set my alarm for the earliest hours of the morning, showered, and put the clothes Liam had given me back on to wear for my early morning trek across the city.

Despite his state-of-the-art flooring, the wooden panels still threatened to expose me with every tiptoed step I took. Even the door let out a groan as I pushed it open to make my escape.

"Please don't wake up." I winced, slinging my bag against my shoulder.

I didn't know what Liam did for work or what time he had to be there, but I figured that no one would want to be woken up at five in the morning by their regrettable roommate creeping around their house. Especially when they were used to being alone.

Holding my breath, I continued my descent down the stairs, counting every step to the bottom until I finally reached the landing and threw my hands up in silent victory.

"Good morning," Liam's voice cut through the silence, and my head snapped toward it fast enough to hurt.

Perched in nearly the same spot I'd left him the night before, Liam leaned against the counter, sipping coffee with a neutral expression.

I might've wondered if he'd slept at all if not for the damp hair and fresh t-shirt that suggested he'd already been up for a while.

"No!" I groaned pathetically. "What are you doing up?"

He raised a brow. "Should I not be?"

"Well, I mean, no! It's five thirty in the morning!" I said, dropping my bag to the floor. So much for tiptoeing around all morning.

"You say this as you're standing here, clearly awake," he retorted, staring me up and down. "Unless you have some sleepwalking issues I should know about?"

I most certainly did *not*.

"Did I wake you up?"

"No. Were you trying to?"

"No, I wasn't!" I countered, slightly insulted.

"So, what's the issue?" he asked, sipping from his coffee mug. Coffee that smelled miraculously enticing.

"The issue is." I stared at the cup longingly. "I was supposed to be gone before you woke up! You know, like I was never here."

"I didn't ask you to do that. I told you, it's fine."

"I know, but—"

"You're staying here, aren't you? At least for a few weeks. So, stay. You don't have to go sneaking around. Just do your thing. I'll probably be gone a lot of the time, anyway."

I crossed my arms over my chest, feeling skeptical about an offer that he had been forced into giving.

"I don't know about a few weeks." I thought about how absurdly long that would feel to both of us. "I think I'll ask around today, see if there are any coworkers I can stay with. Hopefully, I can be out of here in the next day or two."

"Whatever you want." He shrugged. "Just know that you being here isn't a huge deal. I can manage."

But I can't, I thought. *I can't stay here knowing the whole time that I'm imposing.*

Instead, I nodded curtly, offering a smile of thanks because, at the end of it all, it really was kind of him to offer. Even if he didn't mean it.

"Do you want coffee?" he asked. Then, at my bewildered expression, he added, "You've been eyeing mine since you got down here."

Well, he was observant.

"Only if you have enough," I said, finally inching closer.

He grabbed the coffee pot, pouring a fresh cup.

"So, where were you planning on going this early, anyway? I doubt they're sending kindergartners in at this hour?"

I laughed out loud at that.

"I need to go home and grab some clothes. In case you didn't notice, I can't exactly wear this to school." I gestured down to his oversized hoodie and sweatpants, clearly made for someone twice my size.

His face tightened as he gave me the once-over before pushing the mug of coffee across the counter toward me.

"Will he be there?" he asked in a clipped tone.

"Dave?" I asked, taking a sip of the black coffee, reveling in its bitterness. "Yeah, but he'll still be asleep."

"And you're sure you want to go there?" he asked skeptically.

As a matter of fact, I wasn't sure.

I absolutely didn't want to go back to the home we'd shared, the same one I'd woken up in just the morning before, thinking it was just another ordinary day. Now, I had to feel like an intruder, going back to get my own belongings.

But Liam didn't really want to hear any of that, so instead, I shrugged.

"It'll be fine. I mean, I need to get my stuff, don't I?"

"Do you want me to come with you?" He surprised me by offering. "We can bring some of it back here?"

"Uh, no. That's okay." I laughed nervously before quickly adding, "Thank you, though! It's just that I should probably figure out what my plan is before I start moving any of my things out."

"Okay, well." He scratched the back of his head. "I don't have a spare key or anything, but I can get one made today and leave it under the doormat for you."

"Liam." I groaned, dropping my face into my hands. "This is so weird. I can't stay here. Last night was more than enough. I think it's better if I just head out now and get out of your way."

He shrugged. "If that's what you want."

"It is," I said, only partly meaning it.

There was no way I'd find another place as nice as this. Heck, I might not even find another place, period. But I'd rather sleep in my car than feel like a burden to another guy. It was a shame, though, because that guest bed of his was the most comfortable night of sleep I'd ever had.

"Thank you for last night, by the way. And the coffee," I said, timidly taking the first sip. "Oh, my God. This is amazing."

"Oh, shit. Did you want milk or sugar or something to put in it?"

"No, no. I actually drink it like this," I said honestly. "You can actually taste the coffee that way."

His lips twitched with what might've been a smile.

"I agree. And to be honest, I would've judged you if you were the type of girl to pour sixteen packets of sugar into your cup first thing in the morning."

"Well, don't worry. I find other ways to get my sugar in throughout the day."

"Oh, yeah?" he asked, the smirk finally breaking through despite what looked like a valiant effort on his part to fight it.

"Yeah. I do a heavy amount of baking, and that requires a *lot* of taste testing."

"Well, I guess it's a good thing you aren't staying here then," he said teasingly. "Because I'm a cookie fiend, and I can't afford to rekindle that relationship right before the season starts."

"What season?" I asked,

"Hockey season." He laughed.

I nodded slowly, not really understanding this guy's obsession with hockey. "Right. Hockey season. Need to be in tip-top shape to cheer your favorite players on?"

"Sort of." His eyes sparked with amusement that I didn't fully understand.

I downed the rest of the coffee while contemplating the bizarre fascination so much of the male population had with sports.

When I looked up, he was staring at me with an unreadable expression, as if he was confused by the mere presence of me.

"Yes?" I asked, unsettled by the directness of his gaze.

"Nothing," He cleared his throat, looking away. "I was just wondering where you met my sister?"

"Oh!" I smiled brightly, fighting a laugh at the memory of my first encounter with Maggie. "It's actually a funny story."

"I'll bet," he said, leaning back slightly with a shrug. When I shot him a questioning glance, he met my eyes and added, "I know my sister. Most situations she finds herself in are, uh, interesting."

"Well, your sister is an angel," I gushed, "because she actually saved me."

His eyes flared in amusement. "Well, you have to tell me now."

"We were in college together," I explained with a wave of my hand. "I'm sure you knew that. Right?"

He looked at me blankly, making me think Maggie hadn't told him after all. It stung, realizing maybe I wasn't as important to her as she was to me.

"Anyway," I continued, jumping into it. "I was at some frat house party, which totally isn't my scene, but I'd just gotten into a fight with Dave and didn't want to spend the night crying in my dorm, so I went—" Liam frowned, and I started talking faster, not wanting him to get bored by my long-winded tale.

Dave had always told me that I made my stories unlistenable with my rambling, and if my boyfriend thought that, I couldn't imagine a stranger having an easier time with it.

"So, anyway, I was there. It was loud. The music was awful. I hated the smell of weed. I mean, I don't even drink, so like, what was I doing there?" I laughed lightly, remembering how out of place I felt.

He stared, listening intently. It unnerved me to have his undivided attention. I wasn't used to someone paying such close attention to my words.

I cleared my throat, continuing, "So, I was about to leave when some guy grabbed my wrist, trying to strike up a conversation with me. But, honestly? He was gross. His breath stunk of tequila, and he was really touchy. Every time I tried to walk away, he'd pull me back to the corner he had me in." I shuddered at the memory.

Liam's eyes narrowed on me, his hand tightening around his coffee mug. "And no one noticed?"

"No, they did." I laughed dryly. "But that's the thing about parties, I realized. Everyone tends to mind their own business about situations like that."

Liam's frown deepened.

"Everyone except your sister, that is," I told him, biting back a smile. "She shoved her way right between us, staring up at this big guy who towered over both of us, and she told him off."

Liam's posture relaxed slightly, his grip on the coffee mug loosening. "Oh yeah?"

"Uh-huh." I nodded. "She was all, 'Get your hands off of her. Can't you see when a girl isn't interested?' And then, when the guy tried to brush her off, she really let him have it. Started flipping out on him in Russian."

Liam raised his eyebrows in genuine shock. "Maggie speaks Russian?"

"Not really!" I burst out laughing, "She was taking some beginner class, so she was spewing out a bunch of random phrases. Like, 'Hello, goodbye, nice to meet you.' But the point was, *he* didn't speak Russian, so she looked terrifying, staring him down, yelling in another language. He took off, and I didn't see him again for the rest of the night."

Liam snorted. "So she just scared him off with some introductory Russian phrases? Sounds like my sister."

His face was softer than it had been the night before, and I could tell some part of that invisible wall had come down an inch or two.

"Yup." I wiped the tears away from my eyes, "And when I asked her what she said to him, we both laughed until we nearly peed our pants. Said she didn't know any threats yet, so she had to wing it and hope for the best. We were inseparable after that for the rest of college."

"I'm glad she was there for you," Liam said, surprising me with this different version of him from the one I'd met the night before.

"Yeah." I nodded, strangely forlorn. "And ever since then, she's been helping me out whenever she can. I've never met anyone like her."

I looked down at my fingers tracing circles around the coffee mug, needing something to focus on besides her brother and his attentive gaze.

"You're lucky to have her for a sister," I admitted, feeling too exposed to meet his eyes. "I wish she was mine."

My heart ached at the familiar sting of missing something I'd never had. As an only child, with one dead parent and the other one hardly present, being lonely was something I'd grown hauntingly used to. At one point, I thought that maybe Dave's family would take me in and treat me like one of their own, but when that didn't happen, I realized that family was something I'd have to live without.

Until I had my own. That hope was one I clung to, maybe a little too tightly—dreams of a life and family I could finally call mine. But now, it seemed just as far away as everything else I wanted.

I looked up to find Liam still staring.

"I am lucky." He nodded, his eyes a bit distant, as if he were in the process of realizing something. "And for what it's worth, I think you mean a lot to her, too. I mean, I can't imagine her sending any other friend to live with me unless she considered them family."

I felt warmth bloom across my chest as I smiled up at him. "Yeah? For real?"

He laughed at my expression. "Yeah. For real."

I forced myself to look away when I realized I'd been staring into his eyes too long. Here I was, telling the guy about how great his sister was, and meanwhile, I was basically swooning over her brother. Pretty sure Maggie wouldn't love that.

My eyes drifted to the clock above his stove, and I jumped. "Oh my God, I've got to get going before Dave wakes up!" I picked my bag up off the floor and darted toward the door. "Thanks for the coffee!"

"Wait, Cassie," Liam said, his arm extending out to stop me in my tracks.

"Are you sure you want to go there? I can give you money to buy new clothes for the day." His face contorted awkwardly. "Then, you can go get your stuff when you know he won't be home?"

My face flamed crimson, knowing the absolute last thing in the world I'd ever do was take a handout from this man.

"Oh my gosh, *no*," I said quickly. "I mean, thank you. So much. That's really nice. But I'll be fine."

"Cassie," he said firmly, disapproval evident in his voice.

He looked down at me with those sea-glass eyes, and despite the tone, I couldn't help but think it was kind of sweet that he cared, even a little. It said a lot about how much he loved his sister and that he'd even extend a little of that protectiveness to me.

"You've done plenty." I smiled up at him, noticing just how much taller than me he really was. "And I'll pay you for letting me stay in your guest room last night. Is it okay if I send it when I get paid on Friday?"

I'd always been proud of myself for paying my own way. In our whole relationship, I never let Dave pay for a thing for me. I liked being independent and hated the idea of anyone begrudgingly feeling responsible for me, monetarily or otherwise.

Liam, however, did not find it amusing. His face contorted in confusion. "What?" He scoffed, slightly irritated. "You're not paying me for sleeping in a room."

"Plus the coffee and the eggs," I added, mentally calculating how much I owed him.

"Are you kidding?" His brows shot up. "That's insane."

"I'm serious." I looked up at him with determination. "I know you didn't want me here, and the last thing I want is for you to think I'm taking advantage of you."

"You don't owe me anything." He shook his head.

"Whatever you say." I smiled innocently, knowing I wouldn't feel settled until I'd made it up to him. "I've got to run," I said, edging closer to the door. Liam stayed in place, watching me go. "Thanks again for everything. It was really nice meeting you!"

He looked like he was about to say something, but I took off before giving him the chance. In the safety of the hallway, I heaved a sigh of relief, feeling unnerved by how easy it had been to talk to him. How kind he'd been despite everything.

It was strange, the feeling in my chest—like I'd left something behind that wasn't mine to take. I didn't want to hear him say goodbye.

And I didn't want to think about why.

CHAPTER SIX

Liam

I'd known my way around the ice since I was old enough to walk. Hell, I wasn't entirely convinced the skating part hadn't come first. But today? I looked like a man who'd never played a game of hockey in his life.

A bit odd, considering I was known to be one of the best hockey players of the current season. It wasn't cocky of me to state that because it was just a fact. Today though? I was on absolute fire. In the sense that my entire game was burning helplessly down around me.

"Brynn!" Coach roared at me from the sidelines. "Pull your head out of your ass and start skating like you mean it!"

I couldn't believe it. Five years in the NHL, and this was the first time it was *me* getting yelled at for performance.

But he had a point. I was off my game. Actually, that was an understatement. I had lost it completely. Along with my head, which I'd inconveniently left off the ice, back in that moment this morning when I'd watched Cassie walk out the door, assuring me she wouldn't be coming back.

I should've been relieved. It's what I'd wanted. And this way, I didn't even have to feel guilty about it. I had given her every opportunity to stay, but she'd been adamant about figuring something else out anyway. By all accounts, I was in the clear So, why did I feel so crappy about it all?

A puck shot past me, and I swore at my incompetency. It didn't make sense that my head was so clouded over a girl I hadn't even known existed twenty-four hours ago. But after everything, I couldn't help but feel slightly invested. I wasn't pretending to know her, but I knew enough to realize that she deserved better than that guy.

She was probably fine. She was a big girl, after all. Metaphorically speaking. In reality, she was actually pretty tiny. Fragile. I bit back a smile, remembering how small she looked when she came downstairs in my clothes this morning. She had to keep rolling her sleeves up while she was talking to me. I'm not even sure if she noticed herself doing it, but the image of it stuck with me.

No, I scolded myself. *Get your head in the game.*

I skated forward, gaining momentum while trying to get possession of the puck again, like the way she'd gone back to get possession of her clothes. Would he give her a hard time about it? Would he try to apologize and win her back? He would be an idiot not to, but God, I hoped that wasn't the case. For her sake.

Not that I'd ever find out. I'd had my first and last meeting with Cassie, and now I was going to continue on with my life. I'd done my part as a dutiful brother and decent human being when I gave her a place to sleep for the night. Even offered it for longer, but she said no.

Why did she say no?

"Are you kidding me?" Coach hollered, red-faced and furious, as I somehow evaded the puck once more. "That's it. Everyone off the ice and take ten. But when we come back, just know the next few hours we're spending here are because Brynn can't get it together."

A chorus of groans echoed from my teammates, all aimed at me. To hell with that. There were plenty of nights I'd been stuck here after hours on account of one of them screwing around for all of practice. I'd say one bad session in five years should earn me a bit of leeway.

"You good, man?" Brody skated up behind me, slapping my back as we neared the edge of the rink.

"Fine," I bit out.

"You haven't played this bad since… well, never."

"Thanks."

"Aw, come on," he laughed. "I'm just checking in. You're not all uptight because of the girl you've got staying at your place, are you?"

"Nope," I said shortly. "The problem's been solved. She's finding somewhere else."

We made our way over to the benches, where I had a gallon of water waiting for me. I moved to take off my helmet, feeling the sweat plastering my hair down against my forehead.

Collapsing on the bench, I took my gloves off and downed a drink of water, trying to force my mind to refocus back where it belonged—on the ice.

"Oh, well, that's great!" Brody looked relieved. "Because, to be honest, I was nervous for you when your sister pitched that idea. But anyway, about your sister—"

"Why were you nervous?" I asked, narrowing my eyes at him.

"Because I know you. And having someone in close quarters with you does *not* sound like a recipe for success."

I tensed, realizing that on any other day, I would've agreed with him without hesitation. But today, it rubbed me the wrong way.

"What's that supposed to mean?"

"Nothing," he said, his expression shifting to one of surprise when he picked up on the edge in my voice. "Just that, you didn't even want to live with *me* when I was looking for a roommate, and I'm your best friend. Never mind some random girl."

"Because we didn't need to be roommates." I bristled. "It's not like we need someone to split rent with."

"Yeah, but living alone is lonely as hell," he said before waving away the topic. "It doesn't matter, I was saying—"

I rubbed a hand over my face, confused by the prick of annoyance I felt at his words. He was right. I didn't do roommates. Not since college. Not even with him. Hockey was plenty of socialization for me, and after all the noise, rush, and chaos of a game, it was only natural to want to escape home to silence and solitude.

Then why was it that I couldn't get that damn little blonde out of my mind?

"—and I just thought it would be cool if you could arrange that." I looked up to see Brody trailing off, apparently at the end of a long-winded sentence I'd completely spaced out for.

"Sorry, what?" I blinked, feeling worse that my distracted state of mind wasn't solely on the ice but spilling over into normal conversations too.

"I was saying that it would be cool to meet your sister again sometime," he said. "Maybe the three of us could go grab drinks or something one night."

"Are you blushing?" I narrowed my eyes at him suspiciously.

"No," he shot back defensively, cheeks reddening even more. "I just thought she seemed cool, is all."

"Right," I said, my voice trailing off as my mind began to wander.

Where was Cassie right now? Did she find a place to stay? Did she get back together with that guy? I needed to know.

"You're clearly vacant today," Brody observed, making me feel like an idiot. "I'm gonna give you some space to recharge because I sure as hell don't want to spend any more time here tonight than we have to. Come back with a clear head, okay?"

I nodded, knowing there was only one way to clear my head for good. And that was to get answers.

Sighing, I gave in to the urge I'd been fighting all day and pulled out my phone. I had to scroll farther down in my message chain than I thought she'd be before I finally found Maggie's name and shot out a text.

> **LIAM:** How'd Cassie make out today?

Maggie's response was almost instant, thank God, because I honestly didn't think I could go another second without knowing.

> **MAGGIE:** Dave's a dick. That's all there is to it.

A flash of irritation shot through me as I contemplated all the many ways he might've hurt her again today.

> **LIAM:** What happened?

I sent back, trying not to sound too invested.

I wasn't really. More curious than anything else. At the end of the day, it wasn't like it affected me one way or the other.

> **MAGGIE:** He had some girl over at their house when she went to get her clothes. Cassie's devastated.

Okay, *that* pissed me the hell off. Reading the text, I gripped my phone until my knuckles whitened, thinking I should probably just leave it be.

But what type of asshole hooks up with a girl the night after his six-year relationship ends? Had he been seeing her before he ended things with Cassie?

Without thinking, I texted back the most important question running through my mind.

> **LIAM:** Where is she now?

A minute later, the answer came in the form of a picture. I clicked on it to see a shot of Cassie sitting on Maggie's couch. Her blond curls were pulled on top of her head while she stared off vacantly at the TV, hugging a pillow to her chest. I zoomed in, like the maniac I am, and noticed her eyes were red. No doubt from a day of crying over that dick.

I felt something shift in me when I saw she was still wearing the clothes I'd given her last night. Before I knew what I was doing, I sent my reply.

> **LIAM:** Bring her back to my place. I'll be home late.

I watched the three dots appear, disappear, and appear again.

> **MAGGIE:** I don't know. She said something about how it wasn't going to work out.

I clenched my jaw, not knowing anything besides the fact that I didn't want the girl in that photo to worry about where she was going to stay on top of everything else going on in her life.

> **LIAM:** Well, it is. Just bring her over and make her comfortable.

I stared down at my phone intensely, waiting for confirmation from Maggie. A minute passed, then two, and I felt a strange anxiety course through me. It was ridiculous.

Maggie's reply came through a few minutes later, and I felt my body finally relax.

> **MAGGIE:** If you're sure

> **LIAM:** I am.

It was settled. Maggie was going to bring Cassie back, she could take her time recovering from that douchebag in peace, and all would be right in the world.

Feeling more in control of my headspace, I downed the rest of my water, put my helmet back on, and took off for the ice.

This time, the cloud that had been over my mind was gone.

CHAPTER SEVEN
Cassie

I don't know how it happened, but somehow, I ended up back at Liam's for the second night in a row, looking far worse for wear after another emotionally traumatizing day.

Something inside me had broken, shattering whatever delusional hope I'd been clinging to about the possibility of Dave and me getting back together.

I'd been stupid to think he would regret it. To think we'd be fine once we saw each other again. I went in with hope in my heart and a grand speech prepared until I saw him.

And her.

In our bed, sleeping.

I nearly threw up.

And what's worse? He didn't even know I was there. The two of them slept through the whole thing, even though the sound of my heart shattering should've been loud enough to wake the neighborhood.

With tears streaming down my face, I took off, not bothering to grab any of my stuff. All I wanted was to get out of there as fast as humanly possible and never go back.

I sat in my car, sobbing, my heart threatening to burst free from the chest that caged it, while I called the only person I could. At once, Maggie swooped in with a plan. Which is how I ended up calling out of work, driving to her house, and crying on her couch while we watched romcoms all day.

She didn't try to offer me any advice or words of comfort. She knew I wasn't ready for that yet. Instead, we sat in comfortable silence as the September sky turned to night, and I realized that I *really* needed a plan now that everything between Dave and me was officially dead.

"Thank you so much for today, Maggie." I looked over at her from where she sat beside me on the couch, frowning down at her phone as she typed away. "I think I should probably head out now."

Her head snapped up in concern, "What? Where are you going?"

"As much as it sucks," I said, heaving a huge sigh. "I think I just have to go to my mom's."

"No way, Cass," she said in a tone of absolute finality, reminding me of her older brother. "You're not going back there."

"Well, I can't exactly stay here." I forced out a laugh, looking around at her small, cramped apartment that was already filled with her mom's bags. "Shouldn't your mom be here soon, anyway?"

"It doesn't matter." Maggie shook her head. "She'll love you."

"And I love you for offering, but there's no way the three of us can live here in this space for any prolonged amount of time without going crazy," I said honestly. "And besides, I'm used to my mom. It's nothing I haven't already lived through. It's not like I have any other options."

"Well," she said, biting her lip as she looked down at her phone and back up at me. "That's not necessarily true."

I raised a brow, inviting her to continue.

"Liam told me to bring you back there."

"What?" I choked out incredulously. "Why would he say that?"

Maggie snorted and shrugged. "I honestly couldn't tell you."

"No way." I shook my head. "I'm not invading his space like that. He already told me he prefers living alone."

"I know my brother, Cassie," Maggie said, her green eyes that looked so much like her brother's locking onto mine. "He wouldn't offer it if he didn't mean it."

I groaned in frustration, covering my eyes from the cruel reality in front of me. There was no easy solution to this problem. No matter where I went, I'd be a burden to someone.

"Come on, Cass," she coaxed, pulling my hands away from my face. "It's not forever. I'll help you look for apartments every day."

"Rooms," I corrected. "I need to rent a room. There's no apartment in this city I can afford on my own."

"Right," she amended. "We'll find you the cutest little place with the nicest roommate we can find. Okay?"

I twirled a loose piece of hair, mulling over the options in front of me. I hadn't lived with my mom for six years, and going back would be torture. Not to mention, it would be me trying to take care of her when I wasn't even sure I was capable of taking care of myself right then.

If Liam was offering, it would mean my own space. I could keep out of his way, out of sight, and out of mind.

"Okay," I agreed with an exhale.

It might not be the best option, but it was definitely the most comfortable. And if he was offering, it must mean he didn't entirely hate me.

"Good," Maggie said, grinning at me, "because I get the feeling Liam would've been pissed if he got home and found out that I didn't bring you over. He's bossy like that. First child syndrome, you know?"

And that's how I found myself on his couch instead of Maggie's, curled up in the near dark of his apartment, where the only light came from the muted glow of the TV and the city's neon reflections streaming through the massive arched windows.

"What am I going to do, Mags?" I groaned in exasperation. "My life is like a cosmic joke from the universe. My boyfriend dumped me.

I'm staying at your brother's house, a guy I don't even *know,* and I have no idea what I'm going to do next. I don't even have any of my stuff."

"One step at a time," Maggie said, sitting beside me, partially for moral support but mostly because I was nervous to be alone in her brother's house. "I'll get your stuff tomorrow and drop it here while you're at work. And like I said, we'll find the perfect place for you. Okay?"

"Thanks, Mags," I said, feeling a few pieces of my heart slip back into place at the way she was absolutely rearranging her life to help me out. She and her brother. "Where is Liam anyway?"

I bit my lip nervously, feeling like our next meeting would be too awkward to handle. I'd left this morning confident that it was the last of his generosity I'd have to take, only to be back on his couch the very same night.

"At practice," she explained, throwing popcorn in her mouth, distracted by the episode of *Friends* we were watching.

"Practice for what?"

"Hockey," she responded immediately, eyes still glued to the TV.

"What, is he in a community league or something?"

Maggie's head snapped toward me, looking over in bewilderment before she burst into a fit of giggles.

"What?" she asked through laughter.

"What?" I echoed, confused about where the humor was in my question.

"Did you just ask if my brother, Liam Brynn, played community hockey?" Her laughter only grew as tears formed in her eyes.

I stared at her blankly, not really sure how to respond when I was clearly missing some important context.

"Cassie!" She gasped, startled when she realized I was completely out of the loop of whatever she thought I should know. "Are you serious right now?"

"Uh." I stared at her guiltily, "yeah?"

"Liam plays center for the Harbor Wolves," she said slowly as if talking through something with a small child. "I thought you knew."

My face paled, and my eyes looked over the apartment in a new light. All those comments I'd made about how into hockey he was rang in my mind. Humiliation washed through me in waves.

"No, no, no." I groaned. "Why didn't you tell me?"

"I thought you knew! Why do you think I invited you to all those hockey games?"

"We live in the city! Everyone goes to the Harbor Wolves games!" I said, frantically searching the cushions for my phone.

"This is too good." Maggie snorted. "What are you doing?"

"Googling your brother!" I screeched as my thumbs typed his name into the search engine.

Sure enough, his face came up instantly. Pictures of him on the ice, in the locker room. Always decked out in the Harbor Wolves uniform and hockey gear. I couldn't believe it.

Stunned, I scrolled helplessly until articles were popping up about him, showing that not only was he a famous hockey player but apparently a highly sought-after one by women everywhere.

I could've guessed the latter just by looking at him. With his dark hair, tall stature, and those green eyes that felt borderline inappropriate to swoon over, considering Maggie had the same ones, I didn't think I'd ever seen anyone more attractive.

But the hockey thing? That was definitely news to me.

"No wonder he likes his privacy!" I shouted. "He probably thinks I'm some crazy fan who's trying to spy on him or something!"

"What…" Maggie said in a feigned voice, "Noooo."

I raised my brow at her, fixing her with a stare.

"Okay, yes." She sighed, coming clean. "That was the reason for his initial hesitation, but I wasn't lying tonight. He really did want you to come back. Insisted on it, in fact."

I found it hard to believe but didn't say anything. I knew there was some element of him feeling sorry for me at play, but since I didn't have any other viable options, it wasn't worth talking about.

The night drew on, and nine o'clock turned to ten when Maggie stood to leave, asking if I'd be okay on my own. I assured her I would. I had my *Friends* with me, after all. She smiled and told me she'd see me tomorrow and left.

Somewhere between episodes, I drifted off to sleep, right there on the couch, looking out at the comforting city lights that reminded me I wasn't entirely alone in the world.

CHAPTER EIGHT

Liam

Drills had lasted for fucking ever on account of my shitty start to the night. Somehow, I managed to pull it together for the second half of practice, but even still, Coach really wanted to send the message home that half-hearted playing would not be tolerated.

I got it. It was how we upheld our status as one of the best teams in the NHL. It was good for us to be broken down mentally and rebuilt stronger. Tougher.

But I'd be lying if I said that my body didn't feel like it was on the brink of collapsing. The guys blamed me, some for not being able to get home to their families. The younger ones for not being able to make the dates they'd had scheduled.

Little did they know that I had just as much reason to want to get home as they did.

And I'd tried to get us out of there. I really had. The entire rest of practice, I'd been able to lock in, feeling a sense of relief that Cassie had somewhere safe to stay for the night.

But when I walked into my condo later in the night, the darkness made me pause. Had Maggie ignored me? Left Cassie to fend for herself somewhere else?

Then I saw the faint light of the television coming from the living room, and I felt the tension evaporate.

I dropped my duffel bag by the door and walked over to the couch to find her sleeping beneath a blanket. I couldn't help but stare, finding an odd sense of ease in the presence of another person in my usually desolate space.

I hadn't really known what to make of the worry I'd felt at the thought of her not being here. And I sure as hell didn't expect to feel so relieved when I saw that she was.

As if sensing me, she stirred, blinking up at me with bleary blue eyes. Immediately, she shifted into a sitting position as if caught doing something she wasn't supposed to.

"Hi," she whispered, rubbing her eyes.

"Hi," I said, dropping down next to her.

"I'm here again," she murmured, voice guilty.

"I can tell." I smirked to myself, amused.

I sank into the cushions, not able to help the exhale that escaped as my body finally relaxed. I hadn't realized it, but I must've been carrying around an unspoken tension for longer than I thought.

"Sorry for being in your space," she said, voice still thick with sleepiness.

"Sorry you had a shitty day," I responded, grateful for the darkness that would hide the faint smile tugging at my lips.

She sighed, glancing back at the TV. "Nothing a few episodes of *Friends* can't fix," she stated wearily as if trying to force herself to believe it.

I stared at the screen, content to just sit in silence with someone. It was nice. Peaceful, even. We watched for a while, nearly reaching the end of an episode when she broke the silence.

"Who's your favorite *Friends* character?" She stared over at me expectantly.

"I don't know." I shrugged. "I never watched it."

This, apparently, was too much for her to handle.

"What!" she screeched, her posture going rigidly straight. "You've never seen *Friends*? How could you be a—How old are you?"

"Twenty-six," I answered.

"How could you be a twenty-six-year-old who has never seen *Friends*?" she cried in outrage.

I felt my lips threatening to pull up into a smile again and found it odd that, after all this time, this girl, of all people, was the one who was able to pull them out of me.

"I don't know." I shrugged. "I've always been busy doing other things."

Like training, watching hockey, playing hockey, and working out, it kept a guy busy.

She scoffed as if my words offended her. But then, the scene playing out in front of us caught her attention, and her eyes were back on the screen.

Two of the characters were fighting, yelling at each other about how maybe they just needed to take some space from each other. The guy, evidently pissed, stormed off. Cassie, apparently invested, started to get teary. This time I figured, instead of being an asshole, I'd just let her ride out the feelings. Besides, it was a comedy show. I knew that much. It wasn't as if it would end on a sad note or anything.

Then, it got worse. The guy went to some bar and started dancing with another woman. I thought to myself, *This is right when he's going to call his girlfriend.* I mean, that's what I would do if I had one. But instead, he took it a step further and kissed the new girl.

I looked over to the spot next to me, knowing this was probably hitting too close to home for Cassie. Sure enough, there were tears welling up in her eyes. I shifted awkwardly, not knowing what to do if she started crying again. I was sure that pulling her in for a hug would be overstepping, and I had never been one for physical contact with people, anyway. But for some reason, I had the most bizarre urge to reach for her and tell her it would be okay.

Of course, being sane, I didn't.

"I thought Dave and I were Chandler and Monica, but we're Ross and Rachel," she said, starting to blubber. "And I hate Ross and Rachel."

Lost, I scrambled for words of comfort. "You're not Ross and Rachel," I said, trying to follow her analogy. "You can be Monica or whoever it is you want. Dave's just a dick. Not part of the equation."

She wiped the tears away from her face. "Yeah." She sniffed. "You're right. I mean, I'm the same age as they are in season one. My whole *Friends* arc is just starting. I should thank Dave because he probably started my plot line for me."

I nodded along in confusion, but hey, if it was making her feel better, I could go along with whatever code she was using. "Right. Exactly."

"I should get to bed," she said, standing up from the couch. "Don't want to be tired for work tomorrow. I already missed a day." She bit her lip guiltily.

"Okay," I said, feeling a strange sense of regret at the loss of her presence. "Goodnight."

She stood, gathering the blanket around her shoulders as she turned to go, granting me a smile more like sunshine than anything else I'd ever seen in my life. Then she left, leaving me there to linger in the darkness.

I rubbed a hand over my face. I must've been lonelier than I ever imagined. It was the only way to explain why I was so unbothered by her being here. I liked knowing that while she was sleeping in my house, she'd be comfortable and kept safely away from dickheads.

She might be upset right now, but I saw what she couldn't. That the loss of that guy wasn't a loss at all. Unless you counted the dead weight being lifted off her shoulders, I knew before long that guy would be a thing of the past. A blip in her rearview mirror.

I sat there in the darkness of the living room as the next episode started to play. To my surprise, I found myself snorting out a laugh at some of the corny jokes. Not the kind of humor that usually landed with me, but somehow, it didn't seem so bad tonight.

It wasn't going to be so bad having her here, either. I was just being a good guy, helping out my sister's friend who'd had a rough time. I had the space. It'd be selfish not to share it, right? Anyone would want to help out a good person who had already been through enough. That's all it was.

When I finally dragged myself to bed, I found sleep came easier than usual. I told myself it was just the satisfaction of knowing I'd done the right thing. Nothing more than that.

CHAPTER NINE

Cassie

Being back at work felt strangely liberating. It was like I had a part of my identity back when the rest of my world had abandoned me.

I might not have my apartment, my boyfriend, or my sanity, but I still had my job, and I was good at what I did. It didn't hurt that it gave me something else to focus on. An idle mind lets the demons in and all that. At least, mine did.

In the last forty-eight hours, I'd let myself wallow, and I'd let myself cry. Now, I needed to get back into action and figure out my life. Things happened, plans changed, and people let you down. I'd always known that. How could I not, with the upbringing I'd had? But still, I'd been stupid. Six years in a relationship had lulled me into a false sense of security. For some silly reason, I thought it had meant something.

Still, I could treat it as a reminder. *You can't really count on anyone but yourself.* That's just the way it was. And thankfully, I still had me.

Not that I felt very much like myself as I walked into school wearing Maggie's clothes. I'd been too much of a coward to grab any of my own after the fiasco of yesterday morning. Usually, I wore colors or florals or some type of pastel palette, but today, I was rocking Maggie's fierce pencil skirt with a fitted black turtleneck. While she always looked stunning, I felt like I'd stepped out of a Tim Burton movie.

At least I had my coffee, courtesy of my new temporary roommate. I'd woken up at a normal time this morning, resigned to the fact that I'd have to lean on Liam's generosity for a little while longer. After getting ready at a leisurely pace, I'd come downstairs to find that he was already gone.

On the counter, there'd been a note, written short and simply, letting me know he'd gone to the gym. Beside it sat a thermos filled with hot, intoxicating coffee. At first, it didn't register. I thought for sure he'd made it for himself and forgotten it, but he didn't seem the type to forget *anything*. Besides, it smelled so good, and I was in dire need of caffeine. If he'd left it behind, why let it go to waste?

So, with Maggie's clothes on my back and Liam's coffee in my hand, I carried tokens from both of the Brynn siblings with me, like armor that might shield me from the cold, harsh world.

I had just gotten into the teachers' room when I felt my phone buzz in my bag. Holding my coffee up in one hand, I used the other to dig through my belongings until I pulled the device out.

On the screen was a text notification from a number I hadn't saved. I frowned down at the message that didn't give any indication of who the sender might be.

> **UNKNOWN:** Cassie?

The text came from another iPhone.

> **CASSIE:** God?

> **UNKNOWN:** What?

> **CASSIE:** Sorry, lol. Who is this?

> **UNKNOWN:** Oh, sorry. It's Liam. I just wanted to make sure I didn't screw up your number.

My heart jolted. Liam was texting me?

> **CASSIE:** How did you get my number?

I shot back, curious.

> **LIAM:** Maggie.

I hesitated, mulling over what exactly to say to my friend's brother-turned-roommate. Before I could figure it out, another text came through.

> **LIAM:** I just wanted to let you know I made a spare key, and it's under the doormat for you.

I felt a rush of warmth at how unexpected it was. I hadn't pegged Liam as the type to make a spare key for anyone, least of all a temporary roommate he didn't even want.

> **CASSIE:** You didn't have to do that.

I grinned down at the phone, a fluttery feeling spreading in my chest because of the fact he had.

> **CASSIE:** Don't worry. I won't be there long enough to warrant a whole spare key made in my honor.

I saw his response bubbles pop up and disappear. Finally, his text came.

> **LIAM:** I'm not worried.

He was a man of few words, that was for sure. Me? I was more of a verbal sparrer, which usually translated to text. Still, there was something endearing about his simplicity. Maybe that's why I found myself not wanting the conversation to end, even when he wasn't giving me much to work with.

> **CASSIE:** Well, aren't you worried that now I can be in and out of your apartment whenever I want? How do you know I'm not going to make a copy of the key and use it even when I move out just because your guest bed is soooo much more comfortable than anywhere else I've ever slept?

His response was faster this time.

> **LIAM:** I think I'll catch the culprit quickly when I hear the Friends theme song playing in the dead of the night.

I let out an embarrassing cackle, amused by the solemn, withdrawn guy I'd first met now cracking a joke with me over text.

I wanted to respond, but I figured he probably had texted me as a courtesy and surely had much better things to do with his time than sit there responding to silly little words I'd typed on a screen.

But that didn't stop me from smiling down at my phone like an idiot as I reread the messages, which apparently did not go unnoticed by my coworkers.

"What's got you beaming so early in the morning?" Jana's voice startled me back into reality.

I blushed, racing to put my phone away as if I were caught doing something I shouldn't.

"Just happy to be here," I said with a grin as the art teacher peered at me knowingly over her mug.

Dropping my stuff down onto one of the tables, I pulled out my lesson plan book to go over details for the next week. Some teachers dreaded the lesson planning, but for me, it was a reprieve. Lost in thought over crafts to prep and new songs to introduce, I didn't hear Marissa until she was standing directly in front of me.

"No rainbows today?" The fourth-grade teacher peered down at me with a tilt of her head.

"What?" I blinked up at her curiously.

"You're usually all—" She searched for the word, making an exaggerated hand motion toward my clothes. "Rainbowy," she concluded, her tone indicating that it wasn't meant as a compliment.

"But today." She gave me the once over. "You're looking distinctly normal."

Heat rushed to my cheeks at the insinuation that the way I usually dressed wasn't considered normal. I scratched at my collar, suddenly feeling out of place.

"Oh, I had to borrow a friend's clothes," I explained quickly. "I wasn't able to get home because—well, there's been some changes—but I needed something to wear today, so—" I trailed off, cringing at the way I always seemed to word-vomit answers at people.

I didn't have to. I didn't owe anyone the personal, intimate details of my private life. And I was sure they weren't interested in hearing it either. So, why did I always feel the need to explain myself?

Marissa arched a brow at my rambling, nodding slowly at my scatterbrained speech.

Humiliating, I thought to myself, wondering why every encounter with her made me feel like an incompetent idiot.

"I think you look very elegant," Jana offered from her spot across the room.

"Thank you," I answered, deflated, forcing myself not to sink deeper into my seat.

My phone buzzed again, and I jumped at the chance to excuse myself from Marissa's scrutiny.

It was a text from Maggie telling me that she was heading over to my apartment to get my stuff for me. I heaved a sigh of relief and shot a text back, telling her I didn't deserve her. And really, I didn't.

She hated Dave. Always had. Yet, she was sacrificing time out of her day to go over and get my stuff so I didn't have to see him again. Maggie was as selfless as they came, and apparently, as I was beginning to realize, it was a family trait.

Gathering my stuff, I headed to the classroom, taking immediate comfort in the space I'd created to be a warm, inviting, safe haven for my students.

How was it that I could feel so utterly powerless out in the real world, interacting with people my own age, yet totally at ease around a group of kids?

The tension started to bleed off of me with each child that trickled in through the door, their chatter filling the room with life and laughter. Each one had something unique to say, show, or boast about. Soon enough, a bit of life started to pour back into me, too.

Julie, my co-teacher, sauntered into the room a while later, juggling her coffee and scrolling on her phone.

"Good morning." I smiled, feeling only a bit dejected at her usual lack of response.

I took a breath, refocusing my attention back to the kids sitting at the small table around me. The tiny chairs weren't the most comfortable for an adult, but considering I felt about two inches tall today, it didn't really matter much.

"Miss Cassie?" a voice spoke, breaking through my thoughts. I looked beside me, finding Emily staring up at me with large doe eyes.

"Yes?" I asked, smiling down at her while she scribbled on a printout of an apple tree.

Coloring in the lines was not a skill we had perfected, and apparently, neither was understanding what color an apple was, but her neon pink tree was adorable all the same.

"Are you sad?" she asked, staring at me intently.

The bluntness of her question caught me off guard, and I opened my mouth to deny it before realizing I couldn't. Kids were a lot more intuitive than anyone realized, and they didn't take kindly to being lied to. I couldn't blame them. I was like them in that way.

"Why do you think that?" I chose instead, settling on the safer response.

"Well," she started, looking at me intently while trying to figure out the logic behind her very accurate assessment. "Your face isn't smiling like normal and—" She squinted, taking in every detail of my appearance. "—and you're not wearing your colors."

I bit my lip to fight a giggle that threatened to spill out. Her observation was both sweet and painfully accurate. My coworkers might not see the appeal of my usual wardrobe, but it was clear that at least one student appreciated it.

I smiled down at her, nodding my head in confirmation.

"You're absolutely right," I said gently. "I do look a little different today."

I scrunched my nose to show her I was right there with her, missing my normal clothes just as much as she did.

"But I'll tell you what—I promise that tomorrow I'll wear the most colorful outfit you can imagine. Deal?"

Her face lit up, the concern melting away into a wide grin. "Good. Your colors make me happy."

That simple statement hit me square in the chest. My coworkers might think I was odd, Dave might not want me, and my current living situation was temporary at best, but here, in this tiny little classroom, my colors—and maybe even I—mattered to someone.

CHAPTER TEN

Liam

Pacing around the living room, I wondered for the millionth time that day what the hell was wrong with me. There was an anxious energy buzzing inside of me that even the morning workout hadn't burned out of me.

Usually, I was occupied. Satisfied to be at home, on my own, in the peace and quiet of the refuge I had created. If not happy, then at least content.

But today, I'd been restless. Jittery, almost. A fact which was proven when my phone dinged, and I leaped for it with the speed I typically reserved for on the ice.

Get a grip. I demanded to myself, wondering why I'd expected the message to be from Cassie.

I told myself that the irritation of it coming from Brody instead was due to the fact that he was sending yet another link to some TikTok video I didn't want to watch.

LIAM: Can't watch these. Don't have the app.

BRODY: Ur so lame

He responded, and then a minute later, a downloaded version of the video came through.

I clicked on it, only for some horrendous song to start blasting over clips of me on the ice, during interviews, or even just walking down the street. It was creepy as hell, if I was being honest.

> **LIAM:** What the hell is this?

I couldn't fight the scowl that appeared on my face while trying to mute the horrendous music playing from the video.

> **BRODY:** It's called a thirst trap, of which u are the star.

> **LIAM:** Don't send me this shit.

> **BRODY:** Smh. Fame is wasted on the cynical.

I slammed my phone down, disgusted with the state of humanity and the horrific misuse of technology, until someone interrupted.

"Knock knock," a sing-song voice called from the hallway, followed by a noise that sounded a lot like a foot kicking against the door. It was all the alert I needed to know that my sister was there.

I sighed, opening the front door to see Maggie's petite frame dwarfed by multiple bags that she balanced in her arms. They wobbled, and I watched her with an amused expression as she tried to regain balance under the weight of her load.

"Thanks for the help," she muttered, toppling inside the apartment.

"Thanks for the new scuff mark on the door," I countered, looking down at her craftsmanship.

"A little reminder of me." She clicked her tongue and beamed, dropping the bags in the foyer.

"And what's all this?" I asked, gesturing down at the wreckage.

"It's Cassie's stuff," she shot me a look. "What do you think it is?"

"Cassie's stuff…" I trailed off absentmindedly, looking down at the collection of color.

"Yeah, you know, the girl who's living in your house?" she spelled out sarcastically. "Did you not notice that she didn't have any of her belongings with her?"

Unblinking, I stared at my sister.

"Are you coming down to help me get the rest?"

"There's more?" I asked, my face scrunching up in disbelief.

"Duh." Maggie rolled her eyes. "And before you freak out, this doesn't mean she's permanently taking up residence here or anything. But, this way, she won't ever have to go back and see that scumbag again. She can just move her stuff from here into her next place."

It made sense, but the jittery feeling I'd carried with me all day only seemed to amplify with Maggie's words.

"Did you see him?" I asked, feigning casualness. "That guy?"

I had to admit I was curious. Especially now that I'd met Cassie in person, but I wouldn't admit that to Maggie.

"Dave?" She puffed out a breath of air, scowling at the name. "Yeah, I saw him. Charming as ever, the dickhead. He had that new girl plopped on his lap the whole time I was getting Cassie's stuff out."

I clenched my fist at my side, not knowing why every little thing was setting me off today. It wasn't like I cared that much, but what gave that asshole the right to go about his life when the girl he'd spent the last six years with was losing every part of hers?

"What's wrong with you?" Maggie asked, her eyes trailing me up and down. "You seem tense. Is it about that article?"

"What article?" I snapped back coldly.

"You didn't see it?" She looked surprised. "Well, I guess that makes sense, considering you're chronically offline."

"Maggie," I repeated gravely. "What article?"

"Woah, no need to pull out the big brother voice." She raised her hands in surrender. "I'll show you."

She pulled her phone out of her pocket, scrolling down before holding it up for me to see. The title stood out in bold, italicized letters.

Liam Brynn: The NHL's Most Reluctant Superstar.

My eyes scanned the article, irritation growing on me with every word I read.

> The Harbor Wolves have had their fair share of star players over the years, but none perhaps as elusive as their current forward, Liam Brynn.
>
> Since the beginning of his career, Brynn has been notorious for his media reluctance, quiet presence, and what some would call his obsessive need for privacy.
>
> Despite this, he's become not only a star player admired by hockey fans for his speed on the ice and intensity in his plays but also a sort of celebrity amongst young women.
>
> Clips of the Massachusetts native have gone viral on TikTok, and videos of him getting flooded with likes, comments, and shares. With these clips, his social media fans alone have garnered more publicity for the team than any other player in recent years.
>
> Despite his athletic ability and his popularity, rumors swirl that Brynn can be difficult for Harbor Wolves Coach Bryan Dunbar to manage.
>
> When asked about rumors of any potential trading of their center, Dunbar commented, "Look, he's a good kid. As long as he plays well, we shouldn't have an issue."
>
> Though Brynn's social media is scarce and his presence in interviews seemingly disengaged, it's clear that he has a passion for the game and a fair bit of talent to back him up.

> One thing's for sure: Boston doesn't want to lose the player who brought us three Stanley Cup wins in his five-year career.
>
> When asked for comment on how he felt about his celebrity status, the twenty-six-year-old said, "I'm here to play hockey. That's it."
>
> Liam Brynn might be as cold as the ice he plays on, but one thing is for certain: he has Boston backing him.

"ESPN published this shit?" I asked, shoving the phone away. "What a joke. You'd think they'd have something better to write about."

Maggie laughed heartily, pocketing her phone once more. "Liam, you know you've always been the elusive mystery guy. Did you think joining the NHL and becoming one of their best players would, what, *lessen* your appeal?"

"I thought that grown adults would be more respectful of a human being's privacy," I growled. "I mean, what is even the point of that article? It's not covering anything game-related. It's just trying to pin me down."

"The people want to know you." Maggie shrugged. "That's the point."

"Well, they don't know me," I spat out more harshly than I intended. "My job is to play hockey, and I don't owe anyone any more than that. Why the hell do they need to be involved in every other aspect of my life?"

"I knew you'd get like this." She tsked, settling against my couch like she belonged there. "You had to have known that this would be your life when you signed up for this."

"I guess I underestimated the creepiness of people. Or the lack of fucking boundaries," I muttered, thinking about the numerous occasions when random women had gotten hold of my phone number and thought it was their right to actually *use* it.

The amount of obscene messages, photographs, and even videos I'd received had no boundaries. *Nothing* could've prepared me for that, no matter what my sister and everyone else thought I'd signed up for.

"Well, they're going to invade your space whether you like it or not. And to be honest, you're only making it worse for yourself. The less you give them, the more curious they'll be."

She had a point, but that didn't mean I had to like it. Or go along with it, for that matter. I wasn't going to feed the insatiable beast that was the public because, like she said, the more I gave them, the more they'd want. And I'd never been much of a giver.

"Look." Maggie sighed. "I'm only saying this because I care about you. But you're so closed off. Not just with hockey, but with everything. You're letting it bleed into your normal life."

"My normal life? And what's that?" I arched a brow at her.

"Exactly." She nodded as if I'd just confirmed her point. "You don't have one anymore. Your whole life is hockey games and training and isolation, and it's not maintainable. You've been closed off for *years*. It's so hard to even reach you."

"Maggie," I said, about to counter everything she was saying, to tell her that it was just *me*, when she held up a hand to stop me.

"No. Liam, I love you, but you need to let someone in. Anyone. Otherwise, you're going to break, and there's going to be no one around to pick up the pieces. Hockey cannot be your end-all, be-all. You're a person. And people need people."

Without warning, and definitely without my consent, my thoughts wandered off on their own, settling on the image of that little blonde that my sister had sprung into my life.

I'd already let her in. To my home, my life, my thoughts.

I shook the thought away, unsure why it had even popped up in the first place. Cassie was temporary. I needed to remember that.

"Well, anyway." Maggie stood from the couch, clapping her hands together. "You're welcome for the therapy session. You can pay me by coming to get the rest of Cassie's stuff from my car."

And with that, she bounded out the front door, leaving me with no choice but to follow.

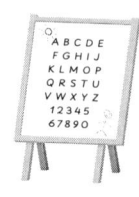

CHAPTER ELEVEN
Cassie

One look at me, and it was painfully obvious to anyone with functioning eyes that I was not, by any stretch of the imagination, athletic. Still, even sedentary human beings required a baseline level of arm strength to navigate day-to-day life.

Unfortunately, somewhere in my genetic code, something had gone catastrophically wrong. My arms weren't just weak. They were useless. Truly abysmal, even by small, unathletic female standards.

This explained why, halfway up the endless stairs to Liam's condo, I was convinced my arms were about to snap clean off. Multiple grocery bags dangled from my hands, their weight pulling on my fingers like they were trying to drag me to the ground.

I looked like an idiot, but at least I was an idiot with a purpose. I'd decided to cook dinner for Liam to prove I wasn't a freeloading leech, sucking up all of the generosity that he had offered me.

Grimacing, I clutched the straps tighter and heaved myself up another step, silently cursing my life choices. By the third-floor landing, my willpower broke.

Reluctantly, I set half the bags down, arranging them haphazardly against the wall where I hoped they'd remain untouched.

"Don't worry," I muttered to the bags like a lunatic. "I'll come back for you. Promise."

With a deep breath, I grabbed the remaining bags and resumed my trek upward, silently praying my arms would hold out long enough to make it to Liam's door.

By the time I got there, I had fresh sweat stains and the revelation that I probably needed to look into a gym membership. But then again, maybe these stairs of his would be enough of a workout.

There *was* an elevator in his building, but considering the number of people already waiting for the lift, I wasn't going to be a jerk by crowding the small space with all my stuff. So, I chose instead to permanently destroy the ligaments in my arms.

Dropping the bags, I made a run for the abandoned groceries I'd left in the stairwell, hoping that no one had touched or tripped over them in my absence.

Heaving a sigh of relief when I found them where I had left them, I grabbed the rest and hurried up the stairs to get started on dinner. I didn't know when Liam got home from work or—training, I guess? But I knew I wanted dinner made and cleaned up before then.

It wouldn't exactly be the nice surprise I was planning if he came home to a huge mess in his kitchen.

The key Liam had made for me was under the doormat where he told me it would be. I used it to let myself in, carrying a few of the bags with me. I unpacked the food on the granite countertops, displaying the ingredients needed to make the perfect homemade chicken parmesan.

Hopefully, this would help show him how much I appreciated him hosting me for a little while. Moving toward the door, I wandered back into the hallway to get the rest of the groceries, letting the door shut behind me. I bent down, scooping them up in both hands, wondering if I'd bought enough food. I didn't *just* want to buy dinner. I wanted to stock his fridge, too. To show him I could pull my own weight and contribute to the household, no matter how briefly I'd be part of it.

Being a burden was the last thing I could handle.

My phone buzzed, and when I saw whose name was flashing on the screen, my heart raced.

Mom.

I didn't have it in me to answer. I'd have to tell her about the breakup, and I wasn't in the right state of mind yet to hear her lecture me about how stupid I'd been to stay with the guy for so long when clearly he didn't want to marry me if it had taken six years of him trying to make his mind up.

I couldn't bear to sink any lower than I already was. Never mind what she'd say about me living with some hockey player I didn't know. For years, she'd begged me to move back home with her, but the time I had spent there had been enough to last a lifetime. There wasn't anything that could make me go back. Not when I finally knew what it was to have peace of mind away from her.

There it was. The pang of guilt that always followed when I rejected the call. Plus, the knot of anxiety because I knew ignoring her would be so much worse than just dealing with her.

I stared at my phone as if it were a bomb about to go off, and then it happened.

The texts started pouring in.

Selfish. Ungrateful. You'll miss me when I'm gone. And a dozen other messages of similar sentiment, the wording getting more colorful with each message that came through.

I inhaled a shaky breath, hating the way my body still tensed in fear despite her being miles away from me.

I muted the message thread with her, knowing that they'd just keep coming for the rest of the night, and I went to make dinner.

Correction: I *tried* to make dinner. But one wiggle of the doorknob told me that I'd messed up spectacularly.

"No, no, no, no, no." I shook my head, willing it not to be true as I frantically twisted the handle back and forth to no avail.

"Are you kidding me!" I groaned, staring up at the ceiling helplessly.

"Uh," A voice called from down the hall, alerting me to the fact that I was not alone. "Excuse me, but you can't be here. This building is residents only."

I looked over to see a middle-aged woman popping her head out of an apartment a few doors down.

"I'm staying here," I told her, figuring it would be enough to satisfy her confusion and send her back on her way.

"Uh, huh." She nodded skeptically. "Sure, you are."

She didn't believe me? I stared at her, dazed, wondering why she was staring me down as if I were some type of criminal. Surely, she'd heard of the concept of people having guests? Then I realized I *was* frantically trying a doorknob that wasn't working, looking more than slightly demented as I tried to get it to open without a key.

"Really," I told her. "I'm staying here. This is Liam Brynn's apartment," I offered, hoping that providing some information might show her that I wasn't some random person trying to break into an apartment.

"I don't doubt that you know whose apartment it is." She snickered. "They all do. But really, he's just a nice young man who wants his privacy, and I think it's despicable that you girls won't leave him alone."

She shook her head, her eyes showering me with buckets of disappointment, the likes of which could rival even my mother.

"*What?*" I said, my voice bordering on screech-like, "You think I'm trying to, what? Stalk Liam?"

"It's not the first time, and it won't be the last, unfortunately." She shook her head sadly. "Now, you get out of here before I call security."

I blanched, panicked by her words. Without the key, I didn't have any other proof that I was actually staying there, and I was horrified at the prospect of being thrown out onto the streets, barred from entry to the place I'd be living for the next few weeks.

"No, honestly. I'm staying here. As his guest. I just locked myself out two minutes ago. That's why it looks like—" I trailed off, staring down at my hands, which admittedly looked guilty as they still were latched onto the handle that would refuse to give way.

"Liam never lets women into his apartment," she said adamantly, her eyes narrowed on me as if the more I said, the guiltier I looked. "No one except his sister, and you're not her."

"Right!" I said, latching onto her words, my demeanor desperate. "His sister! Maggie. She's my friend! That's how I know Liam. I'm friends with Maggie, so he's letting me stay here because he has the room!" I scrambled to explain.

Knowing it might be the only proof I had, I picked up my phone and called her, thanking God when she picked up.

"Maggie!" I cried out manically, pressing the button to put her on speakerphone.

"Hi, Cass," she said, her voice sounding a little scared. "You good?"

"No, actually," I said, eyes still locked on Liam's intrusive neighbor. "I'm locked out of your brother's apartment, and his neighbor thinks I'm breaking in."

"What?" Maggie snorted before bursting into laughter that filled the hall. "Who is it?"

"I don't know," I said, the woman listening in with interest. "But you're on speakerphone. Can you tell her that I'm supposed to be here and I'm not some crazy fan?"

The sound of Maggie's laughter mixed in with her words, making her somewhat unintelligible, but she still tried her best to assure the woman that I was, in fact, staying with her brother, NHL star Liam Brynn, and no, I was not a deranged stalker, but thanks for looking out for him.

The woman tsked as if she still wasn't fully convinced, but she turned on her heel and left without further comment.

"Thanks, Mags. She's gone." I sighed, dropping to the floor with my back against Liam's door. "But how am I supposed to get in?"

"Oh, no problem," she said airily. "Liam keeps a spare key under the doormat."

"I used that one to get in." I groaned.

"No, Liam made you your own key," she said by way of explanation. "The spare key should still be there."

My heart jumped. Maybe I hadn't screwed myself over. I reached down, flipping the mat, finding nothing but the floor beneath.

"Nope." I shook my head. "No luck."

"What?" she asked incredulously. "Look again. It's been there for as long as he's lived there."

In case I'd missed something because I didn't always trust myself, I looked again. Hard. Even looking at the mat itself in case it somehow melded into the fabric. But there was absolutely nothing metallic as far as I could see.

"It's not here, Mags." I sighed. "I can't believe I did this. Your brother's gonna hate me."

"Give me two seconds. I'll call and ask where he moved it," she said before hanging up.

Just two inches of wood separated me from the cold, dimly lit hallway and the warm, inviting apartment where all the ingredients for a mouth-watering dinner were waiting for me. Yet, here I sat, alone with my thoughts, contemplating the way I managed to screw every aspect of my life up, big and small.

I liked to keep busy, to keep my thoughts at bay. When I was forced to sit down in the moments of lull that life always had, it was harder to turn my brain off. The floodgates opened, and the bad feelings came, and all I wanted to do was curl up into a ball and hide.

Surprisingly, I thought of Liam. The way he made me feel… okay. I wasn't so overwhelmed during the brief moments I'd spent with him. It was almost like his presence was so colossal that it distracted me from my own life. He gave me something else to think about. That something being *him*.

Stop, I mentally ordered myself. *You're no better than his fangirls, after all.*

I shook him out of my head, relieved when my phone dinged once more, only to have that relief snatched away by the words written on the screen.

> **MAGGIE:** Looks like you'll have to go to the rink to get his key. Sorry.

Great.

CHAPTER TWELVE

Liam

Nothing like hockey to get your brain jostled up nice and good inside your head.

I'd been distracted for a *second*. One measly second. That's all it took for my teammate to slam me up against the glass, laughing the whole time.

"Ha!" Ryan called, skating away speedily because he knew what was good for him. "I got Brynn."

"Yeah, well, don't think it'll happen again." I scowled, pursuing him on the ice, just until I saw the fear light in his eyes.

As an NHL player, Ryan Thomas was big in his own right, but he was no match for me. At 6'4", I had an inch or three over most of the guys on the team. And while I was on the leaner side compared to some of them, my height definitely gave me an advantage more often than not.

Height and speed. That's what I had going for me, and I wasn't about to let Ryan forget it. Following after him, I feigned left, darted right, and cut him off mid-ice, sending him scrambling to keep control of the puck.

"Okay, okay!" he called, holding up a hand as I closed the distance. "Truce, Brynn. Don't make me regret it."

I smirked, skating backward to let him breathe. "That's what I thought."

"Finally," Coach yelled from the side. "Some camaraderie! This is what I've been wanting!" He clapped his hands together.

"Camaraderie?" Brody skated up beside me, grinning. "If that's what we're calling bullying, Ryan, then I'm all for camaraderie."

"I'm on board with that," Ryan chirped.

As Coach blew the whistle to signal a break in practice, the rest of the team kept their banter going all the way to the locker room, apparently not taking notice of the fact that I wanted nothing to do with it.

"Hey, Brynn," Brody called over his shoulder, his grin as smug as ever. "If you ever decide to write a book on how to take life way too seriously, I'll buy the first copy."

"Sure you will," I shot back, pulling my phone out of my bag. "I'll even sign it for you. 'To Brody: thanks for being the world's biggest pain in the ass.'"

Brody laughed, tossing his towel into the hamper. "Aww, Brynn. You do care."

I ignored him, chugging down an ungodly amount of water before unlocking my phone and scanning for messages. Some twisted part of me was hoping there'd be a text waiting for me from Cassie before I mentally forced the idea out of my head. This girl wasn't my friend. Why would she be contacting me?

What I did have was several missed calls from Maggie. Six in the last five minutes. I dialed her number, mentally preparing myself for her to tell me something crazy, like that she had a second friend who desperately needed to use my car for a week.

"Where's the key?" She asked before I even had the chance to utter a greeting.

"Hey, Mags. What's up? I'm good, how are you?" I responded dryly in an effort to show her the rudeness of her greeting.

"Did you move the spare key?" she repeated expectantly.

"Yes," I said tersely. "Why? Do you need it?"

"Where did you move it?"

"The kitchen drawer," I responded dryly.

"Well, that's a dumb place to keep a spare key," she responded with agitation.

"Why do you need it?"

"I don't. Cassie does."

My body tightened. "I left the one I made for her. Is it not there?"

"No, she used that one but locked herself out after that. Now she can't get back in, and your neighbors think she's some puck bunny trying to break into your apartment."

I stifled a laugh at the thought. Cassie was anything but.

"Well, tell her to come by the rink and pick up my key," I said casually, ignoring the way my heart rate was spiking at the thought of her showing up here.

"Fine, I'll text her. But she might just wait in the hallway for you to get home."

"What?" I asked incredulously. "Don't let her sit in the hallway. I'll be here for a few more hours. She needs to just come and get the key from me."

"Well, I'll tell her she can, but she gets shy about stuff like that. I doubt she'll be too eager to walk into an NHL practice. Especially since she already thinks you hate her."

I stilled at those words. She didn't actually think that, did she? I didn't hate her at all.

"She does?"

"Well, I don't know about hate, but she's definitely picked up on the vibe that you're more of a solo guy."

Damnit, I thought. *Did she feel uncomfortable being there? Did she think I resented her presence?*

I wouldn't blame her if she did. I certainly hadn't welcomed her in that first night. But I didn't resent it anymore, and I'd told her that. I was happy to help while she found her footing again.

"Okay, she just texted back that she's coming," Maggie said in the silence of my contemplation.

"Great," I responded as if my heart hadn't done a tumble at those words.

"Why did you move the key anyway?" she asked.

"I don't know." I tried to shrug her off. "Why does it matter?"

"I'm just curious why you moved a key that's been in the same spot since the day you moved in?" she asked.

"It's just a privacy concern," I responded. "You know how many people try to get in when I'm not there."

"Well, it wasn't a big privacy concern before," she countered, and I could picture the look on her face on the other side of the line.

"Yeah, well, that's when it was just me living there."

"Meaning?"

"Meaning, I'm not going to leave a key to my apartment that anyone can use to let themselves in when I have a girl living with me. It's just not safe."

In Maggie's silence, I mentally chastised my word choice.

"Staying," I corrected quickly, running a hand through my hair. "A girl staying with me. Not living." *Definitely not living.*

"Aww," Maggie gushed dramatically. "Is Liam being protective over his little sister's friend?"

"No," I said in a clipped tone. "It's just common courtesy. I wanted her to feel safe."

Wanted her to *be* safe. I wasn't going to chance some crazy fans being able to get in when she was there inside the apartment. It didn't matter as much when it was just me. I was more than capable of calling security or escorting unruly fans out myself, but I wasn't going to chance that with Cassie there.

"Awww," she repeated in a sickening tone. "You *care!*"

"It's just practical!" I responded, getting worked up. "Have you seen the girl? She's so tiny. I don't want any creepy, hockey-obsessed guys to break in while she's there."

"You looooove her," Maggie droned on.

"Shut up, Maggie." I groaned.

"Awwwww, you're not even denying it!" she squealed into my ear, causing me to hold it away from my face while I recovered from the high decibels.

"Well, I don't!" I responded gruffly. "I didn't think I'd have to say that to you. I don't even know her. It's just a favor for *you,* in case you forgot."

"Calm down, I was kidding," she said, still laughing. "She'll be there in fifteen minutes."

"Okay," I bit out. "Bye, Maggie."

"Bye, *loverboy.*"

I hung up to the sound of her snickering down the line.

Little fucking sisters, man. They were a guy's worst nightmare.

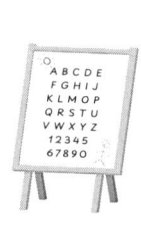

CHAPTER THIRTEEN

Cassie

Who knew people cared so much about hockey?

The way security at the arena gave me the third degree alerted me to the fact that people—strangers, actually, tried to get into a closed practice. I thought only celebrities had that kind of following. Frankly, I was getting sick of being mistaken for a crazed fan.

"I'm here to see Liam," I explained for the tenth time. "I'm his—" *Roommate? Friend? Sister's friend?*

Which one would get me closest to lowering the security guy's scarily high defenses? I mean, really, what did he think I was going to do, even if I was a crazed fan? Any of those hockey players could throw me over their shoulder and toss me out the side door. And I really needed that key.

"You're his what?" he dared me to continue, causing me to blush all over.

"Cassie!" Liam's voice broke through the awkwardness like an angel descending down to earth.

"Liam! Thank God," I said, watching him jog over to me.

He looked *good*. His hair was slick with sweat, and his cheeks flushed with exertion in a way that was undeniably masculine.

"Look, see." I took the liberty of reaching over to Liam when he got close enough and dragging his arm over as if he were my physical proof. "I'm here for this guy." I pointed up toward him. "I'm not crazy."

He smelled minty and somehow fresh despite the fact that he'd clearly been working out pretty intensely.

"Debatable." Liam snickered, peering down at me.

"Hey!" I said, shoving him away, if only because the smell of him combined with the flushed look on his face left me feeling jittery.

"What?" He laughed. "I'm just saying that you standing here convincing someone that you aren't crazy looks a little crazy. I heard you from all the way over there."

"It's not my fault," I pouted. "This guy didn't believe me when I told him why I was here."

"Mr. Brynn?" The security guard looked toward Liam for confirmation of my story.

"She's with me." He nodded, lips twitching in amusement.

The security guy gave Liam a clipped nod, and then I was being led away by Liam.

"Locked out, huh?" he said, bringing us deeper into the arena.

"Yeah," I admitted, shoulders dropping shamefully. "Sorry."

"You're fine." He chuffed out a laugh before leading me toward the bleachers beside the rink. "It happens."

"Woah," I said, my jaw dropping as I watched gigantic men skate around with more grace than I ever thought capable. "They're so fast!"

"They are." He grinned in agreement. "I think that's why the NHL signed them."

"Ah!" I embarrassed myself by squealing but couldn't contain the utter amazement I felt at seeing the way they moved with such ease. "Did you see that? He just…He moves like he was born on blades—fast, smooth, and just cocky enough to make it look easy."

"Haven't you ever watched hockey?"

"Well, yeah. In passing." I nodded. "But this is way different up close. I didn't think people could actually move like this on ice!"

"I'm sure they'll be honored by the high praise," he said, bending over to reach into a duffel bag.

Suddenly, my attention was all on him, taking in the way his broad stature filled out his gear. He really was something, and I was finding it less and less difficult to see why everyone thought I was here to stalk him.

Did I actually just think that? About Maggie's brother?

"What?" Liam turned in concern, fingers working to pull a key loose from its ring.

"What?" I asked back.

"You groaned."

"I did?" My eyes widened.

Crap. I definitely did not mean to do that out loud.

"Yeah." He laughed. "You did. Are you okay?"

"Yes. I'm fine." I nodded. *Besides the fact that I seriously need to get my thoughts under control.* "Thank you."

"For what?"

"Huh?"

"Why are you thanking me?"

"Oh," I said, shifting my weight. "For asking if I was okay?"

He stared at me strangely for a moment before holding out the key for me. I reached up to take it, but he pulled it away.

"You have to promise you won't lose this one because then neither of us will be able to get in, okay?" He looked down at me, feigning sternness.

"Right. No leaving the key on the counter and locking myself out. Got it. I'll only make that mistake once."

He lowered his hand enough for me to grab it, our fingers grazing each other as I took it from him. I snatched it back faster than normal, my heartbeat racing slightly.

He was intimidating. Especially here, in his element, while I was so wildly out of place.

"You sure you're okay?"

I nodded. "It's cold in here." As if that was enough to explain the awkwardness I could feel radiating off of me.

The corner of his lip turned. "It is an ice rink, after all. Didn't you bring a jacket?"

"Locked myself out, remember," I explained. "Didn't exactly think to bring one on my big trip into the hallway."

"Well, here." He reached into his duffel bag once more, this time pulling out a hoodie.

"Oh, that's okay." I shook my head in refusal. "You don't have to do that."

"Stop doing that," he said, putting the sweatshirt in my arms. "Stop saying no to everything I try to give you."

"But I—"

"Cassie. It's cold out. Wear it for the car ride home, okay?"

Home, I thought. *Wish I had one of those.*

But I knew what he meant, so I nodded, mumbling a thanks in response. I pulled it over the top of my head because I really was at the point of trembling from the chill in the arena.

As usual, it fell to my mid-thigh. I rolled the sleeves up a few times so I could have use of my hands. I stared up at him, taking in the full extent of his features in the light. He was beautiful. Dark wavy hair and a few freckles across his nose. A strong jaw. And those *eyes.* Why couldn't I pull myself away from them? And *why* was he looking back at me with similar intensity?

Did he think I was creepy? Could he tell that I'd been checking him out? Oh, God. I was going to ruin the only living situation I had because I was drooling over a big, handsome hockey player who'd already made it clear he hated people who did that.

"Hey, Brynn." We both flinched, breaking eye contact at the sound of someone slamming their glove against the glass. "Get back here, huh? Some of us don't want to be here all night."

I looked over at the hockey player, noticing the way he looked at me in puzzlement before Liam's voice pulled my attention back toward him.

"I'll be right there," Liam told him, his voice gruffer than it had been.

"Mhm," his teammate said distractedly, giving me the once-over.

Liam stepped in front of me, slightly blocking me from view, and I wanted to die of mortification. He was probably embarrassed to be seen with me. Now, he was probably going to hear an earful from his teammates about the girl who showed up at practice, and I knew how much Liam liked his privacy. I was sure he wouldn't be too thrilled to have to explain who I was or what I was doing there.

But he might because he'd probably set the record straight instead of letting his team think I was his girlfriend or something.

Like anyone would believe that, I mentally chastised myself.

"Sorry about interrupting. I'll leave," I scrambled to assure him. "But I have something for you, too."

I pulled the cash from my back pocket, having made a pit stop at the drive-thru ATM. I didn't want to show up empty-handed while I was interrupting his practice and asking for something.

"What is this?" he asked.

"I know it's not a ton," I said sheepishly, holding the wad of $500 toward him. "This won't even cover half your rent, probably, but I wondered if I could give the rest to you later?"

"Absolutely not." He shook his head, causing all the color to drain from my face.

Of course not. I should've known better. His place was so nice. His rent was probably in the high 2000s for something like that in the city. Of course he would want more than $500 while I was staying there, using his space, his shower, and his food.

"Right." I nodded quickly. "Sorry. I'll go get more now and come back—" I mumbled, mentally thinking of how I could come up with the rest of the money fast.

I wasn't sure I had much more in my checking account, but money put toward a place to sleep at night was the best use I could think of for what little I had.

"I don't want your money." He bristled, looking almost offended. "Put it away."

"What?" I asked, trying to process what he meant. "Should I give it to you later when I have the full amount?"

"Cassie, *no,*" he said, staring intently. "I don't want your money, now or ever. I offered you a place to stay, no strings attached. I have the space. It's no big deal. I would never ask for you to *pay* me to sleep in a spare room I already have."

"But I—"

"No buts," he said, grabbing hold of my outstretched hand and guiding it toward my pocket. "Put your money away and get going before you freeze, okay?"

I frowned up at him, feeling caught in a trap. He laughed, taking hold of my shoulders and shaking slightly.

"Stop making that face. You're okay." He looked over his shoulder to where the coach was calling for him. "I've got to go, but I'll see you at home, okay?"

I forced out a nod, and he smiled, jogging away from me, leaving me there staring after him. I turned to go, feeling the soft weight of his hoodie and the slight press of the key in my pocket like reminders of just how much I owed him.

But maybe, just maybe, Liam Brynn wasn't keeping score.

Liam

"Oh, to be Liam Brynn and have beautiful women swarm hockey practice for you." Ryan placed a dramatic gloved hand on his heart and pretended to swoon as I glided back onto the ice.

Choosing to ignore his words rather than feed into the curiosity that was looking at me from nineteen pairs of eyes, I tried to start practice back up.

"Well?" Hudson asked expectantly, "Are you going to leave us hanging?"

"Yes," I responded dryly, sending the puck flying toward him.

He caught it with a grin but made no move to start our drills back up.

"It's okay, guys," Our goalie called out innocently. "Liam's just being protective over his new girlfriend."

A chorus of snickering 'awwws' reverberated through the rink.

"Shut up." I bristled. "It's not like that."

"No? What's it like?" Ryan asked.

"None of your business."

"So, what I'm hearing is, if it's not like *that,* then that means she's single?"

"Hey, leave him alone." Brody laughed. "He obviously plans to marry her, so she's off limits."

"*What?*" My head snapped to Brody so fast I almost pulled the muscle in my neck.

"Well." Brody shrugged. "You gave her your hoodie. That's practically a proposal in girl code."

The resulting laughter from the team pissed me off. Not so much the teasing, but the fact that they'd been watching us at all.

"Don't you guys have anything better to do than spy on me?" I growled.

"Didn't you know?" Hudson grinned. "There's nothing more interesting than *Liam Brynn.*"

"So, who's the girl?" Ryan asked, his persistence pissing me off.

It was a normal question. A valid one to ask even, but I stiffened at his words. I didn't want to explain. I didn't want them to even think about her.

"No one," I said with the tone of closing the conversation down.

But our players apparently had a death wish. They *were* hockey players, after all.

"Well, if she's not yours, then you won't mind passing along her contact info to me," one of the guys quipped.

Yes, I fucking minded, I thought, surprising myself by the way my entire body thrummed with tension.

"She's not interested," I bit out tightly.

Hudson grinned, skating closer. "Come on, Liam. You can't just bring a girl to practice and expect us not to ask questions."

"She was here for five minutes," I muttered, dragging a hand down my face. "And she's not my girlfriend. She's—"

"What? Tell us what she is." Ryan looked at me with a shit-eating grin.

I glared at him. "She's my sister's friend. That's it. Drop it."

"*That's* Maggie's friend?" Brody's shock was evident. "Yeah, good luck with that." He snorted.

"What the hell is that supposed to mean?"

"It means you have an incredibly attractive girl living with you, and for years, you've been determined to keep the opposite sex at a thirty-foot radius."

Brody's words caused an outburst throughout the team as they all descended like wolves with their questions.

"What the fuck?"

"She's what?"

"*Living with you?*"

They all exploded with similar sentiments at once.

"Thanks, Brody," I deadpanned. "That was helpful."

Brody held his hands up in surrender. "We're a team. It's not like they wouldn't have found out eventually."

"They wouldn't have because it's *temporary*," I emphasized the last word with considerable effort.

"Maybe not." Brody laughed lightly. "Considering *that's* what she looks like."

"I'm just helping Maggie out. You know, my sister, who asked me for a favor? Sort of how *you* asked me for a favor recently?" I looked at him pointedly. "I mean, you do want me to put in a good word for you with Maggie, right?"

Brody stilled, looking at me before nodding. "Got it. Right. My lips are tied."

"Well, if you're sure she's not your girlfriend, then that means you're going to be the most eligible bachelor for the gala."

"The what?" I asked with furrowed brows.

"The charity event." Ryan filled in the blanks. "We're all getting put up for auction."

"What the hell does that mean?" I asked.

"It means we'll be there for the mass of women to bid on dates with us," Hudson added. "Kind of creepy, but who am I to deny the women what they want?"

"You already *know* Liam's going to get the creepiest old women to buy him." One of the guys cracked up. "She's going to bring him somewhere sketchy as hell for their date, and we'll never hear from him again."

"I didn't sign up for that!" I scowled, thinking that there was no way in hell I'd ever participate in something so public.

"You don't sign up for it. It's mandatory," Brody said. "The only guys exempt are the ones with wives or girlfriends."

Which was about three guys on our whole team. I, of course, wasn't one of them.

I stared at Brody like he'd grown a second head. "You're joking."

"Not joking," he said with an exaggerated wince. "Coach made the announcement last week. It's good PR for the team."

"It's a nightmare," I muttered. "I'm not doing it."

"You don't have a choice, Brynn," Ryan chimed in, skating by with an infuriating smirk. "Especially since you just loudly proclaimed to us that you definitely *don't* have a girlfriend."

"Just because I don't have a girlfriend doesn't mean I should be forced to give up my privacy for money," I muttered, knowing that none of the guys held the same sentiment.

A lot of them actually thrived off of the attention from fans, the media, and everything else that came with this lifestyle. Apparently, something was wrong with me because I just couldn't get behind it.

Even when the guys moved onto the topic of going out for the night, all I could think about was how much I looked forward to going home.

The image popped into my head of Cassie on the couch the night before, and suddenly, I had a newfound urgency to finish drills so we could wrap it up for the night.

We trained hard for another few hours, and the time passed by quicker once we stopped chatting and got in the zone. I pushed my body to its limit, straining hard enough so I couldn't be distracted by any other thoughts.

When we finally finished up, I found myself moving a little faster as I showered and packed my gear up, filled with an urgent rush I didn't understand.

"So that's a no to going out with us tonight?" Brody asked, still taking his time drying off from the shower.

"Definitely no," I responded.

"Figured." He shrugged. "Just thought I'd ask. But hey, you'll talk to your sister for me?"

I rolled my eyes, thinking that the last person in the world my sister would go for was someone associated with hockey. But to throw him a bone, I nodded.

"Sure. I'll talk to her. Next time I see her."

Brody's eyes lit up, and he clapped me on the back. "Thanks, man. And hey, you know we were all just messing with you earlier, right? I know you're not into the whole relationship thing."

I frowned, not sure what he meant. It was true I hadn't had a girlfriend the whole time I'd been in the NHL, but did people really think I was entirely opposed to the idea?

Was I? Now that I thought about it, I realized I sort of had been. There was no one I'd even entertained the idea of in the last few years. No one interested me enough to think about them that way.

"I'm not against relationships," I said, picking my bag up and slinging it over my shoulder.

"Right, like, for other people."

"No. For me," I corrected.

Brody laughed. "Yeah, okay, Mr. *I-Reject-Anyone-Who-Comes-Near-Me*."

"I just hadn't met the right person," I said before realizing my word choice.

Brody's eyes widened, but I rushed to correct myself.

"I haven't yet, but that doesn't mean I never want it."

"So, do you?"

I thought about it. The idea of one person by my side, doing life with me, sharing private moments with just the two of us.

I could never imagine it before because everyone had always wanted something from me. They'd never liked me in any real way.

Cassie wasn't like that… and with her, I got to feel what it would be like to have someone at home, to sit on the couch with, or have coffee in the morning with…

What the fuck is wrong with you? I scolded myself when I realized where my train of thought had landed. *You don't even know her, and she's reeling from a serious breakup.*

It wasn't Cassie that I was fantasizing about, I realized. It was just because she was the first normal girl I'd met who wasn't after me because I was a hockey player. And she was sweet and shy and kind.

I couldn't lie to myself and say she was nothing to me. I *did* enjoy being in her presence. And I liked the way she blushed or stammered when she was embarrassed. It was cute.

Friends, I thought suddenly. *This must be what it's like to have a girl for a friend.*

That explained why I felt a warm fondness at the sight or even the thought of her. It wasn't anything else but that. And there was nothing wrong with being a friend to someone who had been through a lot.

"Liam?" Brody's voice interrupted my inner monologue.

"What?"

"I asked if you wanted that because I have plenty of girls I could set you up with." He beamed, his face animated as he schemed. "Are you just secretly shy? Do you need a wingman? Because I could be a great wingman."

"No, Brody." I sighed. "I don't need a wingman."

"But you just said—"

"I meant that I'm not opposed to it if it happens. But I'm never going to be hanging around bars trying to pick up women."

"But that's the beauty of being you!" Brody exclaimed. "You don't have to try to pick up women. They'll be throwing themselves at you."

The very thought of it made me cringe.

"Hard pass," I said, itching to get out of this conversation and, more importantly, this whole arena.

"You're killing me, Brynn." He groaned. "Sending me out all on my own."

"You mean all on your own with half the guys on the team?"

"But no one gets me the way you do," he feigned protest. "Man, you having a girlfriend now sucks."

"I don't have a girlfriend."

"Girl roommate. Potential girlfriend. Whatever." He swatted away the air. "Point is, look at you rushing off to get home instead of talking with your best friend. Is this what it comes down to? Have we finally reached the point where I have to share you with some woman?"

"All I'm doing is going home. Like I do every night after practice," I said, edging toward the door.

"Whatever," he called out. "But when the wedding comes around, I'll be rightfully pissed if I'm not the best man, okay?"

And because I knew it was the only way to appease him and close the conversation so I could just get out of there, I told him, "Okay. You'll be the best man."

CHAPTER FOURTEEN

Cassie

I never thought I'd be so ecstatic over ice in my life, but once you're at a certain point in your twenties, the little things start to make a difference.

Like the built-in ice maker that came with Liam's top-of-the-line fridge. I screwed off the lid of my reusable tumbler, doing a happy dance as I pressed the cup against the ice dispenser.

As I filled the cup to the top with cold, crunchy ice, I heard the rattle of keys and the sound of the door swinging open right in the middle of my awkward flailing dance.

"Liam!" I spun around with a guilty expression on my face.

"Am I interrupting something?" he asked casually, leaning against the doorframe as the hint of a smile formed on his lips.

Dressed in his joggers and hoodie, I was startled to realize he looked just as good in that as he did in his gear.

"No, I was just having a moment of appreciation for your ice maker."

"My ice maker?" His brows nearly hit the top of his forehead as a grin overtook the bottom half of his face. "Are you serious?"

"What?" I blushed furiously. "I've never had one before. With the amount of water I drink, this is literally life-changing."

He huffed out a laugh. "Well, I'm glad to be able to provide that weirdly specific joy for you."

Liam dropped his bag by the door before coming closer, filling the kitchen with his larger-than-life presence. I fought the urge to retreat.

"What's all this?" He looked around at the food I had set out on the kitchen island. His eyes scanned the plates of chicken parmesan I'd set out for us.

"Oh!" I said sheepishly. "I made you dinner."

"Dinner?" he asked, uttering the word as if it were a foreign concept.

"Yeah, as a thank you for everything." I shrugged. "And I know you're probably tired from practice, so we don't have to eat together or anything, but I just thought in case you were hungry…" I finished with an awkward shrug.

I stared up at him expectantly, watching closely for his reaction. It was a habit I'd picked up in childhood as a result of growing up with my mother. Even though I was a grown adult now, I still found myself always on edge, waiting to see what a person's next move would be.

Anxiety churned in my stomach as he stared at the plates with an unreadable expression. His hand reached to cup the back of his neck, and I was certain I'd screwed up the precarious nature of our living situation by making him think I wanted him to dine with me.

"I'm sorry. You probably had your own dinner plans already." I moved toward the plates, preparing to clear them. "Really, don't worry about this. I'm sorry."

"No, Cassie," he said, reaching out a hand to stop me in my tracks. "It's not that. I was just surprised."

I paused, looking up at him warily. "Surprised?"

His gaze flickered from where they'd been glued on the plates till they landed on me, and something in his expression shifted.

"I just wasn't expecting this," he started, "No one's ever—" He ran a hand through his hair, his jaw tightening before he tried again.

"This is nice."

I felt my face heat, resisting the urge to hide behind my hands. "You really don't have to eat it if you don't want to. I won't be offended."

"Cassie, it looks great," he said, sitting down in front of one of the plates. "Really, I can't think of anything better to come home to."

"Are you sure?" I pressed, still unsure if I'd done something wrong. "You're acting weird."

He huffed out a laugh. "I'm not acting weird."

"You are," I confirmed with a solemn nod.

"Well, maybe it's because I just trained for hours, and I'm so hungry that I don't know how to function anymore."

I bit my lip to hide the smile of relief that appeared as I settled down across from him.

"Sorry in advance if it's gross," I said nervously as he grabbed his fork. With wide eyes, I watched him take the first bite.

"Well," I asked with a wince, twisting my hands in my lap. "Is it okay?"

"It's great." He stared up at me with warm steadiness in his green eyes as he held eye contact.

I looked down as if I could hide from his gaze. "Good, I was worried."

"Well, don't. It's actually one of the best meals I've had in a long time."

I smiled but didn't respond, feeling too self-conscious to form a coherent thought. I knew he was probably only saying it to be nice, but it flattered me all the same.

We ate in silence for a few minutes until Liam's words broke through the quiet of the dimly lit kitchen.

"You didn't have to do this, you know," he said, watching me cautiously from across the island.

"And you didn't have to let me stay here." I shrugged. "Believe me, you did a lot more for me than a simple meal can make up for."

He shook his head, his eyes boring into mine. "You don't have to make up anything to me. I mean it."

I offered him a smile, knowing that his words didn't erase the massive kindness he'd shown me.

"Hey," he said, clearing his throat awkwardly. "I'm sorry about the other night. I was a jerk. I shouldn't have come at you like that."

I looked up, shocked by the look in his eyes that appeared to be sincerity and... guilt?

"It's okay," I said.

"No, it isn't."

"No, Liam." I held up a hand to stop him. "Really, it is. If you hadn't said all that, I probably would've run back home and tried to beg him to get back together, and I would've walked right into something I didn't want to see. So really, you saved me a little bit of pride."

He stared at me as if wanting to say something more, but I couldn't handle being under the pressure of his gaze.

To escape it, my eyes flicked over to the *Friends* episode I'd left on in the living room while I cooked.

I always had a show playing for background noise. It made me feel a little less alone and was something I'd carried over from childhood. As an only child, TV shows were usually my only companions, and they worked powerfully to ease the loneliness that was my constant companion.

"Do you want us to eat on the couch?" Liam asked, smirking as his gaze scanned between me and the television a few feet away.

"Oh." I blushed. "No, it's okay. I know most people don't like doing that."

Except me because it was the only thing that turned my brain off.

"I don't mind," he said, watching for my answer.

I bit my lip, not knowing what the right answer was. Before I figured out how to respond, Liam was picking up our plates and moving toward the couch.

Wordlessly, I found myself following him. He set our plates down on the coffee table and gestured for me to sit, which I did, pressing against the corner of the couch to give him ample space.

He leaned forward, eating his food over the table, settling into comfort quickly, which allowed me to do the same. He ate, and I watched him, almost in awe of how this could be my life, sitting here beside him.

Despite everything that happened in the past few days, I couldn't find that sense of heartache that had been plaguing most of my moments. In fact, I felt strangely settled in a way that scared me because I knew that feeling couldn't last for long.

We finished our plates, and Liam brought them to the sink for us despite my protest that I would clear up. He gave me a stern look that kept me in place.

I sighed contentedly, feeling the exhaustion of the week washing away as I curled into a relaxed position on the couch. I figured that since Liam had gotten up, that was all the interaction I'd get from him for the night, but after the sink turned off, he made his way back to the couch, leaning against the back of the couch with ease.

I sat in the silence, my eyes fixed on the television. I didn't dare to speak and break the moment, as if he were an animal that might be frightened off by sudden movement.

Eventually, he pulled the blanket off the back of the couch and draped it over me.

"You looked cold," he said when I looked over to him with a raised brow.

I had been a little, but I didn't know how he could possibly notice that. Still, I felt myself dozing off, strangely at peace in the foreign environment I'd been suddenly transplanted into. And in that safety, sleep came quickly.

Liam

I had never resented the sound of a knock at the door more in my entire life.

Sure, I'd never been the type of guy to respond well to unannounced visitors, but at that moment, with Cassie sleeping on the couch, the sound of a fist banging against the door getting louder with each second, I found that there had never been a time I wanted a guest less.

I sprang up from the couch toward the door, determined to send whoever it was away when Maggie piled in as soon as the tiniest crack presented itself.

"Maggie, what the hell do you need?" I groaned, trying to stifle the volume she'd brought with her.

The sound of her purse and keys rang out against the countertop she'd dropped them on, and she was already talking a mile a minute about how she couldn't possibly understand why it took so long to open a door.

"You know, you should really tell someone before you show up at their house at ten o'clock at night."

"Well, I'm here for Cassie, not you," she said with a hand on her hip. "Where is she?"

With a clenched jaw, I nodded toward the couch. "She's sleeping. So, keep it down."

"Well, that explains why she wasn't answering my texts." Maggie nodded, making her way toward the living room.

"Oh, Cassie," she said in a sing-song voice as she approached her sleeping form.

"What are you doing?" I hissed, walking faster to catch up with my little sister before she woke Cassie up.

"I'm here to take her out," she said, exasperated. "What's with you?"

"She's sound asleep. What makes you think it's a good idea to take her out at ten o'clock at night?"

"Oh, please. It's the weekend. The bars are open, and the night is just getting started."

How Maggie and I were related, I'd never know. We had totally opposite ideas of how to spend our time. What could possibly be appealing about sitting in a dark barroom while drunk strangers spilled drinks on you, trying to strike up conversation all night long?

"She's tired. Just come back another night."

"She can wake up." Maggie tsked. "What's it to you, anyway? I figured you'd jump at the idea of having your apartment back to yourself for the night."

"I'm just saying that after the week she's had, don't you think she just needs to relax?"

"No, I think after the week she had, she needs to hang out with her best friend instead of the random brother I've left her alone with all week."

"What's going on." Cassie sat up, blinking in confusion as sleep still clouded her eyes.

She looked exhausted, and my chest tightened at the sight. She was obviously in no state to go out to the bars with my rambunctious sister, who probably had all types of schemes up her sleeve.

"I'm here to take you out." Maggie beamed. "I thought you might like to have a little fun. There's a cool bar downtown, and—"

"Maggie, I don't—" Cassie started before my sister cut her off.

"I know, I know. You don't drink. But they have mocktails, appetizers, and music. Really, it's just a chance to get out of this apartment because I've been a terrible best friend, leaving you here for days."

"If she doesn't drink, then why the hell are you taking her out to bars?" I asked more harshly than I intended.

"Leave us alone, Liam." Maggie turned to glare at me. "Go do whatever it was you were doing. Besides, I know you. I'm sure you're itching for a night to yourself."

Cassie's eyes glanced over to me, emotion flashing in them quickly before returning her gaze back toward Maggie.

"Okay." She shrugged, nowhere near confident enough to convince me that she actually wanted to go out. "I'll go get ready."

"Cassie, you don't have to," I told her.

"Good girl," Maggie chirped, waving her off as Cassie untangled herself from the blanket she'd been asleep under just moments ago.

I told myself that it didn't matter. She was my sister's friend, and I really didn't have anything to do with her other than giving her a place to crash. So why the hell did it feel like Maggie was the one intruding?

"I guess I'll go get ready," Cassie said uneasily before turning toward the staircase and heading up to the guest room.

"What the hell, Maggie?" I spun toward her as soon as Cassie was out of earshot. "What made you think this was a good idea tonight?"

"What's wrong with you? Why are you acting so weird about something that has nothing to do with you?" she pushed back like she always did.

"I just thought that even you would have more sympathy for your friend, who very obviously doesn't want to go out to bars after getting dumped just a few days ago!"

"That's exactly the point! She's never going to want to go out. She needs to be pushed out of her comfort zone. That guy was a jerk. You know that. The best way to move on? Meeting guys who *aren't* jerks."

I scoffed.

"See, you wouldn't understand because you're like morally opposed to relationships or whatever, but Cassie *wants* love, and she's not going to find it being holed up in here."

"Jesus, Maggie. Give her time. She's not going to want to jump into a relationship right away." I found myself speaking for her.

I didn't know if it was true or not, but God, I hoped it was.

Why do you care? My voice of reason questioned.

"Oh, come on, Liam! This isn't about finding the love of her life tonight. It's about having fun. Socializing. Getting hit on by cute guys she'll never see again. It's the first step in a long process, and frankly, you're ruining the vibe."

Getting hit on by cute guys.

The words struck a nerve, sending my instincts into overdrive. I knew what guys at bars were like because the guys on the team *were* those guys. And they made no secret of discussing at length the nights they shared with women they never spoke to again.

Cassie didn't deserve that. I didn't want that for her. It might be irrational, but I pegged it down to protectiveness over my little sister's friend. If I could look out for her, why wouldn't I?

"Fine, whatever." I shrugged, knowing when to pick my battles when it came to Maggie's determined will. "I'll drive."

"You'll *what*?" Maggie's voice reached a decibel that had me grabbing my ear.

"You're telling me this is the first night you don't need a designated driver?"

"And you're telling me that this is the first night you're actually going out? No way, something doesn't make sense." She shook her head, grilling me with her stare.

After a minute, her scrutinizing glare turned into an all-encompassing smirk.

"You're into her, aren't you?" she said knowingly. "I know I was just kidding before on the phone with you, but you actually are!"

"What?" I protested. "No. Absolutely not."

"You are! Why else would you be acting like this?"

"No, I had plans to go out already," I straight up lied. "The guys from the team are already out at a bar." *Truth.* "So, you guys can just come along."

Maggie's lips jutted out as she considered my words. I was betting that she'd buy it, considering I had never lied to her before.

"I don't want my big brother at the same bar as me when I'm trying to have a good night!" she pouted.

"Ew, Maggie. What constitutes a 'good night' that you don't want me there to see?" I groaned.

"Listen." She held up a hand to silence me. "It's been a long week. My best friend got dumped by a jerk. Mom is *living* in my shoebox apartment and has been up my ass for days. And I just want to unwind with my friend. Okay?"

"And I don't see any reason why you can't do that with me there?"

About to protest, I stopped her with another half-truth. "Listen, my friend Brody has been dying to hang out with you, and he's not going to get off my case until I set it up. He'll be there tonight. It's the perfect chance for us all to hang out with no pressure," I told her, hoping she wouldn't see through my flimsy excuse.

"Brody?" She raised a brow. "The guy from the locker room?"

"Yeah, that's him," I confirmed.

"Why does he want to meet me?"

"I don't know, Mags," I said, feeling like I was dealing with my kid sister again, even though we were now in our mid-twenties. "Can you just stop with all the protesting already?"

"Fine," she relented. "You can drive us. But I don't want you doing anything weird tonight because you're seriously freaking me out. Like, I almost think you got a brain transplant or something."

"Fine," I bit out.

"I'm going upstairs to make sure Cassie doesn't pick out something boring to wear," she said, heading for the staircase.

I stood planted where she'd left me in the living room and watched her pause halfway up the stairs.

"And just so you know," she said, eyes squinting at me. "Cassie is *mine*. So don't you go getting all territorial like you do just because she's staying at your place for a few nights."

She disappeared before I had a chance to respond, but I sank back against the couch with her words ringing in my ears.

Somehow, I didn't think her warning was unwarranted.

CHAPTER FIFTEEN

Cassie

Sitting in the backseat of Liam's car was a wild place to be on a Friday night, considering I'd only agreed to go out so he could have his apartment to himself for the first time since I'd moved in.

If I'd known that he had plans to go out for the night, I would've gladly stayed tucked up in his apartment, safe and warm from the horrors of the world.

Going out had never been my thing, but I couldn't think of a time that I wanted to go less than when I woke up from the coziest nap of my life, only to see Maggie standing there waiting for me.

I wasn't in any mood to be out in public. I didn't drink, so it wasn't like I could nurse my broken heart with alcohol.

The only reason I said yes was because I knew that Liam probably needed a break from me, but here he was anyway. I'm not sure if Maggie asked him to come or if he'd been going anyway, but it didn't matter. Now the three of us were sitting in the silence of his car while Liam's fingers thrummed anxiously against the wheel as he maneuvered in and out of Boston traffic.

"So, where are we going?" Maggie asked, her eyes glued to the Instagram feed she was scrolling through.

"The Trap," Liam replied tersely, his body far more rigid than normal.

"No way!" Maggie instantly dropped her phone on her lap. "Are you kidding? That place is always so hard to get into!"

"I told you, the guys are already there." He shrugged. "It'll be no problem."

I stared at his profile, softly illuminated by the glow of the city outside the car. I wasn't imagining it. He was definitely tense. But why?

I tried to focus on something—anything else, rather than being caught staring at him like a creep that he would be forced to bring home with him at the end of the night.

His car was clean with black leather seats and the unmistakable scent of Liam filling the small space. *How do I know what he smells like already?* But I did. He smelled like cedar and ice and cold winter mornings. It was comforting.

But for some reason, he certainly wasn't. At that moment, he looked anything *but*.

"Liam, are you okay?" I couldn't help but ask after a few more minutes of watching him drive with a tight jaw.

At my words, Maggie looked over to examine her brother, scanning his face for whatever she thought I had seen in it.

He looked back at me, startled as if he hadn't expected me to notice him. But how could I not?

"I'm fine," he said before returning his eyes to the road. Somehow, he looked a bit lighter than before.

Maybe I put him on edge. Maybe now he thinks he has to pretend.

"He's fine," Maggie agreed. "Liam just hates going out."

"Why?" I asked. At the same time, Liam said, "I do not hate going out."

"Because he gets swarmed by women. The horror." She giggled. "Though I don't know why anyone would try. He's like the most unapproachable guy in the world."

Something twisted in my stomach. I really didn't want to spend the night watching that. Not that it was any of my business, but it would only exacerbate the feeling of loneliness in the pit of my stomach.

He scoffed but didn't bother denying Maggie's comment as he pulled into a parking lot that had a valet ready to take the keys from Liam.

We all got out, me fumbling awkwardly with my seatbelt while Maggie and Liam hovered, waiting for me.

"Are you cold?" Liam frowned, looking down at the outfit Maggie had picked out for me.

"It's fine," I lied. "We'll be inside in a minute anyway."

"Come on!" Maggie pulled me toward the door, leaving Liam trailing after us with his hands in his pockets.

As soon as we got inside, the stench of alcohol hit me, and I wished we hadn't come at all. It was dark, loud, and, most of all, crowded.

Music boomed from every corner as bodies swayed under the dim lights. Maggie looked dazed, staring in each direction. I'd known since college she was a partier, but my party days had started and ended with that infamous night when I first met her.

Now, I wrapped my arms around my body, feeling totally out of my element.

"Come on," Liam said, as I felt his hand come up to my lower back. "Let's go find the guys."

My body tingled from the sensation of Liam's guiding hand, but I mentally reminded myself that it was only there so I wouldn't get lost in the crowd.

I focused on anything else, taking note of how many people, inebriated states and all, stopped in their tracks to stare at Liam.

"Brynn!" multiple guys called out, attempting to stagger their way toward him.

But he was quicker. As if practiced, he had us lost deeper in the crowd before they could get to him.

"Huge fan, man." Another drunken guy attempted to dab him up as we passed by.

"Liam Brynn," A girl cooed, reaching out as if to grab him and steal him away.

I bristled, immediately uncomfortable by the audacity of people. I knew we were in the Harbor Wolves' home city, but I found myself shocked by how recognized he was in the darkness of a bar. And what surprised me more was how he didn't pay them any mind. Like he was *used* to it.

"Wow," I breathed out, looking up at Liam. "You're like a big deal."

"Not really," He brushed off my comment, his sea-glass eyes looking down at me.

"There they are!" Maggie yelped in excitement, staring at a group of guys at a high booth table in the backroom.

"Do my eyes deceive me?" one of the guys called out with a mocking, open-jawed stare. "Or did Liam Brynn deem to join us for a night out?"

"And he brought some lovely ladies," another commented, despite the fact that they were already surrounded by a handful of girls on the sidelines attempting to chat them up.

"Hi!" Maggie waved, apparently thrilled to be immersed in what appeared to be the busiest bar in Boston.

"Knock it off," Liam ordered, taking his hand off my back to pull a chair out.

I waited for him to sit, only realizing when he looked down at me that he was waiting for *me* to take the seat.

"Oh, thanks." I flushed, hoping it wouldn't be seen in the darkness. Once I was settled, he pulled out the chair next to me and took his place.

Maggie had already taken it upon herself to drag a chair over and was chatting animatedly with the guys, who all stared at her with looks of captivation.

"His little sister," I heard her yelling over the music. "And she's my best friend."

Not knowing what else to do, I waved at them all, uttering a soft "Hi" that I doubted was heard over the thrumming bass.

"Hey, Maggie!" the guy across the table from her said. He extended his hand, nearly sending his beer toppling as he did so. "It's nice to see you again, I'm Brody."

The guy, Brody, stared over at Liam and mouthed what looked like a "thank you" before giving his full attention once more to Maggie.

"So, best friend." The bulky blond guy across the table turned to me. "Do you have a name?"

I felt Liam's arm slink around the back of my chair while I stammered out an awkward, "I'm Cassie."

"Cassie, huh?" He smirked. "We saw you at the rink earlier tonight. And on behalf of all of us, may I say we're all *thrilled* that Liam finally found someone to put a smile on that pretty face of his. Makes the guy a little more bearable to be around, you know what I mean?"

The table laughed, and I was highly aware of Liam stiffening beside me. I felt bad, knowing that these guys probably had the wrong idea about us and how that fact probably bothered Liam more than he let on.

Of course, he was too much of a gentleman to deny it in front of me, but I'm sure the last thing he wanted was for his friends to think there was anything going on between us.

"Oh," I said, not able to hide my blush. "It's not like that. We hardly know each other, really. I'm Maggie's friend."

I pointed to the brunette sitting down at the table, listening intently to something Brody was explaining with dramatic hand movements.

He followed my gaze. "Yeah, he mentioned that," he responded, looking between us, eyes settling curiously on Liam.

I didn't dare look at Liam's expression, but I hoped that my clarification would help show that I didn't expect anything from him.

The bulky blonde across from me downed the rest of his drink in a way that made me shudder before inclining his head toward the open space in the middle of the bar.

"Cassie, why don't you come with me to get another? On me." He flashed a grin.

Oh, great. The worst part of any night out.

Someone would insist on buying drinks, I would politely decline, and we'd then proceed to spend the next handful of minutes discussing why I didn't drink since no one could ever leave it at 'No, thank you.'

But when I opened my mouth to speak the words anyway, a deeper voice responded before I had the chance.

"She's fine," Liam's voice said with little room for discussion.

"But you said—" The blond guy was ready to protest.

"I said she's fine," Liam repeated, and when his friend's eyes landed behind me, I became hyper-aware of the arm draped casually against the back of my chair.

"I get it." The blond guy smirked, holding his hands up in defeat. "No worries."

And even if he didn't *really* get it, I was grateful to Liam, nonetheless. I didn't exactly want to go off with some drunken hockey player in a bar I wasn't entirely comfortable in.

In fact, the only thing grounding me at that moment was the fact that Liam was sitting there beside me.

His teammate got up, no doubt in pursuit of some other girl who would gladly jump at the chance to have him buy her a drink, and I sank back in relief.

Sometimes, I felt defective. I was in my twenties; wasn't I supposed to enjoy nightlife and bars and alcohol? Why, then, did it feel like the only place I wanted to be was curled up in the apartment of some guy I didn't know, who probably didn't want me there?

"Thanks," I mumbled, looking up at Liam, who was already staring at me.

"You don't have to thank me," he said. "I know no girl likes to be hit on by drunk, persistent guys, and Ryan is about the most persistent guy in Boston."

I held back a shudder, grateful to have escaped a scenario like that. That was exactly why I didn't go out. I hated having to dodge guys like that, even if they meant well. Well, that, plus the way being surrounded by alcohol and drunk people always set off my fight-or-flight response.

This brought my attention to the drink in Liam's hand, which looked surprisingly like… water?

"You're not drinking?" I asked with furrowed brows.

"I'm not a big drinker." He shrugged as if it were no big deal. "Especially not when I'm driving you home."

I shifted uncomfortably. I didn't want him to resent the fact that he was driving me or let it get in the way of the night out he wanted to have with his friends.

"Right, but a drink only takes, like, what, an hour to get out of your system? Which means you could have a few beers and be good to go in a few hours," I tried to justify, even though I felt immensely safer being next to someone sober.

"What if you want to leave before then?" he said.

"I can always Uber," I responded. "You don't have to base your night around me. I really don't want to get in your way."

"Cassie," he said, looking at me intently.

"Yeah?" My breath hitched.

"I'm not going to drink," he said. "I wasn't planning on it, and I was telling the truth when I said I really don't do it often."

"You don't?" I asked, feeling a weight off my chest.

Everyone our age seemed to, and it felt like a reprieve to find someone who could handle a night being sober.

"I don't." He shook his head. "I never have. I like being in control of myself too much for that."

I felt myself sag in relief. It shouldn't matter if he liked it or not, but it did. It made me feel safer in a way that I could never admit without sounding crazy.

"That's good." I nodded.

"Is it?" He smirked, raising a brow at me.

"Well, yeah." I blushed. "I mean, drinking is objectively bad, right? So it's good that you don't like to do it a lot?" I fumbled for an explanation, feeling foolish as I rambled.

"Well, I think you're the first person I've met who hasn't called me boring for it, so thanks." He laughed softly.

There was a pause before he said, "So, what about you?"

"Me?" I asked.

"You don't drink at all?"

"No," I admitted almost shamefully. "I never have."

"Why?" he asked softly. "Not that you need a reason not to. But is there one?"

"Uh," I said hesitantly. "I guess I figured my entire family drinks enough to make up for the fact I don't." I chuckled nervously. "In fact, even if I wanted to, there probably wouldn't be any left for me if they were around."

He nodded as if understanding. But I was sure he didn't. He couldn't. Not the full extent of it, at least.

"I always thought it was overrated anyway," he said, changing the topic to himself in a way he must've known I wanted.

Somehow, he was able to pick up on little cues from me. Knowing when I was uncomfortable, tired, or cold, without me having to say anything at all.

"I mean, if you need to be drunk to have fun, then maybe it's more of a you problem."

"Right!" I exclaimed, practically jumping from my seat. I settled back down, embarrassed, before continuing, "I mean, like, why can't we do anything else besides go to a bar? The bookstore, or the beach, or whale watching—"

"Whale watching?" He smirked. "Do you want to go whale watching, Cassie?"

"I'm not opposed to it." I made a face at him. "I'm just saying that there are *so* many things to do, but all anyone in our age bracket wants to do is get drunk."

"Well, don't worry," he said. "I'll take you whale watching, and we can freeze our sober asses off on some boat in the middle of the ocean."

"Yeah, it's getting a little cold for it," I agreed. "More of a springtime activity."

"That's a better plan. We'll go then instead."

I smiled, not wanting to break the comfort of the joke to remark on how we probably wouldn't really know each other better by the time spring came around. Certainly won't be on *hanging out* terms by then, but it felt nice to share a moment with someone.

Cue Maggie.

"Why are you looking at each other like that?"

She looked between us suspiciously.

"We weren't!" I rushed to defend, though I was sure that the blush covering my cheeks made me look a lot guiltier than I was.

Liam, for his part, looked pissed.

I didn't know how he could do that. Look so soft and open one moment and totally hardened and closed off the next.

"Don't mind my sister. She's always been nosy," Liam said, but I noticed the way his chair was pushed slightly farther than it had been.

"It's not being nosy when it's my best friend and brother," she countered before pulling on my arm. "Come on, I need you."

"For what?" Liam and I said at the same time.

"Karaoke!" she squealed.

"Noooo." I resisted her tugging. "No, no, no. I think I've been humiliated enough for this week."

"It's not humiliating!" she whined. "It's *fun*. And I'll let you pick the first song."

I scanned around the room, noticing how engaged people were in their own conversations. I was sure no one would pay us any mind, and if they did, they'd probably be too drunk to remember.

"Fine," I said, letting her pull me off my seat. "But we're doing ABBA."

"I knew you'd say that." She sighed as if in disappointment, but the smirk on her face was all-encompassing.

"Save our seats for us," she called over her shoulder to Liam, who was watching with a smirk of his own before she pulled me away toward the stage.

Maggie sashayed up to the stage, looking far tipsier than I'd seen her in a while.

"DJ," she called out to the guy swaying his head to the music he was projecting into the bar. "We want to do the karaoke!"

Her words were slightly slurred, but I never felt nervous around her the way I sometimes did around drunk people.

Maybe it was because Maggie was never an angry drunk or a sad drunk and never got to a point where I really had to take care of her. She just got silly and laid back, even more so than usual.

He asked for her song request, and she made a dramatic tiptoe across the stage to whisper in his ear.

"Hey, I thought you said I could pick." I laughed when she returned to me, picking up one of the microphones.

"I know what song you'd pick."

She put a hand on my shoulder as if to reassure me. Her eyes looked so much like her brother's in color and shape, but the expression they held couldn't be any more different.

Liam's gaze was sharp and intense as if it could cut through any bullshit, no matter how thick someone was laying it on. Whereas Maggie had an open, uncaring ease to hers, making her far more approachable than her brother.

The opening beats to *SOS* by Abba came on, and I grinned at Maggie, shaking my head at how cheesy her choice was. But she was right. It was my pick. It healed something in my heart to know that she knew me so well.

Maggie swayed across the stage like she didn't have a care in the world, singing, not always correctly, to the lyrics of the song. I didn't have the same drunken courage that was coursing through Maggie's veins, so the idea of singing into a microphone in a bar full of people seemed less than appealing.

Maggie noticed and made her way over to me at once, singing loudly while offering me a disappointed pouty face at my lack of voice.

I looked into the crowd, relieved to see that no one was really paying us any mind. The hockey guys were mostly engaged in trying to chat up women around the bar. There were a few couples already engaged in more than chatting, and everyone else who occasionally glanced our way seemed entirely disinterested.

There was only one person who sat alone with eyes glued to us the entire time.

Liam.

I told myself I didn't have to be embarrassed by what he thought. I was with his little sister, and he probably just viewed me as an extension of her. Little sisters did embarrassing things all the time, didn't they? So why shouldn't their friends? It wouldn't reflect on him in any way.

Maggie pleaded with her eyes, reaching out her hand to me until I finally sighed, found my courage, and started singing along with her. It took a few moments to ease into it, but by the chorus, we were full-on belting, holding each other up to support each other from falling off the stage in a fit of laughter.

Sometimes, life felt like it was falling apart. Sometimes, I didn't know how to move forward when the future I'd envisioned seemed so far out of reach. But moments like this—when a good song played, and a friend stood beside you—made it feel like maybe, just maybe, everything would be okay.

CHAPTER SIXTEEN

Liam

There was a bizarre feeling in my chest. It was uncomfortable and foreign in a way that I couldn't quite name.

But I was certain it wasn't anything good.

Not when the reason for it was the little blonde dancing on stage with my sister.

I shouldn't have feelings in my chest for my sister's friends. And definitely not the one currently living with me.

Shake it the fuck off, I ordered myself, trying to tear my gaze away. But despite my best efforts, my eyes were glued to her.

She was beaming, and I couldn't even be mad at myself for staring so blatantly when it meant that I got to watch that smile overtake her. She'd been so broken that night she came to me, so hurt and small and injured. And now, just a few short days later… well, it looked like she was getting her light back.

It was a testimony to what happened when you evicted dickheads from your life.

Off-key singing filled the bar, and I snorted at their terrible harmonizing, but still, I couldn't fight the smirk that found its way onto my begrudging lips.

Until my least favorite interruption found him.

"Hi," came a sensual voice, and I practically rolled my eyes before I even saw her.

A woman with long, sleek hair and a skin-tight black outfit that I knew would have any of my teammates drooling stared up at me through eyeliner-rimmed eyes.

"Hi," I bit back in a way that I hoped would shut down any further conversation.

Apparently, my acknowledgment of her existence was all the encouragement the girl needed to make her way closer until she was inches away from my body.

The smell of vanilla filled my senses, and I found myself frowning at the audacious girl peering up at me.

"You're Liam Brynn," she stated, eyes flashing.

I blinked at her. It hadn't been a question. She knew who I was, so what did she want me to say about it?

"I'm Sam."

Sam, evidently, was waiting for an invitation to crawl onto my lap.

I fixed her with a stare. "I know that it doesn't look like it now, Sam," I said dryly, "but our table is full."

"Oh?" she said in a way that made it seem like a challenge.

"But if it's a hockey player you're looking for, you'll find plenty of them scattered around here tonight."

"Actually, I think I'm content right here with you," she said, slipping onto the chair beside me.

I fought the urge to abandon our seats entirely as irritation prickled against my skin. What was it about girls at these clubs that made them think everyone there was for the taking? Couldn't people read social cues anymore?

It was why I never bothered to go out anymore. People were too drunk, too touchy, or too bold. I was fine with the peace and quiet of my own home. Even if it meant missing out on team bonding.

"I'm not the best company." I glared at her, screaming without words: *get the point.*

"I like the tough ones," she purred.

I visibly recoiled as her fingers came up toward my arm.

"You know, you're even cuter in person."

My eyes scanned the bar, desperately hoping to connect with one of my teammates so I could shoot them an SOS stare. I knew any of them would come to the rescue, hoping to take the girl off my hands themselves, but everyone was apparently occupied elsewhere.

Even Brody, drink in hand, was up front by the stage, dancing to the song Cassie and Maggie were singing to their crowd of one.

"I'm really not interested," I said, attention focused solely on Cassie and my sister, not sure how to make it any clearer.

"Oh, come on." She pouted, trying to rub circles on my arm before I pulled it out from under her. "I'm sure I could find a way to make you interested."

I jerked toward her, my eyes flaring in barely restrained anger. I knew girls like her. Brody had explained it perfectly. They liked the challenge, the thrill of the chase. Some people couldn't possibly comprehend that a person could be uninterested in their advances.

I wasn't playing hard to get. I just didn't want to be *got*. By anyone.

So I let the lie roll off my tongue, hoping it might sway her in ways that the blatant rejection had not.

"I have a girlfriend."

Predictably, she pulled back. Only slightly, but enough that she was no longer crouched over me, invading every inch of space that should be my God-given right to take when out in a public area. Hockey player or not.

"Who?" Her eyes narrowed on me, her nose scrunching upward as if this piece of information hit her like a bad smell.

"Who?" I repeated, dumbfounded. "Why would you ask that when you couldn't possibly know her?"

"I mean, it's not exactly a secret that you're chronically single."

Chronically single? Ouch.

"You know this how?"

"Rumors." She shrugged. "The internet."

"Well, the rumors are wrong. Because like I said, I have a girlfriend."

It came out more easily than I would've thought.

Changing tactics, I decided to avoid eye contact with her entirely, putting my focus back on the stage where they were now transitioning into the chorus of *Gives You Hell*.

Maggie was sloppily singing, but Cassie was grinning from ear to ear despite her friend's obvious drunkenness.

"Is that her?" the girl's poisonous voice declared.

My back stiffened as I looked over to find her attention fixed solely on Cassie, who was now staring back at us with a watchful look on her face.

"No offense," I said, mustering up as much offensiveness as I could. "But please leave me alone."

The girl, persistent in her mission to work me into a rage, continued. "I haven't seen her in any of your pictures," she retorted.

I didn't know if she meant the paparazzi photos or the social media account that the team media manager ran for me, but either way, she was bordering on stalker territory.

I stood from my seat, realizing that the girl wouldn't be the one to walk away first. Grabbing Cassie's bag that she'd left in her seat, I made my way through the crowd, away from her.

Cassie and Maggie were getting off the stage in a fit of laughter as I moved toward the stage.

"Hey," Cassie said as I approached them.

Maggie was so close to her that she was almost leaning on her for support, sweat glistening on her brow from the exertion of their performance.

"Having fun?" I raised my brows with a smirk.

She blushed, hiding behind her hands. "I hope you didn't watch any of that."

"Oh, I saw all of it," I confirmed smugly.

"We did great, huh?" Maggie giggled. "I never knew we could harmonize like that. We should totally sign up for community theater together."

"Oh, God, no," Cassie blurted, but Maggie had already moved on to her next thought.

With an arm around Cassie's neck and her other one attempting to reach up toward mine, she pulled us toward her.

"Awww," she cooed. "My best friend and my brother. We're all out together. How fun is this!"

She ended with a squeal that had me grabbing the ear that was in closest proximity to her.

"Easy, Maggie," I said through a wince.

"And look, Liam," she continued, letting go of Cassie to put both her hands on my shoulders. "You're smiling! I haven't seen you smile in so long! No, I haven't *seen* you in so long." Her face contorted into devastation. "Why do you always want to be alone?"

I shifted uncomfortably, unsure what to say back to my sister, whom I had never known wanted to spend time with me.

I didn't mean to neglect her. She was always off living her life, doing her own thing. She never needed me. Or so I thought.

"How much did you have to drink in the hour we've been here?" I asked, examining her.

That sent her into another fit of giggles.

Cassie, sensing my discomfort, stepped in.

"I'm going to take her home," Cassie said, pulling out her phone and opening an app. "Because apparently, the answer to that question is *a lot*."

"Wait, what are you doing?" I asked, watching Cassie's fingers type away.

"Ordering an Uber," she answered without looking up from her phone.

"Uh." I laughed, snatching the phone. "Are you forgetting that I drove us here?"

"No." Cassie rolled her eyes. "But I'm not going to make you leave all your friends to drive us."

"I don't mind," I said when I really wanted to yell that I was more than ready to get the hell out of there.

"No," Cassie argued. "It's okay, really. We'll just Uber to Maggie's, and I'll spend the night with her. You're probably itching to have your place to yourself for a night."

What? No. Why would I?

"Ahhhh." Maggie grabbed Cassie's hand. "Sleepover!"

I felt the oddest sensation of disappointment.

"But all your stuff is at my place, and—"

"It's just one night." Cassie shrugged. "I'll manage."

"You sure you want to be stuck with her all night?" I gestured my head toward Maggie, who was repeating the word 'sleepover' on an endless loop.

Maggie stuck her tongue out at me while Cassie just gave a half-smile. Was I imagining it, or did she look sad?

"She's going to need someone to take care of her when the hangover hits."

"Uhh," Maggie drawled. "I'm the queen of not having hangovers. Like, I'm immune to them."

"See." I extended a hand toward my sister. "She's fine."

"Still," Cassie protested, for reasons I wasn't entirely sure of.

Everything in me wanted to fight her on it. To make her come home with me to my apartment. But then, what if she didn't *want* to? She'd told me no. I had to assume she meant it. Otherwise, I was as bad as the girl I'd just escaped.

"Well, at least let me drive you," I argued, not wanting Cassie to pay insane city prices to get an Uber when I had the car waiting outside.

"Nope." Cassie smiled brightly, holding her phone up toward me. "Our driver is almost here."

Well, shit. She *really* didn't want to spend any more time with me tonight. Something about her demeanor had shifted, making her feel distant in a way that she hadn't when she'd been sitting beside me earlier.

Not knowing what else to say, I scratched the back of my head awkwardly, feeling the oddest pang of loneliness at the thought of going home to an empty apartment.

Ridiculous, I thought, thinking how stupid it was to be resenting the solitude that I'd cherished for so long.

"Okay, well, let me know if you need anything," I offered, suddenly feeling unsure of what to do with myself.

"Thanks," Cassie murmured, not fully meeting my gaze.

I slung her bag off my shoulder, handing it back to her.

"Oh, thanks." She took it gingerly, pulling her hand away quickly as our fingers touched. "I hope you have a fun rest of your night," she said, eyes scanning the crowd behind me. "I'll text you before I come back tomorrow so you're not ambushed."

Why would she think that?

"Text me when you're ready to go, and I'll pick you up," I offered, confused by the bizarre tension in the air between us.

She said nothing but smiled in a way that made me think she wasn't going to take me up on that offer.

Before I could pull her aside and ask her what the hell was going on, what was wrong, and how I could fix it, her phone alerted her to the presence of her driver, and she was waving goodbye.

I watched her leave, my sister in tow, feeling that odd feeling in my chest resurfaced in an entirely different way. Somehow, it was even more uncomfortable than before.

CHAPTER SEVENTEEN

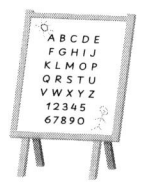

Cassie

I'd spent enough time in my life around drunk people to know that they came in different shades. There were the sad drunks. The mean drunks. The explosive drunks.

But luckily for me, Maggie was what I'd consider a happy drunk. The entire ride back to her place, she'd petted my hair, told me what a good friend I was, and how happy she was that we were going to start a band together.

I decided it would be better to crush her dreams about the band thing when she was sober enough to handle it.

It didn't take too much effort to get her up the stairs to her apartment. She only paused to sing once. As soon as we got inside, I realized how correct Maggie was about the tight living quarters while her mother was staying there.

As I flicked the light on, it illuminated the disaster that had become Maggie's apartment. There were bags and boxes everywhere as if a middle-aged woman's closet had exploded into the heart of Maggie's living room. The couch was pulled out into a futon with the sleeping figure of a woman snoring away in the center.

I was quick to remedy my mistake, switching the light back off and hoping that I remembered the layout of the space well enough to navigate in the darkness.

"Shhh," I shushed Maggie as she continued to ramble on about something at full volume. "Your mom is sleeping."

"Right," Maggie said, lowering her voice a notch in a humorous attempt at a whisper. "Let's be super quiet."

A second passed, and she tumbled over something in our path, narrowly missing a full-on tumble to the floor.

This place definitely wasn't the spotless apartment that Liam had. The apartment that he was probably taking that girl back to at that exact moment.

I'd looked up from karaoke to see that girl from the bar sitting beside him, and something dangerous lurked in my chest at the sight. Anger? Sadness? Jealousy? All things I didn't have the right to feel.

Which gave me the cue that I should probably make myself scarce for a while. It had only been a few days, and already I was taking Liam's kindness to heart.

I didn't have any claim over him, so why the hell did it make my chest ache when I saw him with someone else?

Maybe I was projecting my feelings from my breakup onto Liam. Since I felt safe with him, it was almost like I viewed him as mine in a way.

Which was crazy because he wasn't mine and never would be. In fact, I needed to actually start checking out some of the apartment listings I'd found. Immediately.

I managed to get us to Maggie's bedroom, pulling back the covers of her queen-sized bed and helping her slip in. Once she was settled, I crept to her kitchen and filled a glass with water before raiding her medicine cabinet for something to cure the headache I knew she'd wake up with.

I put it beside her bed before climbing in on the other side, feeling exhausted all the way down to my bones.

"I'm sorry, Cass," Maggie's voice said into the darkness. "I know how much you hate drinking, and then I went off and got drunk on you."

"It's okay, Mags." I shifted on my side to face her. "I'm glad you had a fun night."

"That guy, Brody, is kind of cute." She sighed dreamily. "I think he likes me."

"Yeah?" I perked up, thrilled at the idea of Maggie finding a nice guy.

And I knew he was a nice guy because if he wasn't, I was sure Liam never would've let him near his sister. No matter how much of a distance there seemed to be between him and Maggie, I knew he was the type never to let anyone hurt her.

"Yeah." She yawned. "But I'm scared."

"Why are you scared, Maggie?"

"Because if I see him again, then I think maybe I'll like him back. So I probably shouldn't, right?"

I laughed into the space between us. "Is it really so bad to settle down with one guy?"

I asked the question I never dared before. Maggie never had any issue with getting a guy's attention, but they had the problem of trying to keep hers. It seemed like she was always meeting a guy, hanging out for a few days, and then moving on to the next one. To my hopeless romantic brain, who craved monogamy and commitment above all else, it seemed like self-inflicted torture. But Maggie was different.

"What if once I start to like him, he stops liking me?"

"I don't think that would happen," I said honestly.

Maggie had a long list of amazing qualities that made her the coolest girl in the world—and her beauty was the least important one. She was funny, selfless, and exciting. As far as I knew, the issue in the past had never been a guy not liking her but her not liking any of the guys.

"I really don't like being left," she admitted in a soft, sad voice. "I don't like the way I feel when people leave. I don't think I ever want to feel it again."

"No one's leaving you, Maggie," I said, rubbing a hand down her arm to assure her I was right there beside her.

"I'm glad you met Liam," she responded, her voice drifting off to sleep. "You made him start to smile again."

And then, she rolled over before I could say another word.

What the hell was wrong with Liam Brynn that he'd Venmoed me $150 while I was sleeping?

I woke up to the notification and rubbed my eyes against the brightness of the screen. Surely, it was a mistake. Maybe he'd meant to send it to someone else.

But the words *Uber* were attached to the payment, and I rolled my eyes at the realization.

The man really felt responsible for paying for our Uber just because I was taking his sister home. Right as I started to send the money back, Maggie woke with a groan, and I clicked the phone off to give her my attention.

"There's water by the bed and Ibuprofen," I told her. "I'd offer to go make you food, but I'm scared to run into your mom," I admitted sheepishly.

I was a grown woman who still got shy meeting people's parents. I knew Maggie's mom was nice. Maggie had always told me what a great relationship they had, which always gave me a little tingle of jealousy when I heard. But still, even though Mrs. Brynn was rumored to be kind and delightful, there was always a bit of anxiety in my stomach at the thought of having to interact with someone's parent.

"Oh, yeah," Maggie said, "I forgot about your weird thing with authority figures."

I scoffed. "Your mom is not an authority figure. I'm twenty-four years old."

"Right, well, someone needs to tell *you* that. And anyway, I think she's at her yoga class, so you're in the clear."

I laughed, pulling the pillow out from under my head and throwing it at her before getting out of bed.

"Speaking of," she continued between gulps of water. "How's your mom?"

I bristled, pulling a stray piece of fabric from my clothes. "I don't think she's doing great," I admitted, looking anywhere but Maggie's eyes. "I actually think I need to head over there today to check on her."

"Do you want me to come with you?" Maggie offered, but I shook my head violently before she even got the full words out.

"No, no. It's okay," I assured her quickly. "Thank you, though."

The thought of my mom meeting any of my friends was an idea that had haunted me my whole life. Every time she had, it ended badly. She couldn't control what she said or how she acted, and it always left me reeling with embarrassment, never wanting to see the friend who had to witness her behavior ever again.

Now, I'd come to realize my mother's behavior was in no way a reflection of me, but old habits died hard, and I still somehow felt like the same little girl every time I was around her.

The idea of going back home filled me with dread because, like always, I never knew what I was walking into.

The unpredictability of it was… unsettling. But I hadn't heard from my mom at all in a few days, and she wasn't answering the phone either.

The same familiar tingle of fear settled in my gut. Dysfunctional as she was, she was my mother, and if anything ever happened to her, it would crush me. And the inevitability of that seemed far closer than I would like.

Maggie, for her part, looked at me as if she could see every emotion that played across my face.

"You know I'm always here for you, Cassie," she promised.

I looked at her, feeling the truth behind those words and clinging to it like an anchor.

"I know."

CHAPTER EIGHTEEN -

Liam

> **BRODY:** What the hell happened last night???? I left for two secs to grab another drink and when I got back you guys were gone????? 😭😭😭

I saw the text from Brody the second it came in while I stared at the screen, waiting for a text from Cassie. Surely, she'd need a ride home at some point, and I told her to call me when she was ready. Whether or not she'd take me up on that was anyone's guess. I was starting to realize just how stubborn she could be about things, which would be cute if it weren't for the fact that she was making life harder for herself with these random hills she chose to die on.

I shook my head, sending an apology text to Brody before slipping the phone away. The volume was on. I'd hear the text when it came through. For now, there were plenty of other things I could do in the meantime.

My apartment was covered with traces of her just from the few days she'd been here. It made the space feel warmer somehow. Comfortable in a way that I hadn't managed to make it on my own.

I smiled softly at the sight of her slippers by the couch, her blanket thrown over them, and a mug on the coffee table in front of them.

I noticed that she'd taken up residency in that particular spot whenever she had downtime, making it her own.

Now I sat there, taking note of the things she'd left behind. The coffee table had a few papers spread over it, with a pair of scissors abandoned beside the half-cut-out sheets of paper.

On them were cartoon images of stick figure people with big black phrases of things like **SAFE HANDS, NO BITING,** and **QUIET VOICE.**

"What the hell?" I murmured to myself, staring down in amusement at the pictures.

Was Cassie really going to work and getting bit by small children? And I thought *my* job was tough. At least none of the guys on another team ever sank their teeth into me.

I made breakfast and ate it. Washed the dishes and put them away. I checked my phone again because I was a sadist who couldn't help it, finding no texts waiting for me. And by the time the clock turned 10 a.m., I was already out the door, driving to Maggie's place.

I should've just texted her. I thought as I made my way up the staircase to Maggie's apartment, feeling like a stalker.

In my head, I had justified it. I had even picked up two coffees for Cassie and Maggie, so I had a reason for stopping by other than the real reason: I wanted to put her in my car and take her home before she could use that ludicrous app again to get a ride from a total stranger.

I wasn't going to *force* her to come with me. I was just there to offer a ride if she wanted it.

Which you could've done over text.

I shook the thought away. I was already right outside the door. Technically, I could turn around and drive home before Maggie gave me a ton of shit for how pathetic I was being, but I couldn't bring myself to leave.

I knocked once, then stepped back, wondering why my heart was accelerating after knocking on the door of my fucking sister's house.

There was the sound of shuffling behind the door and muffled feminine voices, and then the door opened.

"Liam!" My mother beamed, her face jumping at once from shock to elation in seconds. "Maggie, your brother's here!"

Shit.

How had I forgotten she was staying here?

"Hi, Mom," I said, shuffling on my feet.

I hadn't seen her in a few months, not because I was avoiding her per se, but just because it was never super convenient to get wrapped up in the attention that came with a visit from her.

"Well don't just stand out there!" She gestured wildly toward the apartment. "Come in, come in!"

"Liam?" Maggie walked out of the bathroom, her brown hair wet from the shower. "What are you doing here?"

"I, uh—" I fumbled for a reasonable excuse.

"Well, he came to visit us, of course! And look, he brought us coffees!"

My mother reached for one of the cups in my hand, looking as if I'd just gifted her with her first grandchild.

"Why would he come visit? I saw him last night," Maggie said, approaching us with confusion.

"You did?" My mother gasped. "My babies are spending time together," she cooed, eyes getting teary at the thought. "It's all I ever wanted!"

Jesus, I felt awkward. And stiff. And filled with an urgency to get out of there.

I craned my neck around, looking for Cassie, but came up short. Maybe she was still sleeping, though I doubted it. She was always up early at my place.

I opened my mouth to ask when my mother's arms came around me, pulling me toward the couch.

"Sit, sit," she ordered, pulling us both down.

Maggie took a spot in the armchair across the couch, and my eyes landed on the many boxes filling the living room with my mother's essence.

Now, sitting beside me, she stared up at me in an expectant way that had me shifting in my seat.

I cleared my throat.

"So, how's the renovations going?" I asked as my mother creepily smiled at me with wide, imploring eyes.

"Oh," She sighed, smile fading. "Fine, I suppose. It's about time, isn't it? I couldn't stand to live in a house your father designed for another minute."

I stiffened. It wasn't often that we spoke about my father, and to hear her mention him so casually set me more on edge than usual.

"Why not?" Maggie asked. "You have for the last fifteen years."

"Why not just move?" I asked the question that had been on my mind since I first heard she was redoing the entire house.

"Why would I do that?" She asked. "The house is already paid off."

"But you're paying the price of a house to have the entire thing gutted and rebuilt." I raised a brow.

My mother was never someone I fully understood, partially because she never really let me. She did things on a whim, making huge life choices in the blink of an eye, and I always felt a little unsettled having to ride along on the waves of her emotions.

"It is a big project, Mom." Maggie sighed. "And a big house to live in by yourself. If I'm being honest, I think downsizing would've been a better idea."

"Oh, if it were up to you two, you'd have me moving into a retirement home." Mom laughed. "And besides, why shouldn't I have a nice home to live in? You two will be thanking me for all the space I have when you want to drop off my grandkids for a weekend at grandma's."

Her eyes twinkled, and I coughed. Neither Maggie nor I was anywhere close to that stage of life yet, though apparently, my mother hadn't gotten that memo.

"Anyway," I said, hands braced on my thighs as I prepared to escape this awkward conversation. "I better get go—"

"I heard from Dad." Maggie's voice detonated the carefully constructed peace in the room. "I figured now's a good time to tell you since we're all here."

I sucked in a breath, watching our mother carefully. Her face remained impossibly neutral, though I swore I saw it drop for just a second.

"Oh," she said, and I wondered how many thoughts were running through her mind at once.

When the man she thought she was going to spend her life with walked out on all of us, she tried to hold it together. For us. But something had changed in her when he left, and it felt like we never really got her back. At least not all the way.

I glared at Maggie, pissed that she'd brought it up in front of Mom when she knew Mom couldn't handle this conversation right now.

"What did he say?" Mom asked shakily, averting her eyes as she pulled at a thread on her sweatshirt.

"Not much. He asked how I was doing. About my life. He wants to meet up." Her eyes landed on me. "And he wants Liam to come."

Fuck that.

A sentiment that I spoke out loud, causing Maggie to furrow her brows at me as if *I* was the offensive piece of shit rather than the guy who abandoned us.

"Why would you even want to see him, Mags?" I asked, standing up. "He left. He didn't want anything to do with us for the last fifteen years. Even entertaining a phone call with him is more than he deserves."

"Liam!" Maggie jumped to her feet, though she was still several inches beneath me. "Why won't you just give him a chance?"

"A chance to do what, Mags?" My voice rose. "Justify why he left and never looked back? Explain why he never bothered to call, or write, or show up for his children? There's no excuse that'll erase all that."

"You're right!" she yelled back. "Nothing's going to erase what already happened, but maybe he wants to do better now."

"We don't need him!"

"Liam," my mother's voice tried to soothe from the sidelines.

"You don't need *anyone*," Maggie's voice broke. "But what about me? What if *I* need someone?"

"Then good fucking luck to you because he's never going to be what you want him to be. He's already proven he can't."

"You don't get it!" she screamed. "You weren't the one crying yourself to sleep every night after he left."

No, I wasn't. Because she and my mom did enough of that for the three of us. Two people crying over that guy were two people too many. I wasn't going to add to that list.

But the worst part was Mom and her waiting. Expecting him to come back. Fuck, I had a feeling she spent years thinking it was all just a mistake, and he'd come walking through the door any day with flowers and an apology.

It just settled the matter more firmly for me.

"Fuck that guy," I told her. "You're not that broken little kid anymore, and seeing him now isn't going to fix her."

Maggie's eyes welled with tears, and I felt like the biggest asshole in the world.

"Maggie," I said softly, wanting to reach out and fix everything I had just broken. But she held out a hand, stopping me in my tracks.

"Just because you're angry at the world doesn't mean I need to be. And if you won't see him, fine. But *I* need this."

I stared at her, determination blazing in her eyes. Then down to Mom, who looked suddenly so small and frail, not saying anything as the news of it all washed over her.

There she was, letting us duke it out like we always did. Dad left, and all of a sudden, she didn't know how to parent. Couldn't figure out the line of discipline between coming across too harsh or letting us off too easy, so she just… left us to do whatever we were going to do.

"I should go," I said, not knowing what else to do, only knowing that they were both better off without me.

"Great idea," Maggie said, following me toward the door.

I didn't know why I couldn't react to things like a normal fucking person. Or why my first instinct was to lash out and board myself up rather than try to listen to what Maggie was saying.

"And Cassie already left, by the way," Maggie said, resentment burning in her eyes. "Because I know you sure as hell didn't come here to see me."

And then she slammed the door behind me, leaving me with the fear that I never allowed my thoughts to linger on for too long.

Maybe I was more like *him* than I ever wanted to be. More like him than I could live with being.

CHAPTER NINETEEN

Cassie

For a long time, I was used to living in a constant state of fight-or-flight mode. Of never feeling truly safe.

When I went back to the house I grew up in, that adrenaline filled my body all over again. Not knowing what I was walking into was an unsettling thing.

I didn't know if I was going to get screamed at, kicked out, or welcomed with open arms. And sometimes, it was a combination of all three in rapid succession.

Today, walking through the front door, there was an added sense of anxiety because if I didn't find somewhere to live soon, I might end up right back there all over again.

"Mom?" I call into the darkness of the house.

The blinds were drawn, the house was trashed, and her figure was sprawled on the couch, sleeping under a pile of blankets while the TV played faintly in the background.

But she was alive.

When I didn't hear from her for a few days, the fear that she might not be alive always sank in. But for now, at least, she was.

I moved through the house, picking up bottle after empty bottle of vodka and putting them all into the overflowing trash. I tied it up, took it outside, and then came back inside to clear up the rest.

This was how we lived for so long. Pizza boxes throughout the kitchen. The stench of alcohol was everywhere. Mess after mess that I couldn't work fast enough to stay on top of.

Her clothes were in a heap on the bathroom floor, so I gathered them all up and started a load of laundry. I washed the dishes in the sink and left them to dry. I scrubbed the countertops and threw out all the old take-out boxes in the fridge that I knew she'd leave to rot.

I was hit with guilt for not being here to take care of her anymore. For letting it get this bad. But what was worse than the guilt, and deeper, was the relief I felt at not having to live like this anymore. Not having to walk into *this* every day of my life.

Her snores filled the house, and I was grateful. I wouldn't have to talk to her, carefully navigating a drunken conversation where something might trigger her at any moment, causing the eruptions of anger I'd grown so used to.

Instead, I did what I could, cleaning as quietly as I was able before stocking the fridge with the groceries I'd picked up on the way over here.

Cans of soup, frozen dinners, cereal, and milk. All foods that were easy for her to make on her own with little effort.

What scared me most was when she was too drunk to eat. Her stomach too full of alcohol to realize that her body was craving nutrients and fuel. If I weren't here to remind her, I knew it had probably been days since she'd had a decent meal, and it hurt to think about it.

When I was home, I could keep track of these things. Now, from far away, all I could do was worry. It was like a chokehold on me at all times, never knowing how far gone she was. If she were one drink away from a hospital visit she wouldn't recover from.

I'd tried a few Al-Anon meetings that were supposedly there to help the families of alcoholics.

It's a family disease, they said. *Because it doesn't just affect the alcoholic. But everyone around them too.*

That was true, but a big portion of Al-Anon's healing methods were a complete detachment from the alcoholic. Not walking away from them exactly, but freeing yourself from the thought that you could control their actions.

I hadn't yet reached that point yet. I'd spent my whole life monitoring my mother's drinking. Trying to hide her alcohol, pour it out, or intervene in whatever chaotic method I thought fit. And even though it never worked, it never stopped the guilt that overpowered me each time she landed in the hospital.

If only I had done better at keeping her away from it. If only the cost of raising me had been less, then she wouldn't be so stressed.

It was one thing to say you understood that your parents' actions were not your own, but accepting that whatever fate she landed at was of her own making and there was nothing I could do about it? That was a level of detachment I would never reach.

I had to intervene. I had to fix her.

Or else I'd have to live in a world without my mother in it. And that was something I couldn't accept.

"Is he okay?" The words on the other end of the phone stopped me in my tracks later that night on my way out of the library.

"Who?" I asked though I knew there could be only one 'he' that Maggie was calling about.

Still, I didn't understand why our mutual 'he' would be anything but okay in the first place. Or why Maggie thought I was the person to call if he wasn't.

"Liam," she breathed his name, causing anxiety to spiral in my gut. "We sort of got into a fight earlier, and now I'm feeling bad about it.

I just wanted to make sure that he didn't, like, take off and leave the continent or something."

"I don't know," I admitted, clutching the papers still warm from the printer in my hand. "I haven't seen him since last night."

"You haven't?" she asked. "He was looking for you earlier. Where are you?"

He was looking for me?

"I'm at the library, printing out apartment listings." I got a glare from a librarian who held a finger to her lips at the volume of my words. "But I'm leaving now."

"Well, could you do me a huge favor and go find him?" Maggie's voice was riddled with anxiety in a way I seldom heard. "I mean, I know he's probably fine and everything, but he gets more upset about things than he lets on. I just want to make sure he's not doing anything self-destructive, you know?"

I bit my lip, wanting to see him so badly while at the same time feeling like he'd view it as an intrusion.

I said as much to Maggie. "I don't know. I don't think I'm the right person to go see him if he's upset. I'm already intruding on every other aspect of his life." I shuffled toward the front door, shoving the papers in my bag and not caring if they crumbled. "Shouldn't I be giving him space if he's in a mood?"

"No!" Maggie cried out helplessly. "Look, I sort of set him off, and I'm not going to forgive myself until you find him and let me know he's alright. Please, just call me when you get home and let me know if he's there."

"I will," I promised, a sudden urgency to my step.

Liam might not need me right now, but some part of me needed him. *Just to see if he was all right*, I told myself, then I'd leave him alone.

CHAPTER TWENTY

Liam

When I was on the ice, everything stopped.

The pressure, the noise, the relentless pounding of my own thoughts in my skull. It all sort of faded into a dull buzz.

It was still there, of course. But it was easier to turn that feeling into something I could use as fuel. To propel me forward, rather than something I had to sit around and take.

It was funny, going to the ice to avoid thoughts of my father when he was the one who taught me how to lace up my skates, hold a stick, and get out there in the first place.

Sometimes, I wondered if I'd become so good just to spite him. Sometimes I wondered if I'd be here at all if he hadn't walked out. Maybe I'd just be another normal, well-adjusted guy who had a good relationship with his parents, working in a cubicle somewhere.

I guessed if I ever saw him again, I might as well thank him for being a shitty father. He had, after all, landed me in the NHL.

I leaned into the shot and sent the puck soaring across the ice, nearly taking our goalie's head off in the process.

He called me a less-than-stellar name, but I didn't care. I had to stay moving. It was like if I skated fast enough, hit hard enough, then the thoughts couldn't keep up with me.

Coach blew the whistle, signaling the end of practice, and I found myself regretting it. Off the ice, it wasn't as easy to hide from all the shit threatening to consume me.

"Hey, you good, man?" Brody's voice sounded as he skated up beside me.

"I'm fine," I bit out.

"Uh, maybe try that again," Brody said, eyeing me. "Because you've been like a machine out there tonight. And you know, normally, that's great for a hockey player. But as your friend? Kind of concerning. You hit the ice, and it's like all traces of human emotion just vanished."

"So?"

"So, it's not good to bottle shit up, man. It makes you get all weird and prone to outbursts."

I scoffed. "I don't have outbursts."

"Well, not yet, but that's why I'm nervous. What if you let all that stuff in your head fester for so long that you go crazy and kill someone? Then their blood will be on my hands because I'm your best friend, and I didn't step in to intervene."

"The only person I'm at risk of killing is you." I shook my head at his ludicrous reasoning.

"You can't kill me." He placed a gloved hand on his chest as we made our way off the ice. "I'm your future brother-in-law."

I raised a brow at him in question. "Is my sister aware of this?"

"Considering she walked out on me that night at the bar, I'd say the plan for making her fall in love with me is going to take a bit more time than I was anticipating, but don't you worry, I'm no quitter."

"Glad to hear it." I chuffed out a laugh.

And to be honest, part of me was.

Maggie didn't really date, at least not in any serious way, and part of me wondered if she was just scared, the same way I was. I wondered if maybe our dad had screwed her up more than she let on.

If so, then I really was a dick because I'd left her alone to suffer with the same things that tormented me when I should've been there for her this whole time.

It might be too late to repair all the ways that I screwed up with her, but if she was willing to give our father, of all people, a second chance, then maybe she would with me, too.

"Hey, by the way," Brody said, nudging my arm. "Your girl's here."

My heart surged at his words, and damn it, if I didn't picture Cassie's face before I even saw her sitting there.

She looked up at me, a smile on her lips as I walked over to her. She was wearing a big pink jacket and blue jeans with a rainbow scarf wrapped around her neck. She waved to me as I approached her, showcasing an equally colorful mitten.

Clearly, she'd remembered how cold it was from her last visit and decided to overcompensate for this one.

"Hey," I said cooly, even though my mind was racing at what she might be doing here.

"Hi." She beamed, jumping to her feet as I got closer. Her smile was wide and genuine, feeling like a blast of sunshine in my direction that I didn't deserve.

"What are you doing here?" I asked, grip tightening on my hockey stick.

"Oh," she said, smile faltering slightly, and I missed it immediately. "Sorry. I probably should've asked you first. Or texted. Or just not come at all." Her eyes darted away.

"No," I corrected, wanting to fix whatever feeling was bubbling up inside of her, causing her to shut down on me. "No. You don't have to ask. I'm glad you're here."

"You are?" Big blue eyes peeked up at me.

"Yeah." I laughed. "I am."

"I've sort of had a crappy day." She sighed and held out her arms.

"Yeah." I nodded in agreement, not understanding what that had to do with her being here and not caring in the slightest as long as I got to keep looking at her. "Me too."

She gave me a half smile.

"Do you want to go get some pizza?" I asked, feeling the weight of the day leaving my chest as I stared down at her.

She nodded up at me—that smile returning to her face as if I'd just offered to take her to the moon rather than a little joint down the street from the apartment.

"I'd like that a lot."

"I don't mean to brag," Cassie said, bells chiming as we walked through the door of the restaurant, "but I'm sort of a pizza connoisseur."

"Oh yeah?" I asked, grinning down at her.

"Mmhm." She nodded. "I can probably put away more slices of pizza than you and your hockey team combined."

I snorted. "Doubtful."

Her eyes flared with the challenge.

"I mean it. There's a hundred percent chance I'll outeat you tonight."

At that, I let out a deep, genuine laugh.

"What!"

"Nothing, it's just—" I said through laughter. "Have you seen you? Or better yet, have you seen *me?*" I gestured between us to our drastic size difference. "In what world do you think you can eat more than me?"

She tsked, waving away my comment with a gesture of hand.

"You'll see." She smiled sweetly.

"Hi, sorry about the wait." The hostess rushed over to the host stand when she noticed us waiting. "Table for two?"

"Yes, please," I said and found myself placing a guiding hand on

Cassie's back as we followed the host to the table.

It was stupid, I thought as soon as I did it. It was a small place and nowhere near crowded enough for her to get lost. But I did it without thinking and then thought it would be weirder to rip it away, so I kept it there, reveling in the feeling of her beneath me and feeling like an asshole for doing it all the same.

"Thank you," Cassie told the hostess as she sat us down with menus.

Cassie said 'thank you' a lot, I'd noticed. Over and over again for the littlest things. She said thank you when the waitress brought us to the table, thank you when she sat us down, and thank you when the waitress left, promising she'd be back soon.

Not to mention the dozens of times she'd said it to me for doing absolutely nothing.

She was really polite, something I could probably learn from, considering everyone loved to remind me what an asshole I was.

But around Cassie, I didn't feel like such an asshole. In fact, I found myself feeling like the type of guy who was nice to people just because I wasn't so damned tense about who they were, why they were talking to me, or what they wanted from me.

Something about her put me at ease in a way that almost scared me because why the hell did a girl I'd only known for a few days make me feel more relaxed than anyone I'd known in my entire life?

And how was I going to react when she was gone?

"So, what's the move?" I asked, shaking the thoughts out of my head.

She was here now, in front of me. I wasn't going to waste the time worrying about what would happen later.

"Um, well, extra cheese is a must," she said very seriously.

"Obviously." I nodded. "What else?"

"Um, I was thinking… mushrooms?"

"Why do you look shy about mushrooms?" I laughed.

"I don't know," she said with a laugh. "Sometimes they're a controversial topping."

"Well, I don't have anything against them, so if you like mushrooms, then load the pizza with them for all I care."

"Okay, your turn to pick toppings." She groaned in frustration. "You're going to be eating it too, after all."

I was about to tell her that I really didn't care, that I'd happily eat anything she could possibly order just because of how excitedly she looked at the menu.

But by now, I knew her well enough that I could predict how she'd react to that. With a nose scrunched and protestations that would leave us going back and forth in circles. So I offered up a suggestion.

"Pepperoni?"

Her face fell. Barely visible, but some of that warmth radiating behind the smile fell away, leaving a distant, insincere look in its wake.

"Great. Yeah. That sounds good." She nodded her head in agreement, but I saw right through her.

"You don't like pepperoni?"

She shrugged her shoulders, looking at me bashfully. "Not really. But, of course, I don't mind eating them if *you* like them."

"I honestly don't care either way," I said, and when she opened her mouth to protest like I knew she would, I shushed her with my next words. "I promise."

"Fine." She relaxed, "Well, if you really want to know, my favorite pizza is mushrooms, black olives, and extra cheese."

"Then, we'll get exactly that," I said, taking our menus and putting them back in their spot. "I figured you should get the advantage of having a pizza you actually *like,* considering all your talk about how you're going to outeat me."

The waitress came back before whatever words were on the tip of Cassie's tongue could tumble out, and I almost regretted that I didn't get to hear what she would've said.

The waitress took our order and scurried off to the kitchen, leaving us alone in a mostly empty restaurant. It was quiet, not in a bad way, but rather the type of silence that made me breathe easily for a bit. It wasn't the dead quiet of my apartment that I used to think was the perfect escape, and it wasn't the overwhelming roar of fans screaming my name in the arena.

It was a reprieve from it all. And I had the feeling it wouldn't be that way if it were anyone else in the world sitting across from me.

The blonde in question had shed her winter attire and was currently tugging on the sleeves of her floral sweater.

She looked cute in her normal clothes. They suited her personality much better than the dark, black outfits my sister had styled her in the last few times when Cassie's clothes had been in limbo at Dave the Dick's house.

Should I ask how she's doing about it all? Should I avoid the topic? Would it be more insensitive of me to bring it up or, worse, to ignore it?

Shit, maybe I really didn't know how to talk to girls.

I felt like I was on a first date, nervous to say the wrong thing, nervous that I'd screw it all up before I even got a chance to know her.

I had to force myself not to shake my head to get the thoughts away because it absolutely was *not* a date. Just two friends eating pizza before going home together.

Fuck.

"How's your hockey going?" she interrupted my inner anguish to ask.

"My hockey?" I laughed at her choice of wording. "It's good.

"When's your next game?" she asked. "I'd love to come to one and see you play! Maggie says you're really good."

I pictured her sitting in the stands, watching me, and the idea of it filled me with warmth. I cleared my throat, annoyed with how idiotic I was being tonight.

Maybe I *did* need a girlfriend because, apparently, I was projecting all my fantasies onto Cassie, which I was sure she wouldn't take kindly to.

"The season hasn't started yet." I smiled.

"It hasn't?" She looked surprised. "But you're gone all the time!"

"Training," I answered. "You live in Boston, and you don't know when hockey season is?"

"I already told you I'm not much of a sports person."

"But you still want to come see me play?" I asked, a feeling blooming in my chest. "Why?"

"Well, because it's you," she answered in a way that made me want to beg her to elaborate.

"How's your school going?" I phrased it the same way she had.

Her eyes brightened as she dove into an explanation of how cute her class was this year, how much progress they'd made in the first few weeks, and how proud she was of them already.

"I mean," she said animatedly, "At the start of the year, they couldn't even walk in a straight line! Now they're doing it with verbal cues only!"

"That's… great?" I offered.

"It is!" Her eyes shone. "So, yeah. The kids are great. The school is great. It's just that some of my coworkers *really* don't seem like they like me."

"Why?" I asked, wondering how it was possible someone could spend five minutes with the girl in front of me and *not* like her.

Hell, I had issues with most of the population, but she drew me in.

"I don't know," she said, shrinking into herself. "I know it sounds stupid, but I feel like sometimes people don't take me seriously just because I try to be happy. It's like they think I'm dumb for trying to stay positive. I don't know, maybe I'm crazy. And a lot of them like to sit around and complain about things—the kids, the parents, the administration, whatever. And it's almost like they hold it against me that I don't."

"You're not crazy," I told her. "Misery loves company."

"That's what they say." She shrugged sadly. "It just sucks to be excluded because I don't want to gossip."

I felt a surge of anger at the thought of Cassie going to work every day feeling anything less than accepted and loved. She had to deal with the shit with her ex, plus shitty coworkers on top of it?

Thank *God* I had come to my senses fast enough and got her to stay with me. If she had to deal with figuring out a living situation on top of it all, I don't think I could bear it.

The pizza came before I could tell her to fuck all those people and keep doing her thing. But somehow, I figured that it wouldn't be the type of advice she wanted to hear.

Cassie struck me as the type of person who deeply cared about people and what they thought of her, and while that wasn't necessarily a trait we had in common, I couldn't fault her for it.

She dug into her slice, making a noise of pure bliss after the first bite. There was enough cheese that it stretched off the pizza in long, white strands, and I had to try it myself to see if it was as life-changing as Cassie's expression made it out to be.

It was.

"So, what about you?" she asked me between slices as she wiped her fingers on the napkin.

"What about me?"

"Well, I just told you about my job, and I think it's pretty clear that despite some minor drawbacks, I'm pretty much living my dream. So, what's yours?"

"Hockey," I answered simply, somewhat confused by the question. "I thought that was obvious."

"Right, but is that all you ever want to do? Like, what else? Any other big ambitions, or goals, or secret aspirations?"

I felt myself withdrawing. Through no fault of her own, Cassie had struck a nerve, venturing into a dangerous topic for me. Because the truth was, I had been grappling with the very questions myself for the last few years.

What's next?

"Being in the NHL is no small thing," I said. "In fact, I think it qualifies as 'dream job' territory."

"Right, of course," she said, quick to correct. "I only meant, what else do you see for yourself in the future? You're more than just a hockey player, you know."

Was I? No one else seemed to think so.

"If I'm being honest, that's kind of a tough subject," I admitted, leaning back in my seat.

"Is it?" Her eyes widened as if afraid she'd offended me, but still, she dared to ask. "But why?"

"Why?" I repeated her question, mulling it over in my mind. "Because I don't know who I am other than that."

"That can't be true," she said.

"It is," I confirmed solemnly. "All I ever wanted to be was a hockey player, and I spent my life working toward that. There wasn't much time for anything else. And now…"

"And now," she pressed softly, willing me to continue.

"Now I only have a few good years left in my career, and I'm terrified of what my life will look like after that."

"What?" She balked, mouth opening in utter shock. "You're only twenty… something years old—"

"Twenty-six," I said. "And most NHL players retire somewhere between now and thirty."

"That's crazy," she admitted. "You're like the fittest guy I've ever seen. You could play for *years*."

I laughed at the way she blushed after she said it.

"The fittest guy you've ever seen?" I smirked.

"Well, in person, yeah," she said, blushing. "But then again, I don't know any other professional sports players."

I was glad she didn't. Guys like my teammates would take way too eager an interest in her.

"But anyway," she rambled. "I mean, even if you had to stop playing hockey, you have all of the opportunities in the world to do *whatever* you want after!"

"But I don't know what I want to do," I responded, uncomfortable with the question.

Life was *long*. It stretched on past the point of being comfortable sometimes. Who would I be when my body couldn't do the only thing I'd ever needed it for? What would my life be like when my hockey days were a thing of the past, left behind in the age of unattainable youth?

"Sometimes," I admitted, "it feels like the rest of my life will be just too much time I have to fill."

"Isn't that exciting? I mean, you could do anything. You could find a new passion or follow a new dream, or if you were really that attached to hockey, you could coach a team or find some way to still be involved in some other way."

She was right, but how could I tell her that everything else would feel so insignificant in comparison to what I had already done? How I felt like I was being demoted into a life of insignificance. That hockey was the only thing that made me feel worthwhile.

"Well, what about you besides teaching?" I deflected. "What else do you want for your life?"

"Oh, you know." She shrugged, apparently doing some deflecting of her own. "The normal things. Nothing as glamorous as the life of an NHL player, I'm sure."

Some part of me wanted to press her, to ask what exactly that entailed... but I didn't know her like that and couldn't bring myself to pry when that was the very thing I hated most that people did to me.

We sat in silence for a moment, both aware that we were creeping around things we'd rather not talk about but content to let it be. For now.

"So, pizza," I said, landing on a safer subject. "Is it like your favorite food or something? Since you claimed to have outeaten the state of Massachusetts in it?"

"Actually, no." She laughed. "It's just the only thing I really ever ate growing up."

"The *only* thing?"

"Well, no," she said. "But it was definitely a top staple in the house. My mom wasn't much of a cook, and pizza was easy to order or throw in the oven with little effort." She shrugged, apparently still enjoying the dish she'd eaten more times than I cared to believe.

The idea of it struck me as… kind of sad. Even in my mom's darkest days after my father first left, she still managed to throw together some type of meal for me and Maggie to come home to.

"Sorry I brought you to have more of it, then," I said guiltily.

"No!" She held her hands up. "I really do love pizza a lot. And this." She held up the last slice in our box. "Is better than most."

Before I could get another word in, Cassie looked behind us toward the back of the restaurant before telling me she was going to the bathroom and would be right back.

I nodded, watching as she disappeared down the hallway before slipping my phone out of my pocket. The guys' group chat was flooded with texts that I didn't bother to sort through, and I had the usual text from Brody that seemed to pop up every time I looked at my phone.

This time, it was a link to some online social media thread. Ordinarily, I wouldn't have even bothered to click on it, except for the text that came along with it.

> **BRODY:** U and ur girlfriend are making the rounds on the internet 👀

My stomach tightened, and morbid curiosity had me clicking the link that brought me to Twitter.

> @sam_3xo: met liam brynn at a bar and he's an asshole.

Pretty tame and consistent with what everyone else wrote about me, but when I clicked on the girl's profile picture and zoomed in to see the redhead from the bar, my blood boiled.

In all fairness, I had been pretty polite about her harassing me. I didn't think it counted as me being an asshole because I rejected her advances, but apparently, I was alone in that mindset.

I read down the thread that had multiple responses, retweets, and likes.

> @hannahbby: nooooooo, he's so hot

The redhead responded,

> @sam_3xo: don't tell him that, apparently he has a gf and can't even have a conversation without letting you know about her.

My jaw ticked. I had only brought out the imaginary girlfriend card after *multiple* attempts to get the girl to back the hell off. Now she got to spread shit on the internet where people would just believe it as fact? It was fucking stupid. And I couldn't say anything about it without getting bad press.

Like a masochist, I kept scrolling.

> @bCassiebuns13: receipts???

> @sam_3x0: oh, I got them

Followed by a blurry photo beneath the tweet that had me sucking in a sharp breath.

It was me, standing by the karaoke stage, my body angled slightly toward Cassie. Our faces weren't visible, but anyone who knew me would be able to tell it was me by my posture alone.

Cassie was barely visible. A blurry face and long blond hair were the only things you could really make out about her figure.

The only thing that was incriminating was how close we stood to each other. I didn't even realize I'd been leaning into her that much.

But it had been loud? Hadn't it?

My grip on the phone tightened, my jaw working as I tried to figure out a solution. I knew better than to believe the story would just die out. Social media was like a curse to humanity, spreading lies and misinformation as rapidly as fire, with no way to drench the flames.

The replies were endless, each comment written by people who clearly had no real lives of their own.

My fingers threatened to crush the phone they held, but still, I couldn't put it away. This wasn't just my life they were messing with now, but *Cassie's*.

Cassie, who clearly would rather hide under a rock than face any type of public scrutiny like the type that came along with my life.

My mind was racing, my blood was boiling, and then, a soft voice cut through the static of my thoughts.

"Hey," Cassie said, sliding back into her seat as she tucked a loose curl behind her ear. "Are you okay?"

I blinked at her, the anger still vividly thrumming in my chest.

Her bright blue eyes were open, searching mine for an answer.

I swallowed anxiously. Did I tell her? That right now, thousands of strangers were likely zooming in, analyzing, trying to track her down, all because of me? That some random girl was spreading rumors about her just because of her connection to me?

Did I tell her the idea of her life getting muddied and messed up with and put under a magnifying glass because of me made me want to throw my fucking phone across the room?

She tilted her head, eyes pinched nervously.

"Liam?" she asked again.

I inhaled deeply through my nose, pocketing my phone once more, though it now felt like more of a bomb waiting to detonate.

"Yeah," I said, voice rougher than I intended. "I'm fine."

CHAPTER TWENTY-ONE

Cassie

Hockey season had officially started. If I didn't know from the fact that Liam was now gone all the time, my coworkers at school would've given me the clue. Apparently, hockey in Boston was a bigger deal than I realized. I guess before, I had always tuned in, but now, I was hyperaware of every mention of the Harbor Wolves, specifically their center, who was apparently a bigger deal than even I imagined he could be.

Liam, who had taken to avoiding me following that night at the pizza place. I don't know what happened, but there was a sense of distance from him after that.

It could be the stress of the season starting and all his late-night games, but I got the feeling it had more to do with *me*. It was obvious I was encroaching on the territory of overstaying my welcome.

I couldn't believe that I'd been there for almost two weeks. The time had slipped by faster than I could've imagined, what with the business of school and the ease I had found myself existing at Liam's.

I had been lulled into a false sense of safety, and I think subconsciously, I didn't want to leave it, which proved to me that I needed to be working on plans to leave immediately.

Which was what I was doing when Liam got home that night. I had the listings I'd printed out at the library days ago spread across the table, accompanied by a myriad of highlighters and colorful pens, when he walked through the door, freshly showered and smelling like bergamot and winter air.

"Hey." I smiled up at him, determined to break the weird tension that had lingered between us the last few days.

I was sure that once he saw I was serious about getting out of his hair, we'd be able to live in relative peace again in the meantime.

"Hi," he said, dropping his duffel bag and walking toward me.

"I wanted to tell you—"

"I wanted to ask you—"

We both spoke at the same time, immediately cutting ourselves off at the other's voice.

I stilled, terrified he was about to tell me I'd been there too long and had to leave immediately. Right then, if possible.

I blinked up, waiting for him to continue.

He arched a brow as if waiting to see if I wanted to say my piece first.

When I didn't speak, fear thick in my throat at the rejection about to come my way, he cleared his throat and started. A little hesitantly.

He looked nervous. Of course he did. Because he was too polite to tell me he wanted me out without feeling a little bad about it. But he shouldn't feel bad. I was the one imposing on him.

God, I was such an idiot.

I stared at him, waiting for the blow to land.

"Um, I just wanted to see if—" He cleared his throat.

If I'd found a place yet? If I knew that it had been two weeks of my being here? If I could get the hell out of his life already?

"If?" I asked shakily, preparing an exit plan as he spoke.

"I have another home game coming up soon, and I was just going to ask if you wanted to come."

His words froze me into silence, and my heart paused, stilling in my chest.

"You wanted to see if…" I trailed off, trying to figure out if I'd misunderstood him.

"I know you're not into hockey," he said, face contorting, "But I thought if you didn't have anything else going on, you could bring Maggie and—" He cupped his neck absentmindedly. "It's probably stupid to ask you. I knew you probably didn't want to. I just figured I'd ask."

His words went over my head as I jumped up and squealed.

"Yes!"

"Yes?" His face morphed into genuine shock.

"Of course I want to come!" I said, bouncing slightly on my feet. "I mean, I don't really understand the games or the rules, but I've really been wanting to see you play! I'm so excited!"

Liam's eyes flicked up to me, and I saw it.

The barely-there shift in his expression. The quiet, fleeting flicker of satisfaction. It was so small that if I hadn't been looking, I might've missed it.

But I didn't miss it.

"You mean it?" he asked, brows furrowed. "You really want to come?"

"Of course! If you're really offering, that is!" I smiled at him, unable to suppress my excitement at the invitation.

Warmth spread through my chest, accompanied by the blissful weight of relief.

Liam Brynn—the most sought-after, most aggressively private player in the league—was inviting me to his game. As if he wanted me there. Like he cared if I came.

Which meant, *maybe* he didn't hate me as much as I feared he did. Maybe he even more than just tolerated me.

"Okay." He nodded, grinning. "I'll set it up."

Then his eyes went to the papers on the table, and his brows furrowed once more.

"What's this?" he said, picking up one of the listings that had my highlighting all over it.

His shoulders tensed as he frowned down at the paper.

"Oh!" I said, my words feeling heavier than I expected. "I was just about to tell you. I'm working my way through apartment listings. It's kind of overwhelming."

His voice was flat when he finally spoke. "You're leaving."

"I mean, yeah." I shrugged, aiming for nonchalance. "I've already been here two weeks. I don't want to overstay my welcome."

His jaw clenched slightly at that.

"I've found a couple of decent places," I continued, utterly self-conscious as he skimmed through listing after listing.

"No," he said simply, dropping the papers to the table.

"No?" I asked, voice airy.

"No," he repeated firmly, a look of displeasure etched on his face. "Cassie, these places are *awful*. There's no way you're moving into any of these."

"Hey, some of them are okay," I defended my listings. "They're all in the city, so I'm close to work."

He scoffed. "In the shittiest parts of town."

I blushed. "Well, my price range isn't exactly getting me into Beacon Hill."

"That's why you're here." He gestured. "Until you find somewhere suitable."

"Uh, that could take a while."

"Who cares?" he countered, tone ringing with annoyance.

"Well, how about this one?" I said, sorting through the papers until I found the one I was looking for. "This is in a decent area, *and* I can afford it."

"*What the fuck.*" He practically snarled down at the paper, squinting at the words. "Did you *read* the part about your potential 'roomie' being a sixty-four-year-old man?"

"We'll have separate bathrooms!" I argued.

"No, you fucking won't because you're not living with some random man!"

"News flash, *I already am,*" I argued, getting worked up.

It's not like I *wanted* to go live in a shitty apartment that I could still barely afford. But I didn't have many options, and I *refused* to be a burden for any longer than necessary.

If I had other options, crappy as they were, I had to take them.

"That's different." He crossed his arms. I hated that I stared at them.

"How?"

"Because I'm not a creep."

"Well, I didn't know that when I moved in."

"Which shows your lack of judgment!"

I pulled away, reeling from the sting of his comment.

"Cassie." He huffed out a frustrated sigh, "Look, I'm sorry. I didn't mean it. I just—"

"You just what?" I glared at him accusingly.

"I just don't want you to end up in another bad situation," he said, voice softer now. "I want you to take your time looking for somewhere you're really going to like. Somewhere you'll be safe and happy."

I stared at him, a thousand thoughts going through my head.

How could I tell him that I'd already found a place where I was safe and happy and that it hurt knowing I had to leave it for somewhere infinitely worse? How could I tell him that anywhere else was going to be a downgrade because he wouldn't be there? How could I admit to myself that the reason I needed a new place so urgently was *because* of how comfortable I was getting here?

I couldn't, so I just stared at him as we lingered in the tense silence that filled the air like a smoke-filled room.

Finally, he spoke, shoulders deflating, the defensiveness in him retreating.

"Just… keep looking. Okay?"

I nodded, afraid of the relief I felt that he was giving me the gift of more time here.

With him.

"Okay."

CHAPTER TWENTY-TWO

Liam

I'd always thought my self-restraint skills were above average, to say the least.

I'd never been the type to indulge in anything I deemed unnecessary. I got my ass to the gym every day. I never missed practice. I didn't spend money on anything that wasn't a necessity. There was nothing that caused me to slip up, to cave into my lesser urges.

At least there hadn't been.

I'd tried to stay away from her. I'd really fucking tried. But apparently, my self-restraint only went so far when it came to the tiny blonde who had taken up residency in more than just my apartment.

She was like an infection that had spread inside me at a rapid pace. I thought about her when I wasn't with her. I wanted to talk to her *all* the time. And worst of all, I was fucking terrified of her leaving.

It took me a minute to realize what the feeling was. I was *worried*.

I didn't trust that she wouldn't end up in some scummy place that she could barely afford. Or worse, she'd end up with some random, sketchy roommate.

Cassie was… delicate. I didn't want her to end up with a random person who left messes in their apartment or brought strangers back to the place Cassie was living. It just wasn't safe.

But what could I do? Beg her to live with me forever? No, I very well couldn't, which left me with one option.

Convince her to postpone until we found somewhere actually suitable. Even though I'd made a big deal of it at the start, it wasn't awful having her here. I didn't mind waiting as long as it took for her to find a safe, affordable apartment.

She had a free place to live, and I could rest assured that she wasn't getting abducted by some guy off Craigslist.

I'd handled it shitty, I couldn't deny that. And I'd been half expecting Cassie to freeze me out afterward or, at the very least, show some type of sign that she was pissed.

But she hadn't.

The next morning, it was like it had never happened. I came out of my room, made our coffee, and waited for her to come down for breakfast.

I'd been prepared to apologize in a way that made my palms sweaty and my body tense. I wasn't in the habit of apologizing. Even when I knew I should. But I couldn't stand the idea of Cassie being mad at me. Or the thought that she might be pissed enough to leave because I'd way overstepped my place in her life by telling her she couldn't move into any of those places.

But when she came downstairs, to my utter shock, she *smiled* at me, said good morning like usual, and started pouring herself a bowl of cereal.

"Ah," she squealed, seeing the coffee I'd poured into her mug. "Thank you so much! I told you that you didn't have to do this every day."

For a minute, I was too stunned to say anything; I just watched her as she went about her routine before sitting at the counter to eat. I went over toward her with an added tension to my step, as if at any moment she might remember she was mad at me.

"You're being weird," she said, furrowing her brows, mid-bite of cereal.

"Am I?" I shook off the feeling, deciding if she wasn't going to mention it, I sure as hell didn't want to be the one to bring up the awkwardness again. Not when I couldn't fully explain my reasoning behind it in the first place.

She was twenty-four years old. She had a right to live wherever she wanted.

For some reason, I sure as hell didn't want to remind her of that either.

"Yeah, you are," she said, her eyes following me. "You're pacing. Are you worried about something? Hockey?"

I laughed softly, amazed at how quickly what I thought had been a fight between us had been brushed off. "No, I'm not worried about hockey."

"Well, maybe you're hungry," she said, gesturing toward the seat beside her. "Come sit down and have breakfast."

"Is this how you talk to your Kindergartners?" I asked with a smirk but did as she said anyway.

"Only when they're acting hangry." She scrunched her nose in a playful tease at me, gulping down the coffee. "Oh my gosh! I forgot to tell you yesterday—"

And then she launched into a series of stories about her workday, the way I'd gotten used to her doing almost every day. She would tell me things the kids said, the way they said them, and the intricate backstories of the kids' lives in order for me to understand the significance of the story.

I felt like I'd gotten to know the personalities of all of these five-year-olds I'd never met just by the way Cassie brought them to life with her stories.

I smiled as she continued. "And then, my coworker said, 'I almost got a speeding ticket getting here today!' and Connor said, 'My dad got a speeding ticket on his way to the beer store!'" Cassie spoke through a fit of giggles as if she were reciting the words of a great comedian rather than her five-year-old student.

"You really love them, huh?" I asked, staring at her in awe.

"So much," she gushed. "I love that I get to be a part of shaping their first experience with the world outside their homes. I get to see them grow and change and form their first friendships. Gosh, I can't even talk about it—" she said, wiping a tear from her eye as she smiled.

"They're lucky to have you," I told her honestly. "Not many people are suited to work with kids."

"I can't understand why!" she said, "They're the most wholesome population in our society. And I get the incredible privilege of teaching them how to be good people in the world. I can't believe how lucky I am to have the job I have."

"I don't know if all teachers feel the same," I said, thinking back to some of the more hardened teachers I'd had growing up.

"Well, yeah. It can be a lot. The pay sucks. I mean, sometimes I have to choose between putting gas in my car and buying stuff for the classroom. It's rough. There have been more than a few times I've driven to school on fumes, praying that I'll make it till payday." She chuckled as if the situation were humorous.

I felt my jaw clench, the idea of her struggling to that degree unsettling something inside me.

As long as she was here, I wouldn't let her go without. She wouldn't have to worry about anything like that.

I would've told her as much, but her words kept spilling out of her, the excitement evident in the way her body nearly vibrated with it.

"Gosh, I can't wait to have my own kids." She sighed wistfully.

"Yeah?" I asked, curious. "You want kids?"

"Of course." She stared at me with those big blue eyes. "I'd have a whole bunch if I could. It's all I ever wanted!"

I grinned at the idea of it. A bunch of little Cassie's jumping around the place.

But then, all the excitement inside of her deflated like a balloon being popped right as it was expanding. Her eyes shifted, staring off into the distance.

"But who knows?" she said nonchalantly. "Maybe it's not in the cards for me. At least I have my kiddos at school."

"Why wouldn't it be?" I asked, hating the way her bubbliness morphed into some weird, insincere masking of her excitement.

"I mean, it just depends on how life goes. The whole breakup kind of threw a wrench in all my plans. Who knows if I'll meet someone who actually likes me enough to want all that with someone like me?"

Her words were like a bucket of ice water, freezing me in place.

How could she even think that? Did Dave really screw her up so badly that she thought she might never meet someone who liked *her?* Honestly, she'd have a harder time finding someone who *didn't* absolutely fall for her the moment they met her.

I could've told her all of that. I wanted to. But I was stuck on something else she'd said.

"What do you mean, someone like you?"

"In case you haven't noticed, I'm kind of a lot." She laughed, trying to pass it off as a joke, as if I couldn't see beneath the surface of it. "Too much for most people." She shrugged.

"What the hell does that mean? 'Too much?'"

"I'm overly emotional." She held out a finger, preparing to count out her flaws to me. "I get too loud when I'm excited. I get excited too often. I'm kind of clingy—" She paused. "And the list goes on."

"Are you serious right now?" I stared at her in disbelief.

She laughed as if about to brush it off once more, but I wasn't about to let her get away with that. Not this time.

"Cassie," I said intently, staring into huge blue eyes, *willing* her to understand what I was about to say. "Do you have any fucking idea what people would do to have someone like you in their lives? Do you even realize how rare it is to find someone as alive as you?"

"Liam, you don't have to—" she stuttered. Her cheeks burned, and she looked as if she wanted to disappear, but I wasn't done.

"No." I shook my head, not letting her escape this. "You think being emotional is a bad thing? It's not. You *let* yourself feel the whole spectrum of emotions that come along with life. Do you understand how brave that is? That instead of shutting yourself down or shutting the world out, you just deal with it?"

She stared at me, mouth slightly agape.

"You're a lot more real than anyone I've ever met," I said honestly. "And if anyone doesn't like that, it's probably because they're terrified of seeing all the ways *they're* lacking when they have to look at themselves compared to you. Okay?"

"Well," she said, staring anywhere but at me in a way that made me want to grab her chin and give me back those blue eyes—to make her accept the truth of my words. "At least I know I'll always have the approval of my best friend's big brother."

Her words extinguished whatever fire had been burning inside of me. I'd forgotten who we were to each other. Forgotten that she was relying on me to be a safe space for her for a while and nothing more.

She thought *she* was too much? Jesus, I'd just basically serenaded her against her will. I was ridiculous.

I couldn't remember the last time I'd felt as passionate about anything other than hockey. How was it possible that this girl was breaking down every single wall I'd constructed over the years, demolishing them with a single, wide-eyed gaze?

"Right," I said, straightening. "Did you talk to Maggie about coming to the game with you?"

Cassie squirmed uncomfortably in her seat, her eyes focused on the soggy clumps of cereal she pushed around in the bowl.

"What is it?" I asked, fear taking hold of me. Did she not want to come anymore? Was she busy? Did she have a date lined up?

What the fuck does it matter if she does? I forced myself not to grit my teeth at my inner monologue. It took all the strength I could muster to remain neutral.

"I know this isn't my place," she said, staring timidly up at me. "Like, at all—"

"Tell me," I urged.

"I just think *you* should be the one to ask Maggie to come to the game."

Whatever I thought she was going to say, I sure as hell didn't expect it to be about my sister.

"Me?" I asked dubiously.

"I mean, I just know that she misses you a lot, and she feels really bad about that fight you guys had the other day."

I groaned, rubbing a hand over my face. "You know about that?" I asked stupidly.

Of course she does. She's *Maggie's* person. Not mine. I was stupid for forgetting that.

"Yeah, I mean, just a little bit," she said sheepishly. "I just think it would mean a lot to her for you guys to smooth things over. And I have the feeling she's too stubborn to be one to reach out first."

I snorted. "You know my sister well."

Cassie smiled.

"So, will you?" She stared at me in a way that made me want to give her whatever the hell she wanted, no matter the cost.

I nodded. "I'll talk to her."

Cassie exhaled a sigh of relief as if she was worried I would say no, and I wondered just how much she cared about my sister to make her worry about the state of our relationship.

"Thank you, Liam," Cassie said, locked in eye contact with me for a moment before she pulled her gaze away.

I watched her stand up and walk to the sink, watched as she washed her bowl and set it to dry. Then she was gone, back upstairs to get ready for the day.

I sat, reeling in the aftermath of that conversation, which for some reason felt more weighted than I understood.

Maggie, I thought.

Smoothing things over would take more than a text or a phone call. It was the type of conversation that needed to be had in person.

I sighed, realizing that I wasn't going to escape the morning without having to face the awkward groveling of an apology, after all.

Maggie was a lot smarter than most people would guess or give her credit for.

She always had been, even when we were kids. She was fast-thinking, sharp, and witty. She always had an answer to anything someone could throw at her, and she *never* backed down from an argument. It was annoying, really. But it was one of the reasons she excelled at what she did.

As a lawyer, Maggie had made a career out of being a relentless pain in the ass, and in all honesty, she had done really well for herself.

Our mother had despaired at Maggie's choice of career, claiming that all lawyers were cold, ruthless workaholics who were only in it for the money. Maggie had proved her wrong on almost every account, choosing to practice family law, specifically cases of trying to reunite families or working out arrangements to grant higher visitation rights to parents who wanted to be part of their child's life.

But there was one thing my mother got right—Maggie *was* a workaholic, throwing herself into every case and not wasting a second before picking up the next. Some people would put it down as passion for her work, but sometimes I wondered if it wasn't something else.

But whatever the reason for her insane hours, it kept her very busy. Meaning, I knew if I wanted to see her, I'd have to go directly to her office, whether she wanted me there or not.

"I'm here to see Maggie," I said to the receptionist, clearing my throat awkwardly as I took in the orderly, polished scene around me.

Business attire, fast-moving people, and sounds everywhere. Phones ringing, the printer going off, and the incessant sound of the receptionist clicking away at her keyboard.

In a way, it seemed so ill-fitting for Maggie to be here in this cold, sterile space.

But then again, Maggie had always been able to adapt to anything.

"Sorry, who?"

"Maggie Brynn?"

"Oh." She typed away, eyes still glued to her screen as she spoke. "You mean Margaret."

I snorted. I was pretty sure the only time someone had referred to Maggie as Margaret was the day our mother had to tell the nurse what to write on the birth certificate. But every moment after that, she'd just been Maggie.

"I guess so," I said anyway.

Finally, she looked up, eyes flickering with something I recognized as she turned her full attention to me.

"And you are?" she asked, a new flirtatious lilt to her voice.

"Here to see Maggie," I repeated, unwilling to engage in any of the bullshit.

"Are you her—"

"Brother," I repeated firmly, with a finality in my tone that I hoped would shut down any further questions. "Is she here?"

I looked around, figuring I apparently needed to find her myself, but all I saw were women trying their best to sneak glances in our direction, not as covertly as I assumed they hoped to be.

"Yes, she's here," the receptionist said, making no move to find her. "Are you-?"

"Liam Brynn?" One bold woman dared to approach. "You're him, right? From the Harbor Wolves?"

I gritted my teeth.

"I'm just here to see my sister," I said, putting up my best attempt at politeness. "Does anyone know where I can find her?"

"Who's your sister?" the daring woman asked.

"Margaret." The receptionist shot her a knowing look.

"Margaret never told us you're her brother."

I thought it was irrelevant but offered a shrug.

"Big brothers can be embarrassing."

The girl laughed, grabbing my arm in a familiar way that had me inching away.

"In fact, I actually think she confirmed you *weren't* related at all… but what are the chances of that? Two Brynns in Boston with no relation to each other?" She laughed airily, her perfume filling the space between us.

Everything about her made me itch to escape, just like I felt around the rest of the women like this, who always proved to make themselves unavoidable. I wondered if they'd do this if I weren't a famous hockey player. I wondered if they'd still care.

But still, her words twisted something inside of me. I get Maggie not broadcasting our relationship to the world, but straight up denying it? Why the hell would she do that?

"*Liam?*" Maggie appeared from behind a corner, her brown hair twisted up, dressed impeccably in a way that seemed to match the atmosphere of the building.

"Thank God," I muttered, pulling away from the handsy woman. "Hey, Mags."

"What are you doing here?" she said, high heels clicking against the floor as she made her way toward me.

"I wanted to talk to you," I said at the same time the woman said, "Why didn't you tell us you have a famous brother?"

Maggie stared at the woman who watched us with evasive eyes, irritation spreading across Maggie's features.

"Because my brother has nothing to do with my work here," she retorted, her lips pursed in the way they used to before she'd erupt when we were kids.

"Because he's, like, a local celebrity," the woman countered. "You could've at least mentioned it."

"Why would I?" Maggie's eyes narrowed on her coworker, waiting for a valid answer to her question.

The woman's laughter faded as if just realizing Maggie wasn't prepared to entertain a back-and-forth with her, and then she excused herself from our presence.

"Come on," Maggie said to me, irritation still lingering. "Let's go talk somewhere private."

I followed her down a hall filled with windows until she led me to a door with her name brandished on a plaque in front of it.

"Impressive," I said, gesturing toward it.

"It's not the NHL, but it matters to me." She shrugged before going inside and leaning against her desk.

What the hell?

"So, why are you here, Liam?" she asked with crossed arms, apparently still pissed.

Cassie had made it sound like her anger had worn off a bit, but of course, Maggie wouldn't have been aggressive toward *her*. Cassie softened people and made them forget why they were upset. Me? I just made them remember. Now it was clear whatever reunion Cassie had been hoping for was going to take a little work on my part.

"I wanted to talk about the other day," I said, feeling stiff and awkward in Maggie's space. The look in her eyes felt like arrows aimed at me.

"The day when you showed up at my apartment, told me I was an idiot for wanting a relationship with my father, and then left?" She stared at me unblinkingly. "Is that the day you're referring to, Liam?"

I cleared my throat. "Yes?"

"Then talk," she said with a resolute jut to her chin.

For fuck's sake, the women in my life were the most stubborn ones alive.

"I handled it badly," I admitted, the feeling of apologizing foreign in my throat. "I shouldn't have gone off like that. It's just… we haven't mentioned him in years, Mags. It took me off guard. I had a knee-jerk reaction."

"So, you're excusing your behavior?"

"No," I said, jaw clenching. "I'm just trying to explain why it happened."

"And now?" she said, willing me to continue.

"Now, I wanted to tell you I'm sorry for how it happened. I didn't mean to hurt you."

She blinked, her hardened features smoothing away to something resembling disbelief.

"You're… sorry?"

"Yeah. I am."

We sat in silence, eyes locked on each other. A moment passed, then another, and then finally, Maggie let out a laugh.

"Maggie?" I asked, slightly unnerved by the reaction.

"I can't believe it took you twenty-six years before you learned how to apologize for something," she said, looking as if she was fighting back another giggle.

I stiffened.

"And, really, it wasn't very good. Just so you know. But I appreciate the sentiment behind it."

"So," I said warily. "You're not mad?"

"I mean." She shrugged. "I'm a little mad, but you're my brother. I'm not going to waste time holding a grudge against you."

"Yeah." I sighed in relief. I didn't want to have any weird tension between me and Maggie, and I was suddenly relieved that Cassie had convinced me to do this.

And while we were clearing the air, I dared to ask, "Why did you tell them we weren't related?" I asked, nodding my head toward the door.

"Oh, that?" she said, her voice sounding guilty. "You saw them. One person finds out you're my brother, and suddenly, every woman in the vicinity is dropping hints on what great sisters-in-law we'd be."

Jesus Christ, some people were weird as hell.

But I wasn't buying that excuse. At least not entirely.

"Maggie." I fixed her with a look. "Tell me the truth."

She stared back at me, her green eyes a mirror of my own, before she finally heaved a sigh.

"Fine," she admitted. "I guess I just hate being known only as *Liam Brynn's sister.* I've had my identity linked to you my entire life. Even before you got famous."

"Bullshit," I argued. "You've always been your own person. Everyone always talks about how you couldn't be any more different than me."

"Right, but even then, I'm still talked about in relation to you. Sometimes I just want to stand on my own, you know? Be looked at for who I am and what I'm doing, not how I compare to you."

"I'm sorry, Mags," I said, now feeling some guilt of my own. "I didn't realize it was like that for you."

"Two apologies in one day?" She feigned a dramatic gasp. "What is the world coming to?"

I laughed, shaking my head at her theatrics.

"But the thing about the woman flocking to me over you was still true. And just so you know, I don't want a creepy sister-in-law, okay?"

"Well, lucky for you, I don't have a wife."

"Yeah, well. Keep it in mind for the future."

"Don't worry. I'll be sure to run her by you before any proposals are made."

"As you should." She laughed, and the air around us felt lighter. Easier to breathe. But I knew if I really wanted to get the point across that I cared, I'd have to make it a little uncomfortable again.

"So," I said, about to detonate the carefully constructed peace. "Did you see him?"

I held my breath, waiting for her answer.

"Yeah, I did," she said, a slight smile creeping across her face.

"Good." I nodded. "I'm glad if that's what you wanted. For closure."

"He really wants to see you, Liam," she said, causing me to scoff. "Please, Liam. Just one dinner?"

"Absolutely not."

"But—"

I cut her off. "Maggie, you can do whatever you want, and I'm sorry I was such a dick about it. But I have no desire to ever see that man again for the rest of my life."

Maggie's face deflated as if, somehow, my words were still a shock to her.

"Don't you think you're being overly harsh?" she appealed.

"He left us, Maggie. And now that we're grown and don't need anything from him, he suddenly wants to be back in our lives? He never even paid child support, Mags," I emphasized, trying to show her not only was he absent but also a deadbeat on top of it all.

"That's on Mom for never going after him about it!" she cried as if my words were an insult to her rather than the guy who abandoned us all.

"No the fuck it's not," I retorted. "Don't you see how screwed up it is? That a man can just walk out on his kids, on his *wife,* and not even worry about how they're going to get by without him? If I had a—" I stopped myself. It was irrelevant. "He fucked up, Mags. And I don't have to forgive him for it, even if you want to."

"Fine," she said with more of a bite than I hoped, but still, I felt the acceptance behind it.

"So, are we good?" I asked, hoping she wouldn't hold this against me, not after we'd already made amends.

"I suppose." She heaved a dramatic sigh but then rolled her eyes in a way that told me I'd been forgiven.

I exhaled in relief, glad to have mended one of the only two familial relationships I still had in my life.

"I really am sorry, you know," I said. "That I've been so closed off. It's nothing personal."

"That's just you." She shrugged as if it was something she'd accepted long ago. "But I really appreciate the effort you've been making lately. I mean, letting Cassie move in has been so huge, and I know you did it for me, so it means a lot."

"No problem," I responded, suddenly tense but trying to shrug it off.

I didn't know why the topic had me squirming. It wasn't like I had anything to hide. But Maggie had a sixth sense for detecting bullshit, and I didn't want her examining me too closely right now.

"But it doesn't seem like you mind her *too* much, right?" she asked, hope glimmering in her eyes.

"No," I said. "I don't mind her."

CHAPTER TWENTY-THREE

Cassie

"You're going to stick out like a sore thumb, you know." Maggie laughed, looking over at me as we walked into TD Garden.

"Why?" I asked, dumbstruck, looking down at myself. I had on an oversized pink, cream, and lavender Nordic-style sweater with a cute snowflake print that I thought was fitting for an ice rink. Plus, a matching pink scarf and lavender beanie to stay warm during the game. "What's wrong with what I'm wearing?"

"Most people wear sports jerseys or team merch, or at the very least their team *colors*. You, on the other hand, look like a human ice cream cone."

"At least I won't be as cold as one," I said, wiggling my mittened hands at her.

"Are those really necessary?"

"Hey, I have an iron deficiency, meaning I'm *always* cold."

"Suit yourself." Maggie momentarily held her hands up in surrender, but when we got through security, I could see what she meant.

The crowd was a sea of blue and gray jerseys, all very aware that they were here to proudly display which team held their allegiance.

"It's not like I have any Harbor Wolves merch lying around," I said, flushing.

That was a lie, though, wasn't it? I had Liam's hoodie still. The one I wore nearly every night to bed and around the house only when Liam wasn't home. But wearing it out, in public—that was very different. Especially when Liam might see. He would probably think I was some stalker if he knew how often I wore his sweatshirt. The one that still seemed to carry the smell of him on it—

"It's not a big deal," Maggie shrugged. "You look cute. And at least we know Liam will be able to spot us from a mile away now."

I was glad I had my scarf to hide underneath.

When Maggie led us to seats right in front of the glass, I gasped.

"We're so close!" I started to sit, flinching as a hockey player zoomed by, the sound of the ice crunching beneath his skates.

"What did you think? Liam would send us to the nosebleeds?"

"Are we going to be safe here?" I cringed, shrinking away each time the players zoomed past. It was like I could feel the vibrations radiating through the glass as they passed. "What if a puck breaks through the glass or something

"Oh my gosh." Maggie gasped. "You're right! We need to alert the NHL immediately because I'm certain they never considered that possibility!"

Then she grinned, a sarcastic smirk replacing the look of horror she'd just worn.

"Ha, ha," I spoke dully.

"Cass, we're good. The glass is like indestructible," she said, glancing at me as I fidgeted nervously. "But if you see a puck coming, duck."

Uneasiness settled in my gut, not as much from the imaginary fear of getting injured but more so from the chaotic atmosphere of the arena.

It was insane. I'd always known the cult following the Harbor Wolves had, but seeing the mass of people gathered for a sports game? It was unreal.

People were yelling and cheering, and the game hadn't even started yet. And more than a few were screaming for Liam.

"Where is he?" I asked Maggie, trying to find his face among the players zooming on the ice. Under their gear and helmets and the speed at which they moved, it was hard to pick him out.

"There." She pointed. "Number 26."

Once she pointed him out, it was obvious. His build, the way he maneuvered his body. But on the ice, he had a grace to him that I wouldn't have expected. Despite his size, he moved effortlessly, gliding like it was more natural to him than walking.

My gaze tracked him on the ice, watching as he used his hockey stick like an extension of his limb, guiding the puck exactly where he wanted it. It was an art form, really. I had to force myself not to drop my jaw in awe.

It was easy to understand why he had the following he had. And some part of me felt unsettled by just how many beautiful girls were sitting in the stands, wearing his name on their backs.

Liam skated by, unaware of the girls nearby, screaming his name as he passed their section. I stared in the direction of the shrieking, eyes narrowing on the poster they held.

"That's a little much, isn't it?" I nodded toward two girls holding a glittery sign that said, "*Marry me, Brynn.*"

Maggie laughed as her eyes landed on the sight. "I've seen worse."

"Like what?"

"Let's just say that one's pretty tame as far as the fangirl signs go."

I shuddered, my imagination filling in the blanks between Maggie's words.

"Does it make you uncomfortable?"

"It does, but not nearly as uncomfortable as it makes Liam," she said.

I stared at him, watching as he was immune to it all. The cheers, the screams of his name, the pleading for his attention. For a minute, it looked like he was scanning the crowd for something, but it was impossible to tell for sure.

"So, he doesn't go for it, then?"

"Hardly." Maggie snorted. "Liam would be a hermit if he wasn't so damn good at hockey. He loves his job—well, the playing part. But everything else that comes with it? The media. The fans like *that*." She shrugged. "Well, I just feel kind of bad for him because as long as he plays for the NHL, he'll never escape that."

"So, why doesn't he just quit? Find a normal job." I squirmed, a newfound understanding of the man I was living with.

"Like I said, he loves the game. Sometimes I think it's the only thing he cares about. He'd never walk away from that. Not for anything."

The weight of Maggie's words settled around me. It was clear that Liam took commitments seriously. Maybe that's why he chose not to have any others. Hockey, apparently, was his end-all, be-all. I didn't know why the thought of it left me feeling so hollow.

"There he is!" the fangirls a few rows away cried as Liam skated closer.

But this time, there was no mistaking where his attention was.

Sea-glass eyes met mine as his gloved hand came up to the glass, knocking twice in front of us and grinning. I blinked at him in shock, holding my mittened hand up in a wave. It was hard to believe that this man I saw in the most intimate of settings was now on display in this huge arena, with thousands of eyes locked on him. I watched him laugh at my surprise, and the sight of it had me smiling back at him before he skated away.

"Well, the fangirls aren't going to like that. He usually pretends the crowd doesn't exist." Maggie laughed as the lights started to dim. "Oh, it's starting."

The National Anthem played, and all the while, Liam's eyes remained straight ahead like a dutiful soldier, though mine were focused solely on him. It was as if I couldn't tear them away if I tried, the heat of his attention still lingering. Seeing him there, in his jersey with his team, it was hard to reconcile the Liam I knew at home with this superstar player.

It made him feel untouchable and very far away in a way that was disconcerting. Why, all of a sudden, was I so overwhelmed? Why did it feel like I was losing him when I never had him and knew I never would?

The puck drop came a few minutes later, forcibly pulling me from my reverie. The teams spread out across the ice as if it were a battlefield, their hockey sticks like blades against the ice, working in perfectly practiced synchronicity.

Though I watched everything, I could barely keep up with what was happening. The sports announcer's commentary might as well have been gibberish for all the sense it made to me. It was too fast, filled with too many unfamiliar terms for me to keep up with.

Liam was locked in and focused, it was clear he had one goal, and he was damn well going to see it through. That was the way he was with everything, even at home. I knew if he wanted something, he'd find a way to get it, no matter what.

After a few moments of watching him, I asked Maggie, "Is Liam captain?"

I was surprised when she said no.

"But why? It's clear he's the best on the team."

She snorted. "Liam doesn't like being responsible for other people. He'd never sign up for a role like that. Plus, all the additional press the team captain gets? The interviews he'd need to do?" She shook her head. "He'd never sign up for that."

I mulled it over, not fully buying it. It was clear Liam loved to provide, protect, and take care of those he loved. It wasn't the responsibility he was running from. It must be something else holding him back. I was sure of it.

My eyes tracked him, noticing how a player from the opposing team was getting close to him, too close.

Why is he so close?

I screamed when it happened, watching as the player wearing the other team's jersey smashed Liam against the glass on the other side of the rink.

"What was that!" I said, not realizing I had grabbed Maggie's wrist in the process.

"Ouch." Maggie winced. "Relax, Cass."

"Is he okay?"

"He's fine." She laughed as if her brother didn't just get his body shoved into the plexiglass. "That's why they wear gear."

"Why isn't that a penalty or foul or something? Don't other sports have consequences for hurting people?"

She shrugged. "It's hockey."

As if that made it acceptable.

But still, he was skating around like nothing happened, apparently used to the barbaric act. I took note of the player who did it, though: #10 on the Titans. I'd remember him.

Regardless of the setback, Liam took control of the puck once more, sending it flying to his teammate, who maneuvered it directly into the net.

The horn blared, sending the crowd into an eruption. I jumped to my feet at the same time Maggie did, suddenly filled with pride over this team I knew so little of. Only knowing that Liam was part of it, and therefore I'd never cheer for anyone else.

They didn't bask in their glory for long, moving on with the game pretty immediately. I guess there wasn't as much joy in a score as there was in an overall victory. They remained focused and steadfast.

The way they moved, all of them, but Liam most of all, was like magic. He had speed and agility; it was something to watch him. He made me understand why people paid such extortionate amounts of money to see these games.

I found myself marveling at what the human body could be trained to do. What *Liam's* body could do.

The Harbor Wolves scored goal after goal. Each time, the horn blared, and celebration spread through the stands.

"Should we do the wave or something?" I asked, not sure about proper conduct during hockey games.

"If you start doing the wave, I'm leaving you here," Maggie deadpanned.

I held my hands up in surrender, a giggle escaping at the gravity of her gaze. It looked just like Liam's.

After a while, I saw what Maggie meant about the players being rough with each other. At every chance, they invaded each other's space, shoving them out of the way with force. After a while, I got used to it. Mostly because Liam hardly gave them a chance to get to him again. He was *fast*.

Still, I noticed the way Maggie flinched when #17 was body-checked against the glass. I examined the player, the last name on his jersey alerting me to his identity. *Brody*.

I raised my brow at Maggie.

"What happened to 'it's hockey'?"

"Shut up," she said, unwilling to discuss the matter further.

When the Harbor Wolves won, the team collapsed into each other, hugging their teammates in victory.

I felt as jittery and excited as if I were one of the players, pride blooming in my chest for the guys down there on the ice. Number 26 most of all.

I watched as he celebrated with his team, understanding on a deeper level now just what this sport meant to him. He deserved this.

I screamed his name, clapping foolishly, my voice getting lost in the roar of the crowd.

And then, for a moment, my breath caught, freezing me where I stood.

Because everyone in the stadium was looking at Liam Brynn.

But he was only looking at me.

CHAPTER TWENTY-FOUR

Liam

In my career, we'd won hundreds of times. The feeling never faded or dulled, but tonight, it felt *different*. I was proud we played like hell if only to show Cassie what hockey could be like.

It was her first game, after all, I told myself when an inner voice of reasoning started to ask why it mattered. Of course I wanted to give her a good impression of the game.

And in my opinion, we'd delivered on that account.

That inner voice was starting to get annoying as hell, though.

Especially when it started bringing up pretty valid points when I went looking for Cassie and Maggie after the game ended.

You have interviews to give. You don't have time for this.

But I knew that Maggie was never patient enough to stick around after a game while I did the media obligations. And I wanted to see how Cassie liked it.

You'll see her at home.

It didn't matter; I wanted to see her now, and no amount of reasoning could talk me out of it. Before I could get roped into an interview, I slipped out of the locker room, promising Brody I'd be back in a few minutes to fulfill any obligations to the team that were required of me.

And then I ran through the arena like a bat out of hell, headed straight toward the exit I knew Maggie usually took.

Without my gear on, I was able to blend in a bit more, wearing only a hoodie and joggers as I maneuvered through the crowds trying to make their way out.

It was mayhem, and I was thanking every God that might exist that no one gave me so much as a second glance. Of course they wouldn't expect me to be here, rushing through thousands of people to try and find one girl.

But I was.

Why?

I saw her several feet away from the exit, finding it impossible to miss a blonde in a variety of pastels among the blue and gray jerseys that filled the lobby.

"What, you guys bailing out on me so soon?" I called out loud enough for them to hear.

I watched as they both turned at the same time.

"I must not have played as well as I thought." I laughed at the bewilderment on Cassie's face.

"Liam?" she asked, eyes lighting up, running toward me.

I fucking melted at the sight of it.

Her eyes had to be my favorite thing about her, not only because they were bluer than any ocean I'd ever seen but because of how expressive they were. I could see every feeling and thought play across them in real-time. And right now? It looked like she was as excited to see me as I was.

"Maggie said you were going to be too busy to talk to us!" Cassie practically bounced on her heels as she approached.

"Yeah," Maggie said, approaching belatedly because she walked at a normal pace, unlike Cassie's run toward me. "What happened to all your interviews?" She sniffed the air. "God, did you even shower yet?"

I ran a hand through my hair, still slick with sweat.

"I have time to say hi quick," I responded to Maggie's skeptical look.

"But—"

"Liam!" A voice behind me called, halting Maggie's words. "They're looking for you now!"

I turned my head to see Brody approaching from behind. *Jesus Christ.*

"I'll be there in one minute," I told him, giving him a look that would ordinarily make him back off.

But this time, he was looking at Maggie, and when I turned, I noticed she was looking right back at him too.

"Hey," she said, more timidly than I'd ever seen her.

Was she blushing?

"Hi, Maggie." Brody grinned. "How's it going? Liam didn't tell me you were here tonight."

"Yeah, Cassie's never been," she said by way of explanation.

"Really?" Brody peeked around me to look over to Cassie. "No shit! Hey Cassie, I didn't see you over there behind Liam."

"Hi." She waved shyly.

I grinned down at her, amused by how bold and timid she could be at the same time.

"You guys played really well tonight," Maggie said nonchalantly to Brody.

"You guys were *amazing*!" Cassie corrected, staring at me in disbelief. "I mean, you were *so* fast. I didn't even know you could move that fast on the ice. And the way you guys managed to be brutally aggressive and graceful at the same time? Crazy."

"Glad you enjoyed it." I laughed.

But I wasn't glad. I was over the fucking moon. Part of me had worried she'd find it all boring and a waste of time. Now I could at least hope she might want to come to more games in the future.

"Are you kidding?" Her voice rose. "I *loved* it. I'm so glad I got to see you in your element. I feel like I sort of get you more now. You know what I mean?"

I did. And my heart clenched because of it. She understood that this was the biggest part of who I was. Maybe that's why I'd wanted her to come so badly. To see all of me.

"I did get scared at one point, though—"

"When?" I asked more intensely than I'd intended. My mind flashed with rowdy fans crowding her space or aggressive drunks spilling drinks on her.

"When that guy slammed you up against the glass. I was really worried." Her eyes were downcast, peeking up at me between words.

My heart paused.

She was scared for me?

"I've taken worse than that before." I tried to joke, but the words came out breathy.

"Well, I hope I never have to see it. That was enough for me."

I didn't notice the way Brody and Maggie had put some distance between us while Cassie was talking. How could I notice anything when she was lighting up my peripheral? Now the pair of them were far enough away that I couldn't overhear their conversation. Fine by me.

Cassie stared at them wistfully, both of us watching as Brody spoke to Maggie with a grin on his face. "He likes her, doesn't he?"

"Yeah," I admitted. "I think he does a lot."

"That's perfect." Her eyes practically turned to hearts as she gushed. "Maggie deserves it. I think she likes him, too. Even though she wouldn't admit it."

I took the moment she was distracted, staring off at them, to fully take her in. Her cheeks were flushed from the cold, her hair was falling down in wisps around her face, and she looked so beautiful. More beautiful than any girl I'd ever seen, that was for sure.

I didn't know how she could be both. So sweet, so kind, and absolutely stunning at the same time. It was enough to throw a man off-kilter. Maybe enough to make him even enjoy the disorientation.

Not good. That pesky voice said. *Not good at all.*

I cleared my throat.

"Hey, um, do you need a ride home tonight?" I asked, stupidly hoping she'd say yes.

Her eyes widened, turning to face me.

"Oh, no." She shook her head. "It's okay. Maggie said she'd bring me."

Yeah, but last time she left somewhere with Maggie, it wasn't my house she ended up back at.

How the hell was I annoyed with my sister for hogging her friend? It wasn't as if Cassie actually wanted to spend any time with me. Of course she'd want to be with her actual friend. But still, I asked.

"Are you sure? If you stick around for a bit, I can try to wrap things up quickly back there." I gestured my head toward the direction of the locker rooms I'd fled from.

I knew I'd have to be getting back soon. Coach would blow a gasket if he couldn't find me, knowing all of the reporters would want to harass me about game interviews.

"Well, if you're sure," Cassie said, tugging at her sleeves. "It would be easier, so Maggie doesn't have to go out of her way."

I didn't know why she got like that sometimes. At first, I thought it was just me because she didn't know me. But even with Maggie, she was still always talking about herself as if she were a burden that needed to be endured. I didn't understand it, and I didn't like it at all.

"Maggie wouldn't care," I assured her, staring down at her intently. "But I do want to drive you home, so I hope you'll wait for me."

"You do?" Her eyes met mine warily.

My breath caught.

"Yeah, I do."

"Okay," she said, a faint smile tugging at her lips.

"That's if you can fit in my car," I teased, tugging the end of her scarf. "You look like one of us with all that padding on."

With her pink puffer jacket over her thick sweater, her earmuffs, and fully mittened hands, she looked puffy enough to survive a few body checks on the ice.

A laugh bubbled out of her, and I wished I could bottle up the sound and keep it forever. It made me want to have a thousand funny lines at my disposal so I could summon the noise from her whenever I wanted.

"Well, if you find any hockey teams who use the color pink in their jerseys, send them my way. That's definitely something I could get on board with."

"No." I shook my head playfully at her. "I don't think I want to see you in any other team's jersey."

Hell, I didn't want to see her in any of *my* team's jerseys unless it was my last name she was wearing.

For a second, the thought made me recoil as the intrusive voice asked me what type of weird, territorial part of me had been unleashed to think up that thought, but I shoved that voice away. I was getting good at keeping it at bay.

"Don't worry," she said, "after tonight, I'm a Harbor Wolves fan through and through."

"Yeah?" I asked, feeling idiotic at the size of the smile on my face. "Or are you just a fan of whoever the winning team is?"

She scrunched up her nose, scoffing at the insinuation. "I'll have you know I am *not* that fickle."

I didn't doubt it. She was as loyal as they came. I had the feeling that once she was in your corner, there wasn't anything on earth that could drag her out of it.

"Besides," she said, "I wasn't cheering because of the team. I was cheering because of *you*."

For a moment, my head whirled. I felt like our conversation was far too intimate to be had in the bustle of the Garden. All I wanted was to throw her in my car and take her home immediately so it could just be the two of us.

I don't know how the hell she did it, but she calmed something inside of me. She made all the noise that was in my head stop. I felt like I could breathe easier around her, and I was scared as hell about what that meant.

"Cassie, I—"

"*Cassie?*" My back stiffened at the sound of her name being called by another man's voice.

Cassie spun, her body freezing when her eyes landed on the owner of the voice.

He was of average build, average height, and average face. Everything about him was completely ordinary. He could've been anyone. But Cassie's reaction made it evident that he most definitely was not just anyone.

"Cassie?" he repeated again, his jaw dropping as he stared at her. "What are you doing here?"

He started to take a step, and when Cassie processed his plan, she turned back to me, eyes wide and frantic, face paler than I'd ever seen it.

"I, uh- I need to go home. Now. Please tell Maggie I'll be outside."

"Cassie—" I started, reaching out for her, but she was already running out the exit.

I could've followed her, but I needed to know what the hell was going on, and the idiot standing a few feet away seemed like the best place to start.

The guy looked as if he were going to go after her, but I stalked over in front of him, grateful as hell for the way I towered over him. Rage radiated off of me toward this stranger who was looking up at me with intimidation in his eyes. I might not know who he was, but I could guess. And Cassie's reaction alone gave me cause enough to hate him with a ferocity that was dangerous.

"Mind backing up?" he asked in a way that pissed me off.

"Mind telling me who the hell you are? And why she just ran out of here at the sight of you?" I lifted my arm, pointing in the direction where Cassie fled.

"None of your business."

He snorted, trying to get around me, but I was bigger and broader, and I knew if he tried to get away, I would punch him right in the face and not care how many reporters printed the story.

"She is my business," I answered. "So start fucking talking."

"I don't know who you think you are, but Cassie and I—"

Those words. The way he still tried to pair himself with her made me see red. I wanted to shove him against the wall and demand that he never utter her name again.

"There is no Cassie and you," I said, grabbing him by the front of his shirt, just an edge away from the tipping point. "So tell me now, who the fuck are you?"

I knew if he didn't answer, I'd hit him. I knew there'd be no restraining myself if he said one more smart-ass comment.

For a minute, his eyes shone with panic as he looked down at the fist that grasped the fabric of his shirt. Then, it was replaced with a scathing look as he jutted his chin in defiance.

I held his gaze, not backing down in the slightest.

It didn't matter who saw. It didn't matter that people were stopping to stare.

Security might be here soon to break up the fight, but it didn't matter. All that mattered was confirming the identity of the dick in front of me.

"I'm *Dave*," he spat out at last, eyes blaring with hatred. "And who the fuck are you?"

"I'm her fucking boyfriend," I seethed, and then I threw the punch.

CHAPTER TWENTY-FIVE

Liam

"Well, didn't take her long, did it?" Dave laughed dryly, blood dripping from his lip. "Didn't ever peg her as one to move on fast."

"Longer than it took you, I can assure you that." I shot him a venomous glare, my fist itching to punch him again.

"That was a mistake," he said, something like guilt clouding his eyes for a microsecond. "I didn't realize it then. I do now. I just need to talk to her—" He looked off as if he might try *again* to go after her.

"You'll stay the hell away from her," I growled, my blood boiling.

There was no fucking way I was letting this bastard anywhere *near* her. He'd destroyed her, not caring how many pieces he'd left her in. He'd wasted six years of her life, treated her like shit, and now? Now that he saw her again, looking beautiful and happy? *Now* he wanted another shot with her?

Abso-fucking-lutely not.

How the hell could *he* ever be with someone like Cassie and not kiss the ground she walked on? Not thank God everyday that he got to have her? It didn't make any fucking sense.

"Why? You scared that she'll come running back to me? She's always been kind of obsessed with me. I'm sure it wouldn't take much of an effort."

I lifted my arm to throw the next punch, but a hand held me back.

"Dude, what the fuck is wrong with you?" Brody hissed in my ear, trying to pull me away from the corner we'd somehow gravitated to.

I didn't take my eyes off Dave for a second, infuriated at the way his eyes seemed to gleam with excitement like he was begging to be hit again.

"Liam," I heard Maggie gasp behind me. "What are you *doing*? Where's Cassie?"

"Hey, Maggie." Dave grinned his bloody smile at my sister. "How's it going?"

"Shut up, Dave." Maggie's voice was venomous.

"She's waiting outside," I said through gritted teeth. "Go find her and tell her I'll be right out to take her home."

"Home?" Dave asked. "Her home is back with me. And I'm sure she'll jump at the chance to get back together if it means getting the hell out of her Mom's house again."

"She's not staying with her mom." I glared, teeth gritted as I tried desperately to restrain myself from throwing another punch. "She's staying with me."

His expression went blank, and I saw the effect my words had on him. He was shocked, and… hurt? Good.

He cackled an ugly sound. "Well, now it all makes sense, doesn't it? I mean, she'd do anything rather than go back to that hell hole. Even shacking up with some hockey asshole."

"Don't you fucking talk about her." My jaw was clenched so hard it ached.

"Liam," Brody's voice said in warning as he tried to tug me back once more.

"Go get my fucking car keys, Brody. I gotta take Cassie home."

"No," Brody said, "What you gotta do is avoid getting fucking arrested. Think about your career, man? Is this worth it?"

Yes.

"Don't worry about your career." Dave sneered. "What fun would it be if I took you out of the running with an assault charge?"

He smiled devilishly at me, *loving* the fact that he had the power to get me in some deep shit if he wanted to.

But I didn't fucking care. I was hardly the first person to punch a guy, and this one sure as hell deserved it.

"She'll come back to me," he said assuredly. "She always does. Some brutish hockey player won't change that."

"Man, you're really asking for it, aren't you?" Brody laughed without humor.

"Doesn't look too good for the Harbor Wolves that two of their players have a fan cornered and bloody, does it?"

At that, I unclenched his shirt, taking a safe step back. This didn't matter right now. Cassie did. And she was outside, cold, and waiting to go home.

I took a breath, stepping away so I could get my car keys and get the hell out of there. Dave stared at me cautiously as if I were a wild animal that might pounce on him at any moment.

"Come on, man." Brody clapped my back. "Let's go."

And I started to, but then, something made me turn, feeling a compulsive need to get the message across loud and clear before I left.

"Next time you come near my girlfriend." I brought my face deathly close to his. "I'll destroy you. And I don't care what the fuck it does to my career. Got it?"

His silence was a good enough answer for me.

CHAPTER TWENTY-SIX

Cassie

I hated my traitorous body and the incessant pounding of its heart. I was *fine*. Everything was fine. I was in Liam's car, and he was driving me home.

My body, however, felt I was an animal being hunted for sport in the wild. I was hyper-aware of everything. The cars going by, the silence in the car.

The tension radiating from Liam.

That was the worst of all.

I wondered if he was mad at me. I'd thrown a fit and run out. It was humiliating to think back on. But I couldn't face Dave. I just didn't have it in me. I'd never been able to do confrontations. Least of all with the man who broke my heart.

"I'm sorry," I finally said after a few minutes of the unbearable quiet, watching the way his fingers clenched the wheel so hard they were almost white.

His head whipped so fast I thought it might've hurt him.

"Why are you sorry?"

"You're mad at me, aren't you?"

He couldn't have looked anymore shocked if I told him I was in the running for the next presidential election.

"Why would I be mad at you?"

"Because I ran out so abruptly?" I said, my fingers twitching in my lap. "I'm sorry I did that. It was so immature of me. To run away like that? I don't know what happened. I just—"

"Cassie, you don't have to explain."

But I did. I couldn't handle the thought of Liam thinking I was some neurotic weirdo who was prone to fleeing conversations at random.

"I just saw someone that I knew, and I guess I wanted to avoid a conversation with them."

"Someone?" Liam bit out tersely.

"Dave," I admitted, cringing at the mere mention of his name.

"Dave," He repeated, the name rolling off his tongue like poison.

"Yeah, my ex-boyfriend. I know it's stupid, but I just couldn't handle seeing him." I looked out the window, embarrassed.

"Why the hell would it be stupid?" Liam asked incredulously. "Most people aren't in the habit of wanting to catch up with their exes. Especially when that ex is a complete dick."

"He wasn't so bad." I shrugged. "We both played a part in it."

Almost immediately, Liam put his blinker on and pulled off over to the side of the road.

"What are you doing?" I asked, wide-eyed and anxious.

"Trying to figure out how you could possibly think that what you just said is true."

"You don't understand," I fumbled, unnerved by his intensity.

Even in the darkness of the car, I could feel the heat of his stare, feel the tension that filled the small space around us.

"What don't I understand?" he asked softly but adamantly. "Maggie's told me stories, Cass. This guy's just no good. And that has nothing to do with you."

"I was… a lot. I can be needy. Sometimes I started fights. And, like I told you, I get way too emotional about things. It's too much for anyone to be expected to handle."

Liam didn't know the half of it. How screwed up I was over my mom? How I'd cry each time I walked in to see the state she'd drunk herself into?

I knew after a while Dave was sick of hearing about it. Of course he couldn't handle it. No one could.

"It's not too much," Liam declared passionately. "*You're* not too much. I want to kill him for making you think that."

But he didn't know. He didn't understand that I'd spent my life walking around the minefield that was my mother's alcoholic mood swings. He didn't know how it caused anxiety to gnaw at me every moment of the day. How each time someone's behavior changed even slightly, I was convinced it was because of me. Something I had done or said or not done enough of.

How I was convinced that everyone in my life was one step away from leaving, so I kept them all at arm's length to dull the pain when they finally did.

If he knew the half of it, he'd run the other way screaming. I'd do the same, but there was nowhere to hide when it was yourself you were trying to run from.

I felt hands reach up to cup my face and was startled at the contact. My eyes flickered up, meeting his as they searched my face, looking for something that I couldn't let him find.

"Why are you hiding from me?" he whispered, his words so soft I could feel his breath warm against my face.

I felt my stomach flutter, and I couldn't tell if it was anxiety or something else. It couldn't be anxiety because I felt... safe. Liam made me feel safe. But feeling seen by him was scary in its own way. He looked at me like he wasn't going to let me run or hide, and I didn't know what to do with that.

I tried to turn my head, to twist away from those eyes, but his fingers kept me in place, his face far too close for comfort.

I stared at him, feeling my resolve breaking, my emotions flooding.

"Cassie," he whispered as his thumb grazed my cheek.

And then, I crumbled.

Tears slid down my face despite my best effort to keep them at bay, and I heard a whimper escape my throat, making me feel pitiful.

"Shhh," Liam said, pulling my head to his shoulder, big hands stroking my hair as he whispered, "It's okay. You're okay."

"I'm sorry," I choked out through tears.

"Don't be." His voice sounded... sad.

"I just don't know what was wrong with me that he needed to find someone else. I tried to be everything for him," I cried.

And underneath my words, the deeper fear, that it would be the same ending with anyone. That because of whatever was broken inside of me, I would never be enough. Not when anyone could go and find someone whole.

"You are everything," he affirmed, fingers still working as my tears soaked the fabric of his shirt. "You weren't the one who wasn't enough, okay?" he said close to my ear, as if his proximity would send the message deeper. "It was him."

And there, on the side of the road under the lights of the city, I felt it in my chest as Liam Brynn put a few of my pieces back together.

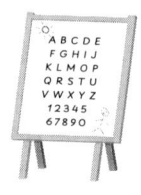

CHAPTER TWENTY-SEVEN

Cassie

The full extent of what Liam's career meant for his life didn't really hit me until I saw the article. I guess I wasn't aware that reporters, even credible sites, could post blatant lies about someone and get away with it.

**Harbor Wolves Star Liam Brynn
Involved In Altercation.**

It was the first time I'd allowed myself to click on something involving him. I guess I wanted to respect his privacy before, so I didn't bother to read anything about him on the Internet. It was too weird.

But this? There was no way I could suppress the curiosity inside of me when I saw that headline. I just had to see how they could justify what I knew was a lie.

I'd been there at the game where this supposed altercation had taken place. I was talking with Liam when it ended, and then he drove me home right afterward. There couldn't possibly have been *time* for him to get into a fight. There just wasn't.

Plus, this was *Liam* they were talking about. Clear-minded, level-headed Liam was far more likely to respond to something with stoic indifference than a punch.

When I clicked the article, it was exactly what I expected. No proof. No evidence. Just a few random reports from "witnesses." None of whom could even confirm that it was Liam for sure.

And that night? It was the one he held me in his car, comforting me as I humiliated myself by crying on his shoulder about the woes and despairs of my life.

There was no way he could be that gentle and understanding after supposedly getting into some hockey brawl moments before?

I rolled my eyes, clicking out of the article while promising myself that I wouldn't bother to read any more clickbait about him ever again.

I don't know why I even searched his name. It was stupid. Also, sort of fangirlish. But I couldn't help it. He was gone for an away game, and the apartment felt so lonely without him… and I guess I just… missed him.

Again, stupid. He wasn't mine to miss.

He may have comforted me the other night, but that was just because he was a nice guy. No matter how much I wanted to think we had stumbled into "friendship" territory, I couldn't fool myself. He just cared about me on Maggie's behalf. That was all. I had to remember that so I didn't go and embarrass myself by breaking down in front of him again.

But then my phone buzzed, and when his name flashed on the screen, I forgot all the promises I was making to myself about keeping my head clear.

> **LIAM:** What's the deal with Ross? Is he like a psychopath or something?

I smiled, fingers typing back rapidly.

CASSIE: Are you…….. Watching Friends?!?!?!?!!

LIAM: We were flipping through the channels in the hotel room. It was on.

CASSIE: What episode????

LIAM: I don't know, Ross is yelling about a sandwich.

CASSIE: Ah. The One With Ross's Sandwich. I know it well. 😂

LIAM: Why did you capitalize it?

CASSIE: It's the name of the episode title. 😂😂😂

LIAM: What? Just a description of the episode?

CASSIE: Yep.

LIAM: ……

LIAM: That's actually genius

CASSIE: *Isn't it, though?!*

LIAM: So, what are you doing? You okay?

CASSIE: Of course, but your apartment is not.

> **LIAM:** ??

I sent a selfie showing the mess that surrounded me. Laptop open, file folders everywhere, glue, and containers of glitter.

I saw the three dots indicating he was typing, then a pause. My heart hammered. Was he going to be mad about the mess? He knew it was a joke, right? That I'd obviously clean everything up before he got back?

But his text didn't say anything about that.

> **LIAM:** Nice hoodie.

I looked down at what I was wearing, realizing with shame that I had on the hoodie he'd given me that first night.

I was humiliated.

I didn't even know what to say. Sorry? I'll give it back? I don't actually wear this all the time when you're not around because it reminds me of you?

But he sent another message before my frantic mind could figure out what to say.

> **LIAM:** It looks good on you.

I blushed, grinning at my phone like an idiot.

I didn't know why I suddenly felt like a middle school girl texting her crush, but just seeing his name appear on my phone made me want to kick my feet and giggle. Which was a dangerous feeling, considering he was my roommate. And my friend's brother. And a famous hockey player that *every* girl had the same exact feelings for.

I was hopeless.

A knock sounded at the door, and I froze. Before Liam started leaving for away games, he warned me to double, triple, quadruple, and quadruple-check who was there before opening because, in the past, he'd gotten some strange people showing up at his doorstep.

He made it sound like they just happened to stumble there accidentally, but after the way his neighbor had treated me, I knew he had some pretty deranged fans out there, so I was more than a little cautious when checking the peephole.

"Ahhhh!" I screamed, jumping back from the door at a huge eye magnified against the peephole.

On the other side, laughter sounded.

"Let me in, you dork. It's me," Maggie called.

"Maggie?" I gasped, fumbling with the intense lock system after the breath returned to my lungs.

The door was open half a second before Maggie was striding in, carrying coffees.

"Wow," she said, spinning around. "You totally Cassie-ified the apartment." Maggie clapped slowly. "I applaud you. It actually looks like a human being lives here now."

"What are you doing here?" I asked, gratefully accepting the coffee she handed me.

"Well, officially I'm here because Liam wanted me to check and make sure you were okay." Maggie rolled her eyes. "Like I need *him* reminding me to do that. But unofficially, I'm here because I need someone to listen to my word vomit about these disgusting feelings I'm having." Maggie groaned at an insane volume, muffled slightly by the hand covering her face.

"Is this about Brody?" I smirked, drawing out his name the tiniest bit. She was silent.

"Maggie," I crooned.

"Yes!" she admitted. "Yes, okay. Fine. I like him. I don't even know how because I've barely even interacted with him. But I have a big, stupid crush on him. Okay?"

I let out an obnoxious squeal.

"This is amazing. This is the first time in our entire friendship that you've ever liked someone!"

"Not true." She frowned. "What about Pete?"

"Tattoo Pete? Who got your name forever imprinted on his biceps after two weeks of dating you?"

"Yeah." She scrunched her nose. "He was kind of weird. Well, what about Kile?"

"You said the way his name was spelled gave you the ick." I laughed, remembering the first time she saw it on his driver's license. She broke up with him the next morning.

"Matthew?" she suggested hopefully.

I shook my head solemnly. "You said he had the fish tank smell."

"Ugh. You make me sound ridiculous."

"No," I laughed. "You're just selective, which is a good quality to have. Now tell me about Brody!"

"Well, we talked at the hockey game the other night," she said. "And then we had that shared traumatic experience of ripping Liam away from the fight—"

"What!" My jaw dropped. "That was *real?*"

Maggie's head snapped backward, her eyebrows arched in question. "Liam didn't tell you…?"

"I saw an article, but I thought it was just lies and rumors that they were spreading. When could he have gotten into a fight? We were with him after the game, and then he drove me home immediately after!"

"Oh, Cassie." Maggie's face paled a bit.

"Is he okay?" I asked. "I mean, I know he's okay because I was with him after, but I mean, what happened? Who did he fight? Did he get hurt?" I was too flustered to form coherent sentences.

"You should ask Liam when he comes home. I don't really know the full story," Maggie said, but the way her eyes wouldn't meet mine left me with more questions and anxieties.

I bit my lip, trying to move past this news. I knew hockey was a rough sport. He'd probably gotten into a heated argument with someone from the other team, and it probably happened so frequently that it wasn't even on his radar to mention it. Right?

"Was it some guy from the other team?" My stomach was twisting itself in knots.

"I don't know, Cassie. Just—ask him, okay?"

She refused to meet my eyes, which did nothing to help my nerves.

"Maggie," I pleaded.

"Nope! Not doing this. Not answering a single question that will stress you out." She grabbed her phone. "Instead, look at my flirty little text messages."

I feigned a growl of frustration but forced myself to move on. If Maggie wasn't going to tell me, there was nothing I could do. She was as stubborn as they came. All I could do was reassure myself that Liam was *fine*.

"Let me see," I relented, hand held out expectantly.

She smiled, handing over the phone after opening their text thread.

I scrolled through message after message. Brody was big on emojis. The angel emoji, the smile emoji, the sun emoji. He sent 'good morning' messages, 'good night' messages, 'how are you doing' text messages, and what was Maggie giving him in response?

One to three-word responses.

"Maggie, why are you barely responding to this sweet angel boy?" I looked at her in shock, scrolling through the texts. "You're giving him the barest of minimum to work with here! He's going to think you're not interested!"

"That's what I'm going for." She smirked. "It drives them crazy."

"Maggie!"

"What?" She feigned innocence. "If they know you like them, they think it's okay to stop trying, or they get bored, or they just totally ghost you."

"Yeah, but Brody isn't like that, from what I can tell."

"No," she mused, staring down at the texts with a slight smile. "He doesn't seem like he is."

"So, what's the problem then?" I asked softly as if the volume of my words could coax the answer out of her.

"You know how hockey players are. They travel a lot. They hook up with random women in every city." She waved her hands dismissively. "It's too much to worry about."

My stomach plummeted a thousand feet. "They do?"

She snorted. "Yeah, they're the sluttiest of all the athletes."

"So, you think right now, they're all just… what, sleeping with a bunch of women?"

"Not right now." She laughed. "It's almost time for their game. But after? Probably."

It made sense, especially if Liam wanted to have no-strings-attached relationships. It would be easier for him to do it in the States half the country away.

My brain was gnawing at itself with questions while my stomach churned uneasily.

"Why do you look like that?" Maggie asked, frowning at whatever she found in my expression.

Instantly, I wiped my face clear of emotion, offering her a smile.

"Oh, I guess I was just worried that I was taking up too much space here, especially if Liam ever wanted to bring a girl home or something. He's probably uncomfortable living his life normally with me in his space."

Maggie threw her head back, laughing dramatically.

"Liam doesn't *talk* to girls, never mind hook up with them."

"But you said all hockey players—"

"Oh no. Liam's the exception to that."

Relief flooded through me. I didn't bother trying to discern *why*.

"He is?"

"Yeah, he doesn't have time for girls in his normal life. Never mind girls in random cities across the country."

"Why?" I asked, dumbfounded and reassured all at once.

"In college, he had a few casual girlfriends." Maggie shrugged. "Well, I wouldn't even call them that. They never really went anywhere. It got worse when he got signed. I'm not even sure the last time he *spoke* to a girl. If I'm being honest, I think the puck bunnies kind of scared him off from our gender completely. He hates girls who are obsessed with him."

Oh.

Right. Like me.

Because I was obsessed with him, wasn't I?

I thought about him all the time, and I talked his ear off whenever we were in the same vicinity. I mean, I was wearing his hoodie, for God's sake.

I fought the urge to visibly cringe. I was just as bad as the rest of them. And worst of all, I was *living in his house.* He couldn't escape from me if he wanted to.

"But he's been different lately," Maggie said, fingers tracing the lid of her coffee cup absentmindedly.

"Different?" My voice was far too curious for an indifferent listener. "How?"

Maggie's lips quirked as if I'd given her exactly what she was looking for.

"Oh, I don't know," she mused. "It's just not like my brother to be, well, as concerned as he's been about you."

"Me?" My face flamed.

"Yes, you."

"No, Maggie, no." I shook my head. "It's not like that. It's just—well, I made a fool of myself. More than once, I might add. Literally broke down into tears in front of your brother multiple times." My words tumbled out faster than I'd intended, all blending together. "If he's concerned, it's only because he thinks I'm the most fragile person in the universe."

"Somehow, I doubt a few tears are what caused my brother to have a personality transplant." She snorted. "I mean, sending me over to check on you? That weird way he insisted on coming with us to the bar. Getting into a fight—"

"What's that got to do with me?" I countered defensively.

"Never mind." She shrugged innocently. "It's probably nothing."

"Maggie, you don't seriously think—"

"Calm down, Cassie." She giggled. "I wasn't accusing you of anything."

"I know, but—"

"Ah, ah, ah." She stopped me with a look. "Forget about it. Let's order takeout and watch a movie," she said, sliding her jacket off and moving toward the couch.

My phone buzzed as another text from Liam came through. My stomach flipped upside down as my fingers fumbled to open it.

"And make sure it's something romantic." She called over her shoulder, "I'm feeling weirdly gushy lately."

Apparently, so was I.

CHAPTER TWENTY-EIGHT

Liam

Two days. I was gone for two fucking days, and that's all it took for me to feel like I was going through withdrawals.

I missed Cassie.

And now that I was about to see her again, I had to check myself back into normalcy. How the hell would she respond to it if I ran up to her like some golden retriever begging for attention?

I forced myself to slow my stride, walking up to our door with an ease I sure as hell didn't feel. I was jittery and restless, and Jesus Christ, were my palms sweaty?

I blew out a breath, turning the knob, readying myself for that first sight of her. I wondered if she was at the kitchen counter, already eating breakfast before work. Or maybe she was sitting on the floor, pulling her shoes on. I smirked at the thought. I had no idea why, but she always plopped to the ground whenever she was putting her shoes on. It was cute as hell.

I opened the door, preparing for the floodgate of emotion to be released from my chest, and came up blank. I blinked, taking in the empty space as if it were an arrow to the chest.

She wasn't here.

For half a second, I panicked.

Was she gone? Had she left? Moved out while I was away?

But no, there were signs of her everywhere. Coffee cup on the counter. School bag by the door. Shoes in the middle of the living room.

But it was late in the morning for her to still be sleeping. Especially when I knew she would have to be leaving to get to work soon.

I dropped my stuff and headed toward the staircase, concern spreading in my chest. She was always downstairs by now. Always.

I was halfway up the staircase when I heard her. Groans of frustration filled the air and then a few thuds. I picked up my pace.

"Cassie?" I called, rounding the corner to her room and coming to a halt in her open doorway.

She was sitting crisscross on the floor, surrounded by a heap of colorful clothes, grumbling so loudly she didn't hear me approach.

"Stupid. Nothing. Maybe I could—" Another groan. "No, that won't work."

"Cassie?" I repeated again, huffing out a laugh.

Her head whirled, eyes widening as she noticed me. She scrambled to her feet like a baby deer learning how to walk for the first time.

Again, fucking adorable.

"Liam!" she said, barreling toward me. "You're back!"

Before I knew what was happening, she threw herself at me, and before my mind could process what was happening, my arms were suddenly wrapped around her.

What the hell is wrong with me? I thought, feeling breathless at the contact. *It's a fucking hug.*

Her arms tightened around my neck, standing on her tiptoes to reach, and I almost groaned out loud at the contact.

Then, at once, she froze. Gasping as she ripped herself away, along with my heart in the process.

"Oh, gosh," she said, mouth forming an 'O' shape. "I'm so, so, so sorry."

My own mouth could barely form words while my arms already ached with the loss of her in them.

Get a fucking grip.

"For what?" I managed to get out without sounding as breathless as I felt.

"For attacking you like that! I just got so excited to see you because I missed you and—" She cringed. "Sorry."

I stared at her agape. "Why are you sorry?"

"That's weird, isn't it?" She toyed with her fingers. "I mean, it was only two days and—"

"Cassie," I tried to stop her.

"Two days is nothing in the grand scheme of things. It's just 48 hours! I mean, like, 16 of those hours are spent sleeping!"

"Cassie—"

"Did you know some guy flew a plane around the world in 46 hours? He literally traveled the world in less time than you were away for hockey," she rambled, words coming out fast as her eyes darted around to look anywhere but at me.

"Which sort of makes 48 hours seem like *more* time than it is, so I'm not making the right point, but that's still crazy, isn't it?"

"Cassie," I tried again, to no avail.

"And I mean, I did end up going to bed super early because I was sort of bored and lonely, so let's say 48 hours total, minus like eighteen hours of sleeping. That's only 28 hours!"

"Cassie!" My hands reached out, grasping her shoulders until those big, oblivious blue eyes finally met mine.

"Yeah?" she said softly.

"I missed you too."

I saw that light spark in her eyes, and it felt like the world was spinning a bit faster beneath us.

"You did?" she asked, as if somehow in disbelief.

As if it wasn't written all over my face.

"Yeah," I answered, voice thick. "I did."

Her cheeks turned a shade of pink as she cleared her throat, taking a step backward. I hated the distance between us, but I knew it was probably for the best.

I knew if she stayed close to me, I would only last so long before grabbing her in my arms again, and who knew if I'd have the strength to let her go so easily the next time I had her there?

"So." I looked around the space that used to be a generic guest room but was now anything but. "Are you going to tell me why I walked into what looked like your closet trying to eat you?"

"Oh." She deflated, moving backward until she was sitting on the edge of the bed, staring down at the mess. "It's Spirit Week at school."

"Well, it's a good thing you're the most spirited person in the fucking state." I snorted.

She still frowned. "I *love* Spirit Week. But I don't have anything to wear because it's stupid sports jersey day, and I own exactly zero articles of athletic gear. Unless you count my shirt that has Snoopy playing tennis on it."

Again, that groan of frustration filled the room, and I couldn't help but laugh out loud at how utterly defeated she looked.

"Why are you laughing?" She pouted.

"Because there's the easiest solution in the world to this problem that you're somehow overlooking."

She shot me a look, waiting for me to go on.

"You do remember that you live with a hockey player, right?" I raised my brows at her.

"Uhhh," she responded, biting her lip.

"Hockey players tend to have a jersey or two in their closet." I filled in the blanks, biting back my own smile.

"No way can I wear your jersey!" she responded, looking appalled.

"Why not?"

"Because you're important! And I work in a Kindergarten class with kids who blow their noses on me and run around with markers in their hands!"

"Have you heard of this thing called a washing machine?" I laughed at the incredulous look on her face.

"Liam." She groaned, like it was some great moral dilemma instead of wearing a piece of fabric.

"Cassie," I said pleadingly, "It's not a big deal. I promise."

But that was a lie. It *was* a big deal. And I wanted her in my jersey more than I wanted my next fucking breath.

I watched as she chewed her lip, wishing I could pull it free and throw the damn jersey over her head. But then, her shoulders relaxed, and a sigh of acceptance escaped from her lips, and I knew I'd won.

Because it wasn't just my jersey she was going to be wearing. But my name, too.

CHAPTER TWENTY-NINE

Cassie

It was obvious to anyone with eyes that the jersey wasn't mine. Down to my knees, I was practically swimming in the blue and gray fabric. I'd paired it with blue jeans and blue ribbons in my hair to go all out.

Spirit Week was big at our school, and I usually went full-fledged for it. In the past, I'd never paid much attention to the sports days, usually borrowing something of Dave's so I could participate. But now? Everywhere I looked, I seemed to spot Harbor Wolves jerseys on the staff and students alike. I noticed Brody's last name on one of them and chuckled, almost having the urge to snap a picture to show Maggie. Others were wearing the jersey of that blond guy who we were sitting with at the bar that night. And some were even wearing *Liam's*.

But the one I wore? It *was* Liam's. Not some knock-off with his name on it that anyone could get in a sports store. No, Liam had bled, sweated, and played in the jersey I was wearing on my body right now. And no one had a clue.

It felt oddly intimate.

Still, they were our city's home team, so I didn't think it would draw much attention.

I rolled the sleeves up to my elbows, wondering if I looked weird in it. I was pretty sure I did based on the way Liam kept staring at me after I changed into it.

Feeling self-conscious, I slipped into the teacher's room to put my lunch away. As always, it was filled with voices swirling together in conversations I could never manage to slip myself into.

I'd been at this school for over two years now, and I'd yet to find my footing with the staff. I was awkward, and my words tended to come out as rambling speeches that most people couldn't keep track of. And usually, I ended up embarrassing myself too much to even bother trying again for a while.

It was the same way when I was in school. I was so hyper-aware of myself and everyone else that I overthought social interactions to the point where I ruined them before they ever began. It was exhausting.

"Didn't peg you for a hockey fan," one of my coworkers' voices sounded.

I didn't realize it was aimed at me until I shut the refrigerator and turned, watching the eyes of everyone at the table on me.

I tensed up, my brain whirling as I tried to think of how to respond. In comfortable settings, I had no problem having conversations. In fact, I thrived on it. I could talk a mile a minute with the right people. But with people, I felt that I hadn't yet proved myself too? Knowing what to say next became a challenge I couldn't conquer.

I wanted to be witty and know how to respond to their small talk that I'd never perfected the art of, like it seemed everyone else in the world had.

I laughed awkwardly, offering a shrug as a response. What else could I say? I *wasn't* a huge hockey fan. If they asked me to name a single sports term, I wouldn't be able to. The only players I could name were Liam and Brody. And if they tried to talk about anything game-related, I'd have no knowledge to offer up.

"I'm not really," I responded as they waited for my answer. "I mean, I just recently started getting into it."

"Because of Brynn?" The art teacher at our school's eyes lit up, nodding toward my #26 jersey.

I froze. "What?"

"I don't blame you. Everyone's a hockey fan for Liam Brynn. I don't know where they found that boy, but he looks like they ripped him out of a Calvin Klein magazine and put him in hockey gear."

"Oh." I laughed nervously, heart racing. "Yeah, he's really good."

"He could be the worst player on the team and still have half the women in Boston showing up to watch him." Another teacher laughed.

"Really?" I asked, forcing out another laugh to appease them, but anxiety gnawed in my gut.

It was strange territory to be in, tiptoeing around the edge of Liam's status.

"I'm surprised you spent the money on a jersey for a sport you're '*just getting into*,'" Marissa said, eating her yogurt and staring me down with equal intensity.

I couldn't figure it out, but whenever her eyes were on me, they felt like a magnifying glass.

She'd never done anything outright to say, '*I don't like you*,' but the sentiment always seemed to be clear, and the stronger I felt it, the more awkward I got around her, as if I could shrink myself down until she couldn't even see me.

"I just needed a jersey for spirit week." I shrugged, not understanding the feeling of having to defend myself.

She stared at me with what looked like boredom before continuing her conversation with the teachers sitting beside her.

This was how it always was. Her attention was on me long enough to make a comment, and then she was moving on as if I didn't exist at all.

I looked down, brows raised, when I noticed she too was wearing a #26 jersey.

"So, Marissa." I slid into the seat across from her. "Are *you* a big hockey fan?"

She looked up as if surprised I was still there and even more shocked that I was talking to her.

"Of course." She laughed. "My family always had season tickets. I've been going to games before I could even talk."

I didn't doubt it. It's how it was for a lot of Boston families. Something about New Englanders made their loyalty to sports teams run thicker than blood.

"Do you happen to know anything about the fight Liam got into the other night?"

She snorted. "I doubt it happened at all. Liam Brynn has *never* been the type to start a fight on the ice, never mind *off* of the ice, with a fan of all people."

"It was a fan he fought?"

"I just told you, I doubt it even happened," she responded, shooting me a scathing look. "I can't possibly think of any reason why he would've punched some guy after winning a game. It's just not like him."

The way she spoke about him rubbed me the wrong way. As if she knew him. A feeling twisted in my gut. Oh my God, was it jealousy? It shouldn't be. He wasn't mine. What did I care if she had some weird parasocial obsession with him?

"Maybe it was over his new girlfriend," the girl next to her, Kendra, chirped.

I felt like I was in an elevator that just dropped ten floors without warning.

"His—" I stuttered, blinking. "His girlfriend?"

Marissa frowned. "Well, that wasn't confirmed yet, either."

Was Maggie wrong? Did he actually have more interest in women than he let on?

"I mean, there was a picture of them on Twitter," Kendra responded. "Isn't that enough?"

Maybe it was someone he met at an away game. Maybe he was just super private about his dating life. After hearing the way my coworkers were discussing him, I would be too if I were him.

"It's not like they were making out in the picture!" Marissa retorted, irritated. "Besides, it was so blurry you couldn't even see anything. It might've been some random waitress he was having a conversation with."

"There aren't any waitresses in *The Trap*," Kendra pointed out, and the realization hit me like a truck.

The Trap. The redhead sitting with him at the booth. Was that his girlfriend?

"What was the picture of?" I asked, voice airy as I felt the oddest, most unreasonable pang of sadness.

"It was actually really cute," Kendra said, "He was leaning into her, bending down to hear what she was saying. He looked way taller than her, which is super hot."

Marissa frowned into her yogurt.

"Well, I doubt it'll last," she said, mostly to Kendra. "He's an NHL player. I doubt he'll be content to settle down with the first girl he's been photographed with."

"You're just jealous because *you* want him." Kendra laughed.

"So what if I do? I have a better chance than most people after him. *I* actually like hockey, and I go to games all the time, so it's not super unrealistic that I might bump into him."

"You'd be the cutest NHL wife," Kendra gushed in agreement.

I snorted, thinking that Marissa seemed like the last person in the world to be Liam's type.

Or was that just this bitter jealousy talking, fueling with me an anger that I couldn't suppress?

Why didn't he *tell* me he had a girlfriend? Was it because he felt bad about kicking me out of the apartment since he knew I'd leave if I knew?

Feeling flustered and sick of the conversation happening around me, I walked out of the breakroom.

I walked a few steps, then paused to lean against the wall, waiting to regain control of my emotions before setting off to teach a group of five-year-olds.

"I don't know," Marissa's voice sounded, drifting out to where I stood. "She's just so jittery all the time. I mean, how can she teach a class of kids if she's so nervous?"

Heat surged through me as I reached some invisible limit that finally set me over the edge.

I was sick of it. Of coming to work feeling self-conscious and out of place when she was around. I was sick of the way she whispered to her friends when I entered a room. I was sick of the way everything she said to me was delivered in a backhanded, condescending manner.

With my heart hammering in my chest, I whirled the corner back into the breakroom, for once ready to hear what she had to say behind the whispers.

For the first time in a long time, I felt angry, and I didn't have the self-control to keep it at bay any longer. Not when I spent every day nervous about navigating conversations with my coworkers as if I were still the shy, awkward girl in high school trying to stay out of everyone's way.

Marissa's eyes widened as I entered as if she thought I'd been long gone, and the look on her face satisfied the part of me that was so used to running away.

"Have you ever thought that if I'm nervous around you all the time, it's because you make conversations incredibly uncomfortable to be part of?" I asked, watching as her mouth opened to respond.

"Or have you not realized that making passive-aggressive comments about what I wear, or how much I talk, or how I'm 'too nice' is probably the worst way to go about giving yourself a confidence boost?" I continued, letting everything I'd bottled up come out at once. "You don't have to like me, and you don't have to be my friend because I'm just here to do my job, and no matter what you say, I *know* I'm good at what I do because I love those kids.

"And you're right. I might not yell at my kids to get them to be quiet, or maybe I don't have that 'teacher voice' you use to scare them into listening to you, but I have managed just fine. So, you don't need to give me any backhanded advice anymore on how to run my class because you've been here longer, or using a louder voice to get their attention, because, timid as I am, those kids respect me. You want to know why? Because I respect *them*."

She stared at me, mouth agape. For once, she was the one with nothing to say.

"What?" I asked, furrowing my brows in confusion. "Did I break the rules of your passive-aggressive game by being too direct? Or was it only fun for you when I didn't say anything back?"

I waited a minute to listen to whatever she had to say back. When she came up with nothing, I turned on my heel and left, feeling better in my own skin than I had in a very long time.

CHAPTER THIRTY

Liam

I was on thin fucking ice.

Figuratively, of course, since the ice beneath my feet was thick enough to hold our entire team, plus my coach, who was currently ripping me a new one.

"Can you give me one goddamn reason why news of this fight you had won't die down?" Coach's face was red and furious.

The rest of the team stood in a line beside me, their faces impassive. They respected Coach enough not to step in when he was laying down the law with one of us.

"Because people have nothing going on in their lives?" I responded, bored by the whole ordeal.

Who the fuck cared if people were still talking about it? No one got anything on video as far as I knew. All that was circulating were a few rumored reports from 'witnesses.' It didn't fucking matter.

"Because you make headlines when you so much as take a piss, Brynn!" Coach fumed. "And you sure as hell know that. So it was *your* responsibility to keep a clean reputation, if not for you, then for your *team!*"

I stared at him. What could I say? That I was sorry? I wasn't.

"And on top of it all, we can't even deny the rumors because the reporters are all attesting to the fact that your ass wasn't in the locker room where it should've been for your mandated post-game interviews!"

I exhaled heavily, rolling my eyes. I was twenty-six years old. Not a kid playing hockey for his high school. The stakes were technically higher, but if I showed up and helped bring the Wolves to victory, then what the hell did it matter what I did outside of the game?

"Brynn, you're a damn good player, and you know that, but goddamn it if that doesn't bite you in the ass. You think you can do whatever you want because you're a good hockey player?" Coach's arms flailed around. "Well, newsflash: the world is full of kids waiting to take your spot. Kids who would jump when their coach told them to fucking jump."

"And what does that mean?" I bit out, a bit of panic rising in my chest.

This game was everything to me. *Everything.*

Was he seriously telling me that I had to participate in the media circus and cater to the vultures just to keep my spot?

No one told me that signing with the NHL meant selling my soul to the fucking devil.

"It means you need to work like hell to fix this mess. It means that at that charity gala, you are going to be on your goddamn best behavior. You're going to be on that stage, smiling and waiting to accept the offer of the highest bidder, you got it?"

"No."

"Damn it, Brynn, you have been a pain in my ass since the day you joined this team. And you know what? Some of the time, it's worked for you. God knows why, but they ate that up. The hockey kid with an attitude. But now? Fighting with a fan?" He shook his head in disappointment. "You need to fix this."

"I didn't *fight* with a fan," I corrected, feeling like steam was about to come out of my ears. "I punched a guy who deserved it, and it wasn't a random fucking fan. It was *private.*"

"Well, you don't get privacy at TD fucking Garden after you win a game! I mean, come on, Brynn! I thought you had a better head on your shoulders than that! Do you want to lose your career because you can't keep it together?"

The answer was no. No, I fucking did not.

"I'll keep it together," I said through gritted teeth.

"I'm holding you to that." Coach nodded, finger-pointing at my chest. "And you're going to prove it at the auction."

Fucking hell.

CHAPTER THIRTY-ONE

Cassie

It was hard to know what feelings were real and which ones weren't when I'd spent so long pretending.

Emotions had been dangerous growing up. It wasn't *mine* that mattered, but my mother's. I'd learned that early, when my tears would bring on her fury, claiming that I was doing it for attention.

Oh, your life is so horrible, isn't it?

I'd then have to listen to how terrible *her* life was, having to raise me on her own, with no money, no husband, no life of her own.

It saddled me with a guilt that emerged each time I felt any type of negative emotion for myself. I realized that usually I *was* being unreasonable.

Sure, my mom yelled at me sometimes, and sometimes her behavior could be a little unpredictable. Sometimes she passed out for entire days at a time, when she had promised me we'd do something together or she'd take me somewhere. But some kids had no parents at all. Some kids got hit or abused.

So, really, she was right. What did I have to cry about?

Now, thinking about the situation, it felt completely unreasonable, but even the knowledge of that wasn't enough to push the feelings down.

I was upset, but I knew how to pretend I wasn't. And that's what I'd have to do to keep the peace. I didn't want a confrontation. I didn't want to fight. I didn't want to get yelled at for feeling something I already knew I had no right to feel.

So, as I walked into Liam's apartment, I told myself I wasn't going to bring it up. Not the fight he got into, not the secret girlfriend he was hiding. None of it. It wasn't my business. And I knew from experience that people didn't like being questioned about their choices. I'd learned to keep the questions at bay.

But then I saw him, and every thought in my head went out the window.

"Hey," he said, looking utterly and completely exhausted.

The air felt different. It always did when someone was upset. I had a sixth sense for that type of stuff, like I could absorb whatever someone else was feeling the moment I laid eyes on them.

"What's wrong?" I asked, staring at him where he sat at the kitchen counter.

His head snapped up. "What do you mean?"

"You're upset," I said, that feeling of anxiety growing inside me like it did whenever anyone was in a bad mood.

But this wasn't just anyone. This was *Liam*. And I wasn't scared of his bad moods. I was concerned for him.

He stared at me, green eyes blazing, before letting out the softest laugh that seemed to lighten some weight off of him.

"How could you *possibly* know that?"

I shrugged, moving to sit on the stool beside him.

"Tell me what's wrong," I pleaded, feeling the strongest urge to fix it for him.

"Don't worry about me," he said, lips parted as if in disbelief. "I'm fine."

"I know you're not." I frowned at him. "Is it because of me?"

"*What?*"

"Are you mad at me?"

"Cassie, no." He shook his head. "Not at all—"

I wondered if he'd gotten into a fight with his girlfriend. Or maybe he was upset that I was still here. It had been nearly a month since I promised I'd only be here for a few days.

I couldn't break a promise I'd made. Not when I knew how it felt to be on the other end of that. I was taking up too much time and space in this man's life, and I needed to rectify it immediately.

"I need to go," I said, standing up, already in motion, planning my escape.

"Cassie." His chair slid back against the floor with a loud screech. "Wait, wait, wait. Where are you going?"

I didn't want to look at him. I couldn't. I needed to get a handle on my emotions, and it was impossible to do that around him.

"I need to leave. I've been here for too long."

"Cassie, stop." He reached out, tugging my wrist until I had no choice but to look up at him. His eyes were wide and panicked, and the look on his face made me feel breathless.

"What?" I asked, voice breaking.

I felt like I was helplessly trying to regain some semblance of control over the situation. I knew the only way to do that would be by leaving on my own terms.

"Hey, hey, hey," he said, his voice low and soft. "What's wrong? Why are you sad?" His hands were cupping the sides of my face, keeping my eyes on him.

I closed my eyes against the sight of him, hating the tear that slipped down my face.

His finger brushed it away.

"I just need to go," I said resolutely. "Please, just let me go."

"No," he said firmly. "Not until you tell me what's wrong."

Finally, I opened my eyes, staring at him through the tears that clouded my vision.

"Why didn't you tell me you had a girlfriend?" The words slipped out despite how hard I tried to hold the question back.

He froze, hands dropping.

"What?" he said, taking a step back.

"Some people at work were talking about how they saw a picture of you online with some girl," I said, willing him to deny it.

He said nothing, his face remaining impassive. He opened his mouth to respond, then closed it shut without a word coming out.

It was as good as confirmation.

"Did you see the picture?" he asked at last.

My heart sank.

"No!" I responded. "I wouldn't betray your privacy like that."

I started moving again, knowing I needed to leave. Now.

"Cassie, stop. Wait," he said, following me through the apartment.

"If I had known, I wouldn't have stayed this long, taking up all this space," I said.

"Cassie," he said, my name a plea on his lips. "Please, it's not like that."

I turned slightly, pausing on my ascension up the staircase.

"Who's your girlfriend?" I asked, hating and not understanding why I felt betrayed and abandoned by this man who had no obligation to me.

"You," he said, and his words froze me in place.

"What?"

"It's you," he repeated, and I stared at him dumbstruck. "No, I mean—" He ran a hand over his face, fumbling for words. "Jesus, not like that. I just mean, you're the girl in the picture. It's you."

My mind whirled, trying to make sense of his words.

"Someone took it that night we were at the bar and posted it online and ran with it. I'm so sorry," he said in an agonized tone. "I didn't tell you because I thought you'd hate me for it. But it's just a really blurry picture. I doubt anyone would be able to tell it's you, so you don't have to worry about that."

My eyes were downcast, processing everything he was saying. I'd never heard him so frantic. Liam, who was always relaxed and level-headed.

"I'm *so* sorry, Cassie. These people—they're crazy. They think they have a right to everyone's private lives. They don't blink an eye about posting that shit on the internet."

I was confused, not understanding why he kept apologizing. The only thing I could process was that Liam didn't have a girlfriend. And that the girl everyone *thought* was his girlfriend—that was *me*.

"Please don't leave," He whispered, voice breaking. "I promise I won't let anything like this happen again."

My eyes snapped up to his, my chest aching at the desperation I found there.

"It's okay," I said, still reeling from the heartache, confusion, and relief I had just experienced in rapid succession. "I don't mind."

"You don't mind?" he repeated, dumbfounded.

"No, I don't mind if people think that." I shook my head.

The article. The photo. The entire internet thinking *I*, of all people, was his girlfriend. This was his life. Strangers writing things, making assumptions about him. About people he was connected to.

It should have scared me, but it didn't.

And now Liam, standing in front of me, eyes searching mine like he still wasn't sure I was going to leave.

"I just hate the idea of people spewing shit on the internet about you," he said, reaching out to push a strand of hair back from my face. "You're not up for debate."

My heart jolted.

"I don't care what people say." I shook my head, realizing that it was true.

Never before in my life could I have honestly said that I didn't care what people said or thought about me. But I was here with Liam, feeling more certain of who I was and who he was than I had ever been in my life.

It didn't matter what people said. I knew who he was. And it seemed, impossibly, like he knew me too.

He blew out the biggest breath of relief, pulling me in for a hug. Before I knew what was happening, I was hugging him back, breathing in the scent of him.

Then, in a small voice, I asked the question that was easier to ask when my eyes were closed, and my face was cradled against his chest.

"What about you? Do *you* mind? That people think I'm your girlfriend."

He didn't say anything for a moment, and my body tensed with anxiety until he finally responded,

"No, Cassie. I don't mind."

A slow breath escaped me, my shoulders loosening as I stepped back from him.

Liam studied me for a beat, then exhaled, running a hand through his hair.

"If you're being serious about the rumors not bothering you," he said, looking as if it were hard to get the words out, "then do you want to save my life by doing me the literal biggest favor in the world?" he asked, his face turned in a way that told me he was expecting rejection.

I stared at him, knowing there was nothing he asked of me that would be too much. After all he'd given me—safety and comfort, and friendship—how could he think there was anything I wouldn't do for him?

"Anything," I responded.

CHAPTER THIRTY-TWO

Liam

I didn't want to read into it too much about what it meant that I'd asked Cassie to be my girlfriend. And I sure as hell didn't want to think too hard about what it meant that she'd accepted.

Because it was *Cassie*.

Of course she'd done it to help me out, like I'd asked her too. It wasn't anything more than that. If I let myself for even a second think it meant something deeper, then I was letting myself creep into dangerous territory.

Besides, it wasn't like it was real, anyway. It was just one night, to save me from being bid off at the charity auction Coach demanded I go to in order to fix the bad press surrounding me and therefore, the team.

So why the hell did I feel like throwing up the whole time I was getting ready?

It's just one night. It's just pretending.

But people around us would think it wasn't, and not only did I not *mind* the idea of that. I liked it. A fucking lot.

Shit.

"Are you ready?" her voice floated in from outside the bathroom door.

I let out an exhale, yanking at the cuffs of my suit jacket as if I could find some minor thing to tweak just to hide in here a bit longer.

The door opened, and all I saw was Cassie standing there in a shimmery rose gold dress that looked like it was made for her and her alone. I doubted it could sculpt to anyone else as perfectly as it clung to her.

I had one of those fucking cartoon moments where I actually did a double-take. Jaw dropped, eyes wide, the whole ordeal.

I remembered those scenes in the movies Maggie used to watch when we were growing up. I always thought they were corny as hell, but here I was, jaw on the floor, staring at Cassie without a single thought in my head, all because of that dress.

"You look—" I started, mouth dry. "Uh—"

"Do I look okay?" she had the audacity to ask.

Understatement of the fucking century.

"You look really pretty." I cleared my throat, nodding in confirmation, but I couldn't tear my eyes off of her.

Or her body.

"You look *so* handsome," she said, running a hand along the sleeve of my jacket. "You always do, but I've never seen you dressed up like this. No wonder every girl's in love with you."

I couldn't breathe.

How could she just casually spew that out, looking like she just stepped out of every guy's most intimate dream and expect me not to grab her in my arms and kiss the shit out of her?

I can't take her to the gala. Not when every man in the room would be staring at her the way I was right now. Not when she wasn't mine.

"Not every girl," I said, feeling in a daze.

But for tonight, I could pretend. Tonight, she was mine, and I could remind every bastard who stared at her exactly that.

"Oh." She raised a blond brow. "*Most* girls being in love with you isn't enough for you? You need every single one?"

Actually, I just need one.

"Cassie," I said, prepared to let everything tumble out of me. To get on my knees and beg her to be my date for real, not for some made-up, stupid event.

But her phone buzzed, and her attention went to the screen.

"They're here!" A noise of excitement erupted from her, cutting off the deluge of emotional word vomit I'd just been prepared to release on her.

Jesus Christ, I would've ruined *everything*.

"Great," I responded, wishing more than anything it was just the two of us driving there together, but knowing it was probably safer for me that it wasn't, considering that I was apparently a fucking liability when it came to this girl.

We'd agreed, or should I say, *Cassie* had agreed that we should carpool with Maggie and Brody, who had apparently worked through their shit and finally were getting out there for a first date.

I was happy for Brody. I really was. But on the other hand, I had the lingering fear that Maggie was going to break his heart.

Maybe it was just in our blood to hurt people the way our dad had hurt us. It was part of the reason why I never bothered seriously with any relationships before. When you looked at the statistics, what was even the point of trying?

I think Maggie guarded herself the same way, though we went about it in drastically different manners. She was fine with hanging out with someone for a while and bolting before it got too serious. But me? I felt like something was broken inside of me because I knew how many beautiful women were out there. Hell, I'd had them *throw* themselves at me, but none of them—not a single one, had ever appealed to me.

Until now.

Cassie opened the front door, welcoming Brody and Maggie inside. I loved the sight of it. I could almost imagine it all being real. Being permanent.

Cassie being here, with me, for good. The two of us having our friends and family over.

I shook the thought out of my head. Cassie and I might not be anything real, but it looked like Maggie and Brody were definitely entering into that territory.

They stood side by side, so close their whole bodies touched as they walked in. He had a hand resting on her back, and what shocked me more than any of it—Maggie didn't pull away.

As happy as I was for them, I was jealous as hell. Brody got to touch her, to be *with* the girl he wanted in front of everyone, no pretenses. Meanwhile, I had to stand next to Cassie and pretend I wasn't losing my fucking mind.

They looked good together, though. Maggie was wearing a sleek black dress with a slit down the leg, her hair done up with a few dark strands framing her face.

"What the f-, Cass. You look *so beautiful,*" Maggie gushed, circling around Cassie, examining every inch of her the way I wished I could.

"Stop." Cassie hid her face, embarrassed by Maggie's attention. "*You* look stunning. You both do." She looked over to Brody with a knowing smirk.

Brody beamed with pride.

"Look at all of us here together, going to an event. Who would've thought?" He said the last part, looking over to me with a knowing look of his own.

Maggie and Brody both knew the deal about why Cassie was going with me tonight, but apparently Brody thought I had *other* intentions.

I rolled my eyes at him, he wiggled his brows, glancing between me and Cassie. I shot him a scathing look, demanding he shut up before Cassie noticed, when Maggie's words had my head whipping in her direction.

"We're totally going to find you the cutest guy to flirt with tonight."

I stiffened. "What the hell, Mags. Did you forget the point of this evening?"

"Yeah, yeah. Cassie's your secret cover story." Maggie rolled her eyes dramatically. "But is that really more important than her landing a cute hockey boy?"

"Why would I want to do that?" Cassie asked teasingly. "You told me all hockey boys are sluts."

I reared back.

"Her words." Cassie held her hands up in defense. "Not mine!"

"I'm personally offended." Brody held a hand to his heart and winced. "I can't believe you would say that, Mags."

My thoughts were still reeling, wondering why my sister was hellbent on ruining my fucking life by trying to set Cassie up with random men.

"Oh, you all know it's true." Maggie rolled her eyes. "But come on, we're going to be late!"

She tugged on Brody's arm with a familiarity I hadn't seen her display with any other guy.

"I'll drive?" Brody chirped over his shoulder, looking all too pleased to be led away by my sister.

"Yeah fucking right." I snorted but still felt stiff and uncomfortable at the prospect of the night before us.

The last thing I needed was to be driven around to an event I didn't want to go to, where every guy in attendance would be trying to steal Cassie away while my sister fucking helped.

Driving gave me a sense of control. It kept me focused and calm. And I knew I'd always have a way out if I felt the need to leave.

Besides, Brody was a shit driver.

We walked behind Maggie and Brody, Cassie by my side, but even that wasn't enough to calm me. Not when she looked so beautiful, it hurt to think about it.

As always, she seemed to know exactly how I was feeling. It was like her own superpower.

"Don't worry," she said teasingly, her hand coming up to touch my arm lightly, and I swear to God that little touch was enough to ignite me completely.

"Worry?"

"About what Maggie said. You don't have to worry about that."

"I don't?" I asked, shoulders loosening in relief.

"Of course not. I'm your girl for the night," she said, winking before turning to climb into the passenger seat.

For the night.

It wasn't enough.

Not at all.

CHAPTER THIRTY-THREE

Cassie

I was in way over my head.

I didn't realize it until the cameras were flashing, and I was clutching onto Liam's arm as if it were a life raft in the middle of the sea of panic I was currently treading.

Liam had warned me about the cameras. In fact, he'd seemed so concerned about them that I started to worry he didn't want any permanent connection to me, like the kind that happened when photos went online. But I told him it was fine, and it was. The issue wasn't me having to pretend to be into him, but the worry I had that *he* wouldn't be able to pretend with *me*.

I kept my head down, noticing how Maggie and Brody had no such reservations as they pranced on ahead of us.

"Hey." Liam's head came down until he was level with my ear. "You're doing great. It'll be a lot calmer once we get inside."

I stared up at him, grateful for the way he was leaning into me, keeping me calm as we walked into the Fairmont Hotel. And that was when a photographer leaped right in front of us, snapping a photo.

Liam's arm tightened around me, pulling me to his side in a protective grip. I didn't know if it was for show, but I knew, at least partially, that he wanted to protect me from all this. The part of the job he hated.

And while it overwhelmed me, I never felt safer than I did beside Liam. It wasn't just that he was tall and big and had that resting expression daring anyone to see what happens if they get too close. It was that I felt some part of him truly cared about me, even if it wasn't in the way I wanted. I knew that if he could help it, he wouldn't let anything hurt me.

"Mr. Brynn." A microphone was shoved into his face. "Who's the lovely lady serving as your date tonight?"

"Private," he said in a clipped tone, moving us along before anyone had a chance to argue.

Thankfully, there were plenty of Harbor Wolves players who *didn't* mind getting their photos taken or being interviewed, but it was clear Liam was the one everyone wanted.

Maybe it was because he denied them so often that all the reporters went after him. Everyone wanted to be the one he stopped for, the one he gave attention to at last. They wanted to be the one to earn the sought-after privilege of being the one Liam Brynn finally paused for.

But he didn't stop. Not for any of them.

"I'm sorry about that," he said when he led us inside the most extravagant lobby I'd ever set foot in.

Everything was shimmering and gold, the glow of the ornate chandelier filling the room with a warm light. It felt more like I was inside the palace of some aristocrat than a place people could pay money to stay at.

"It's fine," I said, honestly, taking everything in. "I know what I signed up for."

He gave me a smile of gratitude, and I had to look away. Not just to take in the breathtaking hotel we were standing inside, but because Liam was so beautiful tonight that it hurt to look at him.

I waited for his hand to fall away now that the cameras were behind us, but it never did. I knew the longer I felt it, the worse it would be when he finally took it back.

Just like how tomorrow would feel after spending a night by his side, pretending to be the one he wanted.

I fought a sigh. Maybe I hadn't thought this all the way through.

"We can still go home if you want." His voice was low, closer than I expected.

I stared up at him, wondering how long he'd been studying me for him to be able to notice the slightest shifts in my demeanor.

"If that were an option, we wouldn't be here in the first place," I teased. Being here with him wasn't the problem. It was being anywhere without him afterward that I was worried about.

"I don't care," Liam said intensely, eyes boring into mine in a way that left me dizzy. "I'll deal with the fallback. If you want to go, we'll go."

"Liam," I said, tilting my head with a smile. "I'm fine, really."

"You always say that." He rolled his eyes, but everything about his demeanor was soft… gentle, almost.

"This time, I mean it," I said honestly. "I promise."

He narrowed his eyes on me, scrutinizing as if he could detect if I was telling the truth or not with just a look.

"Come on," I said, nodding my head in the direction where Maggie and Brody had wandered off. "Let's go have some fun."

"Fun," he repeated with a huff. "You have a great way of spinning things, you know that?"

I laughed, and he led us to the ballroom, but the only thing I was aware of was the way his hand slipped down until it found mine.

Fooling everyone around us of the lie that I knew better than to believe: tonight, Liam Brynn was mine.

Liam

It was loud. There were too many people. And I was being asked a lot of fucking questions. Everything that made up the stuff of my worst nightmare of an evening.

But it wasn't.

And that was solely because of the blonde sitting next to me, who hadn't left my side for even a moment.

I saw the eyes on her. The hunger in men's gazes as they stared her up and down, and while it pissed me the hell off, I had the satisfaction of them knowing she was with me.

Mine.

My eyes said exactly that every time I caught them looking our way.

Yeah, I thought with satisfaction each time some creep averted his gaze, *turn your fucking head in the other direction. She's not for you.*

She wasn't for me either, but no one had to know that.

I don't think she noticed, but I was touching her a lot. In whatever small, inconsequential way I could manage without sending her off any red flags. She'd agreed to pretend to be my girlfriend for a night, not to have my hands all over her body in front of a few hundred people.

So, with every ounce of self-restraint in my body, I kept it casual: a hand on her arm, an intentional brush of our shoulders. Every once in a while, I even dared to brush my hand against hers. Each brief moment of contact was like a jolt of electricity running through me, and I wondered if this was how other people felt, if this was the feeling that made people risk breaking their hearts over.

I hadn't felt it before, not to this extent, and I doubted I ever would again.

Cassie looked lost in thought when I looked over at her.

"What?" I asked, desperate to hear whatever thoughts were spinning around in her head.

"You're not drinking," Cassie noticed, staring down at the untouched drink in front of me. Apparently, she was just as aware of me as I'd been of her.

"Don't need to." I shrugged. "I'm having enough fun with you without it."

She smiled at that softly, as if she were trying not to.

I laughed, "What's that smile for?"

"Nothing." She shook her head. "I just like that."

She was so easy to please. I couldn't understand how Dave had screwed it up with her so badly when the things that made her happy were easier to give her than breathing.

"What the hell, Brynn?" One of my teammates' voices sounded. "You bring a beautiful woman around and don't bother to introduce her to us?"

I turned to see three of the guys standing there expectantly, all dressed in fitted suits. A drastic change from how I usually saw them in their hockey gear.

"This is Cassie," I answered curtly, watching out of the corner of my eye as she waved at them.

"My best friend!" Maggie raised her hand as she sipped her champagne.

Cassie, I noticed, sipped on water, a glass of champagne untouched in front of her.

"And you are?" Shane West asked.

"My date!" Brody beamed proudly, draping an arm around her chair. Weird to see.

"Also, my sister," I added to ensure they didn't have any intention of making comments about her after they walked away.

Guys' dates were usually up for discussion, but they faithfully steered clear of any talk about sisters.

All of them except Brody. But his hard work and delusions had paid off because now my sister was sitting beside him, staring at him with a smile she granted to few.

"Well, we just wanted to come over here and thank you for clearing up the competition." Ryan Dawson smiled cheekily.

"What?" I asked.

"Apparently, you're off the market now." He winked at Cassie, causing me to stiffen. "For the auction at least, right?"

"What's it matter to you?" I asked.

"Now that everyone won't be fighting to the death over you, it gives the rest of us a fair chance with ladies."

"You do know it's usually middle-aged women using their husband's money on these auctions, right?" I responded tightly.

"Age is but a number, Brynn." He shrugged, looking around the ballroom. "Everyone here looks pretty good to me." He laughed. "Though I have to admit, not quite as good as the lovely ladies at this table."

"Watch it," I warned, jaw clenched.

"Relax, Brynn." His hands went up in defense. "It was a compliment."

But Maggie was staring at me with a knowing look.

"Coach is going to be pissed, though," one of the other guys added. "Apparently, you were supposed to be the big money maker of the night."

I cringed, finding the whole idea of a date auction totally bizarre.

"Maybe if they didn't pick the weirdest fucking fundraiser they could think of—" I started, hands balling into fists.

"We would've made less money," Shane added. "And gotten less press about it. I mean, have you seen how many people showed up for this?"

"Not like we need the extra press," I added.

"But seriously, props to you, Liam, for going against Coach like this after he already put you in the line of fire." Ryan laughed. "No one can say you don't have balls."

"I would *not* want to be you when he gets a hold of you," Shane added with a wince.

"What do you mean under the line of fire?" Maggie asked, nosey as ever,

"Coach basically threatened his spot on the team if he didn't start generating better press around his image." Ryan laughed as if it were a joke and not my career on the line.

Cassie tensed beside me.

"Liam!" Maggie said, "Couldn't you have sucked it up for one night if it was *this* big of a deal?"

Why was everyone at my fucking throat *all* the time?

"I—" I started, preparing to spew out some response that would honestly probably get me in deeper shit than I was already in.

"It's not his fault," Cassie suddenly interjected. "Don't blame Liam. I had to *beg* him not to participate, even though he kept telling me how important it was." She gushed, sounding sincere. I gave her a double take at the note of sincerity in her voice, but she kept going, "I hope your Coach isn't too upset. I just get really jealous when it comes to this guy."

Her arm was around my chair, her hand resting on my shoulder in a possessive display. I raised my brows at her, but her eyes remained focused on my teammates.

"I'm sure you guys understand. I just couldn't handle the thought of every woman in Boston fighting each other over the chance to spend a night with my boyfriend."

Boyfriend.

The word hit me like I'd gotten cross-checked on the ice.

It's what we'd agreed on when we talked about tonight. I just hadn't expected to hear her say it out loud. I thought just the sight of us together would be enough insinuation.

A chorus of laughter from the guys sounded, and suddenly they were all around me, throwing light punches on my arm as if I just announced my fucking engagement.

"What the fuck, man. Did Liam Brynn finally commit to a full-on relationship?" Ryan grabbed my shoulders and shook them in what I thought might be congratulations.

"Never thought I'd see the day."

"Maybe you haven't," Brody tossed across the table, knowing the whole thing was for show.

Maggie hit him, but luckily, they were beyond the guy's notice.

Cassie was blushing as if she hadn't expected such a reaction from my teammates.

And who could blame her?

For most guys, getting into a relationship was just another part of life—something that happened, something that wasn't a big deal.

But for me? It was unheard of.

I wasn't the guy people expected to settle down. I wasn't the guy who let someone in.

But here Cassie was.

The first. Maybe the only.

The only girl who'd ever called me that in public. The only girl I could picture ever letting.

Even if it wasn't real.

"Well, we'll leave all you little love birds alone." Ryan snickered. "Who knows? Maybe after tonight, half the Harbor Wolves will be paired off, and we can all take cutesy trips together to the mountains or some shit."

Jesus Christ.

The team was close, but sometimes they were unbearable. I just didn't have the energy half the time to deal with their back-and-forth banter.

Or maybe I just couldn't handle all the conversations about my fake relationship when half of me was over the moon that people thought it could be true while the other half of me was torn to shreds, knowing it wasn't.

Cassie's hand left my arm as soon as they disappeared.

"You didn't tell me what a big deal this was," she said. "Am I going to be the Yoko Ono of the night?"

I arched a brow, laughing at the comment. "What band are you breaking up tonight?"

She groaned. "I just mean, is everyone going to hate me for taking the most eligible bachelor off the market?"

"I'm definitely not the most eligible," I said dryly.

"Yeah!" she exclaimed. "Not now that I've crept in and stole you away from the mass of women who are going to want to murder me!"

"I won't let anyone hurt you." I frowned at the thought. "I promise."

She sank lower into her seat. "I just hate when people are mad at me."

"No one's going to be mad at you, Cass." I tucked my head down to be level with her as she crouched down. "And if they are, I'll beat them up. Okay?"

She laughed, not knowing how true my words were.

"Can I tell you something?" she asked.

"Anything," I said.

"I'm a little intimidated being here with you," she said, making my heart sink. "I didn't realize how big of a deal you were at first, and I feel like I still don't have the whole picture of it."

"I'm not." I shook my head, trying to deny it.

Trying to not let that aspect of my career that I'd always despised ruin whatever precarious thing there was between us.

"You are." She nodded. "I mean, people I work with actually talk about you in the break room. That's crazy, right? Everyone in this state knows who you are."

"You know *me*," I assured her.

"I feel like I do," she agreed. "Sometimes."

Sometimes.

I wanted her to know me. Really, deeply know me. But I played a part in that, and I knew, despite everything, there were still parts of myself I was keeping guarded. Things I tried to shove away, even from myself.

But if I wanted her to know me, to let her in all the way, I had to own up to everything I was keeping buried. And I guess part of that was admitting how I felt about *her*.

"Cassie, I—"

"Brynn!" Coach's voice interrupted, and the both of us sprang apart, apparently unaware of how close our faces had leaned in toward each other.

His voice yanked me back as surely as if he'd grabbed me by the hair and pulled.

I exhaled, turning to face him.

"Coach," I said by way of greeting.

"What the hell is this I hear about you not doing the auction tonight?" His face was contorted in the signature angry scowl that only I drew out of him.

"Didn't you hear, Coach?" Brody interjected with a grin. "Liam's got himself a girlfriend. Pretty serious, too, by the looks of it. He promised I could be his best man."

Cassie shifted beside me, choking on the water she was sipping.

I shot Brody a glare, promising I'd pay him back for that one later.

"Then why is this the first I'm hearing of the girl if it's so serious?"

"Liam's private," Brody offered with a shrug.

"He is. Annoyingly so," Maggie agreed.

"Yeah, right, Hayes." Coach glared at Brody. "Because *you'd* never cover up for him."

"No, it's true," Brody reassured him. "They're living together and everything."

At that, Coach did a double take, finally taking in Cassie for the first time.

"Hm," he said, watching both of us with scrutinizing eyes.

Cassie's chair scraped against the floor as she shifted closer to me,

"Sir, I'm *so* sorry I inconvenienced you tonight. But it really is true. We've been living together for almost a month now. And even though I know it would be good for the team, I just can't stand the thought of him being with another woman, even if it *is* for charity."

At that point, her head came down to rest against my shoulder, and I fucking lost it.

I could smell the lavender scent from her hair as it brushed against my skin. My hand moved up of its own accord to hold her against me as if I could keep her there forever if only I didn't let go.

"Please don't be mad at Liam because of me."

Her hand reached up to cup my cheek while she stared Coach down with those big fucking blue eyes that I knew had to power to melt even the strongest of men.

She was going above and beyond to sell this performance, and all the while, I was sitting there like an idiot who couldn't form a single fucking sentence while she was touching me like that.

"Please don't bid him off on me," she begged, fluttering her eyes at Coach while she cuddled up against me, her hand now tracing circles on my chest.

Coach stared dumbfounded, as if he, too, couldn't process the luck I was having with this beautiful girl beside me.

"All right, fine," He relented at last, tearing his eyes off Cassie and back to me. "Brynn, you're off the hook. And you would've made a damn fortune too, so the only reason is because this is the only time you've ever brought a lady with you to anything in your career, so I have to give you the benefit of the doubt here."

"Thank you, Sir." Cassie jumped to her feet, an enthusiastic smile overtaking her. "You don't know how much it means to me."

She reached her hand out to shake his while introducing herself to him formally. In a daze, he shook her hand back, insisting that she call him Teddy.

I stared in awe at the interaction, watching as one of the most hardened men I knew turned into putty in front of Cassie.

I laughed to myself. Even fucking Coach wasn't immune to Cassie's charms. It was like she was one of those mermaids who sank ships with just the sound of her voice. Only she was wide-eyed and innocent and probably hadn't the slightest clue about the effect she had on people. It was just *her*.

He went off on his way, and Cassie sat down sheepishly, face flaming when she finally looked at me.

"I'm so sorry about that," she said, wincing.

"*Sorry?*" I asked aghast. "You just saved me. What the hell are you sorry for?"

"I was way up in your space, and I know you hate stuff like that," she said. "I just didn't think he'd buy it otherwise."

Was she serious?

And what could I say back?

Don't apologize for touching me? I fucking loved it. Please, touch me more?

Anything I wanted to say, like any of the million thoughts that were rapidly filling my head, would've made me sound like an absolute creep.

"You just did me the biggest favor in the world," I told her honestly. "And you got me out of a world of shit with Coach. You have *nothing* to apologize for."

But I was scared of her refusing to touch me for the rest of the night because of the totally unwarranted fear that *I* somehow didn't want it, so I told her, "Besides, we're supposed to look like a couple tonight." I cringed internally at how desperate I sounded, "So the touching is… good."

"It's good?" She scrunched her nose, still looking bashful and adorable as hell at the same time.

"Yeah, it's good."

"Well, if the *touching* is okay with you—"

More than fucking okay.

"Do you think we could maybe…" She fiddled her fingers nervously. "Dance?"

And then she looked longingly toward the dance floor, where dozens of couples were already swaying with their partners.

"You want to dance?" I asked, feeling my hands go clammy.

"Only if you do," she said nervously.

I hadn't slow danced since the senior prom back in high school, and even then, I'd only been on the floor for a few minutes before choosing to sit the rest of the night out.

But somehow, staring at Cassie, who had just done more for me than anyone else ever had, looking like the most beautiful thing I'd ever seen in my entire life, I knew I'd stand out there all fucking night if she wanted me to.

"Yeah, Cassie." I laughed softly, holding out my hand for her. "We can dance."

CHAPTER THIRTY-FOUR

Cassie

I didn't really understand how I ended up dancing with the man every woman in Boston and beyond wanted to be with, but I was scared that if I thought about it too hard, I might wake up and realize it hadn't been real at all.

For now, I let myself feel the weight of his hands in my mine. I let myself rest my head on his shoulder as we swayed, and in moments when I was sure he wasn't looking, I let myself breathe in the scent of him, as if I could commit every detail of the night to memory.

Because I was sure I'd never have another night of him all to myself like this ever again.

In the background, the soft hum of a love song was playing, making me feel all the more self-conscious about having asked Liam to dance with me. Was that too bold? Was it weird? I let myself focus on the lyrics that were all too relatable at that moment.

It's you and me, and all of the people.

It was exactly how I felt, dancing there with him in a ballroom filled with hundreds of people, but it may as well have been just the two of us.

Somewhere in the distance, Maggie and Brody were falling in love for real, but I couldn't bring myself to focus on anything other than Liam's hands that were trailing down to my waist.

"I'm glad we're here tonight," Liam said, and I was hyper-aware of his hand at my waist.

"Even though I keep stepping on your feet?" I said, trying to repress the urge to tell him how I was more than glad we were here tonight. Or to admit how perfectly at ease I was every moment I was with him.

Or worse, that I was scared I was falling for him.

But I knew he wouldn't want to hear that—maybe he'd even see it as a betrayal after everyone had made it extremely clear how anti-relationship he was, so I locked that secret away and prayed it would never see the light of day.

Besides, I couldn't fall for him. He was a famous hockey player. A superstar in his own right. I was so far beneath his notice that if I hadn't known Maggie, he never would've looked at me twice.

It hurt, but that was life. Besides, I had him here now. As a friend. I needed to be content with that. I couldn't go wishing for things I'd never have. I'd spent my life doing that, and all it caused was pain that could be avoided.

If I just accepted people for who they were, I could've avoided so much unnecessary pain. If I had realized my mom wouldn't stop drinking. If I had noticed the signs when it was clear Dave and I had drastically different visions of the future. If I could just accept the reality I lived in rather than wishing for what it *could* be.

Acceptance. It was one of the teachings of Al-Anon. Coming to terms with the things you couldn't change. And Liam Brynn falling for someone like me? I could never make that happen, so I just had to let that fantasy die.

"I'm a big boy." He huffed a laugh. "I can take you stepping on my toes."

"But your feet are your money makers," I joked.

"What?" He arched a brow, laughing.

"I mean, aren't they? Since your job is skating? Plus all the other stuff. But mostly skating, right?"

His eyes crinkled as he stared at me, the smile never leaving his face. I didn't think people knew what a beautiful smile he had. It seemed it only ever came out in small, private moments like these.

A true shame for the rest of the world to miss out on the sight of it, but part of me was thrilled that they were reserved just for me.

"What?" I asked, laughing nervously at the way he stared at me.

"Nothing," he said. "You're just cute."

My stomach dropped.

Cute. Like a sister was cute?

He cleared his throat as if he hadn't meant to say it aloud. Of course he hadn't. He probably knew how I felt about him. He probably was trying to spare my feelings. He was kind like that.

"Thank you again," he said, "For lying to coach for me. You have no idea what a big deal that was."

What had I said? That it was true we were living together? That I didn't want Liam to be in the auction because I was jealous of another girl having him?

It was a tactic I'd learned throughout my life. Lies sounded more believable when they weren't lies at all. Just selective truths spun to fit your narrative.

It was how I'd survived my childhood.

"You don't have to thank me for that." I shook my head. "Nothing I said was a lie."

Embarrassed by my own admittance, I tried to spin it, feeling the undeniable need to deflect from my own pathetic feelings.

"Besides, it probably did you more harm than good. I doubt it'll be good for your game." My voice sounded higher-pitched than normal.

He drew back. "My game?"

"Yeah," I said, fighting the jealousy that arose in my chest that I didn't have a right to feel. "It's going to be harder now that everyone thinks we're together."

"We are together." He looked down at our entangled bodies swaying in dance.

"You know what I mean," I said, blushing. "They think we're a couple."

"That was the point," he said, looking affronted.

"Right. I just meant if you *wanted* to talk to women, it would be harder now," I said.

"I don't want to talk to any women," he said tightly.

Right. Of course he didn't. I was so stupid. Part of me had been subconsciously fishing for him to admit something, anything, to make me feel like whatever was going on between us wasn't entirely in my head.

But the look on his face and his words reminded me that Liam Brynn was more than content being on his own.

I bit my lip, forcing myself to stop talking before I humiliated myself further.

"What about you?" he asked after a moment. "Are you over…" He trailed off, unwilling to finish.

"Dave?" I asked with a giggle. "It's okay. You can say his name. He's not Voldemort."

"I'd rather not." He grimaced. "The name leaves a bad taste in my mouth."

"You're so dramatic." I rolled my eyes at him. "You don't even know him."

Liam looked off in the distance, watching the other couples. I followed his gaze, noticing for the first time how many women were eyeing Liam.

I clung tighter to his neck.

"So, are you?" he asked again when he finally looked back at me. "Over him?"

I thought about it, feeling awful as the truth settled over me.

"I think I've been over him a long time," I admitted with a sigh. "I don't know if I was ever fully invested, if I'm being honest. It was more like… the idea of *someone* that kept me there. I've always wanted someone to be mine and mine alone. But I don't think he ever really was."

In the same way, I was never really his.

Liam nodded, mulling it over.

"But you were still going to stay with him?" he asked, brows drawn in confusion.

I knew he wouldn't understand how screwed up I was. How I probably had a myriad of abandonment issues on top of some sort of codependency that I hadn't yet acknowledged. But I couldn't bear for him to think less of me, so I tried to explain as honestly as I could.

"I don't think I realized it until I was out of it," I started, trying to find the words. "I think I was so wrapped up in getting to the future I wanted for myself — that I didn't bother to take a look at the person I was building that with." I looked up to him for confirmation. "Does that make sense?"

"You wouldn't ever take him back, would you?" he asked, suddenly grave.

"I hope not," I admitted.

He turned as still as stone underneath my touch.

"What do you mean 'you hope not?'"

"Sometimes I'm scared of being alone," I said. "Sometimes being with the wrong person is better than being with no one at all."

Or being stuck with my mother—the fear I still carried deepest, the one I worried I'd never truly escape.

"Besides." I shrugged, feeling a weight on my chest. "It would be easier to go back to my life than have to start all over."

His jaw clenched, hands firm on my waist as if they were superglued there.

"I'm kidding," I teased. "He doesn't want me back. He didn't even want me when he had me. I wasn't kidding about the convenience, though. Apartment hunting is more brutal than I thought. I doubt I'll find another one that I'll be as comfortable in as my old one." I sighed longingly.

"You can change whatever you want in the condo," he said suddenly. "You know that."

I drew away from him, confused.

"What—"

"Paint the walls, rearrange furniture — hell, buy all new stuff if you want. I'll give you my card."

Blood rushed through me. What was he talking about?

"Liam, Liam, stop," I said, holding a hand to his chest as I stopped dancing.

"You can't go back to him because you're scared of change, Cassie," he said, eyes ablaze with emotion. "That life you had wasn't anywhere close to being good enough for you."

"I know that," I said with a sigh of acknowledgment. "But I can't stay with you forever either."

"Why not?"

My heart fluttered.

Because I'm falling for you when that's the last thing in the world I should be doing. The last thing you would want.

"What's happening here?" I asked, not wanting to overanalyze the way I was so prone to doing.

My head was swimming, and I took a step back to steady myself, but he closed the distance between us immediately.

"I don't want you to be with him, Cassie," Liam said fiercely, reaching for my hand. "I want you—"

"Cassie!" Maggie said, running over to us, saving me from whatever Liam was going to say. "Your phone has been going off non-stop. I figured it might be important," she said, handing the device over to me.

I looked at her, blinking back into reality. My heart was hammering in my chest. Anxiety from all the unknowns around me.

I turned my head back to Liam, his eyes filled with something I couldn't read.

"I'll be right back," I told him, taking the phone from Maggie and stepping away.

I left him behind, along with the tension that had found its way between us. Taking a breath, I let the air return to my lungs at the narrow escape from whatever had just happened.

Because as safe as I felt with Liam, no one in the world had ever made me as nervous, either.

I was scared of what he was doing to me. Scared to get attached to someone else who didn't want me.

I made my way toward the exit, hoping for some fresh air, and my phone started ringing again. This time, I saw the caller ID, and my heart dropped.

I should've known. I should've expected this. After all, I'd spent my life going through the same cycle.

But it didn't matter how vigilant I was. How good I thought everything had been going. The second I let my guard down, my mother was sure to sweep in and ruin the carefully constructed peace I'd found for myself.

"Hello?" I answered the phone call, already knowing what they were going to say,

"Cassie, dear?" my mother's neighbor's voice sounded. "It's me, Kathy. I just wanted to let you know your mom was taken off in an ambulance tonight. I thought you'd like to know."

It didn't come as a surprise. I should've known better. No matter how steady I thought I'd been, this call was a reminder that I'd never been on solid ground to begin with.

CHAPTER THIRTY-FIVE

Liam

Fuck, I'd been about to tell her.

If Maggie hadn't interrupted, I would've told her—hell, I don't know *what* I would've said. Everything that was happening to me regarding that girl was so far beyond my control that it should've scared me.

But it didn't.

The only thing that I was afraid of was the thought of messing it up and scaring her off. But how the hell was I supposed to function when every moment I was with her, I wanted to grab her in my arms and tell everyone who would listen that she was mine?

Would she leave me if I told her? Would she leave me if I didn't?

And which of the two scenarios meant I got to keep her?

"What the hell are you doing?" Maggie slapped me back to reality with the hand that came down hard against my arm.

"What the hell are *you* doing?" I countered, looking down at her scowling face. "Why'd you hit me?"

"Because dumbass," he retorted. "You were just way too close and personal with my best friend. What was that about?"

I paused. I couldn't tell Maggie when I hadn't even told Cassie.

"Everyone's supposed to think we're together," I offered by way of explanation.

What did Maggie even see? It wasn't like I pulled Cassie in for a kiss. *Though I wanted to.*

"They already *did* think that without you staring at her like you're in love with her or something!" Maggie threw her hands in the air. "I mean, what the hell was that about?"

"You're yelling at me for *looking* at her?"

"No, I'm yelling at you because Cassie is way too fragile right now to have her head messed with by you."

"I'm not messing with her head, Maggie. Jesus."

Maggie narrowed her eyes on me, searching for something. I shifted on my feet as she watched me.

"You like her, don't you?"

Deny. Deny. Deny.

"Of course I like her."

"You know what I mean."

"No, I don't."

"Yes, you do! You're wearing your lying face!"

"Okay, so what? I like her. A fucking lot. But I know it'll never go anywhere. So we don't have to talk about it."

"Of course we do!" Maggie exclaimed. "Liam, this is the first girl you've ever really liked, and it's my best friend!"

"Not true," I defended. "Jesus, Mags. I've had girlfriends before."

"What? Those college flings that you got bored of after a week?"

"I didn't get bored of them, Mags. God, you make me sound like a douche. I just—" I paused, unable to explain myself.

Didn't feel a fucking thing for any of them.

But now? I felt everything. Way too fucking much.

"Liam, she's my *best friend*. You can't have a fling or whatever it is you're trying to do with her because it'll just get too messy."

"Jesus Christ, Mags. I never knew you thought I was such an asshole."

"I don't." Maggie sighed, running a hand over her face. "I'm sorry. I'm just worried about her. She has a lot going on."

I know that.

"She can be… vulnerable. She's a relationship girl, and you've never been able to offer that to anyone, so I think it's only fair that you admit that to her upfront. I mean, this is already so complicated. She's *living* with you."

"I know that, Maggie. You're the one who made that happen," I said defensively.

But I'm the one making her stay.

"I know." She sighed defeatedly. "I'm just so scared for her to fall for someone who's not serious about her again. You don't know what it was like watching that for *six years*. And they've only been broken up a month…"

Shit. She was right. Cassie wasn't in any place to start something new. I needed to get a fucking grip on myself and learn how to be there for her as a *friend*.

Suppose that meant never telling her how I felt, fine. But I sure as hell wouldn't stand by and let her go back to Dave the Dick.

"Don't worry, Mags," I lied through my teeth. "There's nothing going on."

She stared at me, her green eyes a mirror of my own.

"I don't know what's happening to you," she said hesitantly. "But you're different with her."

I clenched my jaw. I couldn't deny it. It would be way too fucking obvious if I even tried.

"Just promise me you're not going to hurt her," Maggie said imploringly.

Easiest fucking promise of my life. "I swear."

She nodded, content with my answer, and then sighed again, looking off to where Brody was laughing with a group of the guys.

"You know," I said, trying to lighten the moment. "*I* didn't give you a hard time when you decided to go out with *my* friend."

Maggie rolled her eyes.

"Do you like him, Mags?" I asked. "For real?"

She stared at me. " I do."

"Is that not… good?" I asked, trying to figure out why her admission sounded so sad.

"I don't know." She shrugged. "It's probably not good for him."

"What does that mean?"

"It means I've never figured out how to not hurt people I love," she admitted softly. "I get so scared of them hurting me that I think I try to ruin it before it can get that far."

"Brody would never hurt you, Mags." I shook my head. "*He* pursued you. He was a pain in the ass about it, too."

She stared at me, eyes ablaze.

"Dad pursued Mom. But he still left, didn't he?"

And then she walked off, leaving me with the trauma that we both carried around like a plague inside of us.

"Dude." Ryan Dawson laughed. "I had some woman tell me she was going to bid, like, a thousand dollars on a date with me."

"A thousand?" Shane West snorted. "These are some of the richest women in the city. I wouldn't go bragging about that number if I were you."

I craned my neck, looking around a room that was filled with way too many fucking people, and unable to spot the one I was looking for.

Tuning out the rest of their back-and-forth argument, I scanned the crowd for Cassie. It had been a few minutes and she hadn't come back yet, and honestly, I was starting to get worried.

I grabbed a glass of water from the table, downing the liquid. Brody sat next to me, laughing in turn with the rest of the guys.

"Hey," I said, nudging him. "You haven't seen Cassie around you, have you?"

"You lost your girl?" Brody asked, glancing around the room.

I clenched my jaw, fingers twitching at my side.

How the hell was I going to explain that I was worried she left the room for a few minutes to make a phone call? It sounded insane.

But by now, it had been more than a few minutes, and something in my gut didn't feel right. Cassie looked nervous when Maggie came over with the phone, and Maggie seemed like she knew more than she let on.

"Never mind," I said, standing to go find her.

I just wanted to see her. Once I had my eye on her, I'd relax.

I got up, anxious to move. I'd only made it a few feet into the crowd before someone appeared in front of me.

"Where are you off to, handsome?" The voice was sultry and low, belonging to a woman probably close to my age, give or take a few years.

"Looking for my date."

"Your date?" she asked, tugging on my tie. "Not a very good one if she left you all on your own."

The woman made an expression between a smirk and a pouty face, and honestly, I didn't have the time or headspace to think of a response. I cleared my throat and tried to walk past her.

"Do you want to dance?" she asked,

"I'm here with my girlfriend," I responded, voice thick with agitation.

Out of the corner of my eye, I saw Maggie and didn't bother to stick around to hear the woman's inevitable rebuttal.

"Maggie!" I called out, jogging over before I could lose her to the crowd.

She spun, gnawing on her bottom lip when she saw me.

"Mags, have you seen Cassie?" I asked.

"Uh, yeah," she said, way too fucking shadily for my liking. "I talked to her a few minutes ago."

"And?" I asked, raising a brow.

"She, um, had to leave."

"She *left*?" My heart dropped. "Why? Where did she go?"

"Don't freak out. She had something to do. She wanted me to tell you she's so, so sorry, but she'll see you at home later."

"I drove her here. How the hell did she leave?"

"She Ubered."

She has to stop fucking doing that.

I ran a hand over my face, weary beyond all hell. "Where'd she go?"

"It's not my business to talk about."

"Does this have to do with Dave?"

"What?" Maggie looked affronted. "No!"

"Jesus Christ, Maggie. Just tell me where she is," I said, hearing the sound of desperation in my voice.

"She's at the hospital," she blurted out.

"*What?*"

"Don't worry," Maggie said in a rush. "She's fine. She's okay. She didn't even want me to tell you. She made me promise I wouldn't."

Every nerve in my body ignited in alarm. "Why the fuck is she at the hospital?"

"She doesn't like to talk about it…" Maggie said uneasily.

"What hospital is she at?" I demanded, ready to already be moving in her direction.

"Don't go there, Liam." Maggie shook her head. "She wouldn't want you there."

"What fucking hospital is she at, Maggie?"

Maggie bit her lip, her resolve wavering.

"Maggie, *please*," I begged.

"St. Anne's, but Liam, I'm serious. Don't go there. She won't want you there—"

I was gone before she could finish the sentence.

CHAPTER THIRTY-SIX

Cassie

In some ways, my mother was predictable.

She was predictable in her unpredictability. She was predictable in the fact that she had always and would always drink. And she was predictable in the precarious cycle that our lives had always existed in.

She drank, and drank, and drank until we ended up here. In the hospital filled with the sterile smells of latex gloves and decaying bodies.

But I'd always been able to relax here. Breathe a little easier. In some ways, it was like the worst had already happened. When my mom ended up here, it meant the uncertainty of it all was gone, leaving me with a clear head to navigate the situation.

This was the best place for her. She couldn't drink here, and anything that went wrong they'd be able to take care of. That's how it had always been.

But *I* should've been taking care of her before it got to this point. I should've known how bad it was when I stopped hearing from her. Stopped getting angry texts or phone calls begging me for some request or another.

But a sick part of me had been *relieved*. Every time the phone dinged and it wasn't her name, I felt the tension that had seized me up slowly ebb away.

But still, she was my mother. All I had in the world. I should've been there.

My mother was on a stretcher by the time I arrived, still somehow unruly with the nurses despite the weakened state I'd found her in.

She looked gaunt and hollow, and the sight of her was like a punch to the chest. I hadn't been there to make sure she was eating. To make sure she was drinking something other than vodka.

I wanted her to miss me. To see that I was gone because of her. It was as if my absence was saying to her, *Look. Look at what your drinking has done to us. Now you're alone.*

But, as always, the only one that would end up alone was me.

"Mom?" I called, running to her side, reaching out for her bony hand that trembled violently beneath my touch.

Her eyes were glazed and unfocused, but some part of her was aware that it was me by her side.

"Cassie?" she slurred. "These people won't leave me alone. I just want to go home."

But it was clear she was in no state to do anything of the sort. Her entire body was shaking and she could hardly keep her head up on her own.

I'd seen this before, but each time seemed to be worse than the time before.

"What's happening?" I asked the doctor, needing to be as up-to-date as possible. I needed facts. All the information. It was the only thing that might ground me.

I hated feeling helpless. Out of control. I hated seeing my mother waste away in front of me and being powerless to stop it.

These people saw her like this: matted hair, wild, unfocused eyes, the stench of alcohol radiating from her pores. But I remembered *her* before it got this bad.

When I was a child, she was the most beautiful woman in the world, with golden hair and an intoxicating laugh. The woman everyone wanted to be friends with. The one every man wanted. The one *I* wanted, though that had never meant very much to her.

Alcohol had stolen everything from her. Her beauty, her vibrance, the very essence of who she was. Or who she could've been.

And in turn, it took it from me, too. Because what type of woman could I ever hope to be when my mother—my true mother, had been missing from me for most of my life?

"Her blood alcohol was dangerously high," the doctor explained as if somehow that had escaped my notice. "She's severely dehydrated and in the early stages of withdrawal. We're going to monitor her closely, but sometimes complications can arise."

That didn't worry me. We'd been in this situation before, and she'd always pulled through. What worried me was after.

Staring down at her, I was filled with resentment so hot it burned in my chest. It was the feeling of knowing she had never shown up for me and could never because of what she'd chosen to do to herself.

It was knowing that if I called, needing her, she wouldn't answer. Wouldn't be able to do anything for me. How could she? When she couldn't even help herself?

It had always been this way. Me taking care of *her*. Her needing *me*. But I needed someone, too.

If it were me lying in the hospital, she'd be too drunk or incapacitated to stand beside my bed the way I was here beside her.

And a part of me hated her for it.

But another part of me was so terrified of losing the only person in the world who was really mine.

"What can I do?" I asked desperately. "Are there any rehabs she can go to right away?"

"We can certainly talk about programs to refer her to," the doctor said carefully.

"No." I shook my head. "She won't go based on a referral. We need to put her in immediately after she gets discharged," I explained frantically.

The doctor's expression didn't change, as if he dealt with half-hysterical girls every day. This wasn't *his* mother wasting away, after all. What did he care, at the end of the day?

"Unfortunately, rehab programs are voluntary. If she doesn't want to go, there isn't anything we can do about that."

"But *look* at her. Look at her medical records!" I said in a passion. "This isn't the first time this has happened. It won't be the last, either. Can't we use that to prove she's not capable of making the decision?"

"What you're suggesting would require declaring her legally incompetent," he said cautiously. "That's a long legal process, involving lawyers, court orders—"

I felt defeat wash over me. I didn't have money for lawyers. I didn't know if we even had time for that. With the route she was going, she was a few binges away from drinking herself to death.

"Please," I begged to no one in particular.

I was so broken. So angry. At her, at the world, at the unfairness of it all. And most of all, so completely and utterly out of control.

"I'm so sorry," the doctor said sympathetically. "But, it's not your job to save your mother," he said, as if this would relieve the burden from me.

As if anything would.

"We'll keep you informed of any change to her condition," The doctor said, but was cut off by a voice calling a name.

My name.

"Cassie?" Liam's voice was searching, "Cassie!"

I turned and saw Liam on the other side of the corridor, calling out for me.

"Liam?" I breathed out, the floodgates of emotion I'd been trying to hold back opening at the sight of him.

Still dressed in his suit, he looked so out of place in the dingy gray of the hospital lights. He was the most beautiful man I'd ever seen.

I felt it when our eyes locked, even from a distance, I saw the relief in his eyes when his gaze finally landed on me.

He said my name again and started toward me, but I was already running in his direction, every instinct in my body telling me to just get to him.

Tears were streaming down my face now, but I didn't care. All I knew was that I was throwing myself at Liam, and his arms were open and ready to catch me by the time I got there.

"Liam," I cried against his chest, feeling the weight of his arms lock around me.

"It's okay, baby," he said, his chin coming down atop my head.

I couldn't see or hear or feel anything except Liam's body around mine, as if he was shielding me from everything happening around me.

"It's all my fault," I sobbed, knowing he probably didn't have a clue what was going on or why I was even here, just knowing I needed him in that moment more than I'd ever needed anything.

"Nothing's your fault. Shhh." His arms wrapped impossibly tighter, and he sounded so strong and certain.

"Everything's a mess."

"We'll fix it," he said, and I clung to him even tighter.

"You're okay," he reassured me, and I felt his lips come down hard against the side of my head. "You're fine."

I didn't know why I was falling apart like this in his arms. Maybe it was the feeling of safety that I finally found in his arms after all this time. I knew I could let myself fall apart as long as he was here to hold the pieces together.

"You need to breathe, baby. Okay?"

In a swift movement, he lifted me off the ground and carried us over to the hospital bench. I clung to his neck as he lowered us down, his hands moving my hair back from my face.

I knew how I must look. Blotchy-faced and red-eyed, but I didn't care because I knew *he* didn't care. There was no judgment coming from him. Just concern.

I was vaguely aware that people were staring at him, but I don't even think he noticed.

He was just here with me. Like I was the only thing that mattered.

"What's going on, Cassie?" he asked so softly it hurt.

How could I answer? How could I even begin to explain this big, terrible thing that had plagued me my entire life?

It had always been a humiliating secret I guarded above all else. As if my mother's addiction was mine, too. We didn't talk about it. We didn't tell other people about it. That's how it always was. Even though we were lying to ourselves, anyone with eyes could see the situation as clear as day.

But Liam? He wouldn't judge me. I knew in my bones that he wouldn't. I felt it, and I needed to trust that feeling. Because he'd done something that no one else in my life ever had.

Someone had finally shown up for me. So I told him everything.

CHAPTER THIRTY-SEVEN

Liam

My heart was in fucking pieces. The girl in the car beside me was quiet as she stared out the window. But this time, it was a calm sort of silence. As if a weight I hadn't known she was carrying had been lifted from her.

Now, she just looked tired.

"I'm sorry," Cassie said after a while in the dark of the car.

"For what?" I whipped my head to look at her.

"For leaving the gala. I didn't want to ruin anything for you."

"Jesus Christ, Cassie. You don't need to apologize." I couldn't believe this girl. "But can you do me a favor next time?"

She looked at me, nodding.

"Stop ordering fucking Ubers," I said, exhausted. "I'll take you anywhere you want to go. Just stop leaving without me."

A smile crept onto her face despite everything, and she nodded, healing some fraction of the crack in my chest that had torn open tonight.

"I promise," she whispered.

I reached over and took her hand in mine, and I held it the entire way home.

The apartment was dark when we got home, as if even the city lights that usually illuminated it had gone to sleep.

It was late, but I was wired. My mind was whirling with all the revelations that had taken place tonight about Cassie's past and this secret part of her life I never could've guessed at.

"Are you going to bed?" she asked timidly.

"Are you?" I responded without answering.

She looked utterly exhausted, and I knew she needed to, but God, I didn't want to let her out of my sight.

She shrugged. "I guess so."

But she lingered.

"What's wrong?" I asked, feeling stupid as hell for the question as soon as I asked it.

Everything in the world was fucking wrong.

"I think I'll sleep on the couch if that's okay?" she asked, tugging at her fingers.

"Why?"

It took her a breath before she admitted it, but when she did, the words twisted something inside of me.

"I don't want to be alone."

"You're not," I told her. "You don't have to be."

She looked up at me with hope.

"Come on." I nodded my head toward my bedroom. "You can hang out with me in my room."

If she fought me on it, I'd just carry her there myself. She didn't want to be alone, and I didn't want to be without her.

But she saved us both from the struggle and nodded, sighing in relief as she did.

I gave her my sweatpants and a hoodie, and she disappeared into the bathroom connected to my bedroom to change. She didn't fight me on that the way she used to. She also didn't fight me when I tucked her under the comforter.

But when I turned to leave, she sat up abruptly, eyes wide with something close to fear.

"I'm just getting my laptop," I assured her. "I'll be right back."

She nodded, settling back down in my bed. The sight of it was too much for my heart to handle.

I left the room, dragging in the deepest breath I could before searching for my laptop. My mind was a mess, a fucking hurricane of thoughts, and I needed to make sense of at least one of them.

When I came back, she was already asleep, her hair fanned out on the pillow I slept on every night.

I let myself look at her—the way I couldn't when she was awake. She looked so small like this. Fragile in a way I knew she'd hate me thinking.

I'd only known her for two months, and somehow, she'd carved out the biggest piece of my heart without even lifting a damn finger.

Holy fuck, I'm in trouble.

But for the first time, the thought didn't scare me. If it was going to be anyone, I was grateful it was her.

I changed into sweatpants before sitting on top of the covers beside her. Opening my laptop, I finally typed the search I'd been itching to make since the moment we got in the car.

For the next hour, I read everything I could about alcoholism. The disease, the traits, the fucking devastating effects it had on a person's mind, body, and life.

By the time I got to the effects that children of alcoholics faced, my heart felt like it had been shredded to pieces.

Hypervigilance: Check.
Low-self esteem. Check.
Fear of conflict. Fucking check.
And the list went on.

Fear of abandonment, perfectionism, chronic anxiety, trust issues, and people-pleasing tendencies.

Cassie checked off every single fucking box.

All these things I'd been thinking were personality quirks were signs of fucking trauma that I hadn't even guessed at.

She was fucking traumatized from an upbringing I couldn't protect her from, and it bled into every area of her life.

I slammed my laptop shut, breathing heavily as I looked over to where she slept beside me.

I leaned down on my side, staring at her face only inches from mine, her features finally relaxed in the safety of sleep. I trailed my hand through her hair, feeling so beyond grateful she was here beside me and not anywhere else in the world right now.

I thought back to the promise I'd made to Maggie earlier that same night.

Promise me you won't hurt her.

She had asked me as if I ever would. As if I was even capable of that, now that my heart belonged solely to Cassie.

I would *never* hurt her. I knew that. But I could go one further. I wouldn't let anything else fucking hurt her, either.

Never again.

CHAPTER THIRTY-EIGHT

Cassie

For a minute, I was in heaven.

There was an arm wrapped snugly around my waist, a warmth radiating from the body next to mine, and a feeling of utter security that I leaned into in the early moments of waking up.

But then I realized.

Dave and I had broken up. And he'd never smelled like clean winter air or felt like safety, not like this.

My eyes shot open, seeing that it was Liam's bed I was in, and his arm slung over me.

And then the humiliation hit.

I'd told him *everything*.

Things I'd never even told Dave. Why had I done it? *Because Liam had asked.*

And some part of me had trusted him.

But now, the same fear crept back in. He wasn't permanent. He was going to leave. I had shown him too much, and it was going to overwhelm him, and I'd lose the only good thing going on in my life.

But here he was beside me.

For now.

But last night… his hands had been on me, my body curled around him. He held me and let me cry on him and let me fall asleep in his bed.

That had to mean something, didn't it?

My phone buzzed by the bed and I scrambled away, leaving the room. I wasn't ready to deal with waking up Liam and seeing any regret on his face over the intimacy of last night.

Maybe he had just comforted a girl who he knew was an emotional trainwreck, and that was all there was to it. I didn't know for sure, and I wasn't ready to find out.

In the living room, I looked down at my phone. Maggie had texted, asking if I wanted to grab a coffee. Relief washed over me, grateful for the opportunity to escape a morning filled with awkward conversation with Liam about how I'd dumped an entire life's worth of trauma on him.

Get ready. Be there soon.

Maggie Brynn was probably the prettiest girl I'd ever seen. The type of girl whose hair always shined, skin always glowed, and makeup was somehow effortlessly perfect, no matter what.

But lately, she was radiant. And I think it had something to do with the new hockey boy that she was dating.

She looked happy and healthy and… in love.

And I wasn't going to put a damper on that by talking about my same old issues that never seemed to go anywhere.

So, when she asked about my mom, I tried to give her the briefest rundown, if only so I didn't have to dwell on it either.

"It's the same old thing." I sighed. "She'll probably be out in a few days, then right back in the hospital in a few months."

"I'm sorry, Cass," she said, green eyes welling up with sympathy, the same way her brother's had last night. "It sucks."

"Yeah," I brushed it off. "But enough of that. Tell me about you and the beautiful man you had wrapped around your finger last night."

Maggie beamed.

"It's going good," she trailed off devilishly, leaving much to be desired.

"I'd say more than good." I laughed, raising my brows at her giddy smile.

"He makes me laugh," she said wistfully. "And there's something about him that just feels like a real person. There are no weird pretenses or acts he's trying to put on. He's just him. He actually reminds me a lot of you in that way."

"Maggie Brynn, are you telling me you're in love with me?" I joked.

"You know you're my number one, always." She winked across the table.

Warmth spread through my chest. Sometimes, I tricked myself into thinking I was alone in the world. That if I didn't have my mom, I'd be completely lost. But every time I saw Maggie, it was a reminder that maybe the world wasn't as bleak as my mind sometimes convinced me it was.

"But I have to admit, I am getting a little jealous," she started, smirking at me knowingly.

"Jealous of what?" I rolled my eyes playfully.

"I'm starting to worry that I'm not your favorite

Brynn anymore." She feigned a pout.

I froze, staring at her wide-eyed. "What do you mean?"

"I mean, there's something going on between you and my brother, and you're holding out on me with the details."

"Nothing's going on," I said immediately.

"Bull," she countered. "You sound like him."

Oh my God, had she mentioned something to him? Did he think I had a big, stupid crush on him while I was living in his house?

"Maggie—"

"No." She held a hand to stop me. "You can't convince me that there's nothing going on after I watched my brother flip the hell out the way he did last night."

"It's not like that." I shook my head, flailing as I tried to deny it.

"Okay, then, how's apartment hunting going?" She raised a brow, daring me to answer.

"I—" I paused. "I haven't looked in a while."

"Ha!" She slammed her hands down on the table. "And why not?"

Because I don't want to leave him.

"I'll tell you why," she jumped in. "It's because you looove him, too. Don't you?"

I stared at her. She stared at me. And then I groaned, hiding my hands in my face as if I could make the world disappear around me.

"*I knew it!*" She giggled maniacally. "I knew it, I knew it, I knew it!"

"Please stop," I begged, peeking out through my fingers. "It's so humiliating. I feel like a fangirl with a big stupid crush."

"*What?*" Her jaw dropped. "Cassie, *no*. He's totally obsessed with you. I can tell."

"I don't know," I said while my stomach fluttered at her words. "I mean, weren't you the one telling me how he's not into any of that stuff?"

"That's why I can tell that this is different. I've never seen him act like this."

"Why?" I asked the question I'd been holding back for too long.

"Honestly," she said, "I think it has a lot to do with our dad. Liam would never admit it, but his leaving really screwed him up. It screwed us both up."

I nodded, understanding all too well the trauma that a parent's absence could inflict on a child.

"That's why I thought he'd want to see him now. For closure, or healing, or whatever." She shrugged. "But he still has that wall up."

I didn't tell her, but I understood where he was coming from. There were some things you couldn't forgive, and if he didn't want to, my support was fully behind him in that decision.

"What about you?" I asked, not wanting to touch whatever was going on with Liam and his father. It was none of my business. "How's it going with you guys?"

"Really good," she admitted with that smile that seemed glued to her face lately. "I think that's partially why I'm doing so well with Brody. It's stupid, but I feel like my dad being gone has sort of impacted every area of my life without me even realizing it. And now? I don't know. I feel like everything is falling into place."

I reached across the table to give her hand a squeeze. "I'm so happy for you, Maggie. Really, I am."

"And I'm happy for *you*," Maggie said in turn.

"Me?" I laughed. "Why?"

"Because I have a feeling that Liam isn't going to give his heart away more than once, which means you and I are going to be sisters!"

I choked on the coffee I'd been sipping, feeling it all the way in my nose.

"Don't you think you're jumping the gun a little bit?" I raised my brows at her in bewilderment.

"Not even a little," she said and took a sip of her coffee like her words weren't on the verge of sending me into cardiac arrest. "Just wait. You'll see."

I wasn't going to hold my breath on that.

CHAPTER THIRTY-NINE

Liam

Leaving for an away game almost immediately after all the shit that happened with Cassie felt like a betrayal to her.

She promised she was fine. That everything with her mom was stable and that she'd be so busy with work that she wouldn't have time to think about anything else. Apparently, they were making turkey crafts for Thanksgiving, and it would take a lot of her time and energy.

But the whole time I was gone, I missed her like she was a missing limb. I texted her constantly. I even watched that show she liked so much just to be reminded of her. Not as if I needed a show to do that, but it made me feel like she could be in the same room in some bizarre sort of way.

When we finished the game, I saw a string of texts from her commenting with horribly incorrect terminology on plays I made throughout the game. My heart nearly burst out of my chest.

I'd never had anything like this before. I didn't think I ever would again. Which is why I had to be really fucking careful not to screw it up.

Cassie had a lot of shit going on, and as much as I was prepared to tell her how I felt that night at the gala, I knew now more than ever that the slightest wrong move on my part might send her running out of my life forever.

I couldn't handle that. I just couldn't.

So I had to wait it out and give her time to breathe.

Which is why it made zero fucking sense that I booked a flight home right after the game instead of waiting to travel back with the rest of the team.

I was quite literally feening for this girl and there weren't any options left to reel myself in. It was past that point.

I knew she'd be sleeping when I opened the door, but it settled something inside of me to know that at least we'd be under the same roof. At least I could see her when she woke up instead of another night staring at the ceiling of a hotel room listening to the symphony of Brody's loud-as-hell snores.

Walking into the apartment, I wondered how I could have ever gone home for the past five years without her being here.

But she'll be gone soon if I don't figure out a way to keep her.

The thought had been haunting me. How did I get her to stay? To want to be here with me? I knew everything with Dave was fresh, but if I didn't push her, and if we kept the whole thing in the roommate category... would that help my chances of keeping her here?

I had to figure it out fast before she hit me with more of those apartment listings that felt like I was being served fucking divorce papers.

Wearily, I opened my bedroom door, restraining myself from going upstairs to peek in and make sure she was sleeping okay.

The second the door opened, my heart stopped.

The bed wasn't empty. A small figure was curled up beneath the comforter, only visible by a bump in the dim light.

For a minute, I wondered if someone had broken into the apartment to sleep in my bed. It was out there but not unheard of. I heard it happened to Taylor Swift once.

But then, the figure shifted, and it was Cassie who blinked back at me in the darkness.

"Liam?" She sat up abruptly, panic evident in the tense set of her shoulders. "I didn't know you were coming back tonight."

I bit my lip to keep from smiling.

She was in my bed. Cassie was sleeping in *my* bed.

"Got an early flight," I said, moving closer to the bed to get a better look at her.

I didn't need the lights on to know how deeply she was blushing.

"I'm *so* sorry, Liam," she said, hiding her face in her hands. "This is so humiliating. I thought you were coming home tomorrow. Not that it's an excuse for sneaking into your bed like a creep, but—"

"Shhh," I told her, reaching a hand out to gently push her back down into bed, "It's okay. I'm glad you're here."

More than fucking glad.

"No, it's not. I should leave," she said but remained exactly where she was.

"Are you comfortable?"

She nodded hesitantly. "But now that you're back, you'll be wanting your bed back, of course—"

Had she been in here every night?

"So, I should go."

"Don't," I said, falling onto the bed beside her. "I want you to stay."

"You want me to stay?" she repeated incomprehensibly.

I nodded. "I really do."

Cautiously, she settled back under the covers.

"Are you sure?" she asked, peering over at me.

There was a huge gap in the space between us, but I could still feel the warmth radiating off her. Or maybe it was just my body about to light itself on fire from the pure joy of finding her here.

"Hey, Cass?" I said after a few minutes of silence.

"Yeah?" she breathed.

"I missed you."

She was quiet so long I thought she might be asleep, but then, in a voice so soft I barely heard it, she whispered back, "I missed you too."

And with the slightest motion, she pressed against me until her head was against my chest, and my arm was falling around her torso.

It was the fastest I'd ever fallen asleep in my life.

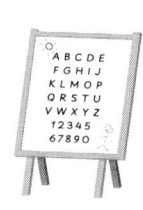

CHAPTER FORTY

Cassie

I wasn't sure when I became a hockey girl, but suddenly every home game the Harbor Wolves had, my butt was in a seat, and Maggie was in one beside me.

Though *she* had a better reason to be here than me. She had a brother *and* a boyfriend on the team. I just had a roommate.

Not that Maggie saw the difference.

"So, any love declarations yet?" Maggie asked a moment after Liam scored a goal.

"Sorry, but no." I laughed.

"Really? I figured by now there would be since you guys have been inseparable lately."

"Not true."

"Oh, you're not?" She raised her brows in a challenge. "What about all the *'Liam and I are cooking dinner,'* or *'Liam and I just ran to the grocery store'* or *'Sorry, Maggie, I can't hang out. Liam and I are watching a movie on the couch like we're a 40-year-old married couple.'*" She rolled her eyes at the last part.

"Stop." I groaned. "It's good to be friends with the person you're living with."

"You're wearing his jersey." Maggie arched a brow with a smirk.

"To support him!" I said in a high-pitched voice. "It doesn't mean anything!"

I didn't tell her that he'd insisted.

I also didn't tell her that I'd been sleeping in his bed every night for a week.

There was no point. Besides some very much-needed cuddling, he hadn't so much as kissed me, which only proved what I already suspected. He didn't like me, and whatever was happening between us was strictly platonic.

"Whatever." She held her hands up. "I'm going to let you two figure this out yourselves."

"Thank you," I said, doing a double-take when something on the ice caught my eye.

As always, whenever we watched a game, my eyes were always glued to number twenty-six. I could spot him in seconds, wherever he was on the ice, no matter how fast he was moving.

That was why, when a player from the opposing team body-slammed someone against the ice, I knew at once that it was Liam.

I let out a shriek, flinching as if I were the one who took the hit. It was drowned out by the sound of the entire arena gasping with me.

"Calm down, Cassie." Maggie put a hand on my knee to stabilize me, but I could see even she looked concerned about the intensity of the crash.

"What the hell was that about?" I asked Maggie, never taking my eyes off Liam, who used the weight of his shoulder to push the guy off of him.

"It's their rival team," Maggie explained, "These games tend to get a bit more… aggressive than most."

"That was a targeted hit, Mags!" I yelled, standing from my seat, wishing I could break the glass to get to him.

The crowd was roaring as Liam and the other player went at each other until eventually, they both dropped their gloves to the ice.

"What are they—why are they doing that?" I asked, panic rising in my voice. "Why aren't they stopping this?"

Both Liam and the other player were throwing punches like wild while the ref just skated around them, watching.

"It's hockey. Fights are encouraged."

To my surprise, the roars of the crowd weren't ones of protest—but, like Maggie said, encouragement.

"This is crazy!" I looked at her in absolute panic. "This is like The Hunger Games! You have to stop them!"

"Cassie, sit down." She tugged me back into my seat. "Before you give yourself a heart attack."

"I can't watch," I said, hiding my eyes. But somehow, not knowing what was happening was worse. Especially when the crowd "oohed" and "aahed" at things I couldn't see.

I opened my eyes just in time to see a fist connect with Liam's face. I imagined the crunch it made and screamed when I saw blood pour from his nose.

I covered my mouth to stifle the gasp, panic settling in my chest. The other guy had gotten his fair share of bangs and bruises, but *he* wasn't bleeding the way Liam was. My hands curled into fists by my side as I watched the refs finally break it up.

"Is he going to be okay?" I frantically asked Maggie.

"It's just a nosebleed," Maggie said. "Trust me, he's had worse."

"*Worse?*" I asked, appalled. "Hey! Why aren't they taking him off the ice?"

"Because the game isn't over," Maggie responded as if it were obvious.

"But he's hurt!" I said, watching as they merely wiped the blood away and sent Liam back out to play.

Maggie laughed.

"I don't know if I can keep coming to these games if it gets worse than this."

"Protective girlfriend vibes." Maggie nodded. "How cute."

I didn't bother to deny it.

The game lasted another excruciating fourteen minutes.

Thankfully, Maggie knew which hallway to bring us to that would lead us directly to Liam. She brought us to a restricted section, flashing her last name to get us past the security guards, but I didn't even worry that we were going to get in trouble the way I usually would. I just needed to see him.

The hallway was crowded with hockey players filtering in and out, staring at Maggie and me like the intruders we were as we infiltrated the space outside their locker room.

A door opened a few dozen feet away, and Liam walked out.

"Stay cool," Maggie said, but I was already running.

"Liam!" I called as I rushed toward him.

His eyes jerked to mine in shock, widening slightly as I moved toward him. My hand came up, reaching out to touch the bruise blooming on his face already.

"Cassie," he breathed, leaning into the palm of my hand on his cheek.

"Oh, God." I bit my lip. "This looks awful."

"Not so bad," he said, green eyes blazing into mine.

"Are you okay?" I scanned the length of him. "I was so worried. I thought that guy broke your nose."

I fumed, anger igniting at the thought of his rival player. If I were five inches taller and one hundred and fifty pounds heavier, I would've let that guy have it.

"I've had worse." He laughed softly.

"So I've heard," I muttered under my breath, still stroking his cheek.

"Hey!" Liam's teammate called. "Get a room!"

Liam scowled at him as he passed by.

"He's just mad because he doesn't have a beautiful girlfriend here to worry about him," another chimed in.

"You're right," The first one sighed dramatically. "That's exactly it. Hey, Cassie. When you're sick of him, want to give me a call?"

"Get the hell out of here." Liam swatted the air where his teammate had been a second before.

Then he turned back to me, face relaxing when he saw the way I was still scanning him for bodily harm.

"Relax," he said, shaking my shoulders. "I'm fine."

"Do you promise," I asked, reaching up just once more to trace the injury.

"I promise," he responded absolutely. "Are you ready to go home?"

Liam always referred to it as home, which made my chest ache as a reminder that I didn't have one of those. At least not a permanent one. But what I did have was a mother who needed to be picked up from the hospital.

She'd called before the game, but I'd risked the wrath she might have for me by not coming the second she called, telling her that I was at a hockey game and would be there when it was over.

Still, the entire time the clock ticked, I panicked, worried about the reaction I would get showing up late to pick her up. For my whole life, we'd run things on her timeline, but now? I figured I needed some things on my own terms if I was going to hold onto any semblance of a normal life.

"Actually, I, uh." I looked around nervously, trying to make sure no one was listening. "I'm not coming to the apartment."

He stilled immediately, face going slack.

"Where are you going?" he asked off-handedly.

I looked around once more before answering. "I have to pick my mom up. She's getting discharged today."

"That's great." For some reason, he let out a breath of air, relaxing his posture. "I'll drive you."

My body tensed at those words.

"No, thank you. It's okay." I shook my head violently.

There was absolutely no way I was letting Liam anywhere near my mother. Her behaviors were unpredictable, and her moods were tumultuous at best.

I knew that after going through withdrawal, she'd at least not be slobbering drunk, but the fear of what she might do was always with me.

"Why?" he asked.

"Because I don't want to put you out."

"Nothing you could do would ever put me out. I want to take you."

"She lives far out of the way. It might take time for them to finish her discharge papers…"

"I don't mind. I can drive you."

"I don't want you to," I blurted out.

He flinched, and I immediately felt like the biggest jerk in the world.

"Oh," he said, "Okay, then."

"I didn't mean it like that." I sighed.

"It's fine," he said, a wall going up between us.

"It's just that I'm embarrassed," I admitted,

"Embarrassed?" His whole demeanor changed, going from closed off to perplexed in seconds. "Of what?"

"Of my mom," I said, stepping closer to him to shield myself because somewhere along the way, *he* had become my safe harbor, and I found solace in his touch.

Even though he was upset with me, he still took me in his arms, letting me hide against his chest as he questioned.

"Your mom?" His voice sounded confused. "Why would you be embarrassed about her?"

"She can be aggressive. And blunt. And sometimes really rude. But other times, she's fine." I groaned. "I don't know. It's complicated. I just never know how she's going to be, so it'll make me more anxious bringing you into that situation when I don't even know what to expect from her."

"She's not a reflection of you, Cassie," he said softly, hands running through my hair. "She could set my car on fire, and I wouldn't hold it against you in the slightest, okay?"

I snorted at his dramatics. "That's only because you have like a million dollars to afford a new one."

"Well, yeah. That helps." He laughed, and I could picture his eyes rolling as he said it. "So, will you let me take you? Please?"

I couldn't fathom it. That Liam Brynn, who had just been a superstar on the ice, whose face had just been blown up on a Jumbotron while thousands of people cheered for him, was asking to be part of my messy life.

"Fine," I relented, sagging against him. "But don't get scared off by her if she's acting up. I promise I won't let her hurt you." I meant it to be teasing but also sort of a warning.

Dave had only ever met my mother a handful of times in our six-year relationship, and those few times had been too much for him. I couldn't bear the thought of Liam taking off because of something my mom said or did in his presence.

But Liam apparently didn't know the extent of what she could be like. I had explained it to him, but that was different than seeing it in person.

"The only woman who can hurt me is you," he said as casually as if it were something he said every day. "Besides, I already took a few hits tonight. What's a couple more?"

CHAPTER FORTY-ONE

Liam

I'd never been much of a fan of hospitals. For me, every time I'd been there was for some hockey injury I'd gotten growing up, which, at the time, always served to remind me that one bad injury could put me out of the game forever.

But watching Cassie walk into the hospital to go pick up her mom reminded me just how lucky I'd had it. I hadn't dealt with any serious injuries or diseases. The most I'd gotten in my life was a broken bone.

But Cassie? I'd gotten the feeling she'd been through this all before. And it put things into perspective about how good I'd had it without ever knowing.

My eyes were glued on the door the entire time since Cassie went in. She had insisted that I wait in the car, and though I wanted to be with her every step of the way, I couldn't begrudge her that request. Not when she'd already let me drive her here.

When they came out together, I stilled. Her mother looked shockingly like Cassie, same blue eyes, same blond hair—but the resemblance only served to make the differences all the more jarring.

Cassie's mother looked weathered in a way that had nothing to do with age. Her face was hollow, her body gaunt. Her skin had a jaundice to it that was painful to look at. One look at this woman, and it was obvious that she'd spent years fighting a battle against her own body.

It was difficult to see her and not imagine how much it pained Cassie every time she looked at her mother. I couldn't imagine looking at my mother and knowing that everything that was wrong with her was her own doing.

They approached the car, and I panicked. Did I get out of the car to help them? Did I stay in so it didn't look like I thought they needed my help?

Shit, I didn't know what to do. I'd never met a girl's parents before. Especially not under circumstances like these.

After a moment's hesitation, I unbuckled my seatbelt, choosing to lean against the car as they approached.

"Hi," I said, feeling awkward as hell when I didn't know how to address her.

Cassie's mom paused in her tracks, looking at me warily and then at Cassie with furrowed brows.

"You didn't tell me you had a friend here," she said, almost accusingly.

"This is Liam," Cassie said, looking every bit as wary as her mother looked. "He offered to drive us."

"No Dave?" she asked.

"I don't want to talk about it now," Cassie said, climbing into the front passenger seat.

"Nice to meet you." I looked her mom in the eyes, noticing the yellow tint to her skin and the wrinkles that framed her eyes as I pulled the backdoor open.

"You, too." She offered me an uneasy smile before getting into the back, looking around as if she were a mouse caught in a trap.

I started the car, following suit with the silence. I decided to let the two of them set the scene for how the ride would go. I was so out of my element that it wasn't even funny.

"Are you still staying with Dave?" her mother asked after a moment, and Cassie tensed.

"No," she said in a way that left little room for questions.

Still, Cassie's mom persisted.

"Does that mean you're coming home then?"

I twitched. No, the hell she wasn't.

She was already home. With me.

She hesitated. "I don't know yet."

My heart sank.

Cassie's hands moved against the radio dials, frantically switching the stations at a rapid speed.

Without thinking, I reached over, sliding my hand over hers. Gently, I guided her fingers away from the dial, back to her knee, and left my hand resting there on top of hers.

It's okay, baby. You're fine.

She turned her attention out the window, but her knee had stopped jittering at least.

"How are you feeling?" Cassie asked, voice thick.

She didn't turn to look at her mother when she asked, just continued staring off at some distant point.

"Oh, I'm fine," her mom answered back. "I'm glad to be out of there. You know hospitals, making such a fuss over nothing."

Cassie stiffened, and I used my thumb to rub circles on top of her hand.

"I was thinking," Cassie started, "that we could talk about some of the rehab programs. I've been researching and found a few good ones—"

"What?" Her mom laughed. "Don't be ridiculous, Cassie. I was in the hospital with a stomach bug."

I paused at that, confused by her words. I looked over to Cassie for confirmation, and she was wearing an expression of absolute outrage.

I'd seen Cassie in a lot of moods. Happy, sad, excited. But never angry. I wished I could smooth the expression off her face.

"Mom," she said in warning. "Stop."

"Oh, don't start, Cassie."

"Haven't we gone through this enough?" Cassie asked wearily. "You need to get help."

"You're being dramatic." Her mom huffed. "I'm fine."

"That's what you always say, but you're only getting worse." Cassie sounded so broken and lost.

"You don't know what you're talking about. I was sick, now I'm better. They wouldn't have let me go if I wasn't," her mom said, sounding pretty damn sure of herself.

"But—"

"You know, honey," her mom said swiftly, "I'm really glad you have a new boyfriend. This one is very handsome," she said, holding a hand up conspiratorially as if she could block me from hearing.

"I—" Cassie fumbled. "Mom—"

"You know, her last one," Cassie's mom said to me, and I caught her eye in the mirror, "dated her for years and wouldn't propose. Aren't you sorry you wasted all that time now, honey? Just like I told you."

"This isn't about me." Cassie was getting flustered.

I didn't know what to do. My mind was whirling at the turn the conversation was taking.

"And she's so bright, but she's stuck in that little job of hers. I keep telling her she needs to go back to school, find something better."

"I like my job, Mom," Cassie said defensively, every part of her voice tight with tension.

"Don't be ridiculous." Her mom shook her head with a smile. "You'll never be able to support yourself on a teacher's salary."

"She doesn't have to worry about that," I interjected, hating the way Cassie's entire being was deflating right before my eyes. "We do okay."

"Still, I don't want her to end up alone and poor," her mom said. "If she couldn't get the last one to commit—"

"Mom," Cassie's voice rang through the car. "Would you give it a rest? Just stop."

"You're so defensive." Her mom frowned. "I'm just trying to help you, sweetheart."

"I'm twenty-four years old. I make my own decisions," Cassie countered. "I'm so sick of you coming at me because you're embarrassed of your own life."

"I'm embarrassing you?" her mom countered angrily. "You're the one making a scene in front of a stranger!"

I tried to interject, to assure her she didn't have to be embarrassed in front of me, but Cassie was fuming, her voice rising to an octave I'd never heard.

"He's not a stranger. He's Liam. He's my—" Cassie paused. "Stop derailing the conversation. You need to get help. I can't keep living like this over and over again. Worrying about you every second of the day. It's *killing* me." Cassie's voice was pure agony, and I gripped her hand tightly as something inside of me broke.

"You'd think you'd be a little nicer to me. I did just get out of the hospital, you know."

"How do you turn everything around on me every time?" Cassie laughed sardonically. "I'm concerned, mom. I'm scared for you. You're going to die if you don't stop drinking. The doctors told me that three hospitalizations ago. You will *die*."

Cassie's mom fumed silently, turning her chin up and out the window. It was as if she put a wall up to shut Cassie out entirely.

"I never knew I was such a burden to you," she said, voice flat and emotionless.

"Mom, I—" Cassie started but then stopped.

I pulled my car up to the address that Cassie had put into the GPS and turned the car off to show Cassie I wasn't rushing her. She could take her time. Go help her mom settle in.

But the second we pulled up, her mom was already opening the door, as if she didn't want to linger a second more than necessary.

Cassie opened her door, too, but her mom held up a hand to stop her.

"Stay in the car, Cassie," she said firmly. "And don't worry. Next time I need help, I'll make sure not to bother you."

And then she was gone.

Cassie heaved a shaky sigh, shutting the door with a reluctant thud.

I watched Cassie as she stared out the window, trembling as she tried to keep herself together as the small figure of her mom walked up the pathway to the tiny, dark house.

Her mom fumbled with the keys, hands unsteady. It took her a few tries, but eventually, the door creaked open, and she slipped inside without a single glance back.

When the door shut, Cassie dropped her head into her hands and cried, defeat evident in the slump of her shoulders that shook with emotion.

"Cassie," I said softly, wanting so badly to pick her up and take her in my arms. To fix everything for her. But I knew that there was nothing I could do. Nothing Cassie could do.

"She's not going to stop." Cassie sobbed. "She might as well be going in there to die all alone."

I didn't know what to say to that, didn't know what anyone could say, so I unbuckled my seatbelt and reached over for her, pulling her against my shoulder.

"What do you need, Cassie?"

"I want to go," she said, wiping the tears out of her eyes.

"Go where?" I asked.

"Back ho—" She paused abruptly. "Back to your house."

I didn't flinch at the way she refused to acknowledge that somewhere along the last two months, it had become her home too. There were bigger things to worry about.

Instead, I took her hand and brought it over to my lap, taking hold of the wheel to take her far away from the pain of the night.

"Okay," I whispered. "Let's go home."

CHAPTER FORTY-TWO

Liam

It was late, the lights were off, and my hands were occupied with Cassie's hair. She was on her side, slightly curled toward me, while my fingers pulled through the soft strands over and over again.

It calmed me to have her so close. To know she was right beside me. She'd been sleeping in my bed every night, seeming to need me as much as I needed her. And now I knew why. Understood it in a way that I had only guessed at before.

And all I got tonight was a glimpse. A fucking glimpse into the life she'd lived for the last twenty-four years. And this was while her mom was *sober*. I couldn't imagine how much worse off it was when she'd been drinking. How much pain Cassie had had to bear on her own.

Not anymore, I thought, my grip tightening on the back of her head.

There was a level of intimacy that had appeared between us almost overnight since the first time she slept in my bed with me.

I didn't fool myself into thinking it was because she had any real romantic attachment to me, but rather knew that she just needed someone.

I was so fucking grateful that someone happened to me. Accidentally, despite all odds. Thanks to Maggie, of all people. It was so strange to think that without my sister, I never would've met this girl lying in bed beside me.

The thought unsettled me that I almost didn't get this life with her. It had me holding her a little tighter.

Her warmth radiated into me from where our bodies touched, and the smell of her hair overwhelmed my senses. I always waited until long after she fell asleep to let myself drift off with her, not wanting to miss a second of the moment.

Especially not when I knew these moments couldn't last forever.

The panic seized me at the thought of losing her, so strong it felt like anxiety had its grip on my throat.

"Cassie?" I asked into the dark. "Are you awake?"

"Hmm?" She breathed out as I felt the rise and fall of her chest.

"I don't want you to leave," I said suddenly.

She yawned, turning against me, eyes closed.

"I'm here." My grip on her head tightened, guiding it down to the crook of my chest.

"You'll stay with me?" I asked, needing to hear it.

It was the only thing that could stop the incessant pounding of my heart.

"Mhm," she murmured, too sleepily for me to be sure she was conscious of what she was saying.

"For good?" I asked.

She didn't respond, but her arm moved around my body, grabbing hold of my vacant arm and using it to drape it around herself.

Was that an answer? Probably not, but I was too much of a coward to ask her in the daylight. Too scared to hear a refusal to what I needed more than air.

"I need you, Cass," I told her, but by then, she was already too far away to reach.

CHAPTER FORTY-THREE

Cassie

"I need to talk to you," Liam said, the words guaranteed to make my heart stop beating in my chest.

It was morning. I had one leg up on the stool while the other dangled lazily as I ate my bowl of cereal. Everything was normal, and I was oddly relaxed, given everything that had happened with my mom the night before.

But those words… they sent something in me into overdrive.

We need to talk.

About what? About how I'd been here almost two months already?

Or maybe about my perverse lack of boundaries and the fact that I'd taken up permanent residency in his bed every night?

He said he didn't mind, but I should've known he was just being polite. I mean, how often did *I* tell people I didn't mind something when I clearly did?

"About what?" I asked, preparing for the blow.

"Thanksgiving," he said, and everything in me relaxed.

"Oh," I said in relief, though my heart still hadn't managed to return to a normal rhythm yet. "Next time, please don't start a sentence with

'We need to talk.' That's practically code for *'I'm breaking up with you.'"* I played it off humorously before cringing and realizing that maybe he'd read too much into that.

He raised a brow at me.

"That was a joke." I blinked at him. "I mean, obviously. It's not like we're dating. I only meant that's a surefire way to get someone's anxiety up."

He stared at me, smirking.

"Anyway," I said, my voice high-pitched, "What about Thanksgiving did you want to talk about?"

He cleared his throat. "I want you to come with me," he said, clearing his throat awkwardly. "To my family's house."

"What?"

Whatever I was expecting him to say, it wasn't that.

"I don't know if you had plans with your mom or whatever. But I was hoping that you'd come with me."

I immediately felt my walls going up. He felt sorry for me. He'd seen my mom, seen our dynamic, and now he was giving me a pity invite.

Heck, he'd probably never kick me out of his apartment because he was too much of a nice guy and felt sorry for me. I couldn't handle it.

"Liam," I said warningly. "No."

"Why not?" he asked.

"Because. It's your family."

"Yeah, like my sister Maggie, who happens to be your best friend."

"She doesn't want me at her family's Thanksgiving!" I said aghast.

"Like hell she doesn't." Liam let out a mixture of a scoff and a laugh.

I shook my head. "No, Liam. I'm not intruding."

"What are you going to do instead?" he asked.

"I was just going to stay here and—"

Watch movies? Eat Chinese takeout? Cry?

"Yeah, to hell with that. You're coming with me."

"No, I can't."

"Fine, then I'll stay here with you."

"Liam, you have to see your family."

"I'm not going without you," he said in a way that let me know this was a hill he was prepared to die on.

I pressed my lips together, wanting to fight him on it but wanting even more to just give in. To finally have a normal holiday for once in my life that wasn't fueled by alcohol and screaming.

"Geez." Liam ran a hand through his hair. "You're acting like it's the most unappealing offer in the world."

"No," I was quick to correct him. "Actually, the opposite."

He lit up. "So, you'll come?"

"Yeah," I agreed. "I'll come."

"Great." He beamed at me as if I'd just gifted him the moon. As if *he* wasn't the one doing *me* a favor.

I exhaled. Holidays were always a time of tension for me. Even before anything happened, I felt it in my body. The anxiety building. Not knowing what would happen or who would be the first to erupt. Not knowing what was going to send my mom over the edge.

But considering how laid back Maggie and Liam both were, they probably had perfectly normal Hallmark movie holidays. And at least for one holiday, I'd get a glimpse into what a normal family looked like. Even if I would never have it for myself.

"And just so you know," he added, "if I ever start a conversation the wrong way again, I promise it won't ever be the kind you were thinking."

The breakup one? I thought to myself, blushing.

Of course it wouldn't.

Because we'd never be dating, right? That's probably what he was trying to say.

It didn't mean anything more than that.

I felt jittery and on edge, all the time again. It was weird, the codependency I had with my mom, even after all these years of being out of the house.

But after a life spent obsessing over what substances another person put inside their body, old habits died hard.

When I was with Liam, it was different. I felt at ease, relaxed. I knew he would take care of me. But the moment I was left on my own, my brain spiraled back into old habits.

Was she at home drinking now? Was she okay? How long until she was back in the hospital?

It made me scattered in a way that started to interfere with my life. Which I guess is why I showed up to work absolutely fumbling my way through the morning.

My bag flung across my left arm was overflowing as a result of me shoving stuff in it rather than taking the time to organize it. My left arm was occupied, cradling my coffee and water bottle while trying to grab my lanyard out of my bag.

All in all, I looked like an utter disaster as I tumbled toward school.

"Do you need a hand?" Marissa asked, coming up from behind.

"No, I'm good, thanks."

"Here, I got the door." She laughed easily, badging us inside and letting me go ahead of her.

"Thanks," I told her genuinely, slightly surprised by the smile on her face.

It wasn't the usual subtle sneer or look of judgment that I'd grown so used to seeing on her. The one that made me squirm under her gaze and try to shrink into myself.

Today, she simply smiled at me. No condescension. No assessing glares.

We walked in together, and I tried to walk ahead to avoid any awkward interactions, but she fell in step with me.

"I just wanted to say, about the other day—"

I froze.

I'd spent my life typically ignoring the aftermath of arguments. I simply followed suit, however they chose to interact with me afterward.

My mom would usually pretend it didn't happen, and we'd go back to normal. Dave was pretty similar.

To be honest, it was easier. Less awkward. Less embarrassing. It made it so you didn't have to dig up the ugly feelings all over again. It was simply swept under the rug.

Marissa, however, didn't seem like that type of person. I should've known, given her history of blunt comments.

"Oh, it's okay," I said, trying to escape from whatever this conversation would entail.

"No, it's not." She shook her head. "I think I've been a little unfair to you. I don't know why. I mean, I don't even really know you."

I paused to look at her.

She let out a small laugh. "Maybe I'm just getting cranky in my old age," she joked, even though she couldn't have been more than her early thirties at the most. "But I think, sometimes, it's hard watching someone who seems like they have it all together when I feel like I'm barely keeping my head above water most days."

"Trust me, I understand that feeling more than you know," I huffed.

"I'm sure you do," she said. "Everyone has shit in their lives they deal with, right? I guess I just never thought about yours when you come in all sunshine and rainbows every day."

I stared at her, shocked by the words coming out of the mouth of the woman who had barely tolerated me for the past few months.

"What I really wanted to say was, I'm sorry I've been a bitch. I really don't mean to be."

"Oh." I exhaled shakily. "It's okay. Really."

"You're not a very good liar, did you know that?" She laughed gently.

I blushed, shrugging my shoulders.

"Honestly, it was hard feeling like everyone here hated me, so it'll be nice to have at least one friendly face around now."

She paused in her steps.

"What?" She gasped. "Cassie, no! Everyone here loves you, which I guess also set me over the edge a little. Everyone raves about how you're the most patient, kindest kindergarten teacher they've ever seen," she gushed. "If anything, people think you're a little shy, but no one hates you. In fact, everyone wishes they had a chance to get to talk to you more."

Was that true? Had I spent my entire time at this school avoiding people I thought hated me for no reason? I could've spent the last few months building friendships, but I was so stuck in my head that I'd gotten in my own way.

"Come eat with us at lunch today," she suggested with a smile. "I think everyone would like that a lot."

"Really?" I grinned, feeling like a middle schooler who'd finally been accepted into an inner circle. "That would be—"

I paused, looking down at the belongings I carried.

"No!" I whined. "I forgot my lunch at home."

She laughed. "That kind of day?"

"You have no idea," I muttered under my breath.

"At least your outfit is fabulous." She gave me the once over in a way that no longer intimidated me. "Where do you find all those cool shirts?"

I looked down at what I was wearing. A graphic tee that said "It's okay to feel all the feels" in huge colorful block letters accompanied by a group of cartoon characters paired with lavender jeans.

"Etsy," I told her, about to go off on a tangent about all the fun websites with teacher shirts when someone buzzed the front door we were currently passing by.

"Holy shit, is that—" Marissa started, but I was already turning to see for myself, my heart stopping when I saw him.

"Liam?" I gasped, staring at his face outside the glass window.

"Why is *Liam Brynn* at our school?" She looked at me with wide, excited eyes. "Dibs on being the one to let him in!" She squealed, running over to the front door while I stood frozen as a statue. Disassociating only slightly.

Marissa opened the door with quite obviously feigned nonchalance, gesturing for him to come inside.

Apparently famous hockey players didn't require a BCI, according to Marissa's logic.

"I'm here for," he said, then spotted me in the crowd of teachers that had paused at the sight of Boston's most recognizable player standing in the lobby.

He looked beautiful in his joggers and backward baseball hat, even in the harsh fluorescent lights of the school.

"Cassie." His eyes landed on me, holding something up in his hand. My lunchbox.

Liam was holding my pink daisy lunchbox, staring at me while the crowd of my coworkers stared at him. Everyone's head whipped from him to me and back to him.

"You forgot your lunch," he said, coming to stand in front of me in an easy stride. "And I know how hangry you get when you don't eat, so I figured I'd better bring it before you burn the place down."

"I do not," I said, pretty sure my face was brighter than a firetruck.

"Yeah, okay." He snorted. "And by the way, I looked inside. A quarter of a bag of crackers and a few slices of cheese is *not* a lunch, so I repacked it for you."

"Not all of us are on an intense meal plan," I retorted, comforted slightly by our easy banter, even though I was hyper-aware of people whispering around us.

"Maybe I should get you on one to make sure you're getting sufficient nutrition," he joked. "In fact, we'll start tonight. I'll make dinner."

"Whatever you say." I rolled my eyes. "Thanks for bringing this." I peeked into the bag. "Liam! Who on earth eats three granola bars?" I sorted through the contents.

A yogurt. A pack of trail mix. A sandwich. The cheese and crackers. An orange, an apple, *and* a banana.

"This is an ungodly amount of food." I cracked up.

"Hey! You get hungry!" He laughed, hands up in defense. "I'd rather you have too much than not enough."

"This was really sweet of you to come out of your way like this," I told him.

"It's not a big deal." He brushed it off, even though it meant everything to me.

"It is," I told him.

I shouldn't have been surprised by anything Liam did anymore, but still, somehow, I was.

"I'll see you at home," he said, reaching out to squeeze my arm once before turning.

"Yeah," I said. "I'll see you tonight."

The crowd that had congregated parted for him as he left and then proceeded to turn to me with wide, expectant eyes as if they'd just witnessed the birth of Christ.

Slowly, I picked up all my belongings, wondering if I could make it to my classroom unscathed, when Marissa came up beside me.

"So *you're* Liam Brynn's mystery girl." She shook her head with a slow-spreading smile. "Okay, so I might hate you again."

But the way she grinned at me told a different story.

CHAPTER FORTY-FOUR

Liam

Something I oddly appreciated about my family was that I wasn't anything special. I mean, not more so than anyone else.

They didn't fixate on my career any more than they would anyone else's. There were passing comments about a recent game or some jokes about how I could be playing better. But honestly? The hockey talk was brief, and I preferred it that way.

I could breathe. Relax. Just be a normal person.

Today more so than ever, because this time, Cassie was with me, and I didn't know what the hell it was about her, but she put me at ease in a way nothing else in the world did.

She, on the other hand, was jittery and restless the entire drive to my mother's house.

"Relax," I told her, stealing a glance. "I promise no one there bites."

"I'm just nervous." She looked over at me with a wince.

"I know," I told her. "But you don't have to be."

She clutched the pie on her lap as if it were grounding her to the earth.

I reached over to interlace our fingers, something I'd noticed always set her instantly at ease. I loved that something as simple as my fingers could have that effect on her.

We pulled up to my mom's and for a second after I turned off the ignition, I just stared at the house I grew up in.

I don't know why, but I'd gotten the hell out of there when I turned eighteen and never looked back. At the time, I didn't really understand why I had the itch to leave as soon as possible. It was nothing against my mom or Maggie. I just felt… resentful, somehow.

Now, I wondered if it had more to do with my dad than I ever realized. I think, on some level, a part of me resented the way we all had to carry on with our lives as if the biggest presence wasn't missing completely. The way we had to go on and pretend the space he'd once occupied was not noticeably empty.

My mom had worked her ass off to raise us, but the memory of him always lingered. Maggie never got over it. Mom sure as hell never got over it. And I guess I hadn't either, much as eighteen-year-old me would've argued otherwise.

But now, the street was lined with cars from various family members, and the thought of going into the house my dad once haunted didn't seem so daunting anymore.

"This is a nice house," Cassie remarked as I came around to open her door.

I snorted. "Who knows what Mom's done to the inside. She's spent the last few months having it redone."

"You don't trust her interior decorating skills?" Cassie giggled.

"No, not at all, actually."

Cassie jumped down from the car, looking on edge as if I were leading her to an execution.

"Relax," I told her, using my hand to guide her to the door. "We're fine."

"It's scary meeting people's families. Especially all at once like this," she admitted.

"They'll love you," I coaxed her.

Who wouldn't?

She smiled up at me, trusting me that everything would be okay.

Before we even got to the door, Maggie was standing there, throwing it open and hurriedly gesturing for us to move faster.

"Thank God you're here," she said when we got to the steps. "I've been waiting by the window for you to pull up."

"Why?" I snorted.

"I wanted to warn you. Mom has gone mental. The entire house looks like a cowboy ranch. She's giving everyone guided tours as if it's Buckingham Palace."

"A cowboy ranch?" Cassie asked at the same time I said, "Guided tours?"

I'd grown up in the house. It wasn't as if I needed to relearn my way around.

But as soon as I stepped inside, I was pretty much eating those words. It was true. The place was unrecognizable.

As if I'd stepped onto the set of an Old West film, the entire place was redone with solid wood, a stone fireplace, a—

"Jesus Christ," I muttered.

"I think it looks… nice," Cassie said.

"We live in Massachusetts." Maggie groaned.

"Is that Liam?" I heard my mother before I saw her. We'd barely entered the threshold, but as always, she had some type of supersense of detecting my presence from a mile away.

"There he is," she gushed, her eyes lighting when she saw me. "My son."

And she pulled me into her traditional hug that always made it seem like she hadn't seen me in years.

"Hi, Mom," I told her, surprised by the strength of a 5'6 woman.

"And Cassie," she said, turning to her beside me. With no hesitation, she pulled her into a hug of equal intensity. "I've heard so much about you from Maggie. I'm so happy you're here with us."

"Relax, Mom, Maggie said.

"Don't break her," I said, only half-joking as I tried to pull Cassie to safety.

"Thank you so much for having me," Cassie responded when she was finally freed of the death grip.

"Thank *you* for coming." My mother waved it off. "It seems you've made quite the impact on *both* my children," she said before turning to me with a smirk.

I hadn't talked to my mom since that day at Maggie's, so I had no idea what she thought the situation was, but it clearly made a hell of a statement that I was arriving here with her by my side.

If Maggie was bringing her friend, that was one thing. But the fact that it was *me*— I had the feeling it sent an entirely different message.

One I didn't really have the desire to contradict.

"Well, what do you think?" Mom gestured around us with eager eyes.

Again, I was forced to take in our setting. Totally unrecognizable from the home I grew up in.

I focused on the antlers above the fireplace while scrambling for something to come up with.

"It's, uh, rustic," I offered.

"It's cozy," Cassie added.

"If you're Butch Cassidy or the Sundance Kid," Maggie muttered under her breath.

"What was that, sweetheart?" Mom asked, still smiling.

"I said you should give Liam the tour while I talk to Cassie all the way over here," Maggie said, lacing an arm through Cassie's and attempting to pull her off into No-man's-land.

Yeah, uh, no.

"Or," I interjected, grabbing Cassie's hand and tugging her back. "I could go introduce Cassie to the rest of the family."

No way was I getting wrapped into one of Mom's all-encompassing conversations on my own.

"Nope," Maggie said. "You have her all the time. My turn."

"Stop it, you two." Mom frowned. "I mean, really. The poor girl isn't a toy for you to fight over."

She looked at Cassie with sympathy.

"I'm sorry you're caught in the middle of my children."

"It's okay." Cassie smiled. "It's nice to be loved."

Then she looked at me and cringed.

"I mean, it's nice to be included. Like part of the family. No—not part of the family like that. But for the day."

"Here's a solution," Mom said, apparently not noticing whatever was malfunctioning in Cassie's brain. "How about I take the three of you on a tour?"

"I already went on the tour," Maggie pointed out grimly.

"And did you think I wouldn't notice how you disappeared halfway through?"

"Halfway through, meaning thirty-two minutes into it," Maggie whispered to Cassie, causing her to giggle. "And I was hoping you wouldn't."

"Come on, let's go," Mom said, charging ahead.

"Giddy-up." Maggie swung an imaginary lasso over her head, and the three of us followed Mom into the depths of her psychotic breakdown.

It got worse the further we went.

"Since when are you into horses, Mom?" I asked, unsettled by the bizarre imagery decorating the hallway walls.

"Oh, you know I've always loved horses," Mom said off-handedly.

"I mean, as much as any other person does, I guess," I mumbled.

"I see the vision you're going for." Cassie nodded along with my mom's excitement. "It's very cohesive."

"Thank you!" Mom beamed.

"You don't have to suck up to her, Cassie." Maggie giggled. "She's going to like you on account of you being the only girl Liam has brought home, ever."

"Anyway," I jumped in. "Here's my old room."

And I opened the door which I was hoping was a portal to another dimension.

But then, I saw that nothing had been changed. It was as if I'd just left last week and not almost ten years ago.

"No redecorating in here?" I asked, voice thick.

"Of course not," Mom said. "It's your space. I wouldn't touch it."

"I just want you to always feel like you have a room here if you ever wanted or needed to come home."

Considering I was an NHL player with a couple of million dollars cushioning me, I knew that Mom knew I would never have to come home.

But still, something about the sentiment touched me.

"Thanks, Mom," I told her, looking around at the time capsule that was my past life.

"Well, now I'm going to be personally offended if you kept Liam's the same and turned mine into a home gym or something."

"Yours is the same too, sweetheart," Mom soothed while she and Maggie walked off down the hallway together.

Cassie trailed behind, lingering with me in the silence of my childhood room.

Posters of hockey players I'd admired still hung on the walls. Trophies lined the shelves. Pictures of me with old high school teammates.

I went over, picked one up, then put it back down with a sigh.

Hockey had been my whole world. It still was... before Cassie entered the scene.

She came up behind me silently, looking over my shoulders at the memorabilia of my life.

"You know," I said, "I spent my entire life praying and working and wishing for what I have right now. And then I spent the entirety of my career scared as fuck to lose it."

"You made it," she said, squeezing my arm encouragingly. "And you're not going to lose it."

"No?" I asked her, suddenly desperate for reassurance. "Do you think there're some things in life we get to keep?"

"I do," She said breathily, staring down at the space between us that was barely existent. "Especially you."

"Why me?" I asked, feeling breathless as I looked down at her lips.

My hands weren't even on her, but I knew in one second they could be. I could grab her and kiss her and make her mine.

Her eyes fluttered, and I could swear she glanced at my mouth, too.

"Because you don't seem like the type to let things you love go easily," she said, and I made up my mind.

I took her by the arms, holding her in place. I let my forehead fall against hers and felt the warmth of her breath against my skin.

I tilted my head, moved toward her, lips hovering an inch away from hers, and—

"Guys?" Maggie's voice came from down the hall, and Cassie jumped away from me as if a bomb had erupted.

"There you are, come on." Maggie's head poked in, staring at Cassie, who looked guilty as hell, and me, who looked—well, I didn't know how I looked, but I felt pissed the hell off, and I didn't doubt my face reflected that.

"Or." Maggie stared between us with assessing eyes. "Maybe don't."

And then she took off like a bat out of hell.

"Cassie—" I started, moving toward her once more.

To explain. To tell her how I felt. Hell, maybe to even try to kiss her again.

"Let's go downstairs," she said in a high-pitched voice. "I can't wait to meet the rest of your family."

I ran a hand through my hair, looking around as I tried to recuperate from whatever had just happened or decidedly *not* happened between us. And what that might mean.

"Yeah." I nodded. "Okay."

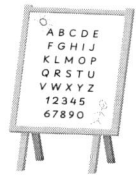

CHAPTER FORTY-FIVE

Cassie

Thank God Liam had a gigantic family because if we had run out of aunts, uncles, and second cousins for me to meet, then I would've had to confront whatever had happened between us in his bedroom, and that was absolutely not something I was ready to do yet.

Yes, I'd been sleeping in his bed. And yes, sometimes we'd hold hands. But that was all strictly comfort. Platonic.

Kissing? There was no way I could fool myself into thinking that was just another way friends comforted each other, the way I regarded everything else we'd been doing.

Because it didn't make sense for him to like me.

It made more sense that I'd made it up in my head, just imagining any tension I'd felt growing between us.

But if I thought busying my mind through conversations with his family would free me from the anxiety, I was terribly wrong.

"How did you two meet?" one of his aunts asked.

I knew right away what she thought. That we were a couple. Because that was a question you asked *couples*. But also, on the surface, it was just a normal question. If I refused not to answer or automatically tried to inform her that we weren't together, that would be way more bizarre. Defensive, even. It would be the type of response that might show Liam every little pathetic feeling I'd been trying to hide.

So I settled on a safe, honest answer.

"I'm friends with Maggie," I offered, hoping that was enough.

"Oh, how perfect." Her eyes lit up. "Well, you two must be awfully certain of each other if you're already living together."

"Oh, no," I said, about to interject and tell it to her straight.

"But when you know, you know. Isn't that what they say?"

"Well, I've got to go introduce Cassie to everyone else," Liam interjected, But he didn't correct her.

Why didn't he correct her?

Was it to save me from the embarrassment of having to tell people the real story of why I was staying with him?

Or maybe he wasn't as bothered by the assumption as I thought he was.

Liam

I felt mechanical in my interactions with my family. Stiff, awkward, like at any moment, one of the screws holding me together would spit out, and I'd crumble.

I could barely focus because the only thing running through my brain was that moment upstairs. I'd been *about to kiss her.* I would've if Maggie hadn't interrupted.

Hell, I wanted to try again right now.

And I could've *sworn* that she was going to let me.

But here, surrounded by my entire family, was *not* the place to unpack that conversation with her.

But my family was apparently hellbent on adding more chaos to the uncertainty of my relationship with Cassie.

"We saw the pictures from the gala," Aunt Kim said. "You two make a gorgeous couple."

"Oh, we—" Cassie started, but my uncle was already cutting her off.

"Can't believe you made an honest man out of him yet." He gave me a wink. "Guess you finally found someone worth leaving bachelorhood behind, huh?"

"Oh, no—" Cassie tried again.

"And look at your beautiful hair," my aunt gushed, "You two will have the most beautiful children."

At that, I actually choked on my own saliva, watching as Cassie turned strawberry red in front of my eyes. I had to drag my gaze away before I did something idiotic—like imagine it.

Oh, wait. Too fucking late.

"Sorry, we know we're embarrassing you," my aunt finally said, noticing the awkwardness that had enveloped the pair of us like a straitjacket. "We're just thrilled Liam is finally settling down."

I should correct him. I should laugh it off.

Now was the time to explain once and for all what the situation was. But I didn't.

Because if she let me, I'd settle down for the rest of my fucking life with this woman.

"Time to eat," Mom called from the other room, sending us the reprieve we so desperately needed.

Cassie visibly breathed out in relief as we walked away from the crowd of relatives drilling us as if they were with the fucking media.

"I'm sorry," I whispered to Cassie. "They're not usually like this."

But what Maggie had said earlier was true. I'd never brought a girl home before, and because of that, Cassie was the biggest deal in my life since I got signed with the Harbor Wolves.

"They're all really nice," Cassie said.

"Nice, but nosey. Just like Maggie."

"You're not like that," Cassie said, almost as a question.

"I'm not nice?" I laughed.

"No!" Cassie blushed. "I mean, yes, you are! I meant the nosey part."

I grinned down at her, squirming.

"You just don't seem curious about, well, anything," she said, hands in the air.

Well, that might be true for most things, but her? I had a feeling I'd never reach a limit on the things I wanted to know about her.

From every detail of her day, to her favorite things to what she thought we'd be doing ten years in the future.

Shut the fuck up. I told my head, knowing I was getting way too ahead of myself.

It's like I was driving a car, and I'd pulled Cassie into the passenger seat and superglued my foot to the gas pedal.

In other words, I needed to chill the fuck out.

"That's because I already know everything." I aimed for light-hearted banter, desperate to mask the route my thoughts had taken.

"I don't doubt that you do." She grinned and then paused in front of the long dining room table.

I pulled out a chair for her, letting her settle into it before sitting in the one beside her.

Maggie slid down into the one on the other side of her, grinning at Cassie as if she were the long-lost sister she'd always wished for when we were kids.

"This is so fun that you're here," Maggie chirped as if she were having a sleepover. "You're going to need to be at every Brynn holiday from now on, just so you know."

On that, we were in total agreement.

"I don't know about that." Cassie laughed. "You don't think it's weird that I'm here with all your family?"

"I'd rather have you here than him." Maggie pointed to me with the fork she'd picked up.

"Thanks, Mags." I huffed out a laugh.

But what I really took note of was the way Cassie fit in between us so naturally. My sister's friend and my... what? I had to know. We couldn't exist in this weird limbo anymore.

Especially not after today, when I saw that look in her eyes. The one that gave me hope there might be a chance for us after all.

"Before we all start eating," my mother's voice pulled me from my thoughts and toward the end of the table where she sat, "I just wanted to get everyone's attention to thank you all for coming again. I know everyone has their own busy lives going on, so it really means a lot to have the family together like this for a meal. Especially my busy children who are living their lives in the city, far away from their mother, who misses them dearly." She dabbed at her eye, apparently already emotional.

"Mom, you literally were living with me for the last three months." Maggie rolled her eyes over the table, sending the relatives into a chorus of laughter.

"Well, I'll miss you all the more now that I'm here by myself," Mom defended. "Okay, okay. Everyone eat. And if you don't like it, pretend that you do to spare my feelings."

The table sounded with the clinking of silverware against plates, and arms were moving haphazardly as everyone reached for food across the table.

While everyone was caught up in conversation, I let myself look at her. Really look at her without any preconceptions.

I watched the way the glow from the chandelier caught in her hair, turning the ends of those curls golden. The way her blue eyes, which I loved so much, went soft when she was listening, sharp when she was amused. I noticed how every emotion she felt could play across her face in such a distinctly *Cassie* way.

And then she turned, looking up at me with a smile that made me know for certain.

Whatever it took, whatever I had to do, I would do it to make sure that Cassie sitting next to me like this wasn't something temporary.

CHAPTER FORTY-SIX

Cassie

Everything felt strangely like home.

With Dave's family, I always felt distinctly other. As if they knew at any second, he might get rid of me and treated me as such. Hey, maybe they had known all along. They even kept me out of the family photos, even though I would've sworn up and down that we were going to be together forever.

Well, I guess they made the right call.

But here?

I didn't feel as out of place as I feared I would. No one treated me like I was this weird intruder crashing the family party.

And I was sandwiched between Liam and Maggie, who were the two people I loved most in the world.

Cared about. I mentally chastised myself before realizing there wasn't anything particularly wrong with *loving* your friends. That could still be a platonic emotion.

But my feelings for Liam were *anything* but. I realized that now, which is why I couldn't go throwing the "L" word around so casually, even in my head. Otherwise, I'd have another slip-up like earlier in the day and ruin everything.

I didn't get to dwell on my feelings for long because Liam's family had a way of drawing me into the conversations and engaging me completely, so the only thing I focused on was what they were discussing.

This was what normal families were like. This was how it should feel. I wanted it someday. For myself.

Would I ever have that? Sometimes, it seemed like the most unlikely thing in the world, and the thought of never getting it broke my heart more than anything else.

Absentmindedly, I reached for a pot in the middle of the table while listening to one of Liam and Maggie's cousins tell a story from when they were all kids together. I didn't notice how hot it was until my fingers burned at the contact. I winced, pulling my hand off of it and shaking my fingers.

"Careful, baby." Liam reached out, guiding my hand back before taking the pot himself to bring it closer to me.

I blinked up at him, frozen by the word he'd let slip so casually from his mouth. But he avoided eye contact, instead making a sound of clearing his throat before jumping into a conversation with someone across the table.

"So, Maggie. I hear you've been in contact with your old man again," one of the many uncles in attendance said. "How's that going?"

Instantly, I was aware of Liam stiffening beside me while Maggie squirmed uncomfortably in her seat.

Weird. I thought.

"It's fine," Maggie said, trying to shut it down.

Even weirder.

Last I saw her, she'd been over the moon over her recent coffee dates with her dad. I'd never prodded Liam about it, but he was decidedly less than pleased by Maggie's recent contact with their father.

"How's he doing? I'm sure you two had a lot to catch up on." One of the aunts smiled encouragingly.

"Yeah, like twenty years' worth."

Liam's mom had downcast eyes, very focused on the food she was moving around on her plate.

Liam was rigid beside me.

Under the table, I reached out a hand and settled it on his knee. Giving it a squeeze of encouragement.

He relaxed slightly until a moment later when his hand came atop mine and held it in place.

"He's good. It's going good," Maggie said in a flat tone.

Apparently, Liam and Maggie's family were able to pick up on the shift that was taking place in all the Brynn's in the room, and suddenly, the conversation shifted to safer topics.

Liam relaxed fully, but his hand stayed on top of mine. Maggie's eyes were glazed over with some emotion I hadn't seen from her in a long time.

And I wondered if maybe Liam had been right not to reconnect with their father after all.

"Someone needs to take your license away," I shrieked. "Because you are an absolute menace!"

Maggie cackled while her Bowser sent a shell flying directly into the path of my Princess Peach.

We were on the third lap of Mario Kart, and we were neck and neck, but Maggie apparently had the same supersonic athletic ability that Liam was blessed with because she leaned forward and took the lead in the last possible minute.

"I won!" she said, flipping her hair behind her.

"You're a maniac." I shook my head with a laugh. "And I'm done playing."

"Sore loser." She pouted.

"I'm not a sore loser. I played six rounds with you!"

"Well, don't you want a chance to win at least once? I'll go easy on you," she offered in a singsong voice, dangling the Wii remote in front of me.

"Fine, I'll play one more game." I gave, in partially because Maggie was impossible to say no to, but also because I wanted to get a chance to talk to her while the rest of her family was occupied elsewhere.

"So," I started while she set us up for another game. "Not that it's my business, but you seemed a little off when everyone brought up your dad earlier. I thought things were going good?"

She exhaled. "It had been. It is, I guess. I don't know. It might be all in my head, but I feel like…"

"Like what, Mags?"

"I feel like he's only using me to get to Liam. It's, like, all of a sudden, the only thing he ever wants to talk about. How Liam's doing, and if Liam's asked about him, and if he can have tickets to come see Liam play."

"*What?*" I asked. "Does he know that Liam wants nothing to do with him?"

Maggie groaned. "I sort of hinted that Liam wasn't ready yet, but I sort of made it sound like he'd be open to it in the future? I was just so scared of doing something wrong that would send him running again, so I didn't want to be the one to tell him his son never wanted to see him again for the rest of time."

"I'm sorry, Maggie. It sucks that you're in the middle."

"It's whatever," Maggie said.

"I mean, that's crazy, though, that he thinks you'd get him tickets to see Liam play. That's kind of nervy of him, don't you think?"

"Yeah," Maggie said after a minute's hesitation, but her eyes stayed fixed on the screen. "Maybe it is."

Liam

I don't know what my sister did to Cassie, but when I came inside from a game of touch football with my cousins, she was slumped against the couch like she didn't have the willpower to even lift her head for a second longer.

"Post-dinner slump?" I asked, sliding down beside her.

"That combined with the stress of your sister's driving." She groaned.

"What?" I laughed.

"Nothing," she said. "I just need to close my eyes for a second."

"Go for it," I told her, watching the football game flickering across the flat screen in front of us. "We're not getting kicked out any time soon."

The den was empty save for the two of us, the rest of my family no doubt congregating in the more eclectic areas of the house. I watched the game with passing interest for the sake of the holiday. I'd never been much of a football guy, clearly.

I didn't notice how quickly Cassie had fallen asleep until I felt her head fall down against my shoulder. I didn't really realize either that my fingers had been trailing absentmindedly through the strands of her hair, twirling the curls at the end before starting again from the top.

At some point, she shifted, nuzzling closer as she let out a sleepy sigh. My chest vibrated with quiet laughter at the way her face scrunched up in sleep, and before I even thought about it, I leaned down and pressed a kiss to the top of her head.

Shit, did I just do that?

I froze, waiting for her eyes to open and ask me what the hell I was doing. When she didn't, I relaxed.

Thank God she was sleeping because I'd have no words of explanation to offer her. I did it without thinking, like my body was acting of its own accord.

"Look at you guys." Maggie snorted, prancing into the room with knowing eyes. "Practically married."

I stared at her as she sat in the chair across from us.

"You could thank me, you know." She flicked her hair behind her shoulder.

"Maggie," I warned.

"Remember how hard you tried to fight it when I asked if she could stay with you?"

"Would you—"

"And now, look," she interjected, "I found my brother's wife for him."

I couldn't deny anything. I was grateful as hell.

"Soooo," she drawled, "What do you have to say?"

I exhaled, blowing out a breath. I looked down at Cassie at my side for a moment before meeting Maggie's smug gaze once more.

"Thank you, Maggie," I said gruffly.

"Hey, I guess I did have a say in picking out my sister-in-law after all." She laughed and then turned to face the TV.

"Ugh, football." She stuck her tongue out. "Let's watch the Gossip Girl Thanksgiving episode instead."

I didn't get a word in before she reached for the remote, taking control of the television.

But honestly, I was too content with my situation to even care.

Cassie

The sky was an explosion of orange outside the windows of Mrs. Brynn's house, and I wondered if I'd ever grieved a holiday ending as much as this one.

Who knew if I'd ever have another one that gave me the same warm, Hallmark feeling that this day had.

I could lie to myself and chalk it up to the simple lack of tension or argument that had been so commonplace in my family's homes growing up, but I knew better.

It wasn't *just* that. It also had everything to do with the man sitting beside me, looking more like a goofy boy eating his pumpkin pie than the NHL star I knew he was.

"So, you guys," Maggie started around a bite of her apple pie. "What's the move?"

"The what?" Liam asked.

"The plan for tonight. Brody wants to see me after and I thought it would be fun if we all went together."

I stifled a groan. I was exhausted and didn't really have any desire to go to some loud bar or club in the city after the perfectly quaint day we'd just had. Especially not when the idea of going back to the place I was living was now such an appealing concept.

But, still. If Liam wanted to go out with his friend and his sister, I would suck it up and handle it. I looked to him as if he could understand with just a look that I was going to follow his lead.

And what surprised me most was that he was looking at me in the same way. As if searching for confirmation of what I wanted to do. I gave him the slightest shrug and a smile, trying to prove that it was up to him.

He turned to Maggie, and when he opened his mouth in what I thought was going to be confirmation of the plan, he shocked me by saying, "I think we're just going to go home."

Home. I thought, sagging in relief, dumbfounded that somehow Liam could read me like a book in a way no one ever had before.

"Ugh, boring," Maggie said. "You guys really are like an old married couple."

But the way she said it didn't make it sound like a bad thing at all.

CHAPTER FORTY-SEVEN

Cassie

Sometimes, I think I became a teacher to hold onto whatever part of my inner child had been lost to me at the expense of my mother's drinking.

School had always been safe. Predictable. Structured. I didn't have to worry about what anyone was doing but myself. In fact, there were adults there to worry about *me*.

Teachers who noticed if I came without a lunch or walked me down to the cafeteria in the morning to make sure I was eating breakfast.

People who cared about me. People who were responsible. Who made me feel safe. I think some part of me wanted to return the favor, to be that for some other child out there.

And it was true that it still was a safe haven of sorts for me. Kids were gentle in a way that adults weren't. They hadn't yet been burned by the world and hadn't learned yet that they had the power to hurt and be hurt by others in ways that a band-aid wouldn't fix.

But the second I walked out of school for the day, I heard a voice that made every feeling of safety disappear completely.

"Cassie," Dave said, standing in the parking lot outside of my school.

I stared at him, feeling panic settle over me as I thought of an escape route. I could go back inside and wait for him to leave. I could try to book it past him to get to my car and hopefully speed away, but there was always the chance of him coming back another day.

Besides, I was tired of running. Of avoiding confrontation. Especially from someone like him. Whatever he had to say wouldn't be able to affect me because I wasn't giving him any power over me any longer.

I knew it when I finally let myself look at him. The memory of the pain was there, but though I thought seeing him would make the wound reopen, I was slightly surprised to realize that it hadn't.

"What are you doing here?" I asked.

"I've been waiting for you to call," he said, standing there as if I should have a response for whatever the hell he meant by that.

"Why would I call?" I asked, dumbfounded. "We broke up, remember?"

"Yeah, but I thought," he started. "I don't know. Maybe it was a mistake."

His words stopped me dead in my tracks.

A mistake.

The word settled over me.

Had it been a mistake? I'd been with Dave for six of the most formative years of my life. The period between adolescence and adulthood, when I was becoming my own person, discovering who I was and what I wanted.

Some version of me would've married the man in front of me, but now? She felt far away in the deep crevices of the past. She certainly wasn't present for this conversation.

"Don't you think so?" he asked, realizing I didn't have a response. "Haven't you missed me?"

"No," I admitted.

"No?" he countered. "We were together for years, Cass. I thought that meant something to you."

"It didn't mean anything to you when you dumped me over the phone and told me to find somewhere else to live," I snapped.

"I told you, it was a mistake. I didn't realize how much I needed you."

"I don't want someone who needs to lose me to realize they want me.

"Give me a break here, Cass," he pleaded. "We'd been together so long. It's normal to want to know what else is out there."

When he said it, I realized that if it weren't for Liam, I probably would've believed him. I would've sat here and let him convince me that I should take him back. I would've listened to him explain how, after he'd gone out and been with other women, he realized I was who he truly wanted.

But now that I knew what it felt like to be cared about genuinely and completely? I couldn't fool myself into thinking Dave was what I wanted.

"I can't," I said. "You were right to break up with me. Our relationship—it wasn't right. We weren't right for each other."

I didn't tell him that I realized that because of how right it *did* feel with someone who I wasn't even dating. But even if Liam disappeared out of the picture forever, being alone was better than being with a person who I never felt on equal footing with.

"Does that hockey guy really have you wrapped around his finger that tightly?" Dave snapped as if he had read the direction my thoughts had gone to. "We're broken up for a minute, and you jump right into bed with the next available guy?"

At first, I figured he'd seen the pictures. Heard the rumors swirling on the Internet, and then it all made sense. He didn't want me until he thought someone else did. And that hurt more than anything because it wasn't even true.

"It's not like that," I explained, not wanting to let him believe the lie or rub it in his face that I'd moved on with someone else. I just wanted him to be securely in the past. "He's not—we're not," I trailed off, not knowing how to explain. "Liam and I are friends, that's it. He's Maggie's brother. He offered me a place to stay when *you* told me to get lost."

"That's not what he said." He snorted viciously.

"*What?*" I drew back. "When did you see Liam?"

Half of me was convinced it was some type of mental warfare that Dave was weaponizing against me, but I couldn't see the point of it. On the other hand, I couldn't understand why Liam would ever lie to Dave like that and not tell me about it.

"At some hockey game a few months ago," he said. "I figured that you'd get tired of him eventually and come back to me, but apparently, I was wrong. What, are you just after the guy with the fattest wallet, now?"

"I told you," I bit out. "I'm not with Liam."

"And I told you to cut the bullshit because he told me himself that you were."

I stilled. "What are you talking about?"

"Oh, he didn't mention it to you? How he punched me in the face after warning me to stay away from you? Nice guy, you've got there, by the way."

I would've denied it. I would've told Dave to his face that he was a liar, but I couldn't because I remembered the articles that came out about the fight that Liam had gotten into. I remembered Maggie bringing it up herself.

I just didn't know the guy in question was *Dave*.

I had a million questions running through my head. *Why did Liam punch him? Why did he lie about us dating? Why didn't he tell me about any of this?*

But I didn't want answers from Dave, which was strange because he was probably the person I'd spent more time with than anyone else in my whole life.

But he wasn't the person I felt closest to anymore. He wasn't the person I cared about.

That was Liam.

"I have to go," I said, walking past him to get to my car.

"Come on, Cassie," he yelled. "You can't just walk away. You're throwing away everything we had!"

Without wasting my breath for another second on Dave, I drove away, leaving him exactly where he belonged. Behind me.

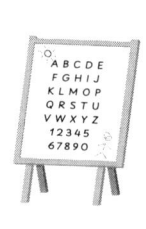

CHAPTER FORTY-EIGHT

Cassie

I hadn't meant to ambush him.

I'd spent the car ride rehearsing what I would say without making him defensive, how I could say it without coming across too strong. How I could segue into it in a natural way without irritating him after he'd already had a long day.

God, I didn't want to ask him. The thought of confrontation always left me a little shaky, but this was Liam. Cool, level-headed, calm, and collected Liam Brynn, who must have an explanation for why he punched my ex-boyfriend in the face.

But I needed to know.

Apparently, I needed to know so badly that the second I opened the door and saw Liam sitting there at the counter, my entire plan of nonchalance went straight out the window.

"You're home late," he said, staring at me with a look of concern. "I was getting worried."

"Did you punch Dave?" The words flew out of my mouth, and before I could apologize and take it back, because of course he wouldn't punch *Dave*, I watched as his face went pale, and I knew.

"What?" he asked, his face expressionless.

"He told me you did, so I'm asking you."

"You talked to him?" His jaw clenched.

"I saw him," I said, feeling a little breathless as I watched Liam stand up and pace. "Just now."

He was silent for a minute, pacing back and forth with both his hands on top of his head. I followed his movements, heart racing in my chest.

"Why?" he asked, pausing to look at me.

"Why what?"

"Why did you see him?"

"He showed up at my work. He wanted to talk."

"I'm sure he did." Liam snorted. "But why would *you* give him the time of day after everything?"

"I couldn't just walk past him and pretend he didn't exist. I owed it to him to hear him out."

"You owe him *nothing*," Liam countered, angrier than I'd ever seen him. "I can't believe he even had the audacity to show up and try."

"So, it's true then?" I asked, holding my breath. "You hit him?"

"Yes," he bit out.

I held my face in my hands. "Oh, Liam. You shouldn't have done that."

"Why not?" he asked. "You care about him that much still? After everything he did to you?"

"No, you idiot," I yelled. "I don't care about him. I care about *you!* You could've gotten arrested for that! It already made headlines because of who you are."

"It doesn't matter." He shook his head. "I don't care."

"You should," I told him. "It's your career."

"It's *you*."

My breath hitched; not sure what he meant by that.

"You told him we were dating?" I asked.

"Yeah, I did," he said without apology.

"Why?"

"Because I wanted him to leave you the fuck alone, but clearly he didn't get the message."

"It doesn't matter." I shook my head. "He didn't bother me."

He couldn't bother me even if he tried because Dave didn't mean anything to me anymore.

"So, what did you tell him?" Liam asked.

"I told him the truth."

Liam let out a sardonic laugh. "And what's that, Cass?"

"That you're my friend's brother and you're letting me stay with you."

Liam's face tightened, and he walked in the opposite direction. I followed him, needing to understand whatever piece of this story I was missing.

"Why do you care if he talks to me? Are you trying to protect me? Because I don't need you to save me from Dave. Not at the cost of your reputation or your career!"

"No, Cassie." Liam spun. " He doesn't get to do this! He doesn't get to want you when it's convenient for him. That's not how love works."

"It wasn't your call to make."

"Are you seriously telling me you would've taken the guy back?" His face dropped. "Did you?"

"No, I didn't!" I said, crossing my arms. "But it would've been nice to know that I had the option if I needed it."

"Screw that, Cassie." He fumed. "You don't need that asshole as a safety net or whatever the hell you think you needed him for. He's a dick, and the best thing he ever did for you was let you go."

"Oh, yeah?" I asked, furious. "If you don't want me to be with him, then tell me who you think I'm supposed to be with."

"No one!" Liam shouted. "I don't want you to be with anyone! And I sure as hell don't want you to think of me as just your friend's brother!"

It was my turn to walk away because I couldn't bear to let him see the look on my face at that moment.

"Wait," he said. "Cassie, I'm sorry."

But I kept walking. I didn't know what was happening between us and I was scared. I was scared of how I felt about him, scared of not knowing how he felt about me. Scared of losing it all the way I seemed to lose everything.

"I'm fine," I told him, "I'm tired."

"Don't do that," he said, voice right behind me.

"Do what?" I asked.

"Don't pretend you're not pissed when I'm the one who screwed up. You *get* to be mad, and you don't have to worry that I'm going to walk away just because you're upset with me."

I froze. How did he know? How did he *always* seem to understand what I was feeling and thinking and worrying about? How had he managed to cut through the surface of everything I was without even trying?

For my whole life, I'd wanted to be seen and understood and noticed, and here was the most beautiful man I'd ever met looking at me like I wasn't some puzzle he had to learn but some innate thing he'd always known.

"So yell at me," he continued, staring down at me with eyes so soft I could melt. "Scream at me. Hit me if you want. I can take it."

"I don't want to hit you," I whispered.

"No?" he asked, bridging the gap between us, until we were chest to chest. "So what do you want, Cassie?"

For a second, something flickered in his eyes—like he was *scared* of the answer I might give.

I let myself look at him, at this face that had become so familiar to me, and before I could stop myself from doing something that had the potential to ruin everything, I surged forward, grabbing hold of him like a life raft in the sea, and I pulled his lips to mine.

For a horrible, agonizing moment, he stilled. Like a statue beneath my touch, Liam froze, and I was convinced my worst fears had come true. I'd ruined everything. I'd made assumptions that were wrong, and now I had destroyed the one good thing I had going for me.

Face flaming in shame, I moved to rip my lips off of his, to apologize, and run immediately to the closest place I could change my name and identity.

But then, he was pulling me in. Impossibly closer and, oh God. He was kissing me back.

I whimpered against his lips, and he groaned, fingers lacing through my hair as if he wanted me the way I wanted him.

I couldn't handle it, couldn't get enough oxygen to my lungs as every fiber of me was overwhelmed with the feeling of him.

I pulled away, looking up at him to try and make sense of what was happening. He stared down at me, green eyes wide and glazed over as if he didn't know where he was or how he'd gotten here.

Somehow, I understood the feeling.

"You kissed me," he stated as if he hadn't processed it yet.

"You kissed me back," I said, letting a finger come up to touch the lips that had just been on his.

"Do it again," he said, breath warm against my face.

That was all it took for us to collide once more.

CHAPTER FORTY-NINE

Liam

Cassie. Cassie. Cassie.

My hands were still tangled in her hair like she'd disappear if I loosened my grip even for a second. Half of me was convinced I'd wake up and find this wasn't real at all—just something my mind had invented to cope with wanting her so badly.

Her lips moved urgently against mine, clutching the fabric of my shirt like she was feeling the same way. Like, maybe she was scared of losing me, too.

"Cassie," I groaned, trying to pull her impossibly closer.

She tasted like summer air and strawberries and fucking sunshine, and I could not get enough of her. And she was mine.

For this moment at least.

The thought made my brain short-circuit because *fuck,* I'd do anything in the world to ensure we could keep doing this for the rest of my life.

"Wait, wait," I said, pulling back slightly, even though it caused me physical pain to break the best kiss I'd had in my life.

"Do you want to stop?" she asked, looking up at me with fluttering eyes.

No. In fact, I very much wanted to do the exact opposite of *stopping*.

"We need to talk about this," I said as she stilled in front of me. "I just want you to know where I stand before we keep going," I said, struggling to string words together when she was staring at me with flushed cheeks, wide eyes, and swollen lips that I'd just claimed as my own seconds ago.

But she needed to know this couldn't be a hookup for me or some type of passing fling. If we were really, truly going to go through with this, there'd be no going back.

"Right," she said, nodding frantically. "I'm so sorry. We should talk. Definitely."

"Jesus, Cass. You don't have to be sorry," I emphasized.

How could I even begin to explain to her that this was what I wanted all along, and now that we were here at this point, I needed to do everything I could to ensure we got to where we needed to be?

"Shit," I said, looking over at the clock. "I have to go." We had a home game tonight and I was already going to be late for the 4:30 time slot Coach wanted us to arrive at.

One thing was for certain, I wasn't going to screw this up with a half-assed conversation. I'd never been good with words, or feelings for that matter, but she deserved for me to lay it all out bare. No questions, no guessing. I needed to tell her flat-out what I wanted from us.

"Right, you should go," she said, backing away as if to give me space that I didn't want.

"Will you come tonight?" I begged, attempting to reach out to her. "We can talk after the game."

"Yeah," she said, but she seemed so far away all of a sudden. "We'll talk later."

Maybe it was because I'd just had her exactly where I wanted her, and now I had to leave. It was unbearable.

"Okay." I nodded, every part of me in overdrive from the turn the night had taken.

I was sure she was feeling a similar type of way, probably needing time to process what had just happened. But *she* had kissed *me*, erasing any lingering doubts I'd had about the two of us.

We were going to do this. We were going to make it work. I knew we would. I could feel it.

"I'll see you tonight," I told her, fighting the urge to kiss her one more time before I left, but I knew if I did that, I'd never get out of this apartment tonight.

"Bye," she said and I wanted to stop and just lay everything bare right then and there.

Stop. I told myself. *You'll see her tonight.*

And then, we'd talk. And after we did, everything would be different.

CHAPTER FIFTY

Cassie

I was no stranger to panic.

In fact, it had become so second nature I was almost comfortable with my spiraling. It let me be aware of any possible dangers that might be lurking where I least expected.

But if I was always expecting something bad to happen, then nothing could truly hurt as much, right?

But tonight, I had lost control completely. I had forgotten to be cautious. I had forgotten to worry about what could happen if I made the wrong move.

And I had. I really, truly had.

I'd kissed *Liam,* and for the life of me, I couldn't understand what had propelled me to do it. And for a moment, I let myself believe he wanted it, too.

Maybe he had. But it probably didn't mean the same thing to him that it did to me. He knew it, and I knew the moment the words left his lips.

We need to talk about this.

I knew what that meant. He was going to let me down easy. He probably saw that I'd fallen head over heels for him completely, the way he saw *everything* about me.

I was an idiot. The next time I saw him, we were both going to have to endure some pity let-me-down-easy conversation about how he really appreciated the kiss, but at the same time, I'd crossed over some major boundaries that there was no way for me to erase.

He wouldn't even be able to avoid me the way he could dodge all the other girls who were obsessed with him because *I was living in his house.*

Which meant he was probably going to ask me to leave, which I should've done a long time ago. I'd stopped looking for apartments which meant I didn't even have a lead on somewhere to go next.

Maggie's mom had been out of her apartment for weeks now, but somehow, I never thought to go stay there instead.

Why? Because I didn't want to impose on her. My best friend. But apparently, I didn't have the same issue about imposing on her brother.

Not anymore. I couldn't stay here another minute after what I'd just done.

I picked up my phone and called Maggie. She answered on the third ring.

"Maggie?" I asked, voice cracking the same way my chest was. "I need to stay with you."

CHAPTER FIFTY-ONE

Liam

Cassie was nowhere to be found, and I was playing like shit. I guess that's what happened when you were too busy scanning the crowd instead of watching the puck.

Where the hell was she?

I missed two clear shots—because apparently, scouring the stands had become my biggest priority.

Maybe something came up.

Maybe she got busy.

Maybe she was in trouble.

"Get your head in the game, man," Brody muttered, whirling past me to cover my mistakes.

But I didn't. We lost by four points, and no one bothered hiding who they blamed.

I didn't care. The second I hit the locker room, I grabbed my phone. Called Cassie. Felt my stomach drop when it went straight to voicemail.

I showered fast, then checked again. Nothing.

I waited as long as I could before trying again, which ended up being two minutes.

Phone to my ear, my knee started bobbing up and down as the sound of her voicemail filled my ear once more.

"Hey, Cass?" I said into the phone, trying to keep my voice even. "Just wondering where you are. Call me back, okay?"

The guys side-eyed me on their way out, but I didn't give a damn. Panic was taking hold of me fast and I needed to get home. If I could just see her, I'd be fine. But damn it, why wasn't she answering the phone?

"What's going on with you tonight?" Brody came up behind me, drying his hair with a towel.

I ran a hand over my face. "Where's Maggie?" I asked him, realizing she hadn't been there either and feeling a thousand times worse about the whole situation.

"She sent a last minute text." Brody shrugged, the picture of casualness. "Said something came up, and she wasn't gonna make it."

Shit. *Shit*. Shit. Shit. Shit.

"What?" Brody asked. "What's wrong?"

"I can't get ahold of Cassie." My voice sounded rough, even to me. "We kissed before I left and now she's not answering her phone."

Brody blinked. "Jesus. Calm the hell down, man. I'm sure she's fine. They're probably off doing whatever girl stuff—"

"No." I shook my head. "You don't get it. Cassie and I kissed tonight. And now I can't find her."

Brody stared at me, processing. "Wait. Hold up. Are you telling me that was the first time?"

"Yes."

"What the hell took so long?" He scoffed. "You've basically been a couple for months."

"We have not," I snapped, barely able to stand still, let alone have this conversation.

He raised an eyebrow. "Dude, according to everything Maggie's said? You sure as hell have been. Or at least something damn close."

"It doesn't matter," I snapped. "I just need to go find her."

"Relax, she and Maggie are probably together. Girls love talking about stuff like this. Trust me. It'll be fine."

"How do you know?" I asked, wanting reassurance of that fact more than I wanted air.

"Because anyone can tell by looking at you guys that you're totally and completely obsessed with each other."

Was it true? God, I hoped it was.

"Now go find your girl and breathe, dude."

I didn't need to be told twice.

"Hey baby," I said shakily into the phone, probably breaking every speeding law in the state as I drove like hell home. "I'm not sure what's going on, but I'm trying really hard not to panic, but I'm kind of freaking the fuck out over here. Please call me back and let me know you're okay."

I pulled into the parking garage, not bothering to bring any of my stuff in as I took the stairs two at a time. I couldn't be bothered to wait for the elevator in the state I was in.

And I couldn't ignore the feeling that something was seriously and utterly wrong.

When I opened the door to the apartment, I saw just how right I'd been.

"Cassie?" I yelled into the darkness.

If she were home, the lights would be on. If she were home, there'd be a candle burning, or the smell of food, or the TV flickering. *Something.* Because she left signs of her behind wherever she was.

Then I flicked the light switch on and felt the breath leave my lungs in a sudden, fell swoop.

She was gone. Not just momentarily. But completely gone. There wasn't a single trace of her to be found. Everything she owned was missing, and I felt it.

"Cassie?" I called out anyway, as if it were all somehow a joke. "Where are you, baby?"

And I ran up the stairs to the bedroom she hadn't slept in for weeks. Empty. Just like the rest of the apartment.

Just like me.

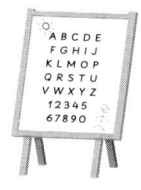

CHAPTER FIFTY-TWO

Cassie

"You've got to tell me what's going on, Cass," Maggie said, sitting beside me on her couch. "You can't just show up with everything you own and then take a vow of silence."

"I just said something a few minutes ago."

"You saying, 'I like this episode' doesn't cut it for the current situation," Maggie deadpanned.

It was eerily similar to the last time I'd showed up at her place after fleeing Liam's. I was teary-eyed, emotional, and absolutely did not want to talk about the chaos existing inside of me at that moment.

"I can't talk about it," I said. "It's too much."

"What's too much? Cassie," she said, but then a pounding knock whipped both our heads in the direction of the door.

"Open the door, Maggie," Liam's panicked voice sounded from the other side.

I froze, wide-eyed and helpless. I wasn't ready to see him yet. I didn't know how to explain myself.

I'd run and hidden like a kid, and even knowing how wrong it was, I couldn't bear to deal with the aftermath of my decision right now.

"Please don't let him in," I begged Maggie in a whisper. "*Please.*"

"What did he do to you?" Maggie's eyes narrowed on me. "I'll kill him."

"No." I shook my head quickly. "He didn't do anything. It's all my fault."

"Maggie!" he called again, sounding desperate.

"Please," I said again, and she nodded in quiet acceptance.

"Okay," she said quietly, even though confusion flickered in her eyes. She didn't know what was going on, but she respected my request anyway. "I'll just tell him to leave then."

Somehow, it sounded like it hurt her as much as it was hurting me.

She padded to the door and stepped out into the hallway, leaving the door cracked behind her.

"I can't find Cassie, Mags," he said breathlessly. "I can't—I don't know where—she was supposed to be at the game, but now I can't get in touch with her."

"Liam—"

"I need to see her, Mags."

"Liam, breathe. She's fine," Maggie said.

"How do you know?" he asked.

"Because she's here."

"Thank fuck," he muttered, relief flooding his voice. "Let me see her—"

"No." Maggie stopped, and from the slight crack, I could see her moving in front of the door. "She doesn't want to talk to you."

"Don't say that," Liam said, breathing out as if it hurt to do so.

"Just give her a little space. I'm sure she'll talk to you when she's ready."

"All her stuff is gone, Maggie!" Liam shouted. "She moved out! And you're telling me I can't talk to her? What happened?" His voice broke at the end.

"I don't know, Liam," she replied, sounding on the verge of breaking herself. "She hasn't told me anything."

"Please, just let me talk to her. I can fix this if I talk to her," he pleaded, and I felt agony rip through me that I was the cause of it.

"It was always supposed to be temporary, Liam." Maggie sighed. "Remember?"

"*No.*" Liam's response was raw and guttural.

"No?" Maggie responded.

"It can't be. I—" he started and stopped. "I fucking love her, Maggie. You have to let me see her."

The breath left my lungs as a pain I'd never known settled securely around me. Did he mean that? Did he really love me, and I'd left him like that?

For a second, I thought she was going to give in and open the door for him, but a moment passed, and her voice responded so quietly I could barely hear it.

"I can't. I'm sorry, Liam."

I wiped the tears that were streaming down my face when I realized she was crying, too.

What had I done to the two best people in my life? I'd ruined everything, like I always do. I was so scared of rejection that I ran off before I'd give anyone the chance to deliver it.

"Just tell me she's okay, then," he said, and I wanted to run to him more than anything.

"She's okay. She just needs time," Maggie said.

"Time for what?"

"Maybe to realize that you aren't going anywhere?" Maggie offered, and a sob came out of me.

Was that true? Did this man outside the door really love me, and I'd upped and left him because I was scared of something that hadn't even happened?

He deserved better than me. He deserved someone who knew how to love him properly. Not me, saddled with anxiety and guilt and coping mechanisms that only hurt the people around me.

I couldn't be what he needed. And he'd realize it sooner than later.

"I'm not going anywhere," he said adamantly. "Tell her that."

"I think she knows already," Maggie said. "She just needs time to trust it."

Before I could hear anything else that broke my heart further, I slipped into Maggie's room and cried.

Liam

I drove to Brody's house.

I couldn't stomach the thought of going back home without her there. Or her stuff littering the place, even though she tried so hard to put things away.

Fuck, if I couldn't get her to come back, I was pretty sure I'd have to just sell the place rather than be there without her. But where could I go that the pain of her absence wouldn't follow me?

What the hell happened?

I'd tried so fucking hard to play it safe. To leave things on her terms, to wait until *she* was ready.

Had she realized after kissing me that I wasn't what she wanted? That she didn't feel the same way about me that she had about Dave? Had seeing him ruined all the progress I thought we'd been making toward each other the last few months?

Or was I just the type of guy that wasn't worth sticking around for?

I'd learned early that people were fleeting. Even the ones who were supposed to stay. I'd realized that if you didn't let people close to you, it wouldn't hurt as much when they went away.

Halfway to Brody's, I pulled over to the side of the road, convinced I was going to vomit from nerves. When I walked into my apartment earlier, it was the same feeling I had the day I'd come home from school to see that our dad had cleared the place out of everything he owned.

He hadn't said a word to me or to Maggie, and based on the image burned into my brain of my mother sitting at the table red-faced and sobbing, I was guessing he hadn't filled her in on his plans, either.

But Cassie? The way this hurt was like nothing I'd experienced before. No gash, concussion, or dislocation was comparable to the pain of losing her. What made it worse was that I hadn't seen it coming. When we kissed, I'd let myself think I'd gotten her. I'd let myself think I could keep her.

And despite everything, I wasn't giving up. I'd thrown myself entirely into this girl, and now that her name was carved across my heart, there wasn't any amount of time I wouldn't wait for her on the chance that she'd change her mind.

"This might not be as bad as you think," Brody said, cracking open a can of Coca-Cola as I stood in his kitchen.

"How the fuck do you figure that?" I shot him a look.

"I mean." Brody sipped, considering. "Have we considered the possibility that she might've just been totally overwhelmed by the epicness of your perfect fairytale kiss and got freaked out?"

"Why would she get freaked out?"

"I don't know, Liam." Brody made a "duh" face. "Maybe because she just got out of a long-term relationship that she thought was going to be forever, and maybe she's having a little trouble believing what's going on between you won't end up the same?"

"It wouldn't," I defended adamantly.

"But how is she supposed to know that?" Brody asked. "I'm sure the last guy told her the same thing."

"The last guy was a dick, and I'm glad I punched him in the face."

"Okay, let's tone it down a notch," Brody ordered. "I'm just saying, it sounds like this girl has been used to a lot of disappointment in her life."

He didn't know the half of it.

"So, just maybe, it's harder for her to accept that something in her life might be going right as it is for you."

Shit. Maybe he had a point.

Hadn't everything I read about her trauma pointed to exactly that fact?

I exhaled, feeling something heavy loosen in my chest. Hope. Terrifying, stupid, idiotic hope.

"What? Are you retiring to become a therapist now?" I deflected with a laugh. "How the hell do you know all this anyway?"

"I told you before, dude. Sisters will make a guy hella self-aware."

"Don't say 'hella.' You're twenty-five." I shook my head with a smirk.

"Don't nitpick all the wisdom I just bestowed on you because of word choice." Brody winced. "So, are you going to fight for your girl or what?"

"Like hell." I nodded in confirmation.

Because I might be a lot of things, but a quitter had never been one of them. Not in arguments, not in training, and not when it came to fighting for my spot in the NHL.

And sure as hell not when it came to winning over the love of my life.

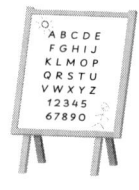

CHAPTER FIFTY-THREE

Cassie

Maggie didn't let me wallow. The second she came inside, it was with guns blazing and questions flying before I even had a chance to brace myself for Hurricane Maggie.

"You need to explain to me what's going on because, in twenty-four years, I have never in my life seen my brother look the way he just did in that hallway." She pointed in the direction of the front door.

"I messed everything up." I groaned into her pillows. "Now, you both hate me."

"I don't hate you. I *care* about you," Maggie shot back, clearly affronted. "And if you think that my *brother* is anything other than completely in love with you, then you didn't see the guy standing out there in the hallway."

I looked up at her with cautious eyes.

"Do you think he meant that?" I asked, replaying the words I heard him say that stopped my heart. "That he loved me?"

"*Loves,*" Maggie corrected. "Present tense."

My heart fluttered.

"What happened, Cass?" she asked, sitting down on the edge of the bed.

"I kissed him," I admitted, watching warily for her reaction.

To my surprise, there wasn't one.

"And then…" she prompted, waiting for me to continue. "You had an allergic reaction to him or something?"

"Maggie!" I hit her with the nearest pillow.

"What?" She held her hands up to block it. "I'm just having a hard time understanding how you went from kissing Liam to ending up here with everything you own." She stared at me imploringly. "So?"

"So, I freaked out and left."

"*What?*" She leaped to her feet. "Why the hell would you do that?"

"Because *I* kissed *him*," I said for emphasis. "I crossed a line. Put him in an awkward position. He was probably about to kick me out."

"Let me reiterate the fact that the guy is *in love with you*." She sighed.

"If he wanted to kiss me, he could've done it at any point," I said, embarrassed.

"You're really oblivious sometimes, Cass." Maggie laughed. "Then again, so is he since you're both equally responsible for this weird little dance you've been doing together."

"Huh?"

"He's into you. That's clear as day," she said. "You're into him. Again, also obvious."

I tried to protest.

"But, neither of you have been able to figure that out because you're both shackled by all these little lies you've both convinced yourselves of."

"What are you going on about, Mags?" I shook my head in a daze.

"Cassie," she deadpanned. "Do you really think running away from Liam has *nothing* to do with your mom?"

"My mom?" I pulled back, dumbfounded.

"I only know bits and pieces, but it sounds like she was pretty inconsistent at best, neglectful at worst, throughout your life." Maggie looked to me for confirmation.

"So?" I said, unable to deny it.

"So," she said, "maybe you're scared to have someone dependable and reliable and let me scream it one more time—totally in love with you because you haven't had that before, and that's the part that freaks you out."

I lingered in it, letting the realization wash over me.

"I was with Dave for years, and that didn't scare me," I defended, though I had to admit what she said made some sense.

"Don't even get me started on all the ways Dave screwed you over." She held a hand up to pause me. "But the quick version of that is Dave kept you in the same up-and-down cycle your mom did. That was familiar to you. Comfortable. Doesn't mean it was right."

"Where'd you learn all this anyway?" I stared at her with a laugh.

"Uh." Maggie gestured down to herself. "I'm brilliant and self-reflective, that's why."

I snorted.

"And I might be well acquainted with my therapist," she added at the end with a smirk. "Who, by the way, I'll be referring both you and my brother to immediately."

I let out a soft laugh, lingering in the warmth that Maggie's presence brought.

"If you have all the answers, what do I do now?"

"Glad you asked." She grinned, pulling me off her bed to my feet. "You sleep here tonight, recover from all the drama while we eat copious amounts of food and watch *One Tree Hill*."

"You don't think I should talk to Liam?" I frowned. "Apologize… explain."

Hear whatever it was he wanted to tell me in the first place.

Good or bad, I could handle it. For his sake.

"There'll be time for that tomorrow," Maggie said. "We'll both go to the game, and after they win, you guys can have your little rom-com-style make-up moment. Okay?"

"I don't want to put it off that long," I told her, jittery at the thought of him being upset somewhere over me.

Even though the idea of a girl's night with Maggie sounded like the perfect remedy to the hell that the day had been.

Maggie waved away my concerns.

"He's got forever to sort it out with you, Cass. He can spare one night. Plus, you can send him a text. You'll see him tomorrow," she offered as if it were as simple as that.

"Forever?" I asked skeptically.

"I know these things, remember?" she said, already leading the way out of her room. "Like I said, I'm super smart."

For my sake, I hoped she was about this.

CHAPTER FIFTY-FOUR

Liam

Amazingly, she texted me first. I was staring up at Brody's ceiling when the phone dinged. I swear, I'd never dove for something faster in my life.

The message was simple and to the point and left me wanting a hell of a lot more.

Can I come to your game tomorrow?

Why was she even asking? She could go anywhere I was, anytime, no questions asked.

My fingers wanted to type a hundred messages that I couldn't send:

Can you come home tonight? Can I come pick you up right now? Can I be wherever you are?

But I didn't know where the hell her mind was at, so all I typed back was a simple, *Yes.*

She didn't answer, but a while later, Maggie texted, saying, *"I fixed all your problems. You're welcome."*

That couldn't be true because Cassie and all of her stuff were still at Maggie's house instead of where they belonged.

I spent the rest of the night tossing and turning on Brody's couch, trying to figure out how to convince her that she was supposed to be with me. Because I knew she was. Even if she didn't.

By the time morning came, I was ragged and weary and wasn't sure how the hell I was supposed to play another game tonight with all the chaos in my head.

I stayed with Brody all day, obsessively checking my phone for messages that never came and going through my usual game day routine with him by my side to keep me in check.

When it came time to get ready to go to the game, I realized I'd screwed myself. I didn't have a clean suit with me, and Brody's would've fit me like a second layer of skin the absolute worst way.

The logical thing would've been to run home and grab one of the many I already owned, but I couldn't fucking do it. I couldn't go there alone.

Instead, we left early and bought one on the way. It might've created some mayhem in the local Hugo Boss, but the employees were good about getting me in and out of there in record time.

"Now, remember," Brody said in the locker room as we changed into our gear. "Everything with blondie is going to be fine, but everything with Coach will *not* be if you don't keep your head in the game tonight."

I knew he had a point, but suddenly, hockey wasn't the biggest deal in my life anymore. It wasn't real. It was my career, and I loved it. But if I lost it? It wouldn't destroy me. Not the way it would destroy me to lose someone I loved.

Cassie was real.

This? It was a game.

I'd used it as a distraction from real life for so long that I'd stopped building a world outside of here. But now I had, and I was scared like hell to lose it.

The crowds were seated, and even from here the volume of the Garden was thunderous, but it had nothing on the noise in my head.

"I'll be right back," I told Brody, beelining for the tunnel.

Brody called after me, but I knew I had time before my absence would be noticed. At least a few minutes' worth of it.

I shot Maggie a text, telling her where to meet me away from the eyes of the rest of the stadium. She answered immediately, telling me she'd be there.

Cassie. Cassie. Cassie.

My thoughts screamed her name on a loop as I raced to meet Maggie. Would she be there with her? Would I get to talk to her before I went on the ice?

Every question was answered when I saw Maggie standing there alone, looking breathless and a lot more anxious than I was comfortable with.

"Liam, I—" she started, looking behind her quickly.

"Is she here?" I asked. "I thought she was coming." I couldn't hide the way my voice cracked at the question. "What happened?"

"She is here, but I have to tell you something."

"Are you sure?" I looked around, relief flooding my chest. "Where is she?"

"She's in the bathroom, but Liam, I really need to—"

And then my heart stopped as another figure appeared behind her, approaching us

I didn't know what to do at first. Couldn't process what was happening as I looked at their face.

"Liam," the voice said, and my blood ran cold.

I was staring at the man whose face I would wear in thirty years. I hadn't realized it when I was a kid, and certainly not in all the time he'd been gone, but I saw it now. How eerily similar everything about us was, as if his genes were copied and pasted onto me.

I wondered if that's why it hurt Mom so much to look at me, the way I knew it sometimes did when I watched her avert her gaze from me.

I resented that I could have gotten so much genetically from a man who provided so little to my life.

I clenched my jaw hard enough to break it.

This was too much.

All of it was too fucking much.

"What is he doing here?" I looked at Maggie, the sting of betrayal settling over me as I stared at her for answers.

"I was trying to tell you," Maggie said, having the decency to at least look guilty.

"Liam," his voice said to me for the first time in fifteen years. "Son—"

"Don't call me that." I scowled, my focus snapping to him. No part of me wanted anything to do with the man standing in front of me.

"Why would you bring him here, Mags?" I bit out. "Why?"

"I—" She opened her mouth but came up empty.

"I wanted to see you. Talk to you." He stepped in as if he had the right. "To tell you how sorry I am and explain what a mistake it was to do what I did."

I laughed humorlessly.

"Abandoning your family isn't a mistake. It's a fucking choice."

"You don't understand," he said, infuriating me to my core. "It wasn't supposed to happen like that. I needed space. Time away from your mother."

"And your children?" I asked coldly.

"Let him talk, Liam," Maggie snapped as if I were the bad guy here.

He swallowed. "I thought if I wanted to see you kids, I'd need to deal with your mother, and I just… wasn't ready. But then time went by. Too much time. By then, I figured it was too late. Six months had passed. I was scared you wouldn't want to see me."

I shook my head. "Well, if you thought I wouldn't want to after six months, I bet you can imagine how much I don't want to after fifteen fucking years," I snarled vehemently.

I was disgusted by his presence, feeling my skin physically crawl as I looked at him. I'd resented him since the day he left, and seeing him in the flesh only amplified that feeling tenfold.

"Don't say that," he pleaded, shooting a heartbroken look that did nothing to soften me. "I'm proud of you, Liam. I tell all my friends about what you've accomplished."

"No," I spat. "You don't get to be proud of me. Nothing I've done has anything to do with you."

He tried to interject, but I didn't let him. Didn't want to hear another word. "It might be your last name on my jersey," I told him, staring him dead in the eye, "but I created a name for myself without you."

He faltered,

"And I can promise you," I said, enunciating each word to ensure he heard loud and clear. "When people hear the name Brynn, they sure as hell aren't thinking of you. And neither am I."

He flinched. Maggie had her head in her hands. And I needed to get the hell out of here. I'd wasted too many minutes on this guy already.

"Enjoy the game," I tossed over my shoulder as I left, hoping to God that I would never see that man again for the rest of my life.

I'd never taken a drug in my life, but I felt wired as if I'd taken a hit of something. My brain was fried—between the confrontation with my father, the anger I felt toward Maggie for bringing him here, and the cyclone of a mess going on with Cassie, it was a wonder I managed to play the game at all.

I paid enough attention to get by, but I'd be lying if I tried to claim that most of my focus wasn't on the stands.

Did I see a blond head anywhere? It was hard when so many were screaming for my attention, holding up crazy signs that seemed borderline illegal to be shown in a public setting.

But finally, I spotted her a few minutes into the night. The last time I saw her, her lips had been on mine and everything was perfect. Then she was gone before I had a chance to process how it happened.

She sat beside Maggie in a replica of *my* jersey, with a long white-sleeved shirt underneath. She looked so beautiful it hurt to breathe, even as relief flooded through me.

She really was here tonight. Everything would be fine because I was going to talk to her and make things right. It didn't even matter if she wasn't ready for a relationship or any of that. I'd rather have things go back to the way they were before than not have her at all. And if she was here, it meant she wasn't giving up on me yet.

I played like hell to prove a point to myself and to my father, who was there in the stands beside Maggie. I didn't need him and never did. But most of all, I played like hell because of that girl in the stands watching who held my heart in the palm of her hands.

I hoped she'd go easy with it.

We were unstoppable for the first half of the game, to the point where I was entirely locked in, concentrating only on what I needed to get done in front of me.

The guys and I moved like clockwork, seamless, unstoppable. The rest of the world faded into a blur—just noise beyond the rink. The puck belonged to us, and we made damn sure the other team knew it. Score after score, the crowd roared louder, the announcers raving about how this game would go down in Harbor Wolves history.

But I barely heard them.

I was locked in, breathless, running on pure muscle memory. Somewhere between passes and checks, I remembered why I loved this game. How it shut everything else out. How it let me forget, let me escape, let me feel nothing at all.

Lately, I hadn't wanted that. But tonight, I let the adrenaline drag me under—just until the game was secured.

Then, somewhere in the third period, as the energy swirled around me, I glanced up for a glance at Cassie, only to come up short.

Fans screamed in every direction I turned, but I ignored them, searching for the one face that wasn't there.

Where the hell had she gone?

As soon as I was able to look in the direction of where Maggie was sitting, I mouthed the question through the glass.

"Where is she?"

She mouthed back, "Her mom."

That was all it took to take me out of the game. Like a bucket of ice water dumped over my head, I was done. I skated off, Coach yelling, trying to block my path.

"Where the hell do you think you're going?" he shouted. "This game is going down in the books. You'll see it through to the end!"

"I can't." I yanked off my helmet. "It's Cassie. I have to go."

"Who the hell is Cassie?"

I met his eyes dead-on. "My girl."

Whatever he saw on my face made him step back. He clapped my shoulder, letting me pass.

As I stalked down the tunnel, the announcer's voice echoed behind me.

"Liam Brynn is leaving the game due to a family emergency."

And then I was gone.

CHAPTER FIFTY-FIVE

Cassie

Over and over and over. Repetition. Cycles.

There was a reason why the same thoughts raced through my brain at all times, and my anxieties played on a constant loop.

It was because I was living in the same cycle over and over. My bad scenarios weren't a matter of *if* they might happen but a matter of when. I knew that as I stared down at my mother's comatose body, hooked up to more wires and machines than I could count.

She'd been doing well. I'd talked to her just a day ago. Or maybe two?

I let my head fall into my hands. Two days was apparently plenty of time to drink yourself into needing to be sedated.

I didn't fully understand everything the doctors were saying, only that her body had gone into some kind of shock from not having alcohol in her system. They said it can happen when someone dependent stops drinking suddenly—but in her case, it wasn't like she chose to stop. Either she ran out, or her body just got too sick to keep going. And that was enough to send everything spiraling.

Seizures. Skyrocketing blood pressure. Heart failure.

I couldn't fathom it.

Her body physically craved alcohol so strongly that it was trying to destroy her when it wasn't in her system anymore. Part of me was heartbroken. But another part of me, that angry monster that lurked inside, was furious that she let her addiction get to a point where not having a drink would kill her.

That was why I never felt safe or secure. The reason it was so hard for me to let my guard down. She was the one who was supposed to protect me from the world, not the reason I was afraid to really live in it.

And because of that, I ruined everything with Liam. And then I took off from the game tonight. I was sure he was sick of me running and crying and all the emotional whiplash I was sure I had given him. I wouldn't blame him if he was done with me for good after this. Even as a friend.

The room was dim, and I was glad for it. It hurt too much to see her like this. I'd seen her barely conscious or passed out from alcohol. But now it felt eerie, like she was gone for good.

The doctors had medicated her into the state of sedation she was currently in, but I was worried that this was something she wouldn't wake up from. Part of me wondered if I'd spoken to my mom for the last time without ever knowing it. The thought had tears springing to my eyes all over again.

Alone, again.

I was always alone.

Until the nurses came in, just passing by. A round on their shift. Nothing memorable or special. Even though my world was crashing down around me, this was routine for them.

So, I tried to pull myself together.

"Is she going to be okay?" I asked again, begging for reassurance that no one had been able to concretely give.

As always, I was met with a tight-lipped response that did little to settle my nerves.

"I don't want to lie to you," a man in a white coat said. "Your mother is critically sick."

I felt it like a punch to the gut.

"We're doing everything we can, and there's a possibility of recovery, but she's not out of the woods yet."

I nodded grimly, staring up at him with a trembling lip.

"But there's still a chance, right?"

"Yes." He nodded, looking at me with something like pity. "There's a chance."

That's all I needed. Just a shot at everything being okay. I just needed her to make it through.

I stared up at the muted television playing in the corner of the room, if only to distract myself. I didn't want to watch as they cared for someone who, by all accounts, should be able to care for themselves.

The Harbor Wolves game was playing. The one I'd been at just an hour ago. It was hard to believe that I'd been there, watching Liam play the game of his life, only to now be sitting here, watching my mother fight for hers.

I scanned the figures, so impossibly small on the screen, looking for the number twenty-six. They moved so fast it was hard to tell, but after a few moments of searching, I started to panic.

Where is he?

They wouldn't take him out of the game. He was the star player. He'd been on fire tonight. He was going to secure their win.

"Can I turn this up?" I looked to the nurse for confirmation.

"Of course," they confirmed, nodding toward a remote on the bedside table.

I clicked it a few notches up, just enough to hear faint murmurs of the announcer's frenzied voice.

"There's never been a game like this in all my years," one said with an almost manic energy. "The Harbor Wolves are still holding it together and coming out ahead even after the departure of center Liam Brynn."

"What?" I asked out loud.

The nurse looked over and huffed a laugh.

"Crazy, right?" he responded. "They said he had a family emergency or something. Hell of a game to have to walk out of, though." The nurse shook his head sadly.

Family emergency?

It couldn't be Maggie. I'd been with her just an hour ago. She was fine. Was his mom fine? Was it the stress of seeing his dad?

I stood up, walking out of the room with urgency, needing to find out what was going on. I could call Maggie. She would know—

Phone in hand, I started dialing the number when I heard him.

"Cassie Dwyer, she's here for her mom," his voice said, demanding. "Please, just tell me what room she's in."

There, just a few feet away at the nurses' station, stood Liam Brynn. Still in his jersey and hair matted down with sweat, he looked every bit the fantastic hockey player featured on posters across the city.

The nurses looked a bit starstruck, staring up at him. I couldn't blame them. I was feeling the same way myself.

"Liam," I said, barely loud enough to be heard.

But somehow, he did.

He spun, facing me, looking me up and down before closing his eyes shut in what looked like relief.

"Cassie," he breathed.

"You're here," I said, frozen in place.

He took a few wary steps closer, the same tension lingering in the air from all the unsaid words between us. But still, he was here. He'd shown up despite it all.

"I'm wherever you are," he said.

And I threw myself at him.

"You shouldn't have come," I said, even though I was clutching him so hard he probably couldn't get away if he tried. "You're supposed to be at the game."

"It doesn't matter." He held me back, smelling like the ice rink and Old Spice Gentleman's Blend deodorant I knew he wore because of the time I peeked inside his medicine cabinet. "I'm exactly where I need to be."

"I'm sorry I left," I blurted out, staring up at him as if I could convey the depth of my regret with just a look. "I shouldn't have—"

"Cassie, it's just a game. It doesn't matter," he said.

"No," I shook my head, "Not the game. Your apartment. The other night. I was scared, and I ran and—"

"It's okay." He shushed me when I started to get worked up again. "It's not important right now."

"It *is* important," I assured him. "*You're* important, Liam." *The most important.* "I—"

Oh God, was I going to admit it?

I had to. I couldn't let myself be scared anymore. Not of my feelings, not of rejection, not of being left.

Because if I ran from those things, I'd end up alone anyway. And Liam deserved to hear just how much I felt for him.

"Liam," I started again, staring into his eyes. "I lo—"

"Cassie Dwyer?" a doctor spoke from down the hallway. My mother's room.

I spun my head, staring at him with wide, terrified eyes.

"Yes?" I croaked out, but he couldn't hear me. My voice was barely a whisper.

"We're here," Liam called out, an arm securely around my shoulder while the other was waving to get the doctor's attention.

The doctor made his way toward us, eyes widening in surprise when they landed on Liam, but he smoothed his features after a moment, maintaining an impressive air of professionalism despite Boston's runaway hockey player being right in front of his eyes.

"Your mother is—"

"Dead?" I blurted out, covering my mouth.

"Waking up," he offered with a soft smile. "If you want to go see her."

I looked at Liam, scared to leave and have him vanish in the meantime. He gave my hand a squeeze and nodded at me.

"Go," he said, "I'll be here."

So I did, nodding at the doctor to lead me to her.

"She's going to be groggy for a while," he explained, walking beside me. "The sedation is still wearing off, so she might fall back to sleep soon, but you might get a few minutes to talk to her."

"So, what does this mean? That she's waking up?"

"She's stable for the most part, but there are things we're keeping an eye on," he said, causing hope to bloom in my chest. "She'll still be here for a while, but if all goes well, she might be moved out of the ICU soon."

And then we walked in, and I saw my Mom sitting up, blinking at her surroundings as if she wasn't quite sure how she got there.

"Mom," I said, a million pounds lighter at the sight of her blue eyes open once more.

"Cassie?" she asked, stretching her body away from the wires and cords that connected her to the machines.

Her voice was dry and brittle from disuse, but it was *her*.

I ran beside her bed, holding her hand as a few tears of relief escaped my eyes.

"I'm so happy to see you," I told her.

"I was dreaming about you," she said, disoriented. "I missed you."

"I missed you too, Mom."

And I did. Not her physically, but mentally.

I missed having a lucid moment with her, where I knew she was in the right frame of mind to remember what we were talking about. I missed all the moments we'd lost to her drinking.

But maybe, maybe, that was all over now.

This had to be rock bottom. She'd been sedated, on oxygen. And she'd survived it for a reason. This was our second chance, I knew it. I felt it.

But for now, she needed to recover. She needed to rest. And when she slipped back into sleep, I stayed right beside her.

"I'll be right here," I told her, as her eyelids started to flutter.

We had all the time in the world to fix what had been broken.

CHAPTER FIFTY-SIX

Liam

Vending machines were a pretty evil contraption. They preyed on the hungry, desperate passerby who had no choice but to buy their garbage that would do nothing to fill their growling stomachs.

I was sure as hell that, at least in my case, a bag of chips or a few M&M's would have no effect on mine.

I sighed, settling on a skimpy bag of trail mix that was probably filled with more sugar than anything that might replenish me after those ruthless two hours I put into the game the night before.

What time was it now? Late in the night? Early the next morning? All I knew was that I was starving and jittery and praying to God that Cassie was going to be okay after her mother's latest—and apparently most dire—health scare.

I watched as the mechanical arm pushed the snack forward, and it dropped to the bottom. I bent over to reach for it, jerking back when a voice came from behind me.

"I thought you left," Cassie's voice said and I turned to see her standing behind me, arms crossed across as she watched me. She looked slight in the dim fluorescent lights. So fragile, though I knew she was far stronger than most people I'd met.

"I told you I'd be here." I watched her as if she might disappear if I looked away for a second.

"Yeah," she said. "You always do what you say you're going to do."

I didn't know what to say to that, so I held the bag of trail mix as an offering. She smiled and shook her head.

"I'm okay, thanks." She looked toward a pair of empty chairs. "Can we talk?"

"Uh oh," I said lightly, trying to laugh it off. "The dangerous words."

"No," she said, staring up at me. "Nothing bad."

Relief hit me like a tidal wave.

I walked with her toward the chairs and sat down beside her, watching as she breathed in and out as if trying to hype herself up for whatever she was about to say.

She looked at me for a minute, unspeaking, and then off to the TV in the corner of the waiting room. I didn't notice at first that it was a recap of the game playing until she spoke.

"I can't believe you left," she said, staring at the headline of how the Harbor Wolves won scrolled across the bottom of the screen.

Good, I breathed. They'd stayed strong and secured the win even without me there. I didn't have to feel guilty about leaving. Not that I did, but at least I didn't have to act like I was when I saw everyone.

"Looks like it didn't make a difference." I nodded up toward the screen. "They did okay without me."

"I wouldn't." She turned to look at me, eyes shining. "Do okay without you, I mean."

I stared at her, a thousand questions on the tip of my tongue. Cassie was like this butterfly that had landed in my life, and any wrong step could send her fluttering off.

"I wouldn't do okay without you, either," I told her the honest-to-God truth.

Hell, it had only been a day, and I'd fallen apart.

"Aren't you going to regret not being there, though?" She bit her lip. "They said this was a pretty important game."

I laughed, causing her to startle.

"What?" she asked.

"Nothing," I assured her. "I just can't believe you're talking to me about a hockey game right now."

"It's important to you," she protested.

"You're important to me," I said, reaching up to touch her cheek. "Don't you know that?"

She pressed her eyes shut, leaning into the palm of my hand. When those blue eyes opened, they were blinking back tears.

Fuck, I loved those eyes.

"Did I mess everything up with us?" she asked.

"No, baby," I told her, "Not even close."

I wanted to tell her that we could take things at her pace. That everything was going to be okay, and we would work out everything together because honest to God, I couldn't imagine a life without her in it anymore.

But as I opened my mouth to tell her that, another doctor approached, pulling her attention away from me. I couldn't begrudge him for it. Right now, her mom was our priority.

"Cassie?" It was the same one from before. "Your mother's a bit more lucid now. She wanted to speak to you."

Cassie stood up, looking at me as if it pained her to leave the same way it did me. Maybe she was just scared of going to see her mom. But I knew from the determined set of her shoulders that this was something she wanted to face alone.

"I'll be waiting right here. I promise," I told her.

She nodded, offering me a smile, and then she was gone.

CHAPTER FIFTY-SEVEN

Cassie

The sun was rising, filling my mom's room with a soft amber glow that made me feel like everything was really going to be okay. Liam was there. My mother was alive. And I was going to be there to help her through her recovery.

"Hi, baby." She smiled up at me as if nothing were the matter with her at all.

I wanted to cry, hearing her voice so lucid, seeing her smile without the lazy, drunken tilt to it.

"Mom." I beamed, sitting beside her. "You're okay."

I hugged her, squeezing tight while being careful of the wires still connected to her.

"These pesky things." She laughed, scrunching her nose up as if they were an inconvenience rather than the reason she was alive.

"How are you feeling?" I asked.

"Oh, I'm fine," she said, and though her face was pale and her body still far too thin for comfort, she looked alive. And that was good enough for me.

"You have no idea how worried I was," I told her with a huge exhale. "This time was really bad, Mom."

"I know, baby," she said. "I'm sorry I scared you."

"It's okay," I told her. "I'm just glad you're okay."

I wiped away a tear. Everything was really going to be fine. I looked around to the bedside table where I'd left the pamphlets that the doctor had given me.

"So, the doctors were telling me about some really good programs that you can go to once you're strong enough—"

"For what?" She blinked up in confusion.

I stared.

"For rehab, Mom."

"Oh, honey." She laughed. "I don't need that."

"B-but," I stuttered, brain freezing in confusion. "But you do, Mom. Do you know that you almost died this time? This wasn't just withdrawal. This time it was bad."

"Honey," she said. "I love that you worry about me, but you don't need to. This isn't going to happen again, I promise."

"You promise?" I asked numbly.

Those words.

I'd heard them my whole life.

About everything from showing up for one of my school events to coming home on time to taking me somewhere because we hadn't spent time together in days. Each one more painful than the last until I learned that promises were nothing more than empty words made to be broken.

And then it clicked. I couldn't help her if she didn't want me to.

"I'm glad you're okay, Mom. I really am," I said, voice detached. "And you know that I love you. I've loved you more than anyone for my whole life." *Myself included.* "But I can't keep doing this over and over. It's killing me."

"Cassie, stop being dramatic." She rolled her eyes. "You're always so dramatic."

I stood up mechanically, feeling the finality of the moment settle over me. The acceptance I'd never quite felt before now.

"I hope you get better, Mom. I really, really do."

She needed me. I knew that. But she needed alcohol more. And if that's the choice she was making, then I had to make one of my own. Even if it broke my heart to do it.

"But, if you don't, well, I won't be here to see it." I turned to leave.

"Cassie," her voice cried out indignantly. "Cassie, stop."

"Bye, Mom," I told her, vowing to myself that it was the last time I let my life be pulled in by the chaos of her drinking.

And while my mother wasn't very good at keeping her promises, I needed to keep this one to myself. For the sake of my own life and my future.

My past had been consumed by my mother and her needs, and I'd spent my life loving and hating her in equal measure. I thought if I loved her hard enough, I could fix her. Change her.

But she couldn't be my everything anymore.

And I knew now, in a way I never really understood before, that I couldn't be hers, either.

Liam was exactly where he said he would be.

And I surprised myself when I realized I didn't expect anything different. Not everyone would let you down in life. He had proven that to me time and time again.

But somewhere along the way, I had let him down. And now I needed to rectify that.

I'd been so caught up in my own hurt that sometimes I didn't stop to think that I might be the one doing the hurting.

And as I watched Liam dozing in that waiting room chair, I knew I never wanted to hurt that beautiful boy again for as long as I lived.

"Liam," I whispered gently so as not to scare him.

He stirred immediately, opening his eyes. It must not have been a restful sleep at all.

"Hi," he said, standing up.

"Hi." I smiled back.

Part of my heart was broken that I didn't have the power to change my mother. But if I had stayed in that cycle, I would never get to experience the rest of what my life could be like without her. What it could be like with him, if he let me.

"Are you okay?"

"I will be." I nodded, knowing that even if nothing happened the way I wanted, I could at least know in my heart that I tried my best.

I couldn't control her. I couldn't control what happened with Liam. I could only control me. And somehow, it was freeing.

"I'm scared," I admitted to him.

He waited, letting me go on, eyes burning into mine.

"I'm scared because I don't know what's going to happen here." I gestured between us. "And that's a really scary thing. I can't control what happens. I can't control how you feel about me or if you'll ever stop."

"I won't," he cut in, and I loved him for it, but I kept going, knowing I needed to say everything in my heart if we were going to move forward together.

He needed to know me. To understand the way my brain operated. The fears I harbored about losing everything I loved. Of not being able to control the outcomes.

"Honestly, Liam," I breathed out, trying to find the words. "The way I feel about you scares me more than anything because if it goes wrong, I don't know if I have it in me to recover from that. It's almost easier to not get you at all than to lose you."

"You're not going to lose me, baby." His hand came up to cradle my face again, and I sank into it. "Do you know why? Because *I'm* not going to let myself lose *you*."

My heart cracked clean open. I was done for.

"Can I tell you something?" I whispered, heart thudding wildly.

"Anything. Everything. Whatever you want," he spoke quickly, words tumbling out of him in rapid succession.

I stood on my tiptoes, leaning up toward his ear, knowing I'd only have the courage to whisper the confession to him.

"I'm completely in love with you," I admitted, hearing nothing but the sound of my own heartbeat sounding through my ears.

Liam went still underneath me, rigid as a statue, and I wondered if I was wrong. If maybe he liked me, but my feelings were too fast, too soon for him to be on board with.

But I couldn't take it back. It was the truth, and I wasn't going to lie to myself anymore. Not about anything.

But then, miraculously, his hands clamped down around my waist, and he picked me up until my feet weren't on the floor but spinning around as he twirled me in his grip.

"Thank fucking God for that." He exhaled like he'd never breathed before and then slammed his lips against mine until I was consumed by Liam and love and whatever magic had brought this moment to me.

When his lips finally broke from mine, and my eyes finally opened, I stared into his green ones that looked like they'd just seen sunlight for the first time.

"Because I can't live another day of my life without telling you how absolutely and totally in love with you I am."

Everything inside of me malfunctioned at that, as if my lungs suddenly forgot how to breathe, my heart forgot how to beat.

Was it true? Was he being honest?

I could never be sure, but I could learn how to trust. To do the thing I'd been scared of doing for so long.

And part of that started with me.

"I want to be yours," I admitted, even though it was scary to ask for what I wanted. "And I want you to be mine."

"Baby." He laughed as if it were the funniest request in the world. "I've been yours the whole time."

And then he kissed me again, slower, like we'd have all the time in the world to keep doing this forever.

"What else do you want?" He smiled against my lips.

I thought about it and knew there was only one more thing I wanted. One more thing I could ever hope for.

I looked up at the man who had seen me—all of me—and somehow was still choosing me exactly as I was. He was mine. I was his. And now, there was only one thing left to ask for.

"I want to go home."

He was more than happy to oblige.

EPILOGUE

Liam

Three Years Later

It turned out that game I walked out on that night a few years ago *did* go down in history.

To Boston, sure. But more than that, it was the game that changed everything for me and Cassie.

That night was the one I stopped hiding in the game and started running toward her. You could say it paid off in the long run.

"You ready, Cap?" Brody asked as we got ready to skate onto the ice for the next game in our unstoppable season.

For years, hockey was all I had. My entire life, my purpose consisted of what I could do on the ice. But now?

The game is still important to me—but I recognize it for what it is. A game. It wasn't my world. And I knew when the time came, whether it was in one year or ten, I'd be ready to walk away.

Because my whole entire heart? They were right over in the family box, cheering me on no matter how the game turned out.

"Just about ready," I told Brody, scanning the crowd until my eyes landed on them.

My eyes locked on her immediately. How could they not? She was the most beautiful girl in the whole damn arena.

She smiled, somehow excited enough to see me that she bounced as she waved. And even though we'd done this a million times, I still felt it in my chest when she did.

The same way it still made me giddy to see her in that jersey with the last name that now belonged to both of us.

Us and the perfect little human Cassie held up to plexiglass as if somehow baby Lily had any idea that her Dad was about to play for and hopefully secure the Stanley Cup.

"Hi, baby," I mouthed to Cassie as I waved at my beautiful family.

And then the team was swirling around the ice, warming up for the game that I knew would make or break the spirit of more than half of them.

Don't get me wrong, I wanted to win. I wanted to win so bad I could taste it. And I was prepared to play like hell for this game I loved, that had given so much to me in my life. This game that had kept me stable and balanced during the worst times of my life. But if we didn't win? It would've hurt like hell, but my world wouldn't end. It didn't matter the way it used to. What mattered was my real life—the one that happened entirely off the ice.

And as I looked at my family—my beautiful wife, our gorgeous daughter, my stupid, impulsive sister beside them who had brought them both to me—I knew I had already won.

Acknowledgements

This book is the product of so many experiences, people, and places that I can't possibly fit them all here—but I'll try to name a few I especially want to thank.

To Wesley—who convinced me I had the ability to write something worthwhile when I didn't believe I ever could. I love you more than anyone.

To all my literary heroines who shaped my dreams and ambitions—Anne Shirley, Jo March, Rory Gilmore. I wouldn't be who I am without the countless fictional women who lit up my imagination growing up—because fictional characters do matter.

To my earliest ARC and beta readers—your feedback and encouragement meant the world.

To Megan Jayne, for designing the most gorgeous cover I could've hoped for. To Stephanie at ALT 19 Creative—thank you for making me weep with joy over the beauty of the interior formatting (and for patiently answering all my first-timer questions!). To my editor, Sherri—thank you for combing through every line of this book with such care and for helping me polish it until it shone.

To Kristen Nace, the first person to read this story from start to finish, and the first to make me feel like I had something worth putting out in the world. To Karen Ramsey, for your guidance, tips, and kind words every step of the way. To my friend Kat, who has read a dozen of my stories over the years and always lovingly lied to me by telling me she liked them all. I probably would never have finished a whole book without her kindness.

To Mom and Nana, who always knew I'd write a book someday.

To the little girl in me who never thought she'd be holding a book with her name on the cover—we did it. And we made it through every experience we thought we wouldn't.

And finally, most importantly—to you, the reader. It's surreal to think that my characters now live in someone else's imagination. I hope you loved spending time with them. Thank you for choosing to hang out in their world for a little while.

About the Author

Emma O'Dea is a Rhode Island-based author with a wild imagination and a soft spot for fictional characters. When she's not working in a special education preschool, you can find her drinking obscene amounts of iced coffee, running by the ocean, or daydreaming cinematic montages in her head set to the soundtrack of Taylor Swift songs. Though she dreams of living in Ireland one day, for now she's content at home with her partner, Wesley, and their calico kitty, Nala.

Off the Ice is her debut novel.

Made in United States
North Haven, CT
04 October 2025